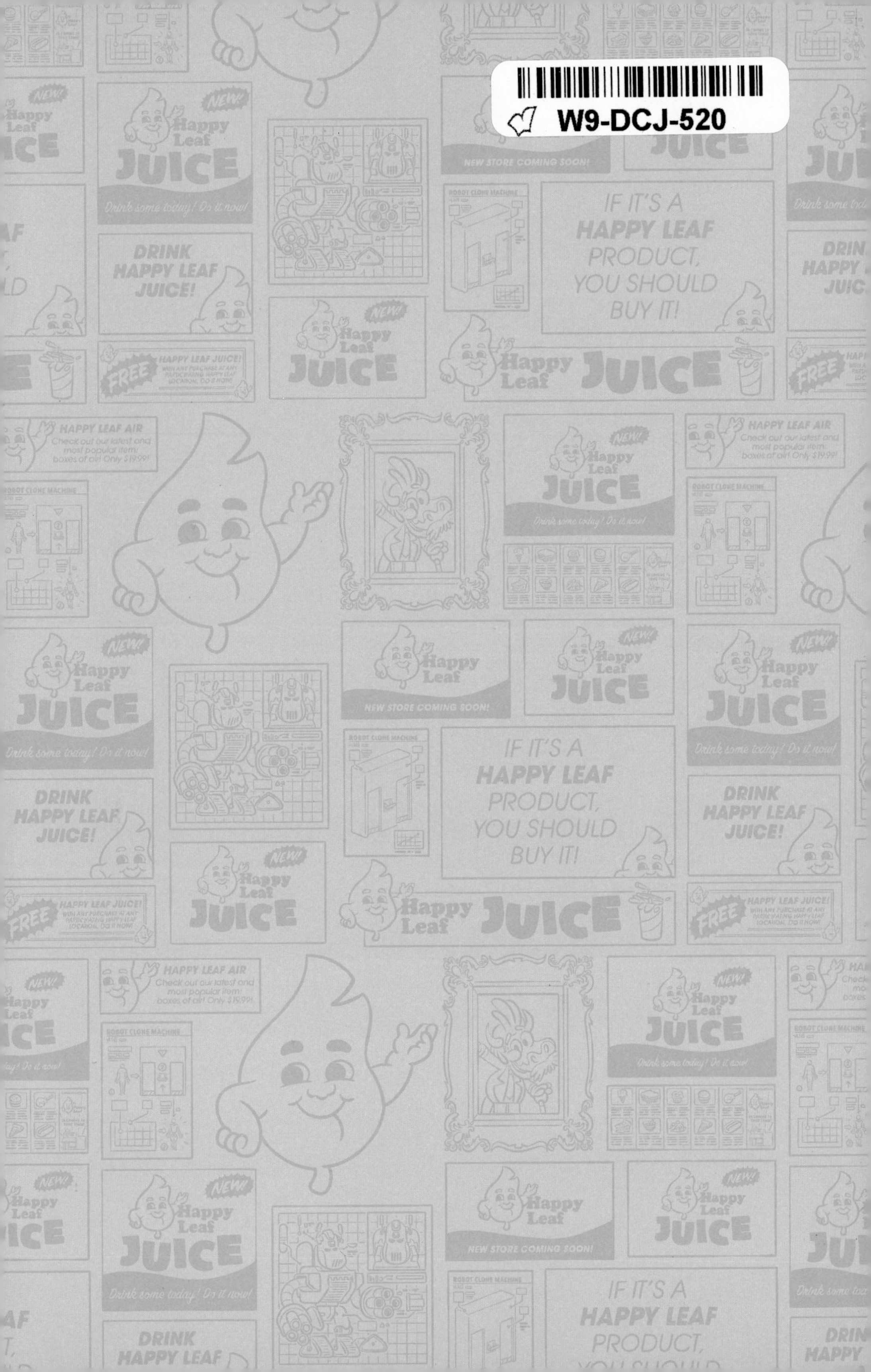
NEW!
Happy Leaf
JUICE
Drink some today! Do it now!
DRINK HAPPY LEAF JUICE!
IF IT'S A HAPPY LEAF PRODUCT, YOU SHOULD BUY IT!
NEW STORE COMING SOON!
ROBOT CLONE MACHINE
FREE
HAPPY LEAF JUICE!
HAPPY LEAF AIR
Check out our latest and most popular item: boxes of air! Only $19.99!

JOEY ELLIS

WOLFIE MONSTER AND THE BIG BAD PIZZA BATTLE

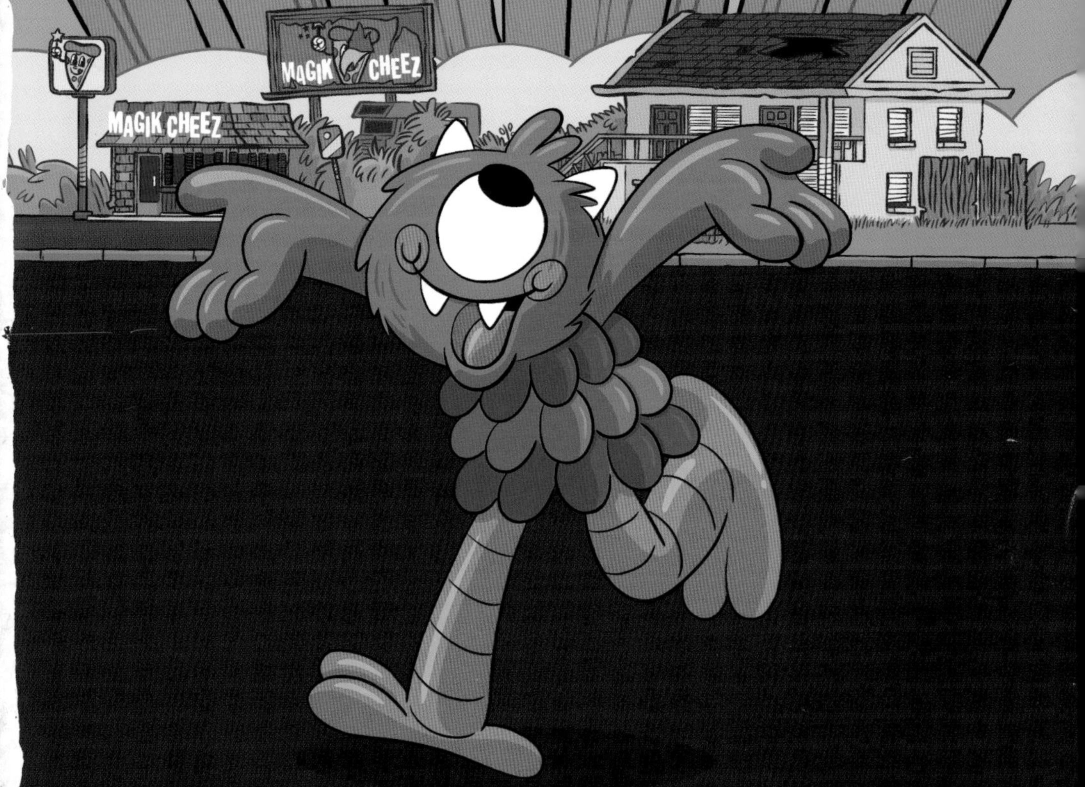
MAGIK CHEEZ
MAGIK CHEEZ

graphix

An Imprint of

SCHOLASTIC

All rights reserved. Published by Graphix,
an imprint of Scholastic Inc., *Publishers since 1920.*
SCHOLASTIC, GRAPHIX, and associated logos are trademarks
and/or registered trademarks of Scholastic Inc.

Library of Congress Control Number: 2018949525

ISBN 978-1-338-18604-8 (hardcover)
ISBN 978-1-338-18603-1 (paperback)

10 9 8 7 6 5 4 3 2 1   19 20 21 22 23

Printed in China   62
First edition, July 2019
Edited by Adam Rau
Book design by Phil Falco
Publisher: David Saylor

TO JAMES AND MICHAEL —
REMEMBER THAT BROTHERS STICK
TOGETHER, NO MATTER WHAT.

AND TO ERIN —
YOU ARE THE LOVE OF MY LIFE.

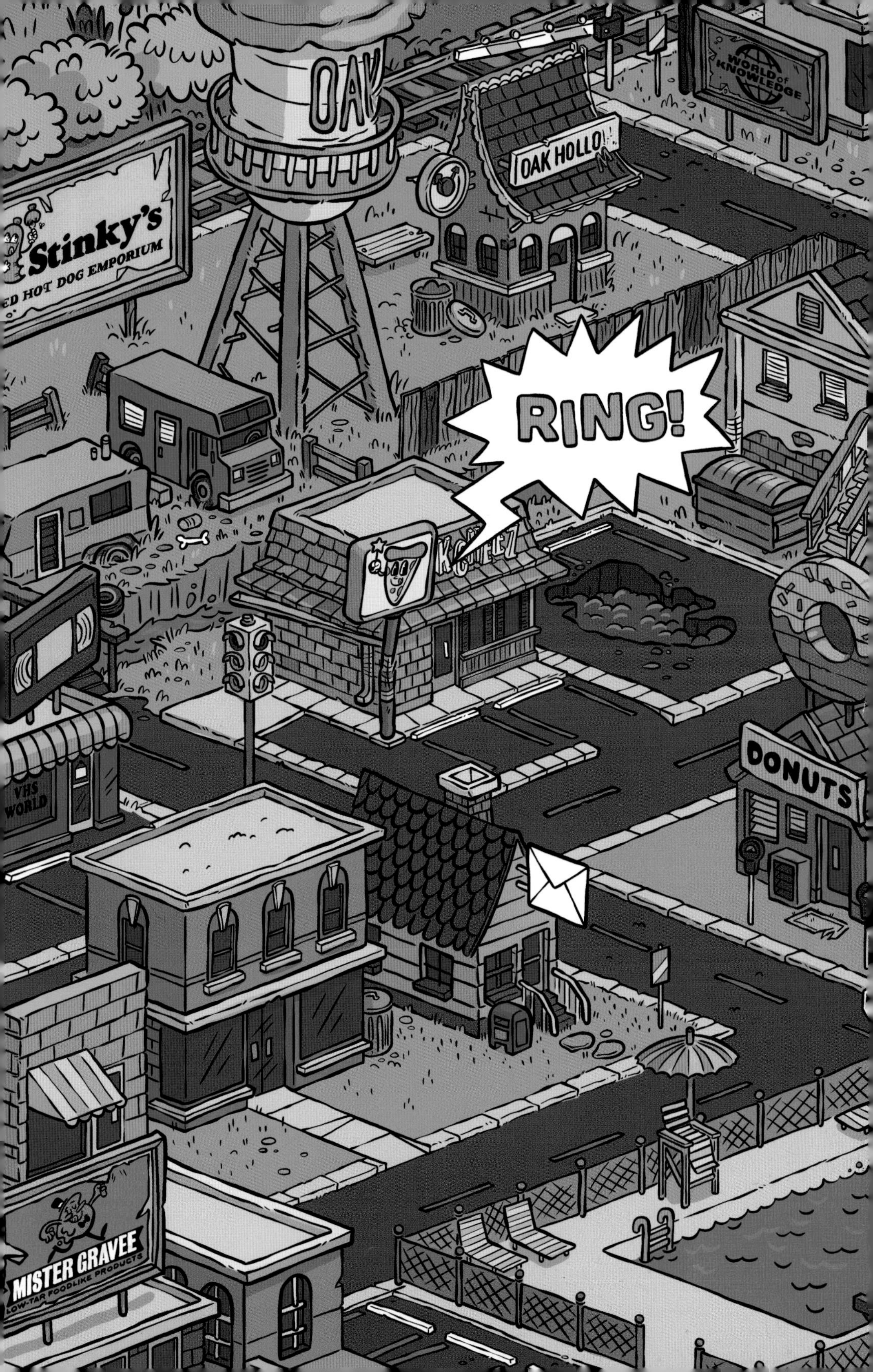
OAK
OAK HOLLO
WORLD of KNOWLEDGE
Stinky's
ED HOT DOG EMPORIUM
RING!
VHS WORLD
DONUTS
MISTER GRAVEE
LOW-TAR FOODLIKE PRODUCTS

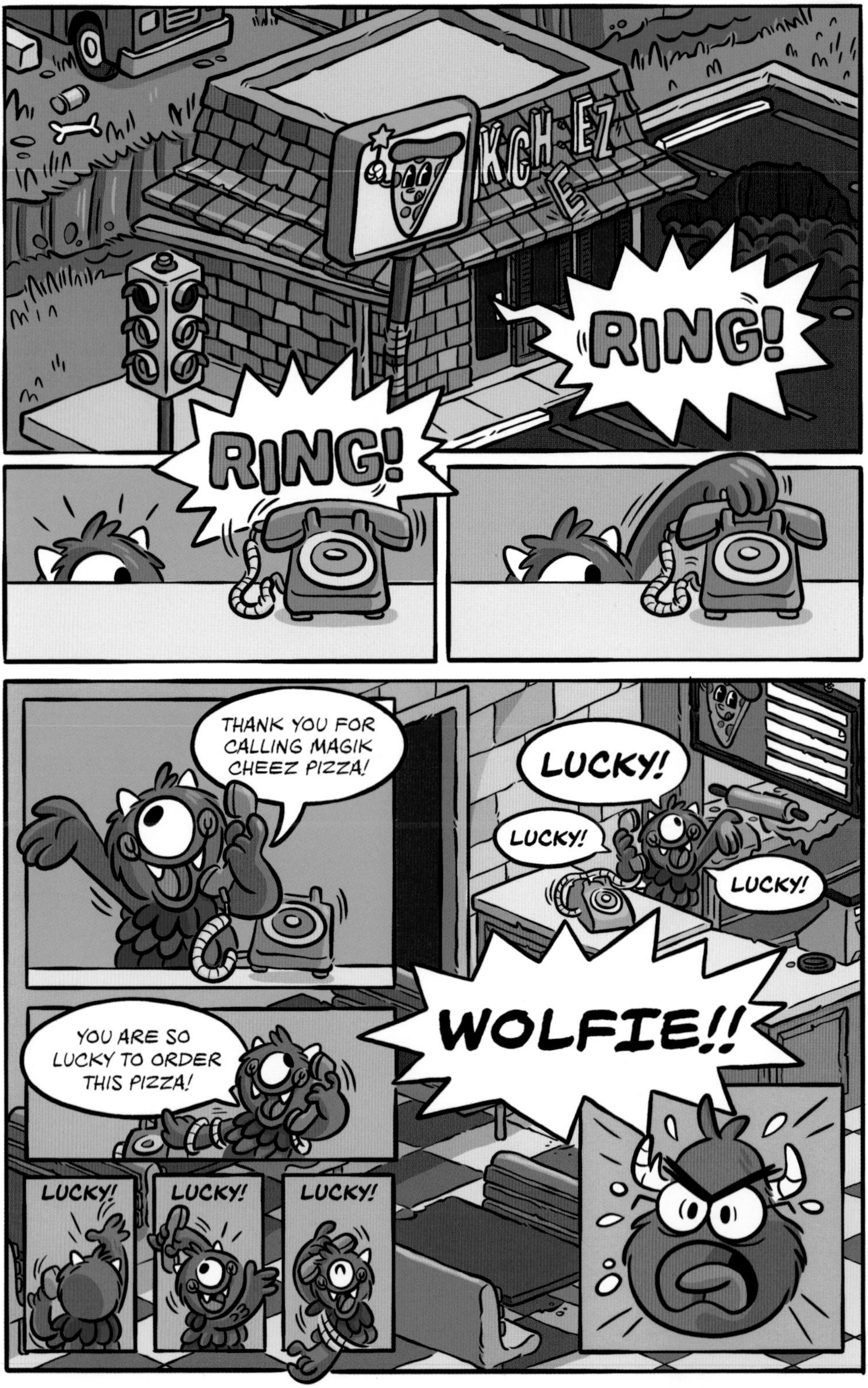
RING!
RING!
THANK YOU FOR CALLING MAGIK CHEEZ PIZZA!
LUCKY!
LUCKY!
LUCKY!
YOU ARE SO LUCKY TO ORDER THIS PIZZA!
LUCKY!
LUCKY!
LUCKY!
WOLFIE!!

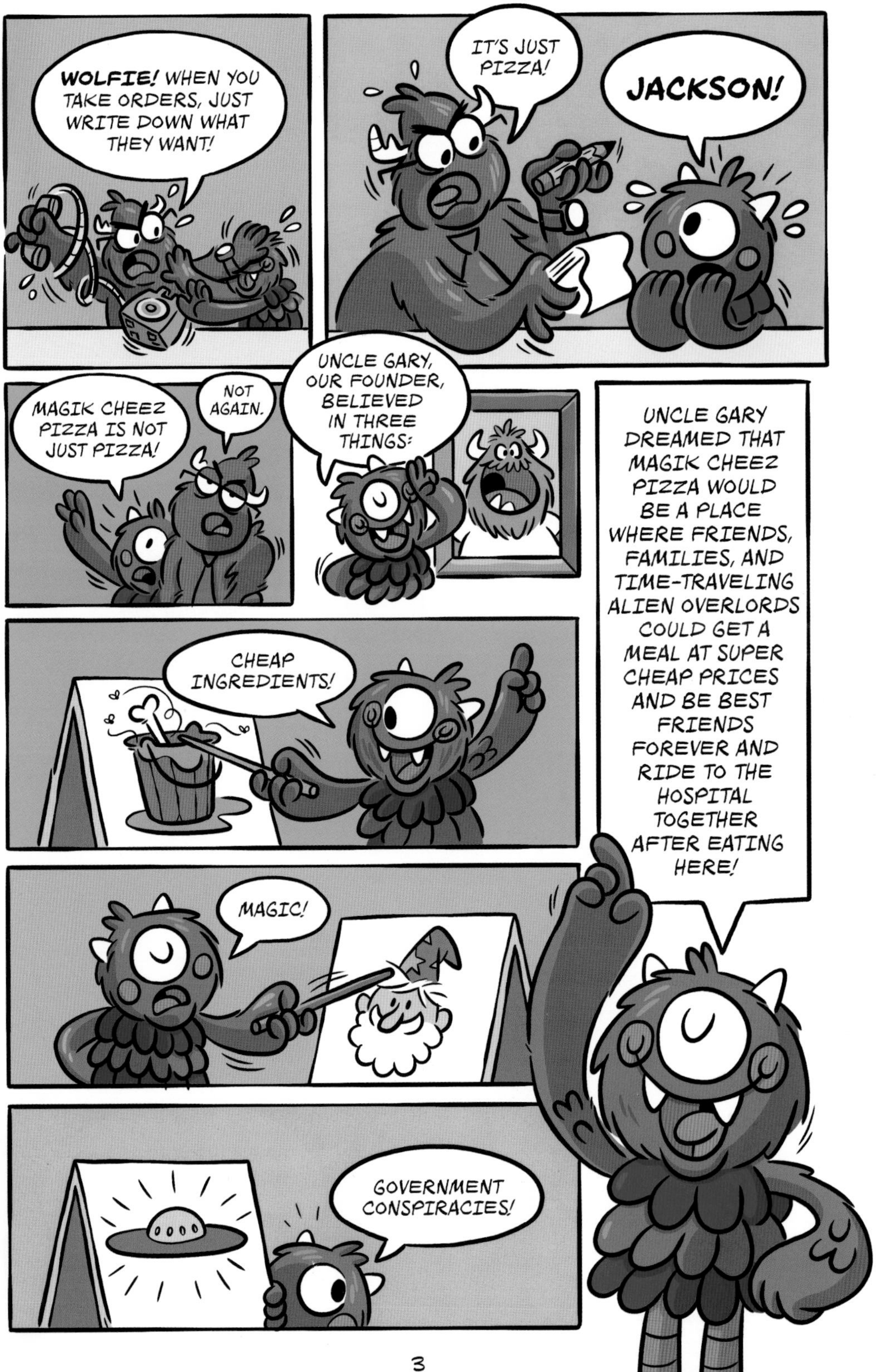

WOLFIE! WHEN YOU TAKE ORDERS, JUST WRITE DOWN WHAT THEY WANT!
IT'S JUST PIZZA!
JACKSON!
MAGIK CHEEZ PIZZA IS NOT JUST PIZZA!
NOT AGAIN.
UNCLE GARY, OUR FOUNDER, BELIEVED IN THREE THINGS:
CHEAP INGREDIENTS!
MAGIC!
GOVERNMENT CONSPIRACIES!
UNCLE GARY DREAMED THAT MAGIK CHEEZ PIZZA WOULD BE A PLACE WHERE FRIENDS, FAMILIES, AND TIME-TRAVELING ALIEN OVERLORDS COULD GET A MEAL AT SUPER CHEAP PRICES AND BE BEST FRIENDS FOREVER AND RIDE TO THE HOSPITAL TOGETHER AFTER EATING HERE!

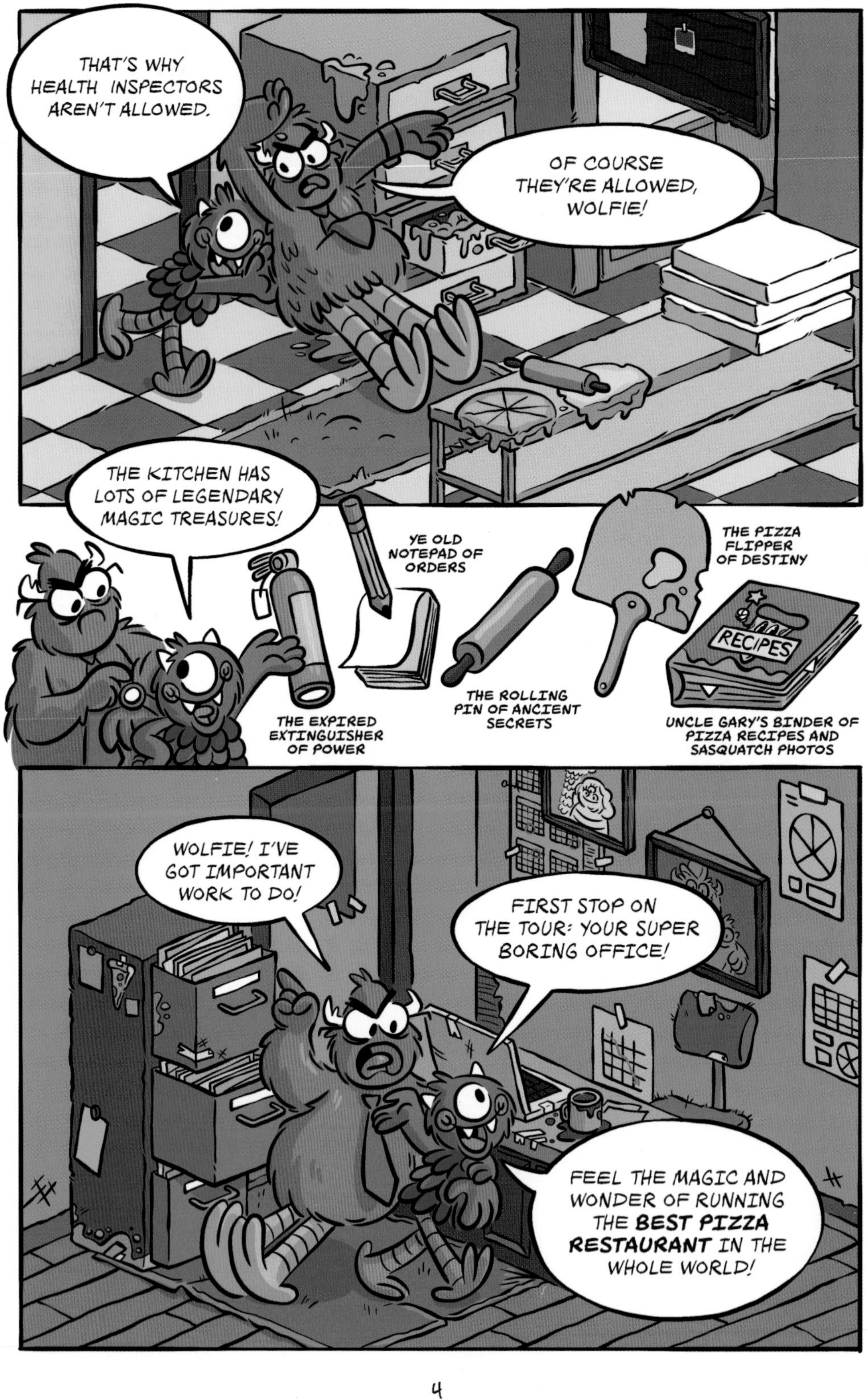
THAT'S WHY HEALTH INSPECTORS AREN'T ALLOWED.
OF COURSE THEY'RE ALLOWED, WOLFIE!
THE KITCHEN HAS LOTS OF LEGENDARY MAGIC TREASURES!
THE EXPIRED EXTINGUISHER OF POWER
YE OLD NOTEPAD OF ORDERS
THE ROLLING PIN OF ANCIENT SECRETS
THE PIZZA FLIPPER OF DESTINY
RECIPES
UNCLE GARY'S BINDER OF PIZZA RECIPES AND SASQUATCH PHOTOS
WOLFIE! I'VE GOT IMPORTANT WORK TO DO!
FIRST STOP ON THE TOUR: YOUR SUPER BORING OFFICE!
FEEL THE MAGIC AND WONDER OF RUNNING THE **BEST PIZZA RESTAURANT** IN THE WHOLE WORLD!

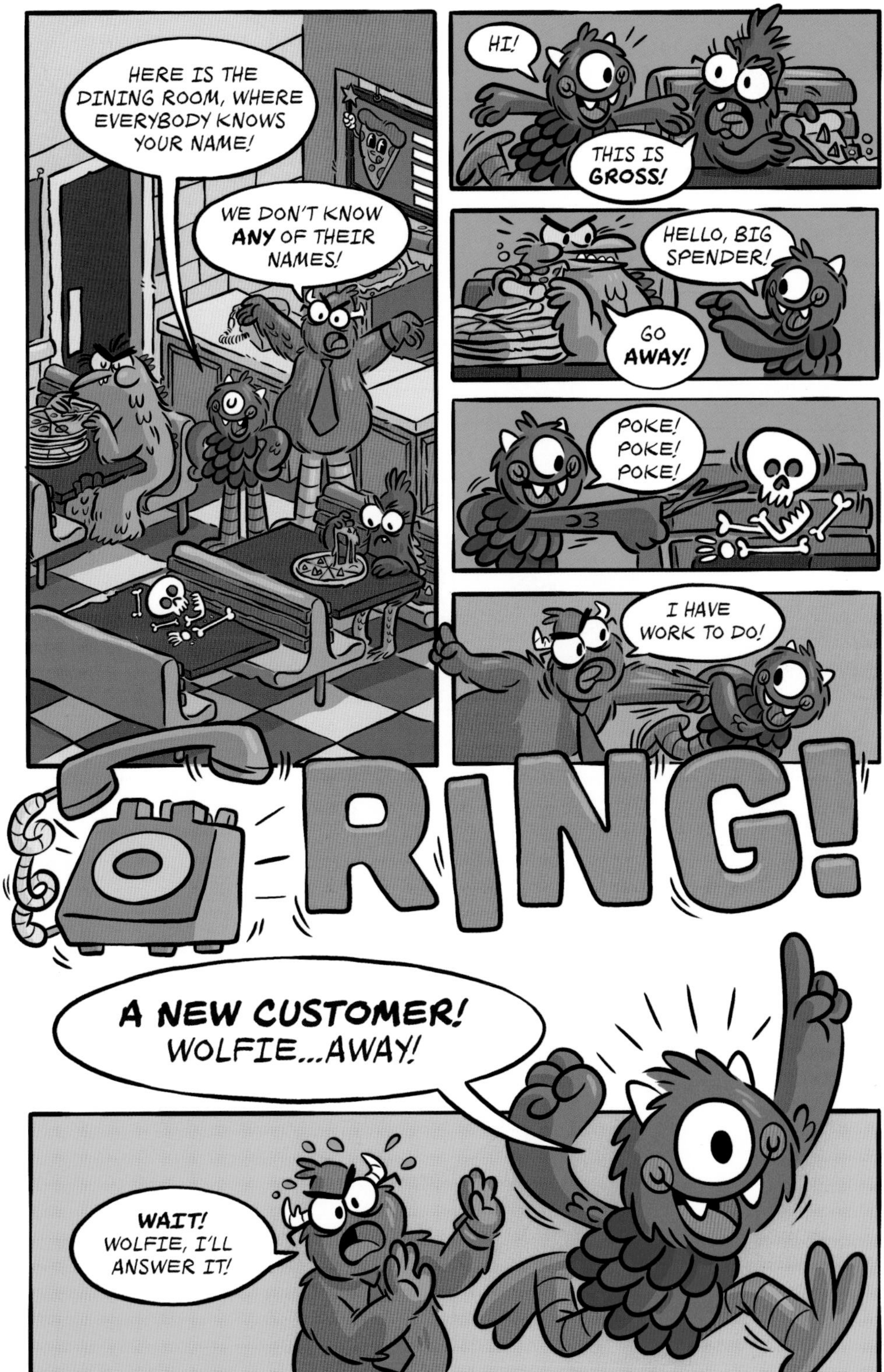

HERE IS THE DINING ROOM, WHERE EVERYBODY KNOWS YOUR NAME!
WE DON'T KNOW **ANY** OF THEIR NAMES!
HI!
THIS IS **GROSS!**
HELLO, BIG SPENDER!
GO **AWAY!**
POKE! POKE! POKE!
I HAVE WORK TO DO!
RING!
A NEW CUSTOMER! WOLFIE...AWAY!
WAIT! WOLFIE, I'LL ANSWER IT!

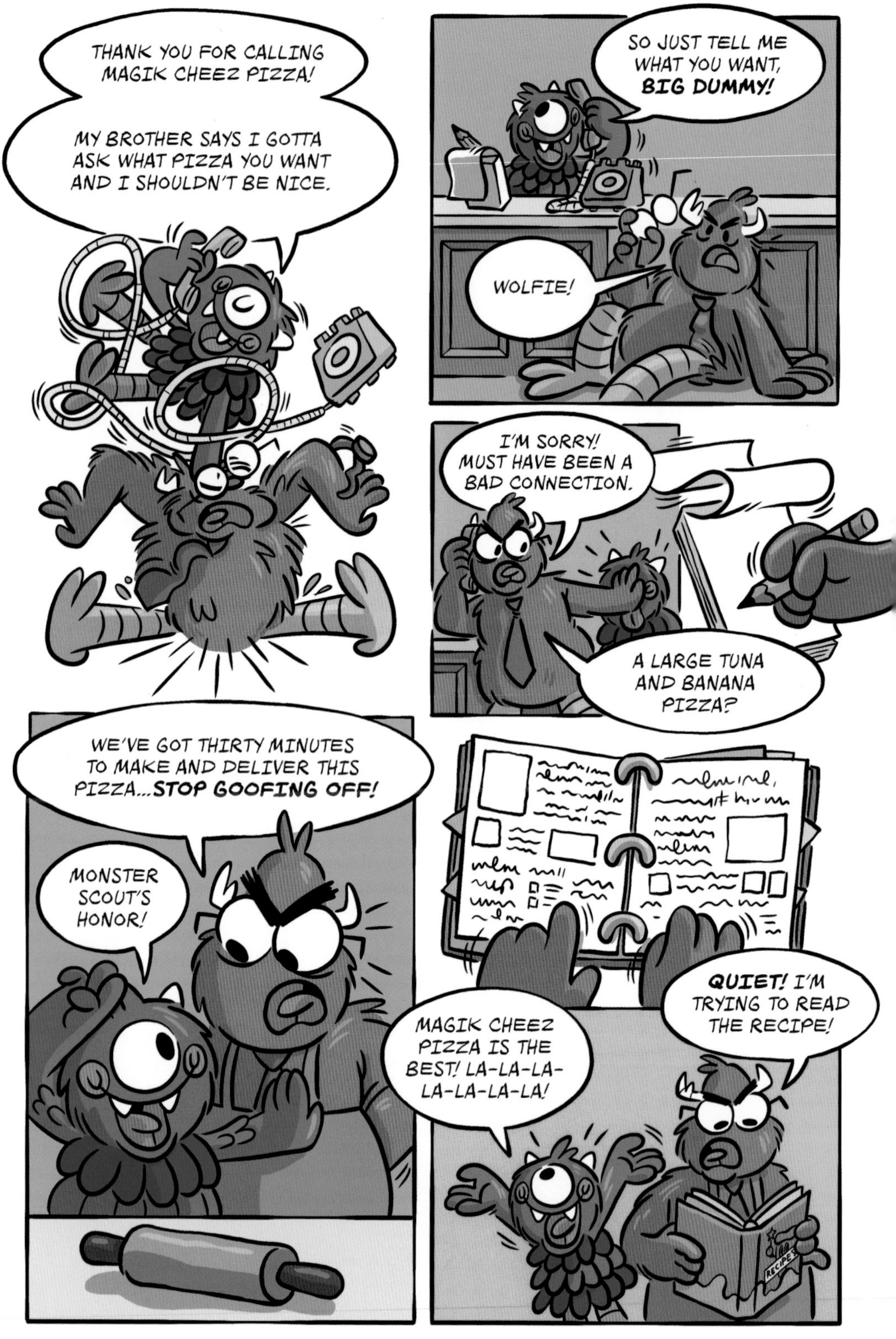

THANK YOU FOR CALLING MAGIK CHEEZ PIZZA!
MY BROTHER SAYS I GOTTA ASK WHAT PIZZA YOU WANT AND I SHOULDN'T BE NICE.
SO JUST TELL ME WHAT YOU WANT, **BIG DUMMY!**
WOLFIE!
I'M SORRY! MUST HAVE BEEN A BAD CONNECTION.
A LARGE TUNA AND BANANA PIZZA?
WE'VE GOT THIRTY MINUTES TO MAKE AND DELIVER THIS PIZZA... **STOP GOOFING OFF!**
MONSTER SCOUT'S HONOR!
MAGIK CHEEZ PIZZA IS THE BEST! LA-LA-LA-LA-LA-LA-LA!
QUIET! I'M TRYING TO READ THE RECIPE!
RECIPES

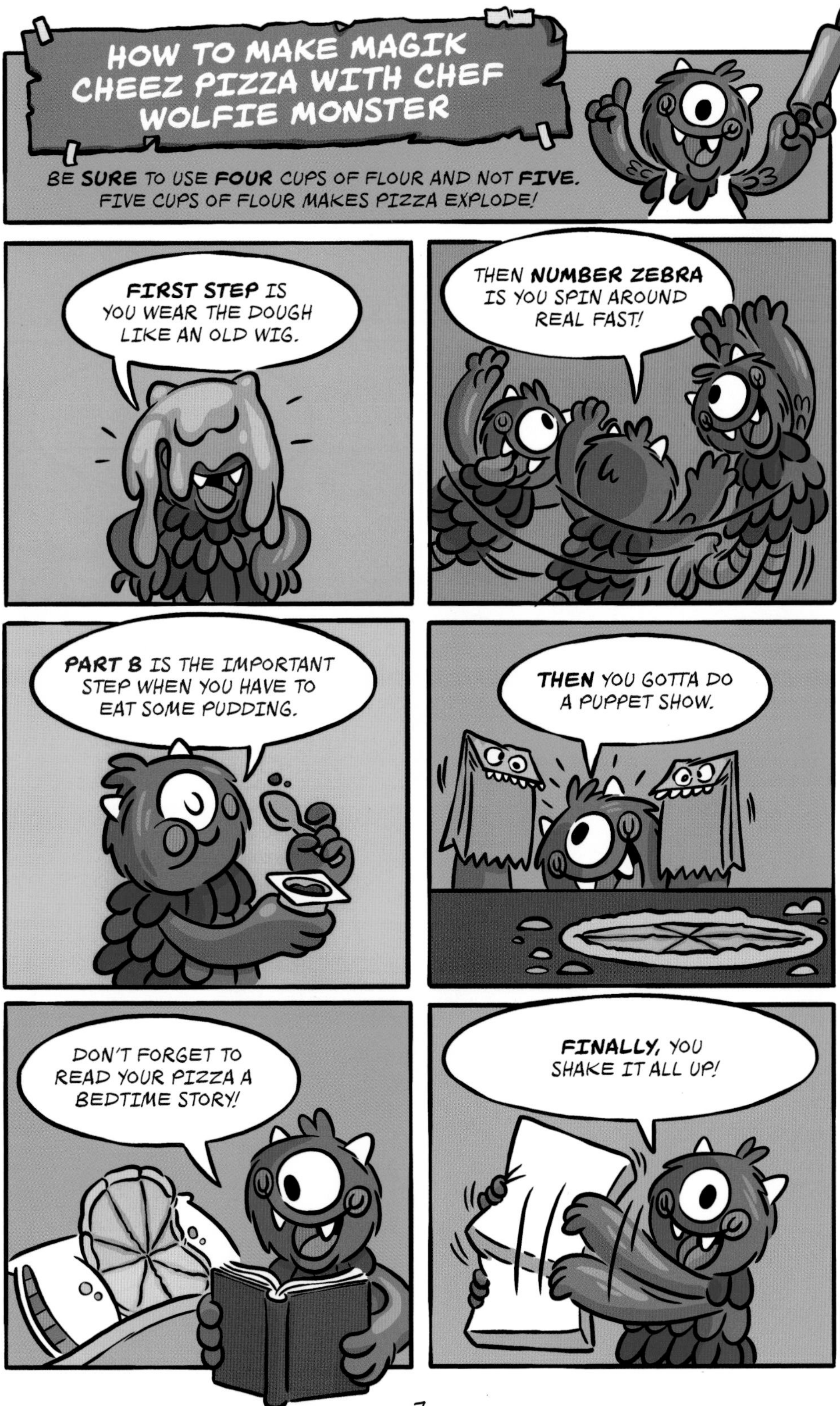
HOW TO MAKE MAGIK CHEEZ PIZZA WITH CHEF WOLFIE MONSTER
BE **SURE** TO USE **FOUR** CUPS OF FLOUR AND NOT **FIVE.** FIVE CUPS OF FLOUR MAKES PIZZA EXPLODE!
FIRST STEP IS YOU WEAR THE DOUGH LIKE AN OLD WIG.
THEN **NUMBER ZEBRA** IS YOU SPIN AROUND REAL FAST!
PART B IS THE IMPORTANT STEP WHEN YOU HAVE TO EAT SOME PUDDING.
THEN YOU GOTTA DO A PUPPET SHOW.
DON'T FORGET TO READ YOUR PIZZA A BEDTIME STORY!
FINALLY, YOU SHAKE IT ALL UP!

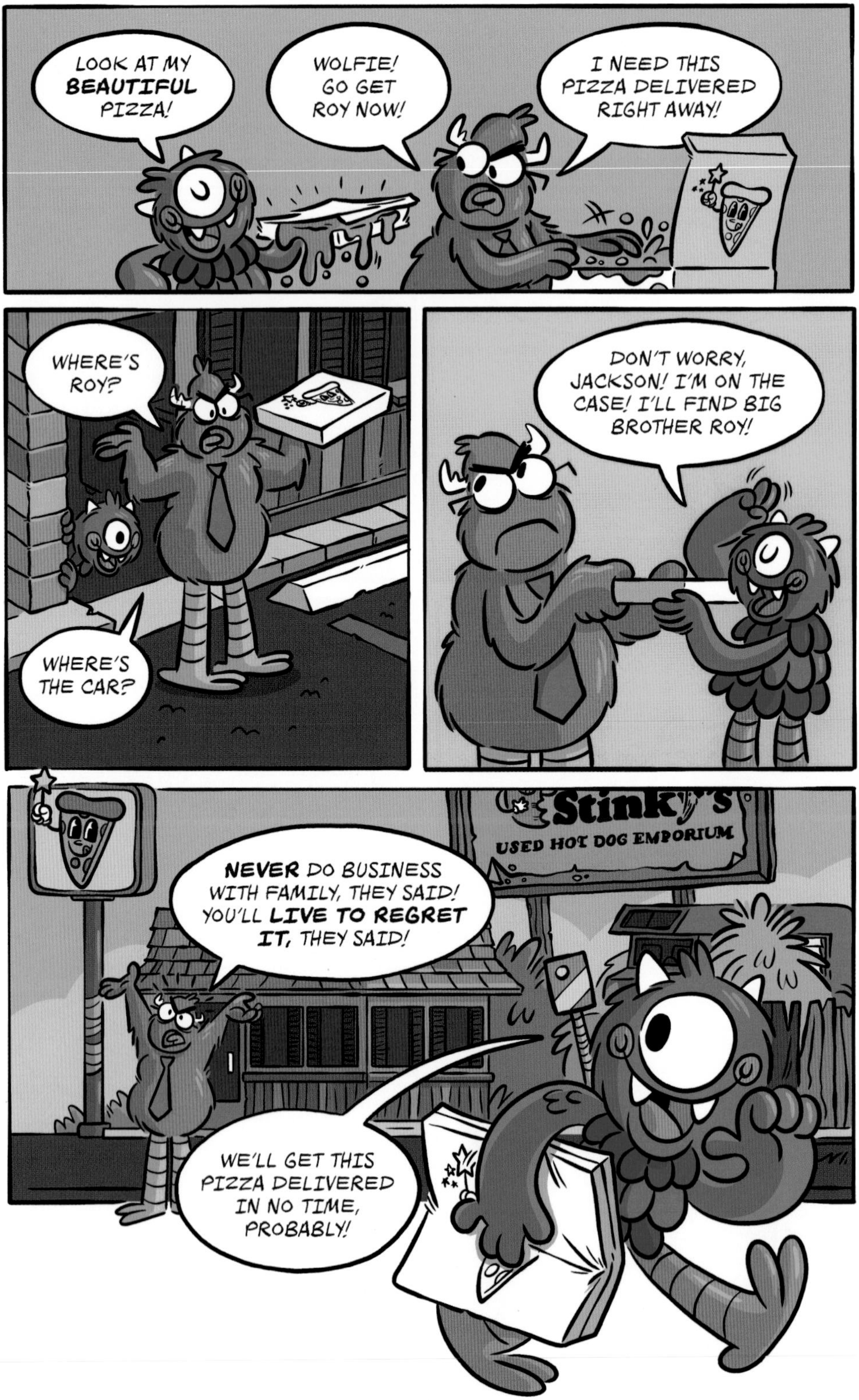
LOOK AT MY **BEAUTIFUL** PIZZA!
WOLFIE! GO GET ROY NOW!
I NEED THIS PIZZA DELIVERED RIGHT AWAY!
WHERE'S ROY?
WHERE'S THE CAR?
DON'T WORRY, JACKSON! I'M ON THE CASE! I'LL FIND BIG BROTHER ROY!
Stinky's
USED HOT DOG EMPORIUM
NEVER DO BUSINESS WITH FAMILY, THEY SAID! YOU'LL **LIVE TO REGRET IT,** THEY SAID!
WE'LL GET THIS PIZZA DELIVERED IN NO TIME, PROBABLY!

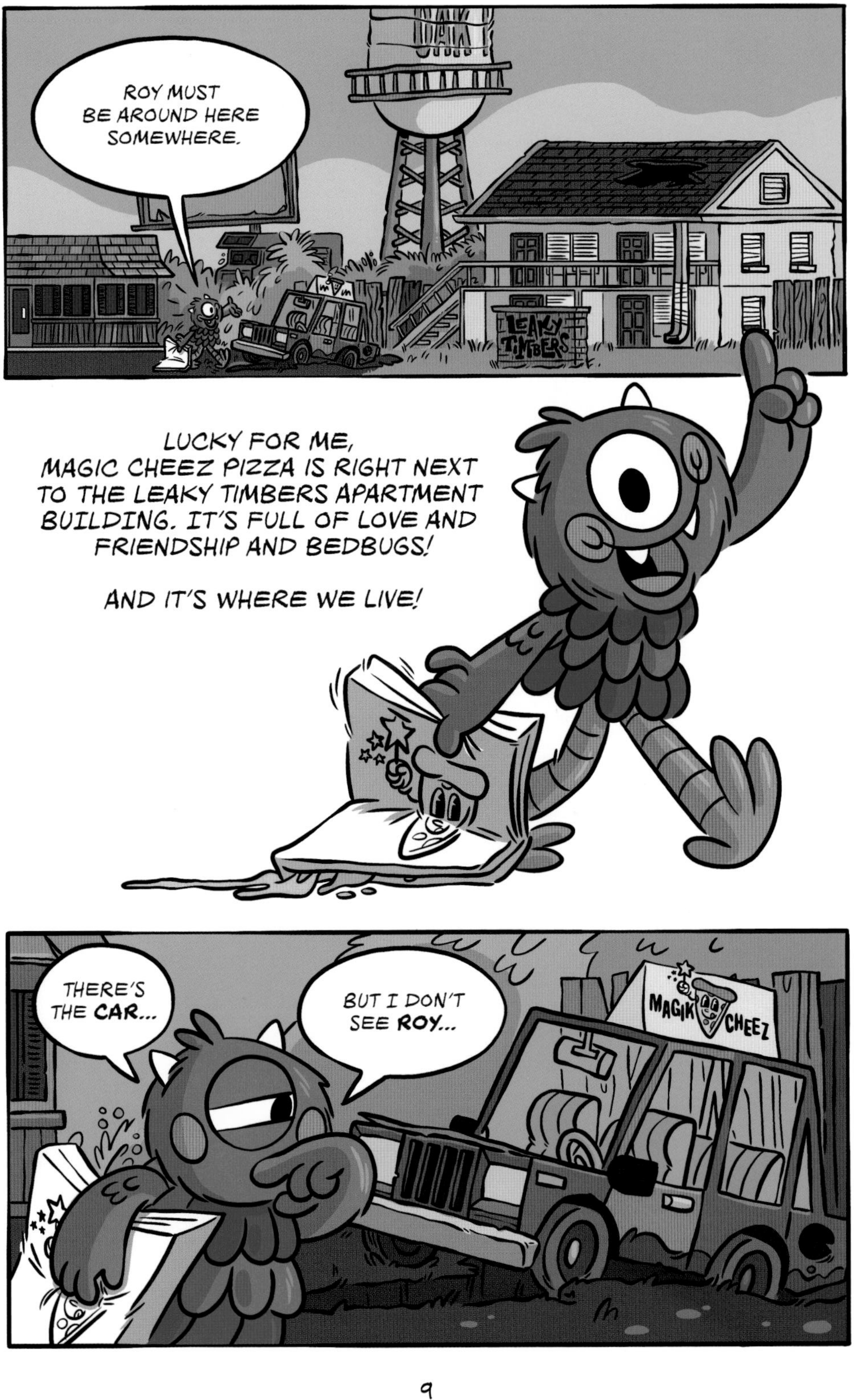
ROY MUST BE AROUND HERE SOMEWHERE.
LEAKY TIMBERS
LUCKY FOR ME, MAGIC CHEEZ PIZZA IS RIGHT NEXT TO THE LEAKY TIMBERS APARTMENT BUILDING. IT'S FULL OF LOVE AND FRIENDSHIP AND BEDBUGS!
AND IT'S WHERE WE LIVE!
THERE'S THE **CAR**...
BUT I DON'T SEE **ROY**...
MAGIK CHEEZ

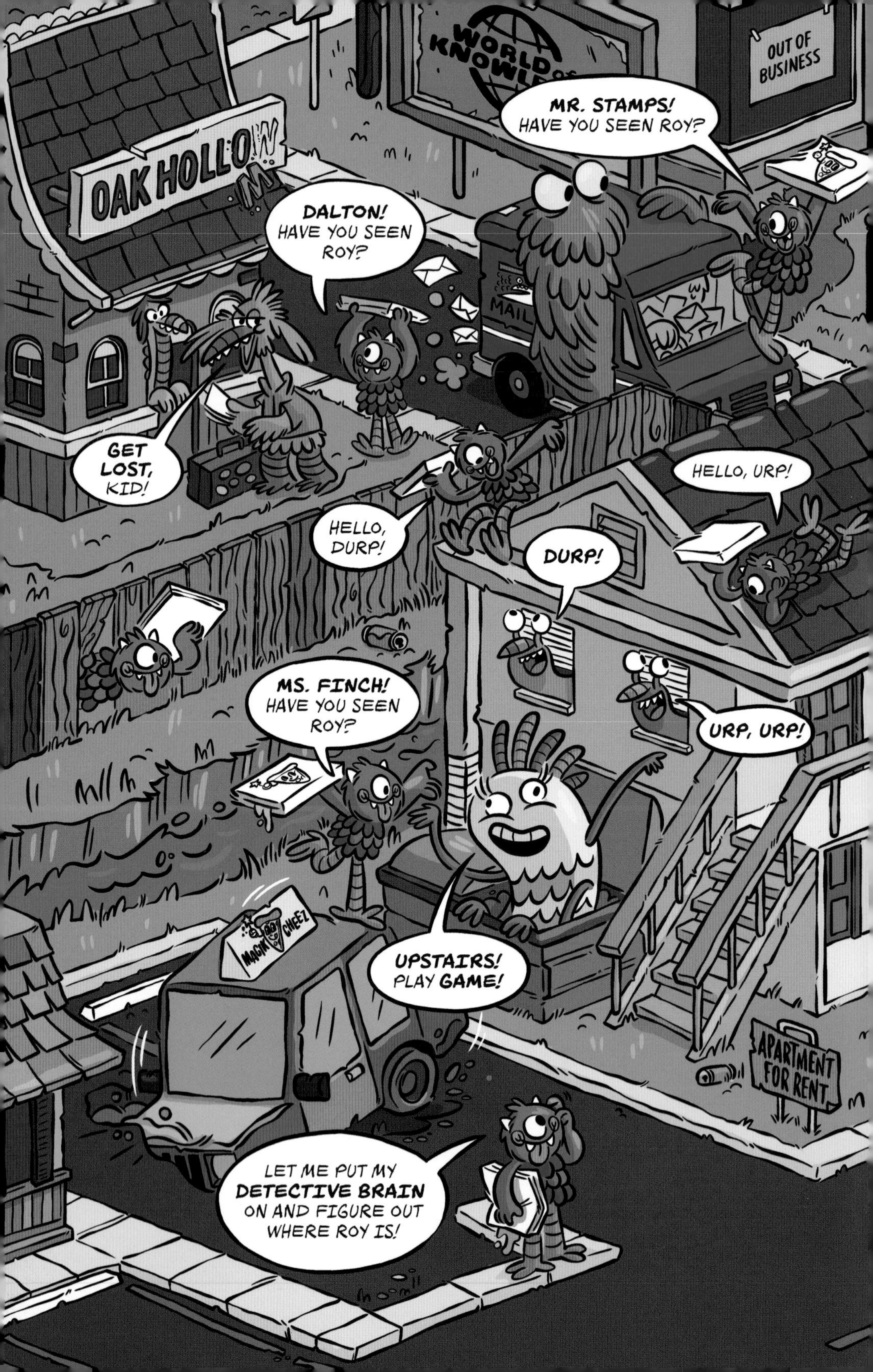
OAK HOLLOW
WORLD OF KNOWL
OUT OF BUSINESS
MR. STAMPS! HAVE YOU SEEN ROY?
DALTON! HAVE YOU SEEN ROY?
MAIL
GET LOST, KID!
HELLO, URP!
HELLO, DURP!
DURP!
MS. FINCH! HAVE YOU SEEN ROY?
URP, URP!
MAGIK CHEEZ
UPSTAIRS! PLAY GAME!
APARTMENT FOR RENT
LET ME PUT MY DETECTIVE BRAIN ON AND FIGURE OUT WHERE ROY IS!

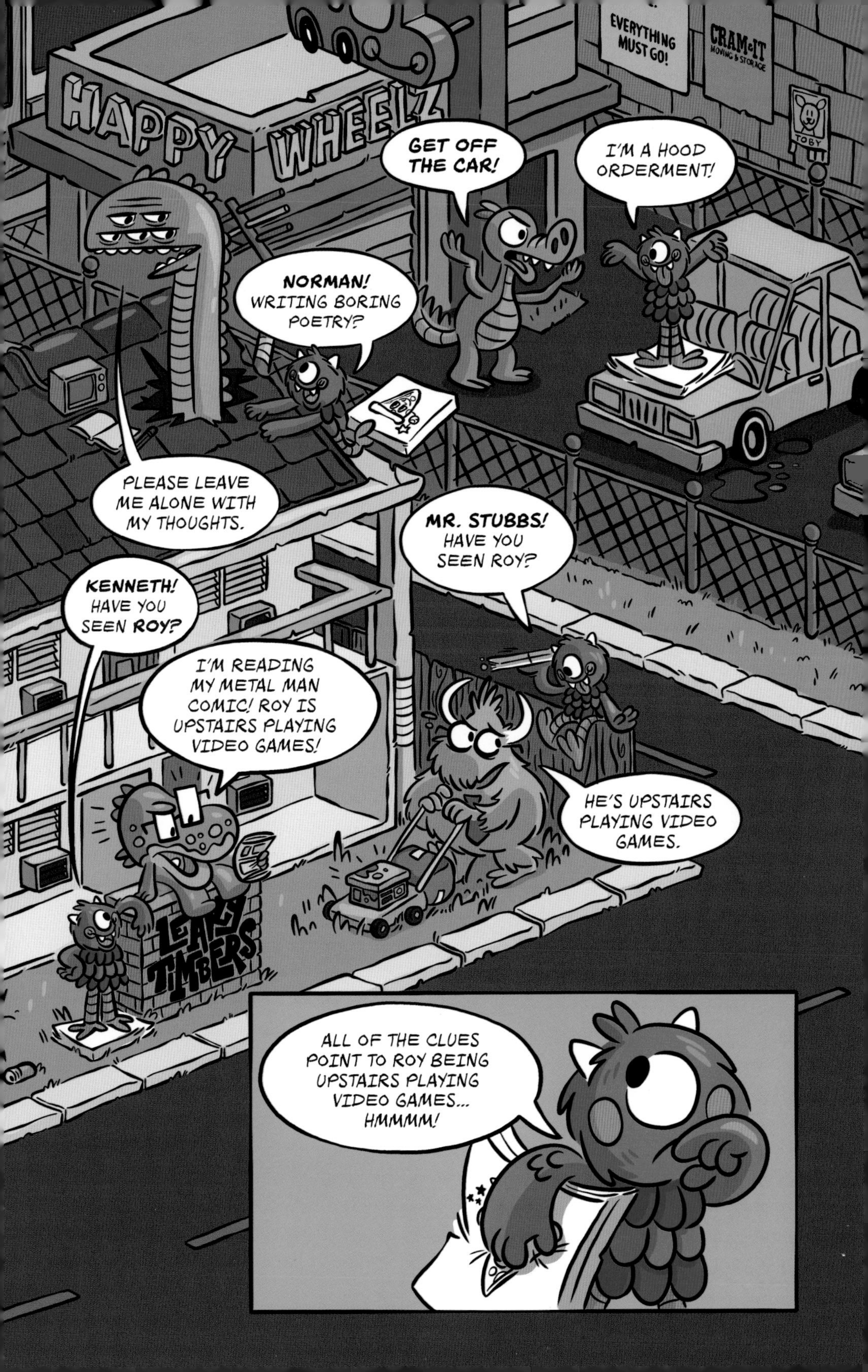
HAPPY WHEELZ
EVERYTHING MUST GO!
CRAM-IT MOVING & STORAGE
TOBY
NORMAN! WRITING BORING POETRY?
PLEASE LEAVE ME ALONE WITH MY THOUGHTS.
GET OFF THE CAR!
I'M A HOOD ORDERMENT!
MR. STUBBS! HAVE YOU SEEN ROY?
HE'S UPSTAIRS PLAYING VIDEO GAMES.
KENNETH! HAVE YOU SEEN ROY?
I'M READING MY METAL MAN COMIC! ROY IS UPSTAIRS PLAYING VIDEO GAMES!
LEAKY TIMBERS
ALL OF THE CLUES POINT TO ROY BEING UPSTAIRS PLAYING VIDEO GAMES... HMMMM!

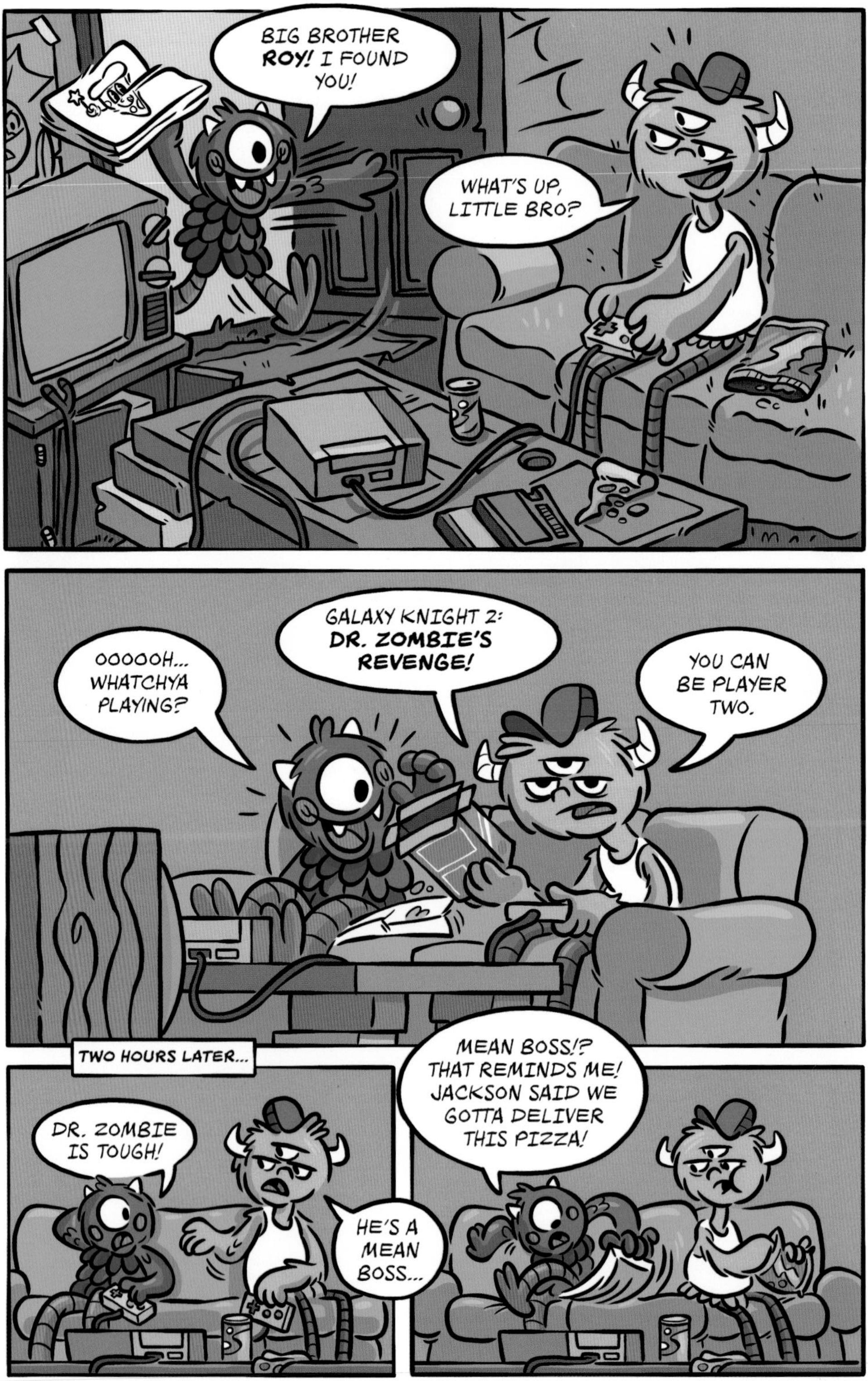
BIG BROTHER ROY! I FOUND YOU!
WHAT'S UP, LITTLE BRO?
OOOOOH... WHATCHYA PLAYING?
GALAXY KNIGHT 2: DR. ZOMBIE'S REVENGE!
YOU CAN BE PLAYER TWO.
TWO HOURS LATER...
DR. ZOMBIE IS TOUGH!
HE'S A MEAN BOSS...
MEAN BOSS!? THAT REMINDS ME! JACKSON SAID WE GOTTA DELIVER THIS PIZZA!

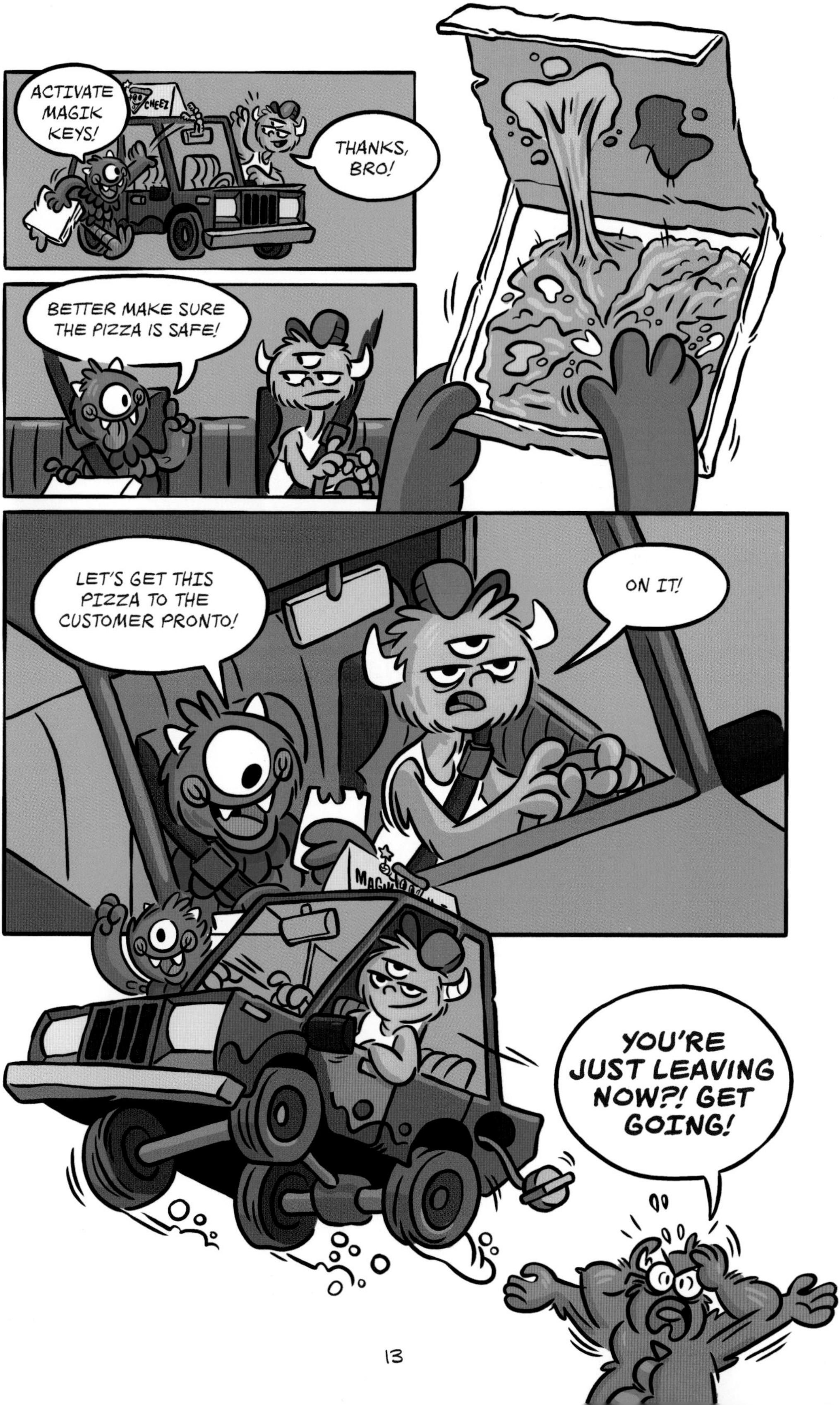
ACTIVATE MAGIK KEYS!
CHEEZ
THANKS, BRO!
BETTER MAKE SURE THE PIZZA IS SAFE!
LET'S GET THIS PIZZA TO THE CUSTOMER PRONTO!
ON IT!
YOU'RE JUST LEAVING NOW?! GET GOING!

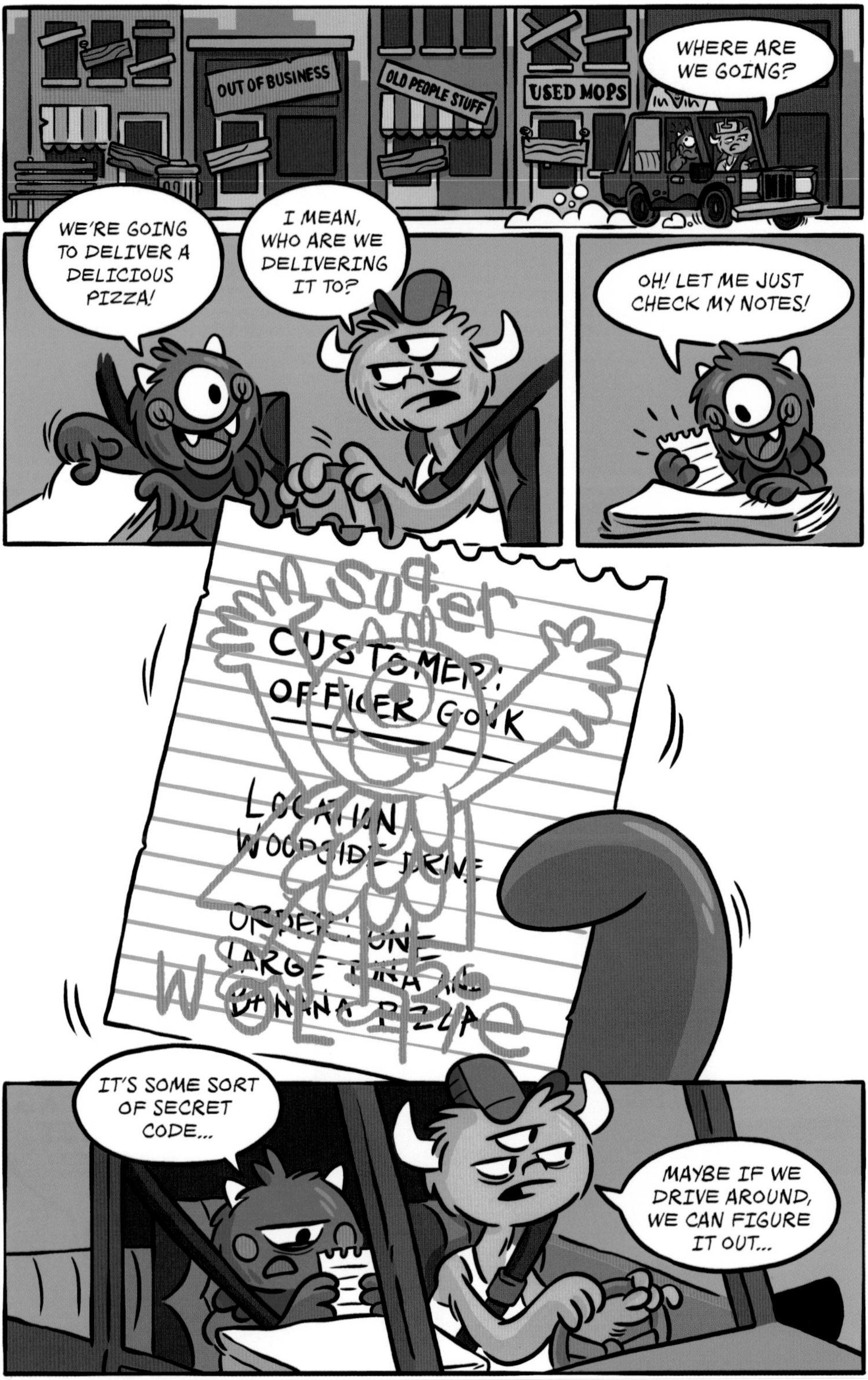
OUT OF BUSINESS
OLD PEOPLE STUFF
USED MOPS
WHERE ARE WE GOING?
WE'RE GOING TO DELIVER A DELICIOUS PIZZA!
I MEAN, WHO ARE WE DELIVERING IT TO?
OH! LET ME JUST CHECK MY NOTES!
CUSTOMER:
OFFICER GONK
LOCATION
WOODSIDE DRIVE
IT'S SOME SORT OF SECRET CODE...
MAYBE IF WE DRIVE AROUND, WE CAN FIGURE IT OUT...

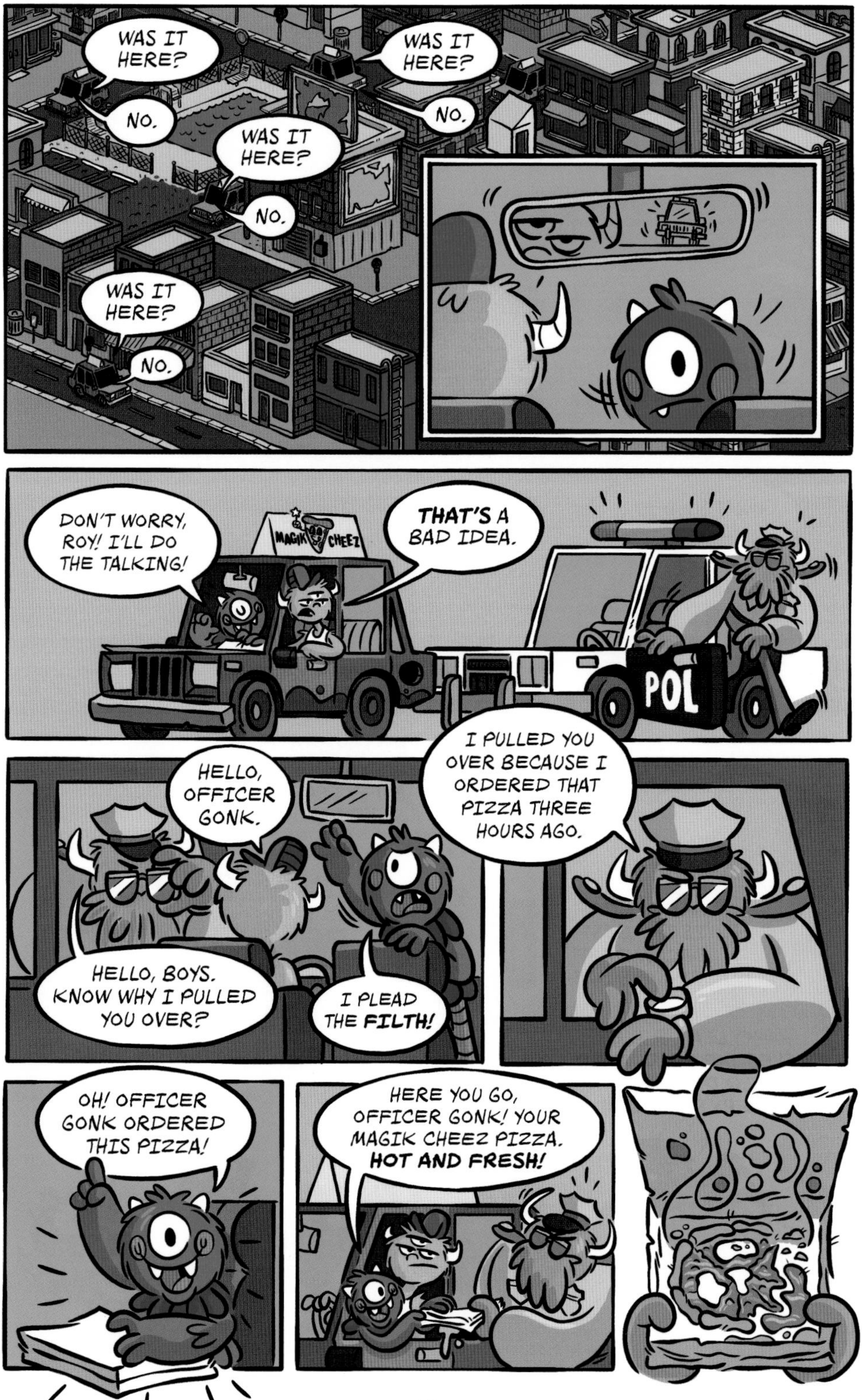
WAS IT HERE?
NO.
WAS IT HERE?
NO.
WAS IT HERE?
NO.
WAS IT HERE?
NO.
DON'T WORRY, ROY! I'LL DO THE TALKING!
MAGIK CHEEZ
THAT'S A BAD IDEA.
POL
HELLO, OFFICER GONK.
HELLO, BOYS. KNOW WHY I PULLED YOU OVER?
I PLEAD THE FILTH!
I PULLED YOU OVER BECAUSE I ORDERED THAT PIZZA THREE HOURS AGO.
OH! OFFICER GONK ORDERED THIS PIZZA!
HERE YOU GO, OFFICER GONK! YOUR MAGIK CHEEZ PIZZA. HOT AND FRESH!

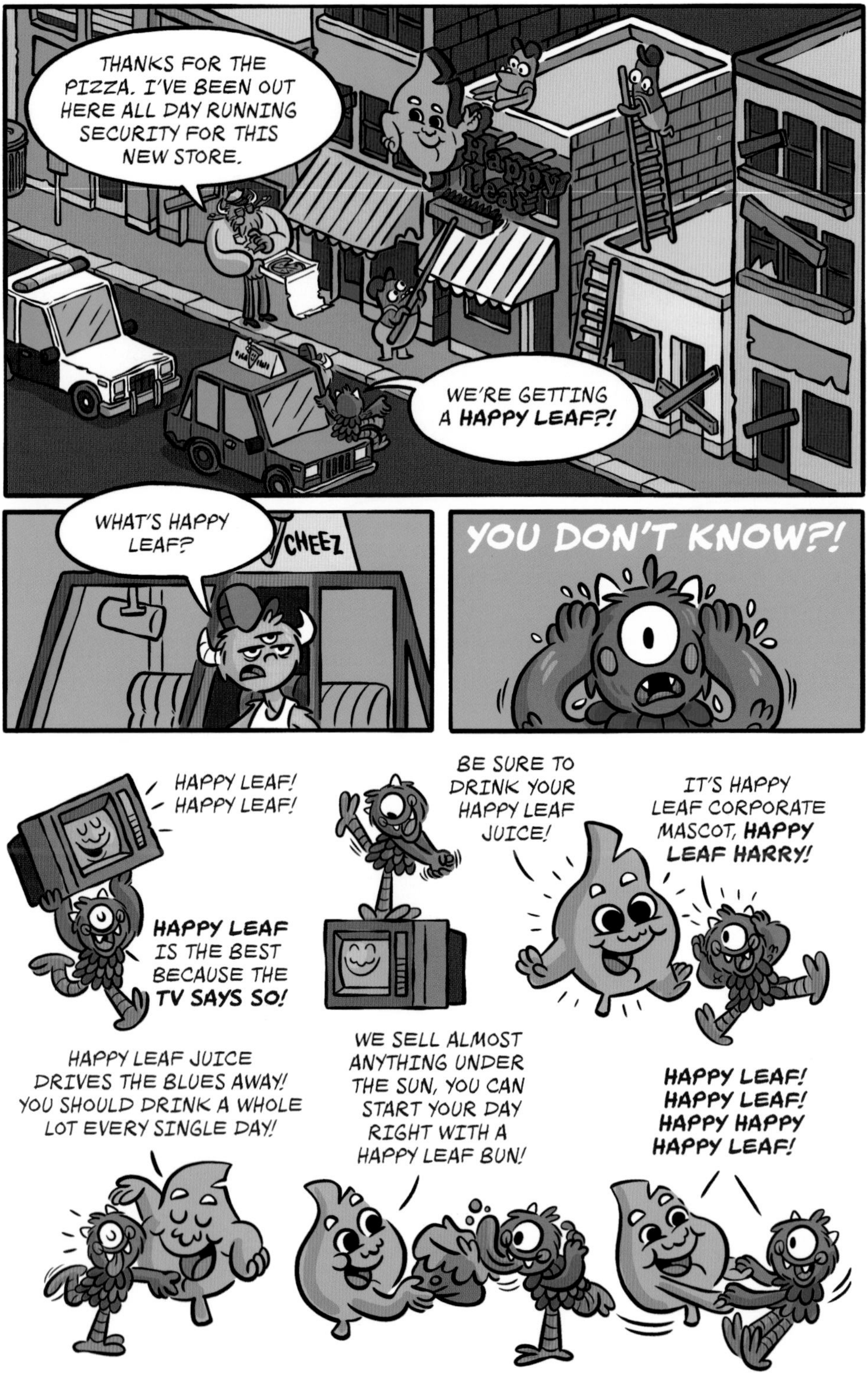
THANKS FOR THE PIZZA. I'VE BEEN OUT HERE ALL DAY RUNNING SECURITY FOR THIS NEW STORE.
Happy Leaf
WE'RE GETTING A **HAPPY LEAF?!**
WHAT'S HAPPY LEAF?
CHEEZ
YOU DON'T KNOW?!
HAPPY LEAF! HAPPY LEAF!
HAPPY LEAF IS THE BEST BECAUSE THE **TV SAYS SO!**
BE SURE TO DRINK YOUR HAPPY LEAF JUICE!
IT'S HAPPY LEAF CORPORATE MASCOT, **HAPPY LEAF HARRY!**
HAPPY LEAF JUICE DRIVES THE BLUES AWAY! YOU SHOULD DRINK A WHOLE LOT EVERY SINGLE DAY!
WE SELL ALMOST ANYTHING UNDER THE SUN, YOU CAN START YOUR DAY RIGHT WITH A HAPPY LEAF BUN!
HAPPY LEAF! HAPPY LEAF! HAPPY HAPPY HAPPY LEAF!

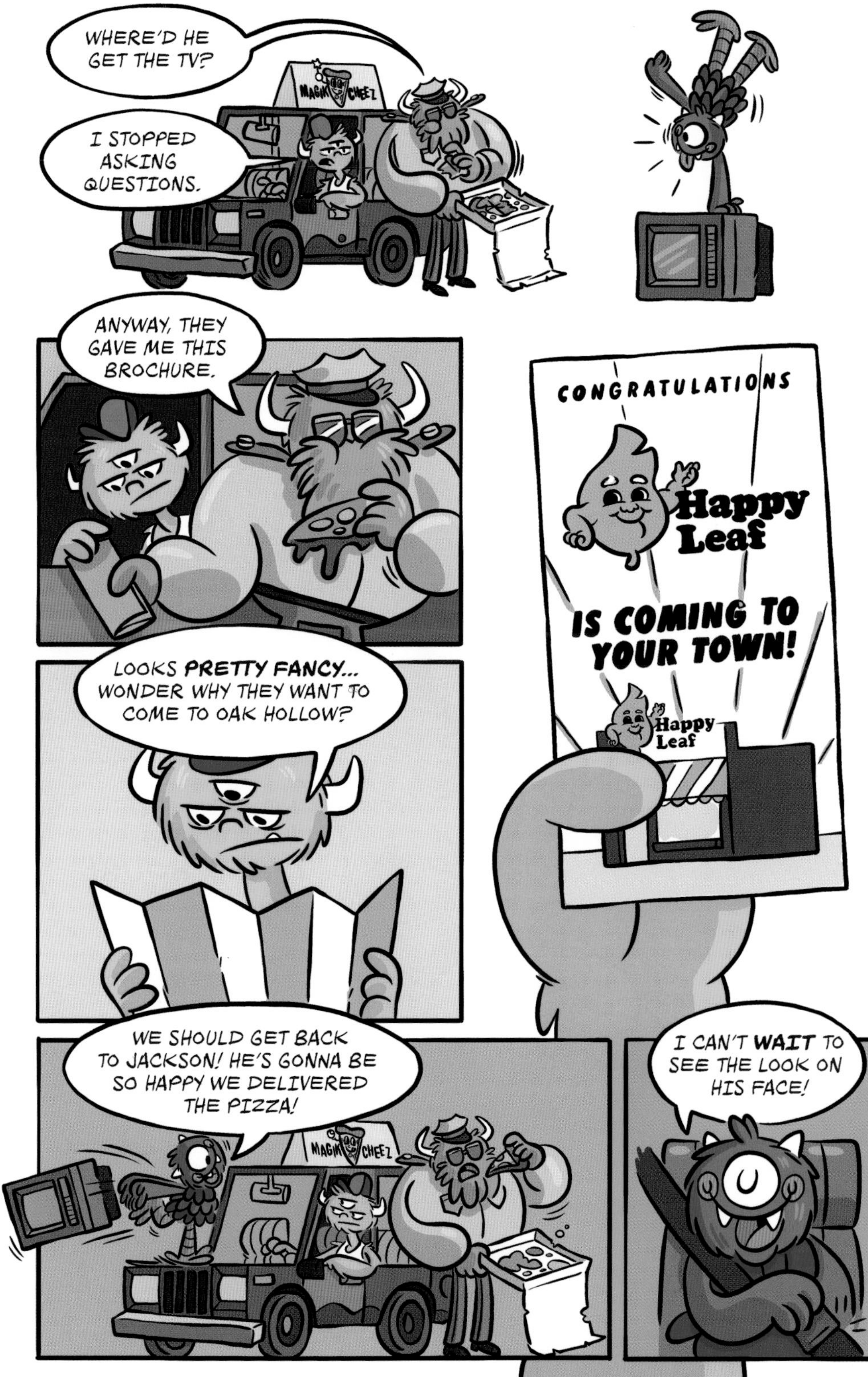
WHERE'D HE GET THE TV?
MAGIK CHEEZ
I STOPPED ASKING QUESTIONS.
ANYWAY, THEY GAVE ME THIS BROCHURE.
CONGRATULATIONS
Happy Leaf
IS COMING TO YOUR TOWN!
Happy Leaf
LOOKS **PRETTY FANCY...** WONDER WHY THEY WANT TO COME TO OAK HOLLOW?
WE SHOULD GET BACK TO JACKSON! HE'S GONNA BE SO HAPPY WE DELIVERED THE PIZZA!
MAGIK CHEEZ
I CAN'T **WAIT** TO SEE THE LOOK ON HIS FACE!

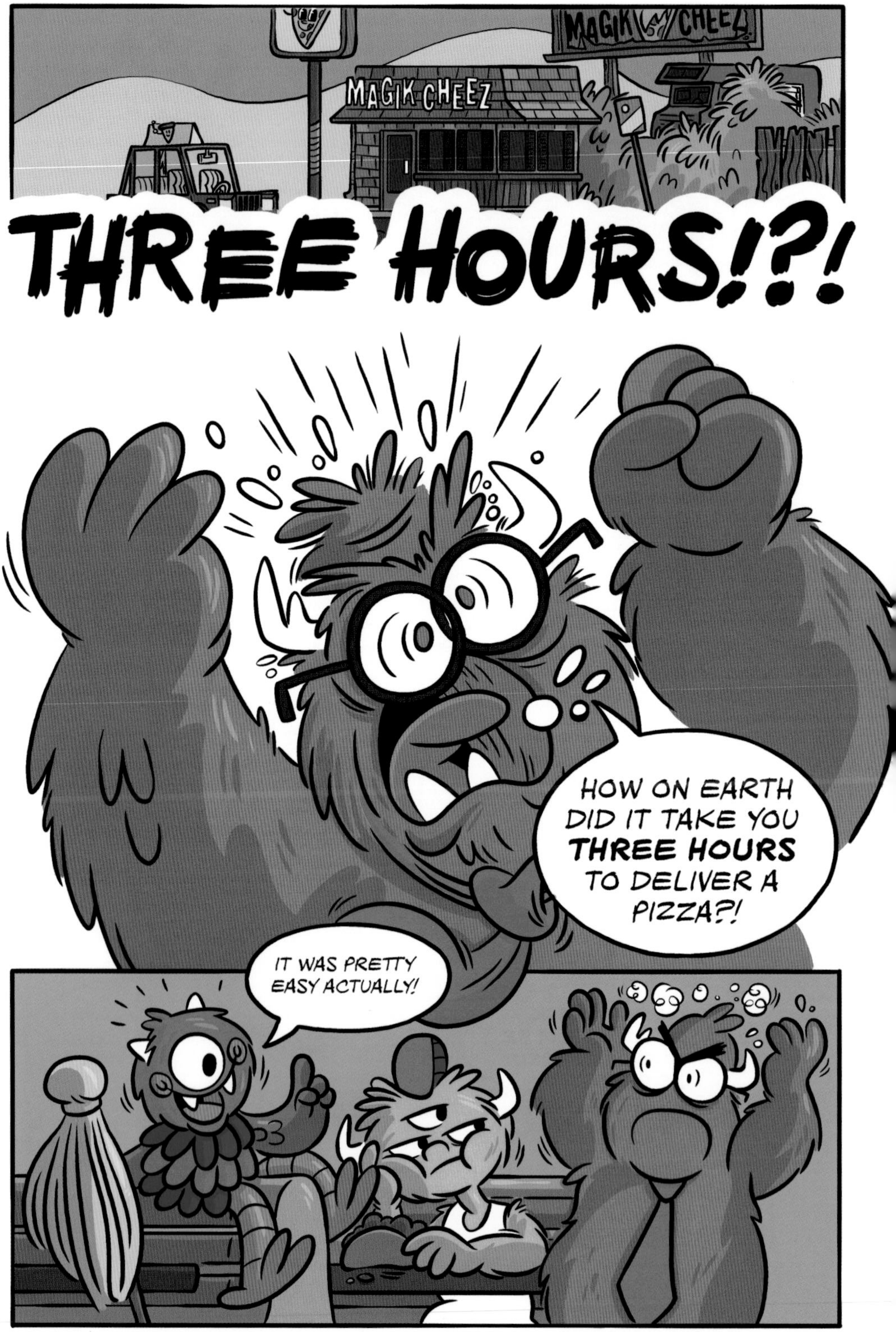
MAGIK CHEEZ
MAGIK CHEEZ
THREE HOURS!?!
HOW ON EARTH DID IT TAKE YOU **THREE HOURS** TO DELIVER A PIZZA?!
IT WAS PRETTY EASY ACTUALLY!

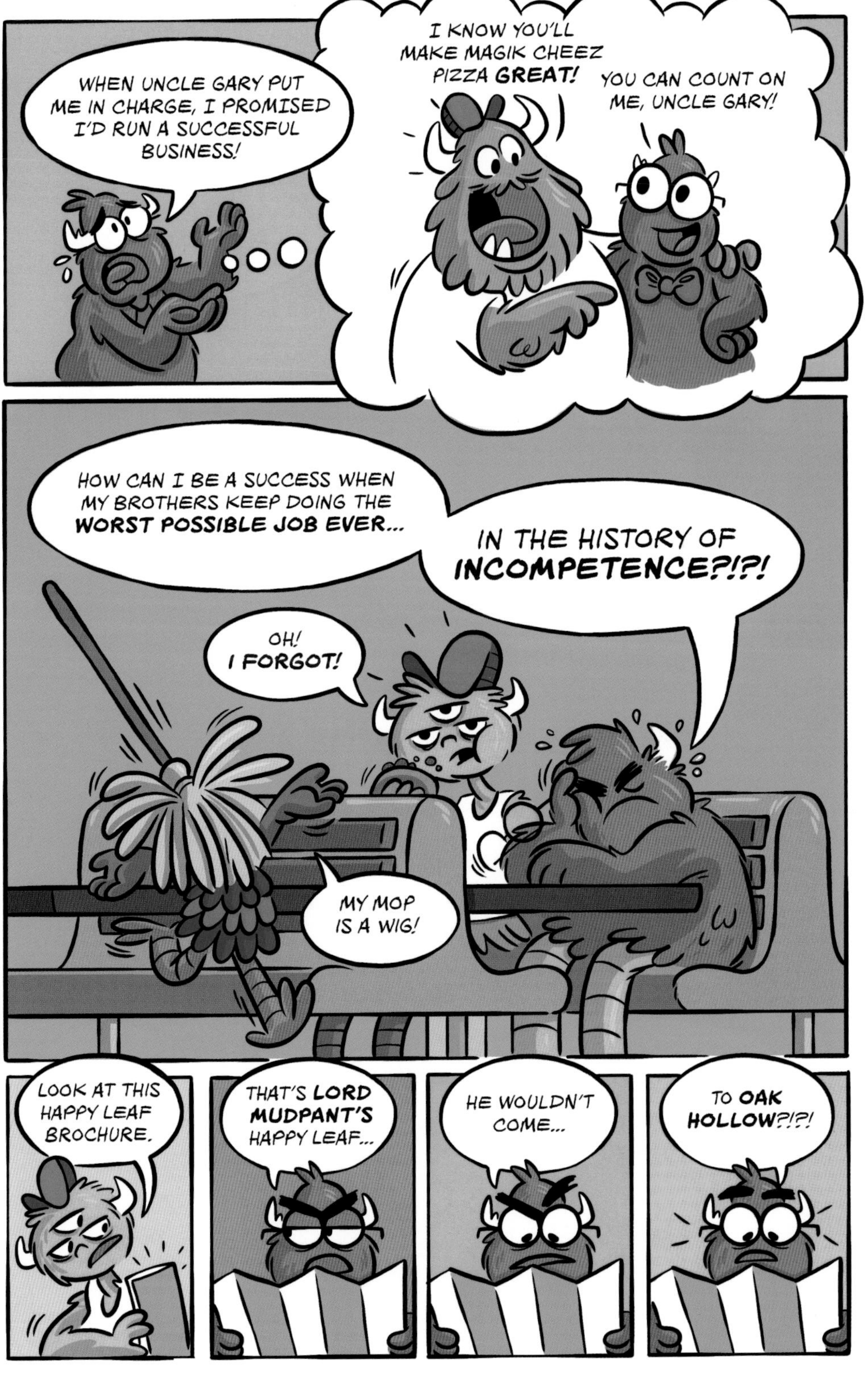
WHEN UNCLE GARY PUT ME IN CHARGE, I PROMISED I'D RUN A SUCCESSFUL BUSINESS!
I KNOW YOU'LL MAKE MAGIK CHEEZ PIZZA GREAT!
YOU CAN COUNT ON ME, UNCLE GARY!
HOW CAN I BE A SUCCESS WHEN MY BROTHERS KEEP DOING THE WORST POSSIBLE JOB EVER...
IN THE HISTORY OF INCOMPETENCE?!?!
OH! I FORGOT!
MY MOP IS A WIG!
LOOK AT THIS HAPPY LEAF BROCHURE.
THAT'S LORD MUDPANT'S HAPPY LEAF...
HE WOULDN'T COME...
TO OAK HOLLOW?!?!

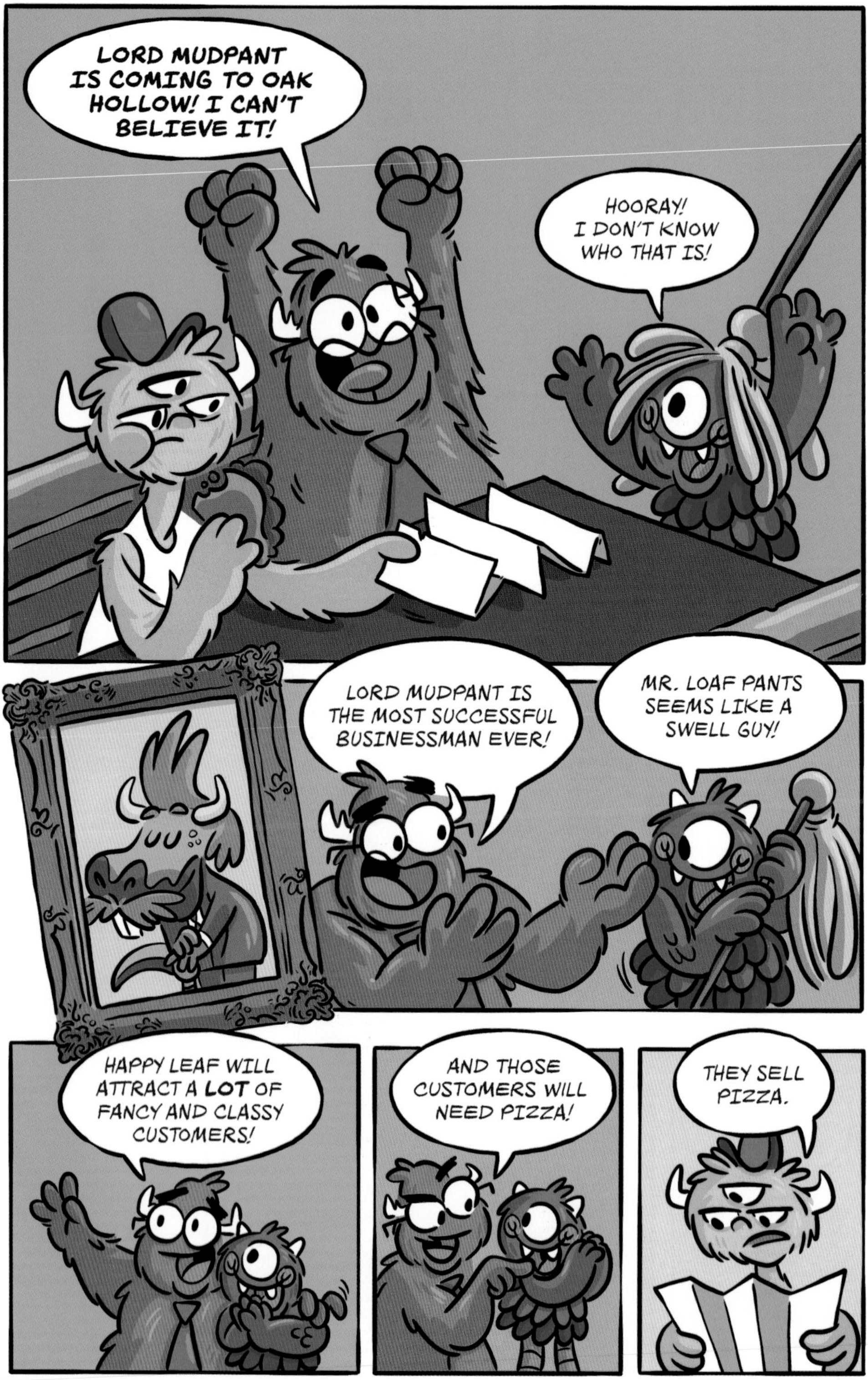
LORD MUDPANT IS COMING TO OAK HOLLOW! I CAN'T BELIEVE IT!
HOORAY! I DON'T KNOW WHO THAT IS!
LORD MUDPANT IS THE MOST SUCCESSFUL BUSINESSMAN EVER!
MR. LOAF PANTS SEEMS LIKE A SWELL GUY!
HAPPY LEAF WILL ATTRACT A **LOT** OF FANCY AND CLASSY CUSTOMERS!
AND THOSE CUSTOMERS WILL NEED PIZZA!
THEY SELL PIZZA.

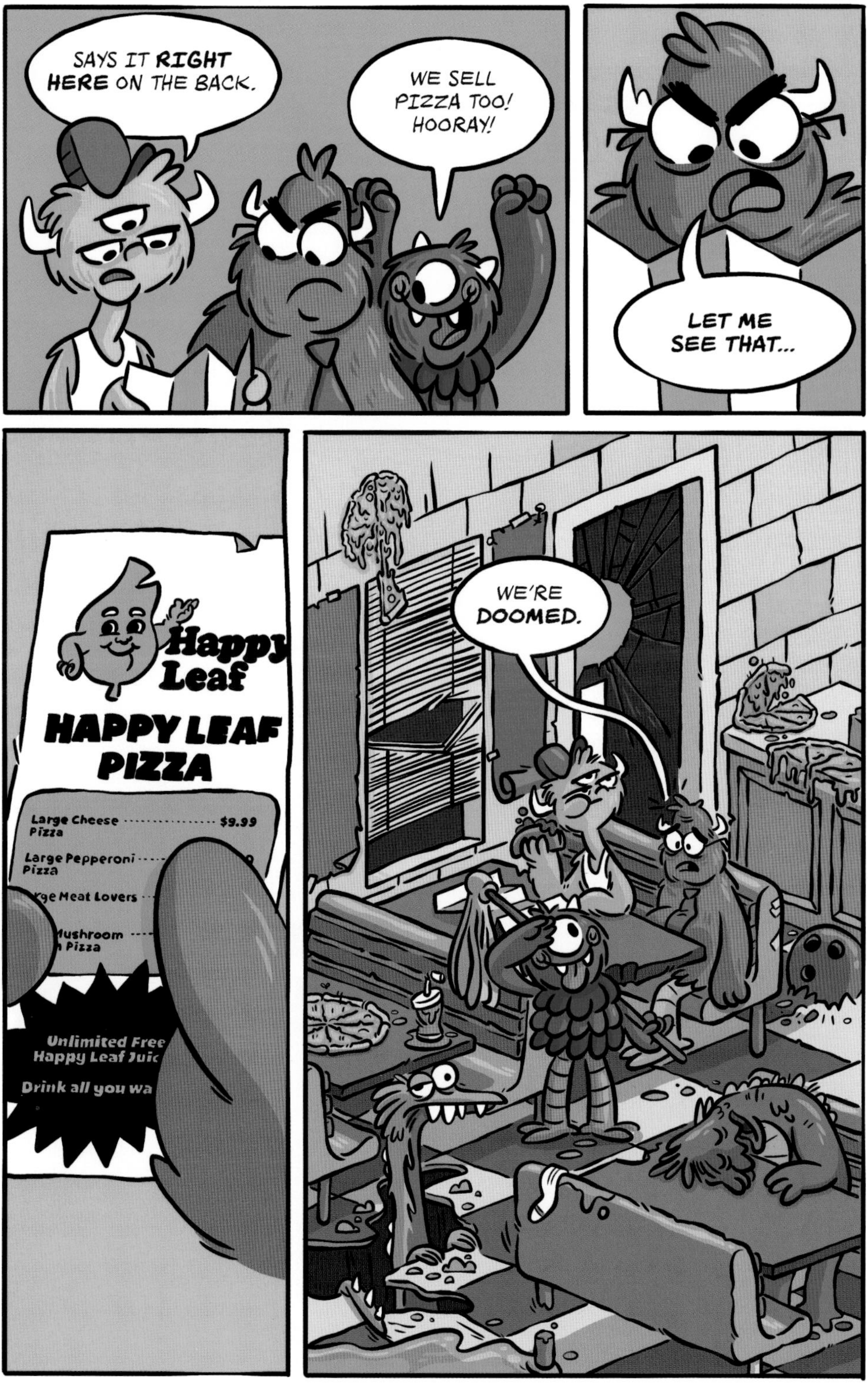

SAYS IT **RIGHT HERE** ON THE BACK.
WE SELL PIZZA TOO! HOORAY!
LET ME SEE THAT...
Happy Leaf
HAPPY LEAF PIZZA
Large Cheese Pizza $9.99
Large Pepperoni Pizza
WE'RE **DOOMED.**

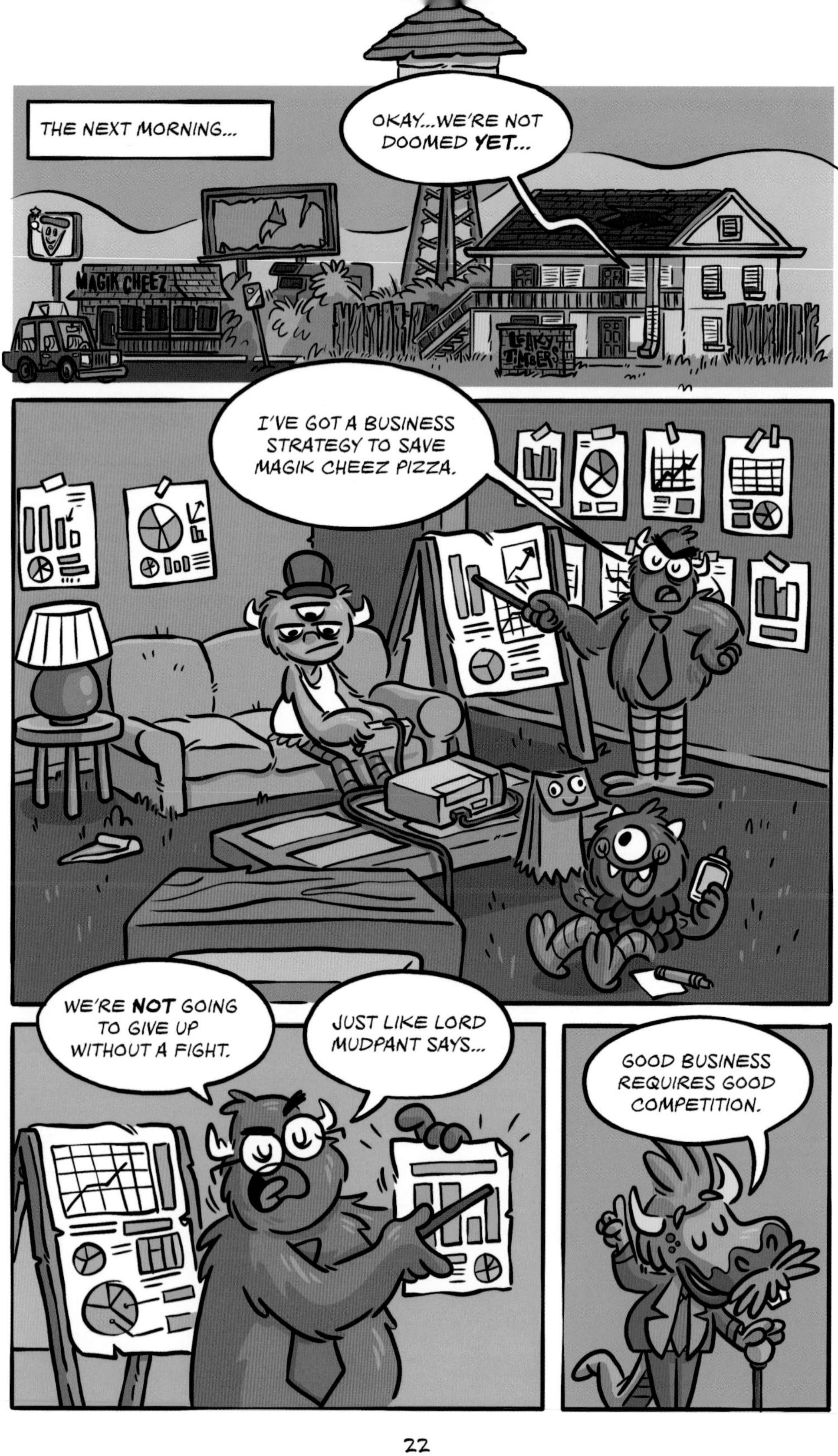
THE NEXT MORNING...
OKAY...WE'RE NOT DOOMED **YET...**
MAGIK CHEEZ
LEAKY TIMBERS
I'VE GOT A BUSINESS STRATEGY TO SAVE MAGIK CHEEZ PIZZA.
WE'RE **NOT** GOING TO GIVE UP WITHOUT A FIGHT.
JUST LIKE LORD MUDPANT SAYS...
GOOD BUSINESS REQUIRES GOOD COMPETITION.

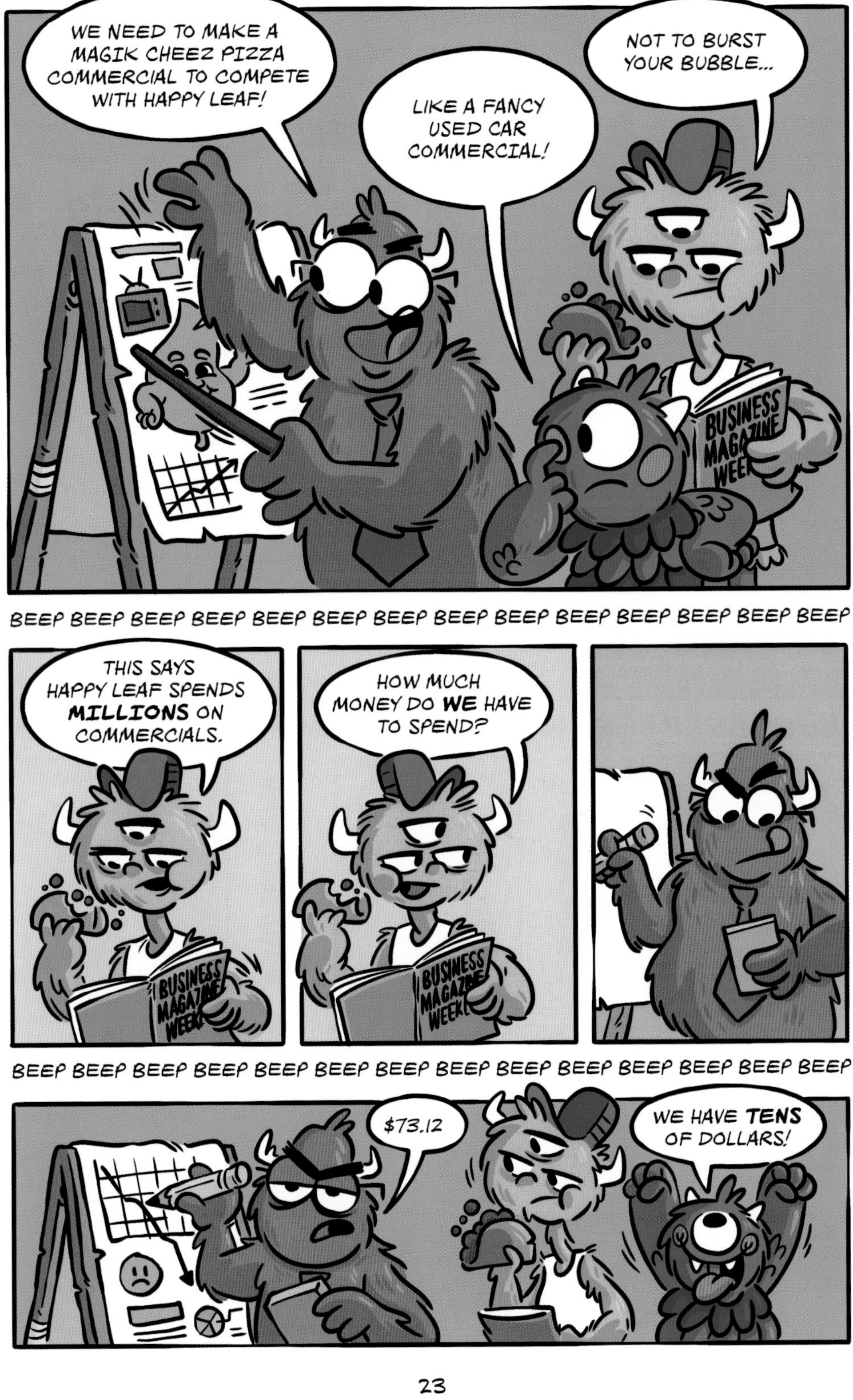

WE NEED TO MAKE A MAGIK CHEEZ PIZZA COMMERCIAL TO COMPETE WITH HAPPY LEAF!
LIKE A FANCY USED CAR COMMERCIAL!
NOT TO BURST YOUR BUBBLE...
BEEP BEEP BEEP BEEP BEEP BEEP BEEP BEEP BEEP BEEP BEEP BEEP BEEP BEEP
THIS SAYS HAPPY LEAF SPENDS **MILLIONS** ON COMMERCIALS.
HOW MUCH MONEY DO **WE** HAVE TO SPEND?
BEEP BEEP BEEP BEEP BEEP BEEP BEEP BEEP BEEP BEEP BEEP BEEP BEEP BEEP
$73.12
WE HAVE **TENS** OF DOLLARS!

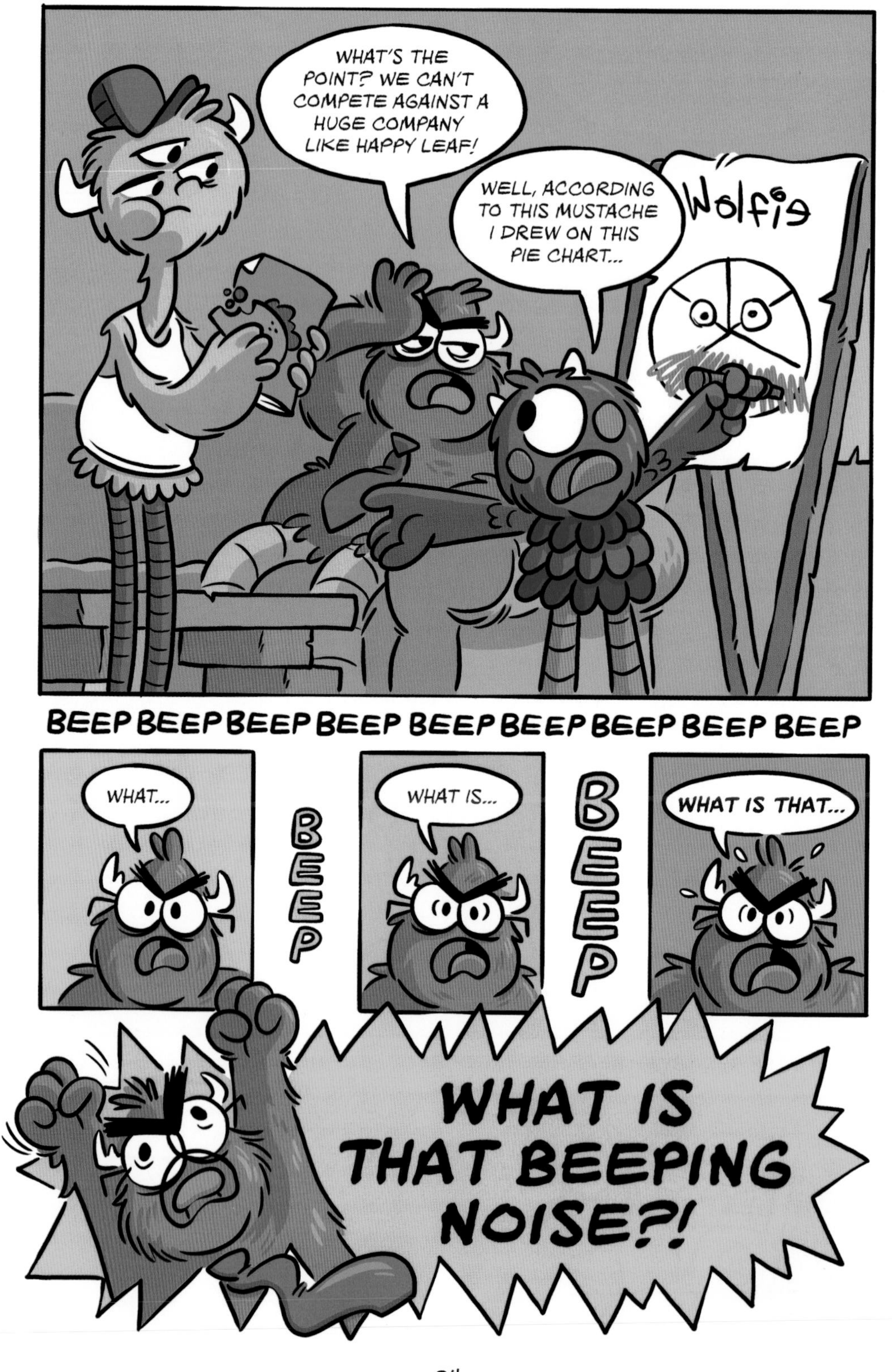

WHAT'S THE POINT? WE CAN'T COMPETE AGAINST A HUGE COMPANY LIKE HAPPY LEAF!
WELL, ACCORDING TO THIS MUSTACHE I DREW ON THIS PIE CHART...
Wolfie
BEEP BEEP BEEP BEEP BEEP BEEP BEEP BEEP BEEP
WHAT...
BEEP
WHAT IS...
BEEP
WHAT IS THAT...
WHAT IS THAT BEEPING NOISE?!

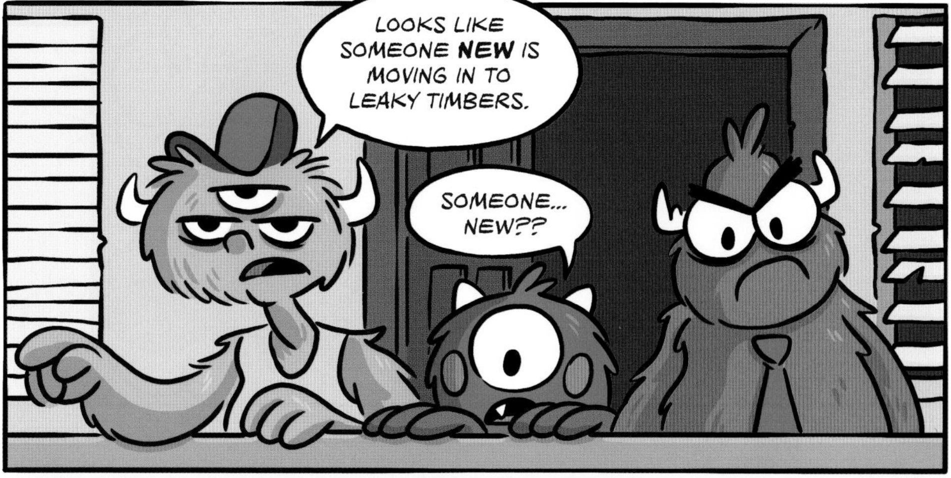
LOOKS LIKE SOMEONE NEW IS MOVING IN TO LEAKY TIMBERS.
SOMEONE... NEW??

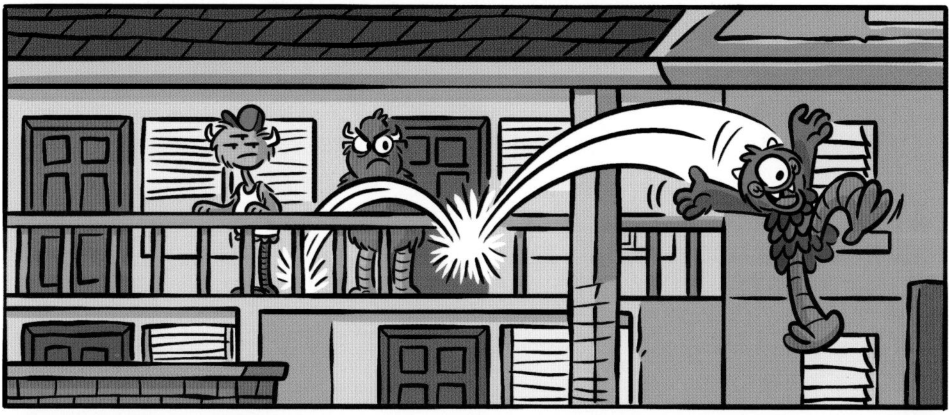

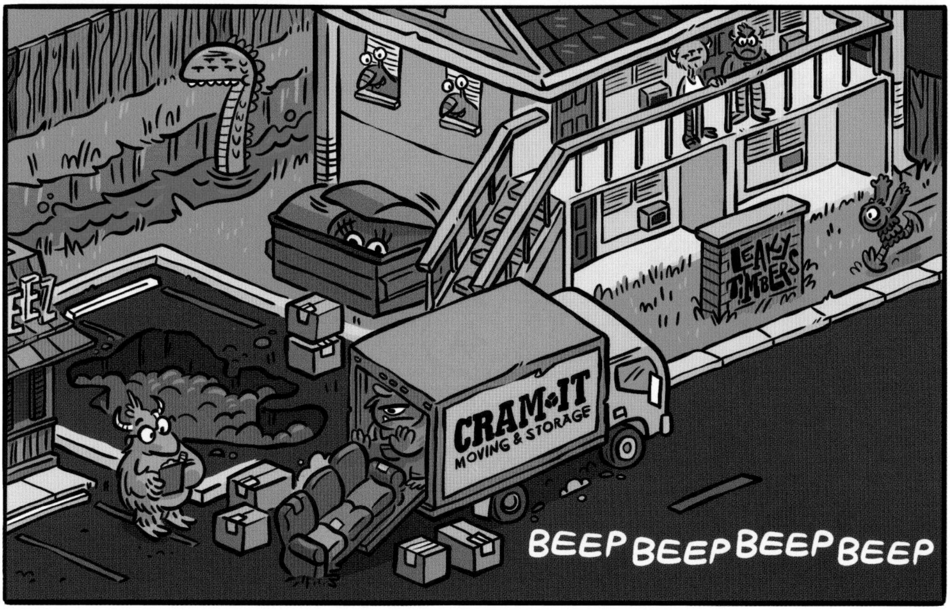
LEAKY TIMBERS
CRAM-IT MOVING & STORAGE
BEEP BEEP BEEP BEEP

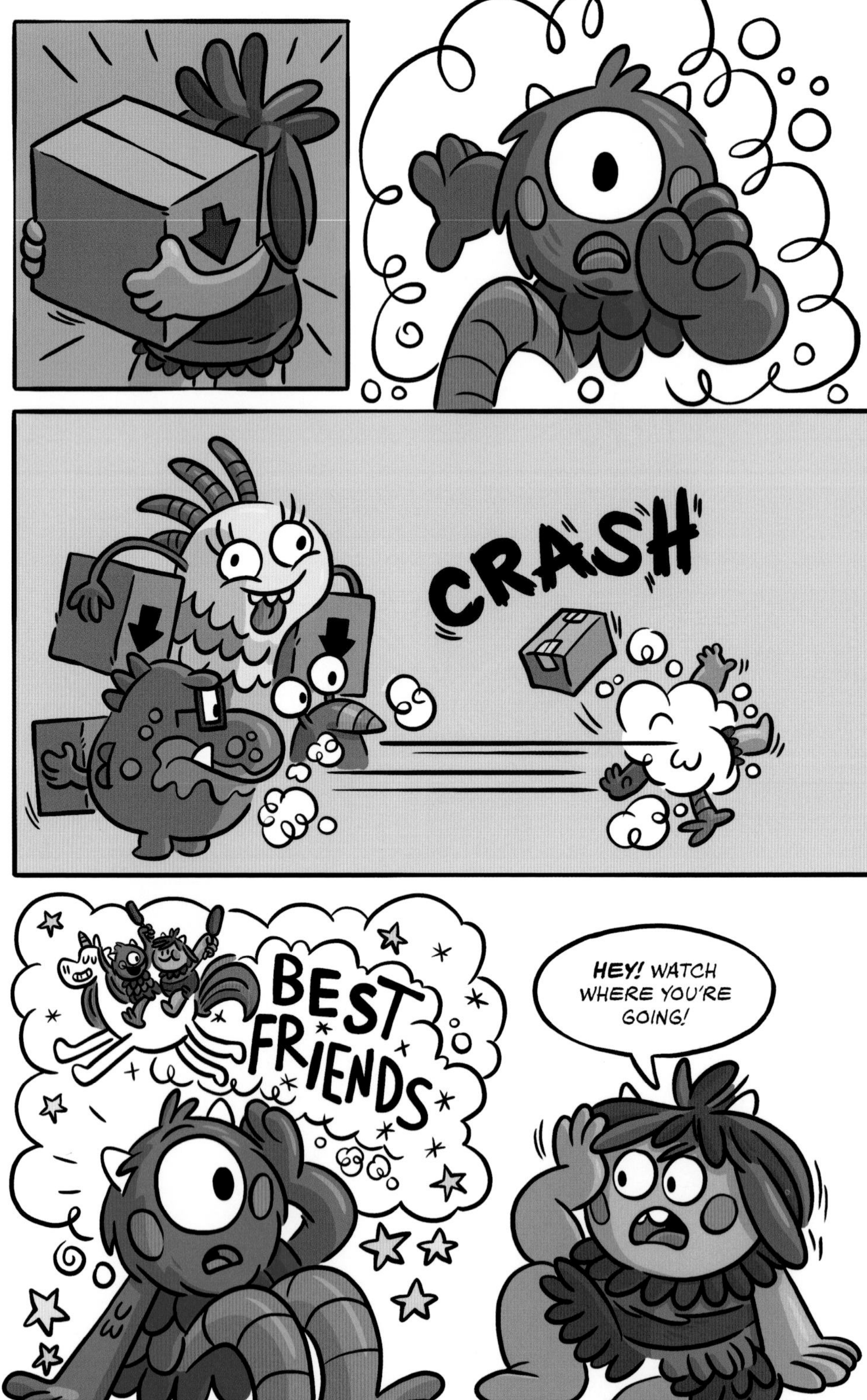
CRASH
BEST FRIENDS
HEY! WATCH WHERE YOU'RE GOING!

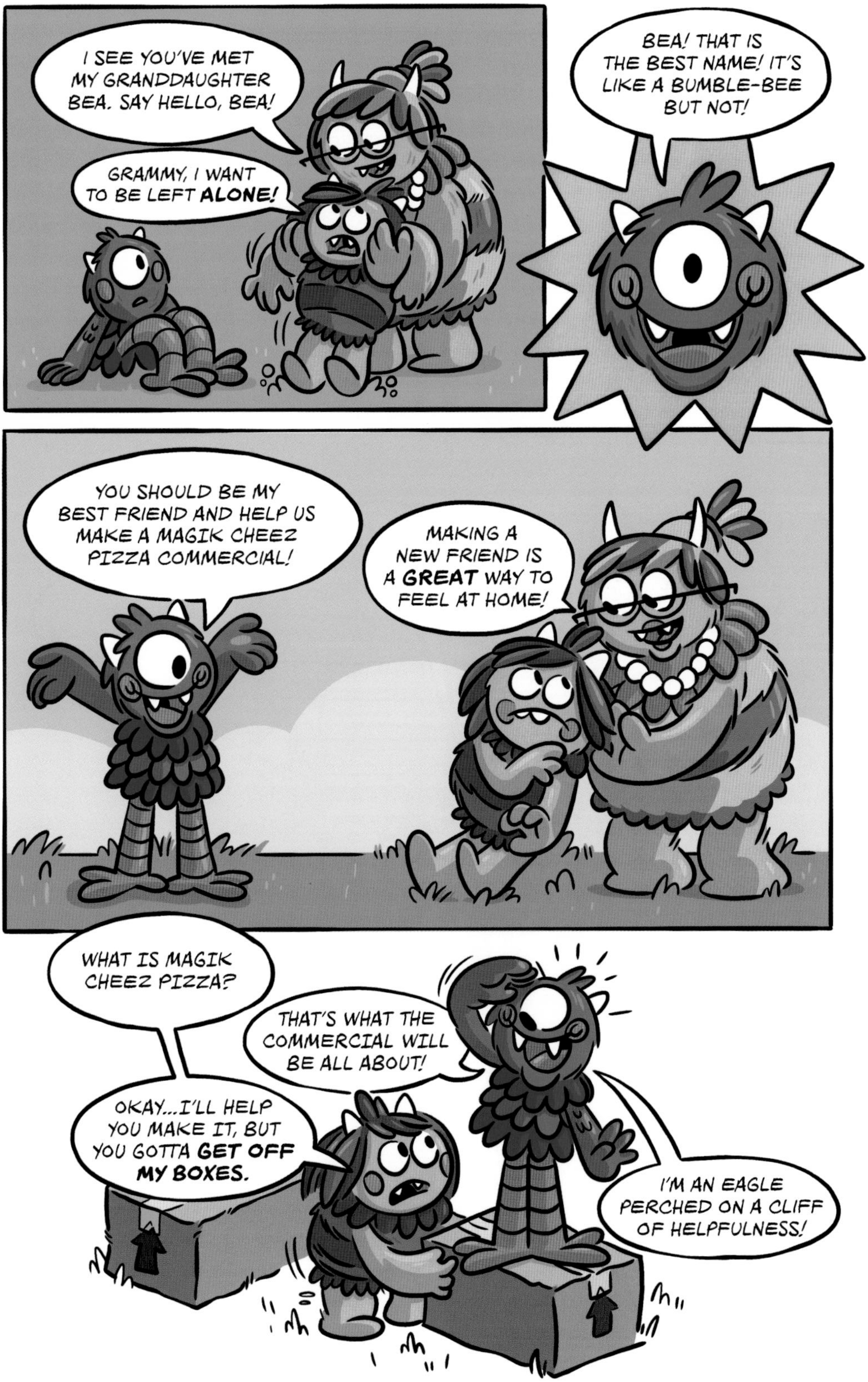
I SEE YOU'VE MET MY GRANDDAUGHTER BEA. SAY HELLO, BEA!
GRAMMY, I WANT TO BE LEFT **ALONE!**
BEA! THAT IS THE BEST NAME! IT'S LIKE A BUMBLE-BEE BUT NOT!
YOU SHOULD BE MY BEST FRIEND AND HELP US MAKE A MAGIK CHEEZ PIZZA COMMERCIAL!
MAKING A NEW FRIEND IS A **GREAT** WAY TO FEEL AT HOME!
WHAT IS MAGIK CHEEZ PIZZA?
THAT'S WHAT THE COMMERCIAL WILL BE ALL ABOUT!
OKAY...I'LL HELP YOU MAKE IT, BUT YOU GOTTA **GET OFF MY BOXES.**
I'M AN EAGLE PERCHED ON A CLIFF OF HELPFULNESS!

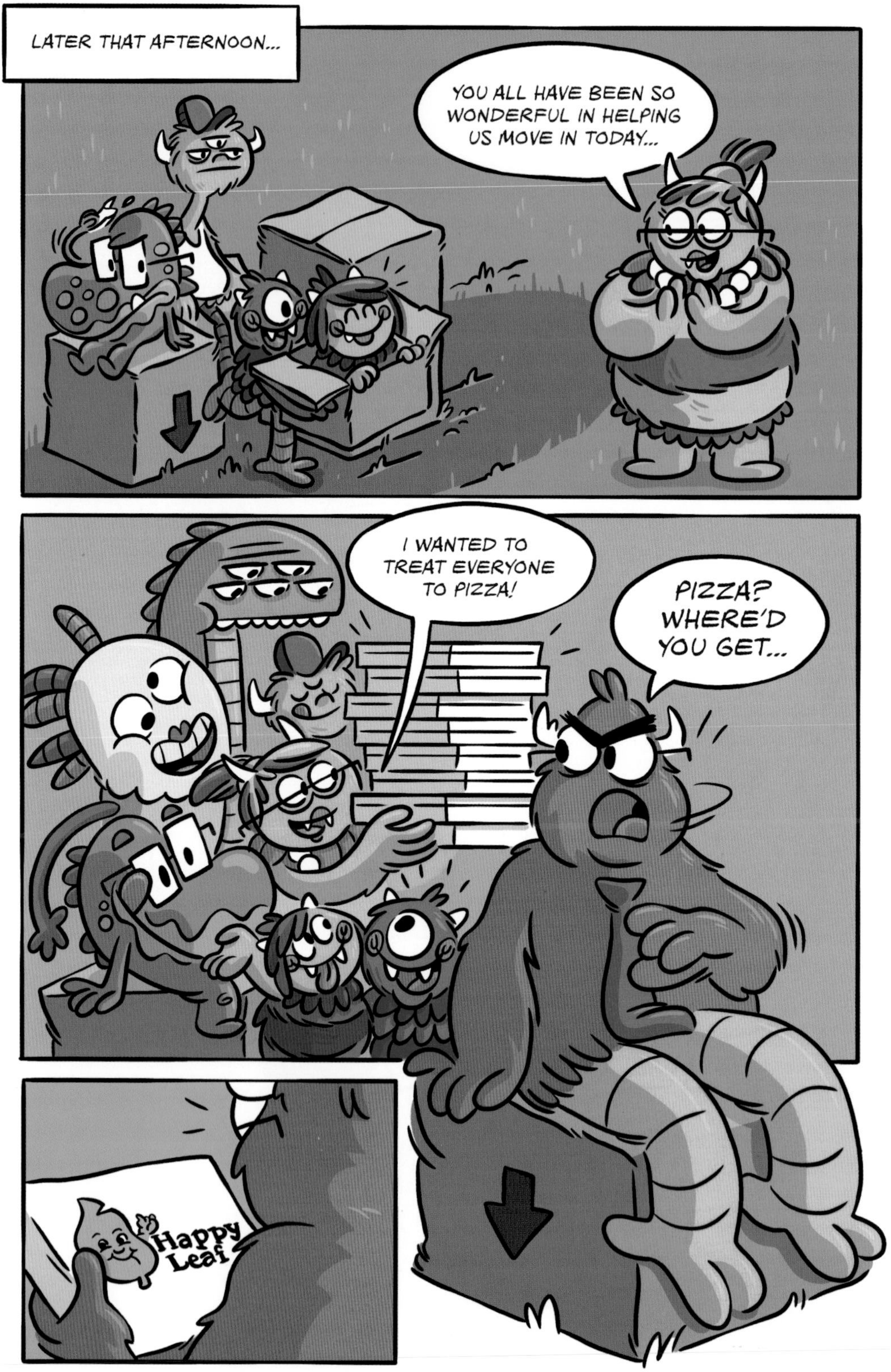
LATER THAT AFTERNOON...
YOU ALL HAVE BEEN SO WONDERFUL IN HELPING US MOVE IN TODAY...
I WANTED TO TREAT EVERYONE TO PIZZA!
PIZZA? WHERE'D YOU GET...
Happy Leaf

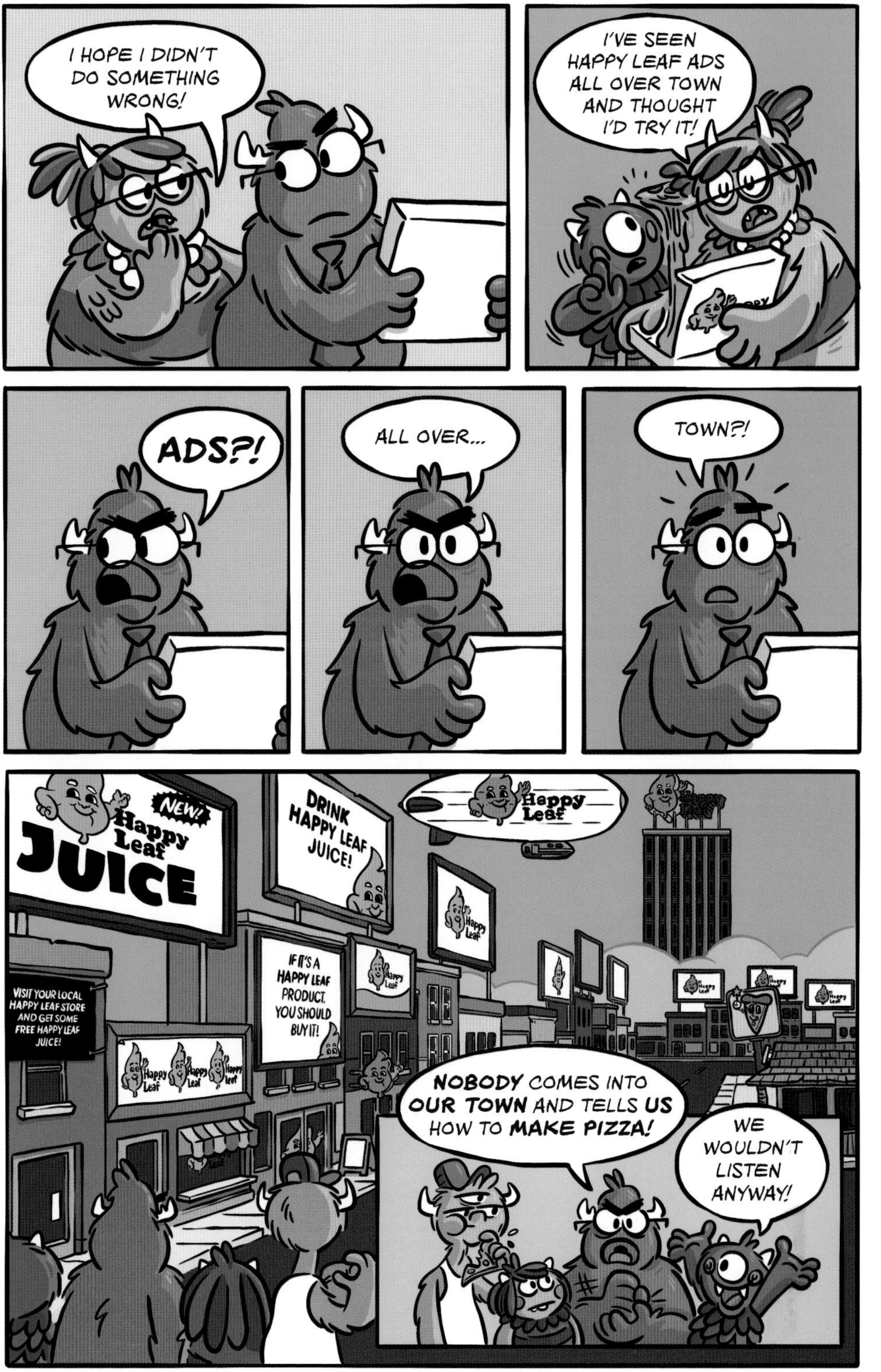
I HOPE I DIDN'T DO SOMETHING WRONG!
I'VE SEEN HAPPY LEAF ADS ALL OVER TOWN AND THOUGHT I'D TRY IT!
ADS?!
ALL OVER...
TOWN?!
NEW!
Happy Leaf
JUICE
DRINK HAPPY LEAF JUICE!
Happy Leaf
VISIT YOUR LOCAL HAPPY LEAF STORE AND GET SOME FREE HAPPY LEAF JUICE!
IF IT'S A HAPPY LEAF PRODUCT, YOU SHOULD BUY IT!
Happy Leaf
Happy Leaf
Happy Leaf
NOBODY COMES INTO OUR TOWN AND TELLS US HOW TO MAKE PIZZA!
WE WOULDN'T LISTEN ANYWAY!

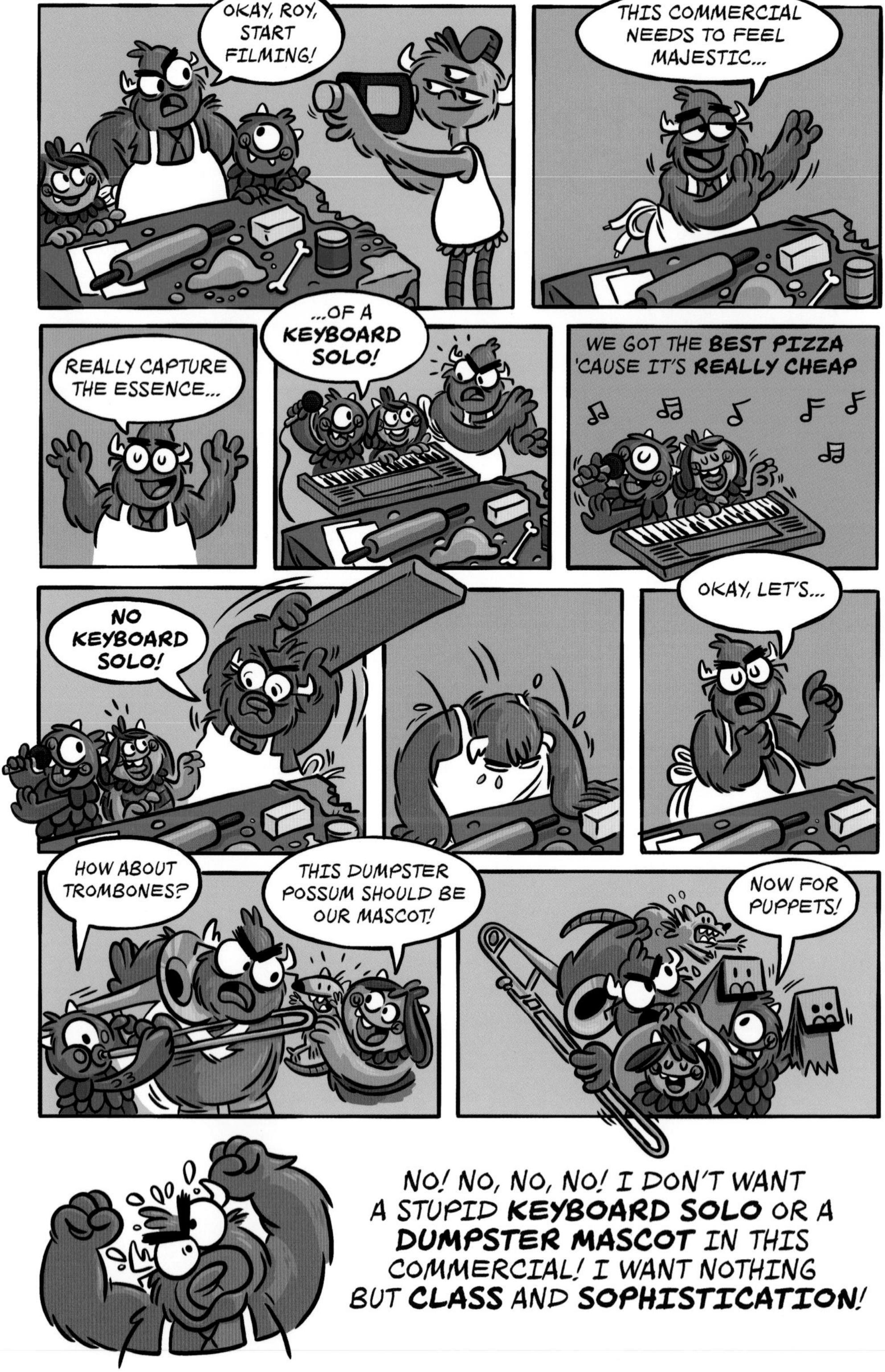
OKAY, ROY, START FILMING!
THIS COMMERCIAL NEEDS TO FEEL MAJESTIC...
REALLY CAPTURE THE ESSENCE...
...OF A KEYBOARD SOLO!
WE GOT THE BEST PIZZA 'CAUSE IT'S REALLY CHEAP
NO KEYBOARD SOLO!
OKAY, LET'S...
HOW ABOUT TROMBONES?
THIS DUMPSTER POSSUM SHOULD BE OUR MASCOT!
NOW FOR PUPPETS!
NO! NO, NO, NO! I DON'T WANT A STUPID KEYBOARD SOLO OR A DUMPSTER MASCOT IN THIS COMMERCIAL! I WANT NOTHING BUT CLASS AND SOPHISTICATION!

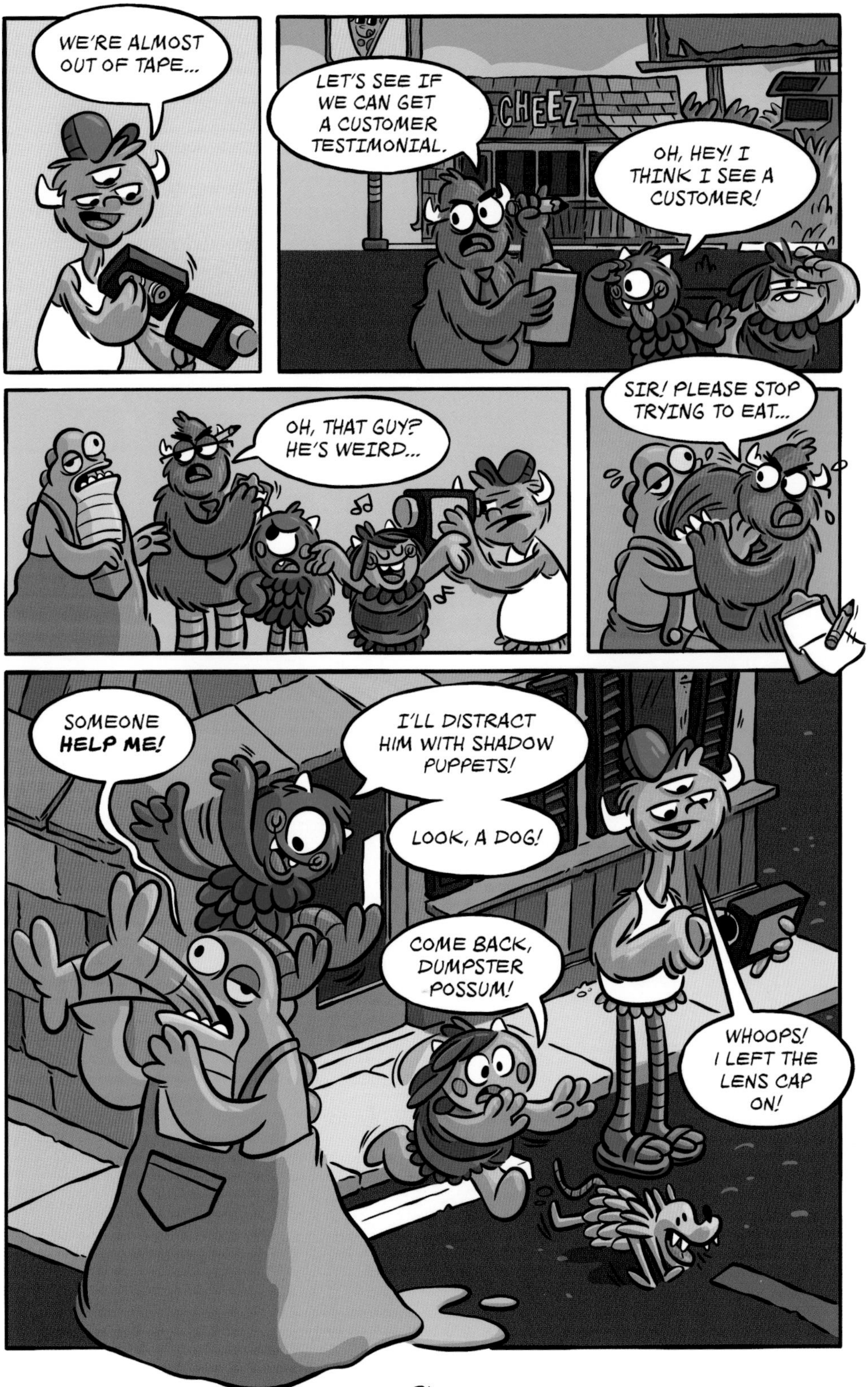
WE'RE ALMOST OUT OF TAPE...
LET'S SEE IF WE CAN GET A CUSTOMER TESTIMONIAL.
CHEEZ
OH, HEY! I THINK I SEE A CUSTOMER!
OH, THAT GUY? HE'S WEIRD...
SIR! PLEASE STOP TRYING TO EAT...
SOMEONE **HELP ME!**
I'LL DISTRACT HIM WITH SHADOW PUPPETS!
LOOK, A DOG!
COME BACK, DUMPSTER POSSUM!
WHOOPS! I LEFT THE LENS CAP ON!

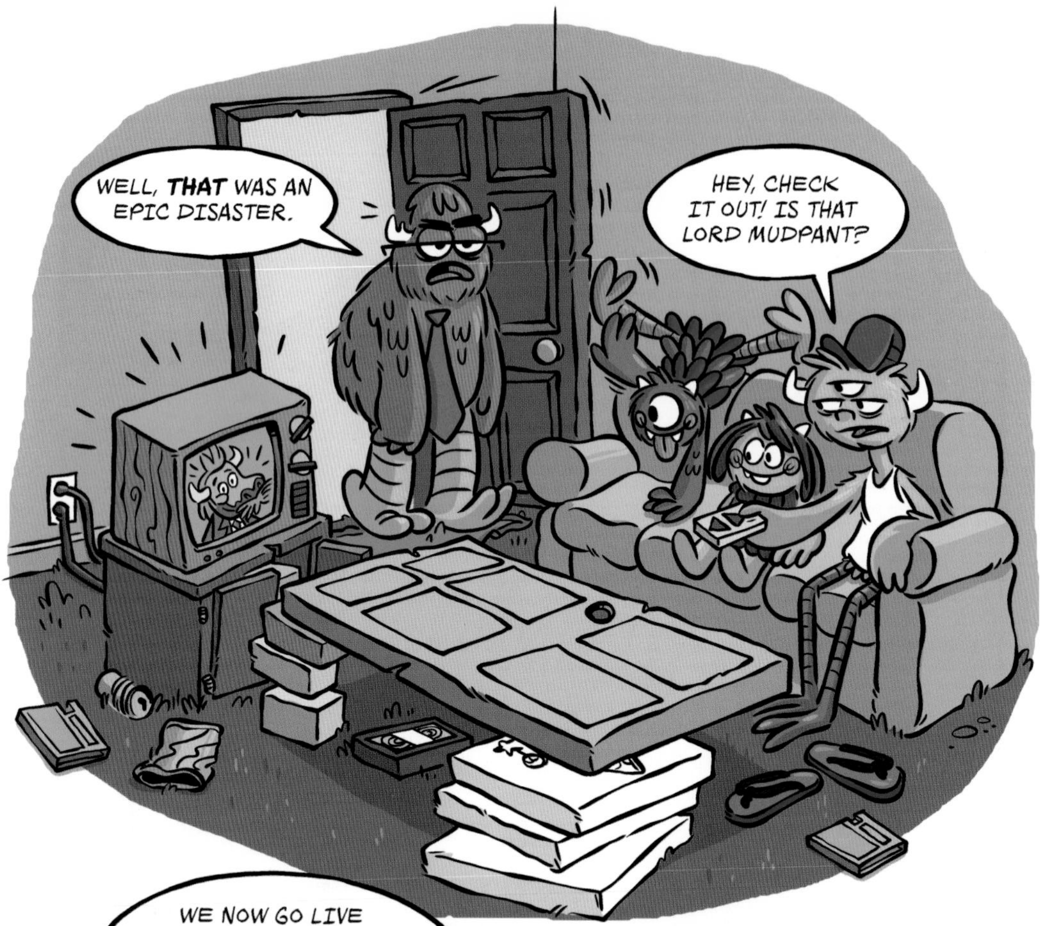
WELL, **THAT** WAS AN EPIC DISASTER.
HEY, CHECK IT OUT! IS THAT LORD MUDPANT?

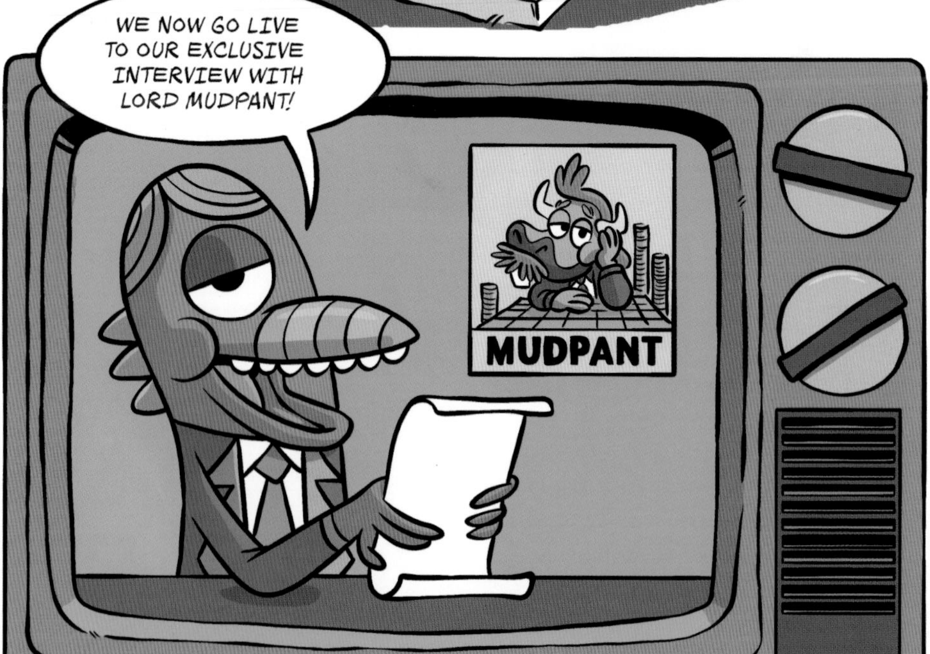
WE NOW GO LIVE TO OUR EXCLUSIVE INTERVIEW WITH LORD MUDPANT!
MUDPANT

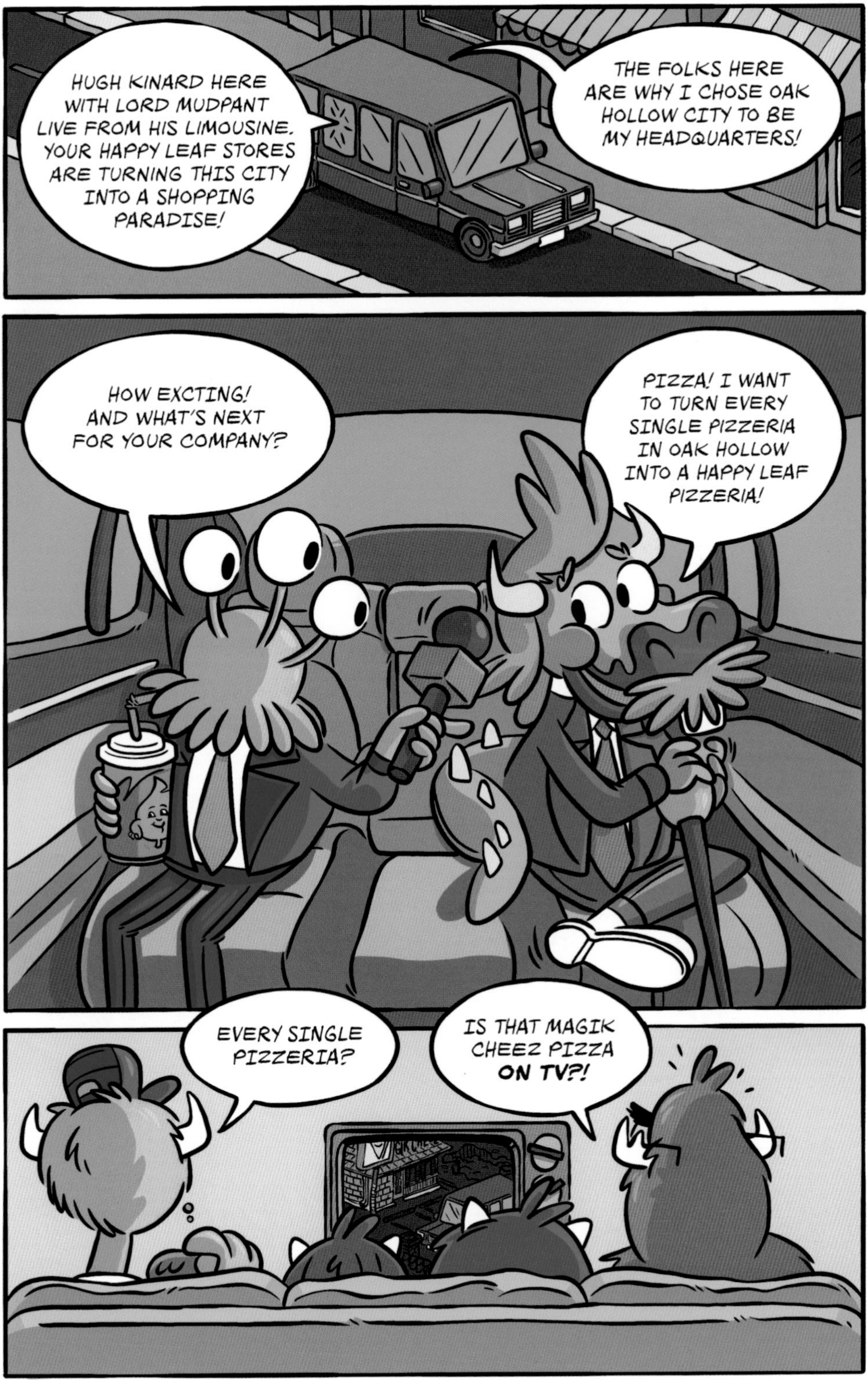
HUGH KINARD HERE WITH LORD MUDPANT LIVE FROM HIS LIMOUSINE. YOUR HAPPY LEAF STORES ARE TURNING THIS CITY INTO A SHOPPING PARADISE!
THE FOLKS HERE ARE WHY I CHOSE OAK HOLLOW CITY TO BE MY HEADQUARTERS!
HOW EXCTING! AND WHAT'S NEXT FOR YOUR COMPANY?
PIZZA! I WANT TO TURN EVERY SINGLE PIZZERIA IN OAK HOLLOW INTO A HAPPY LEAF PIZZERIA!
EVERY SINGLE PIZZERIA?
IS THAT MAGIK CHEEZ PIZZA **ON TV?!**

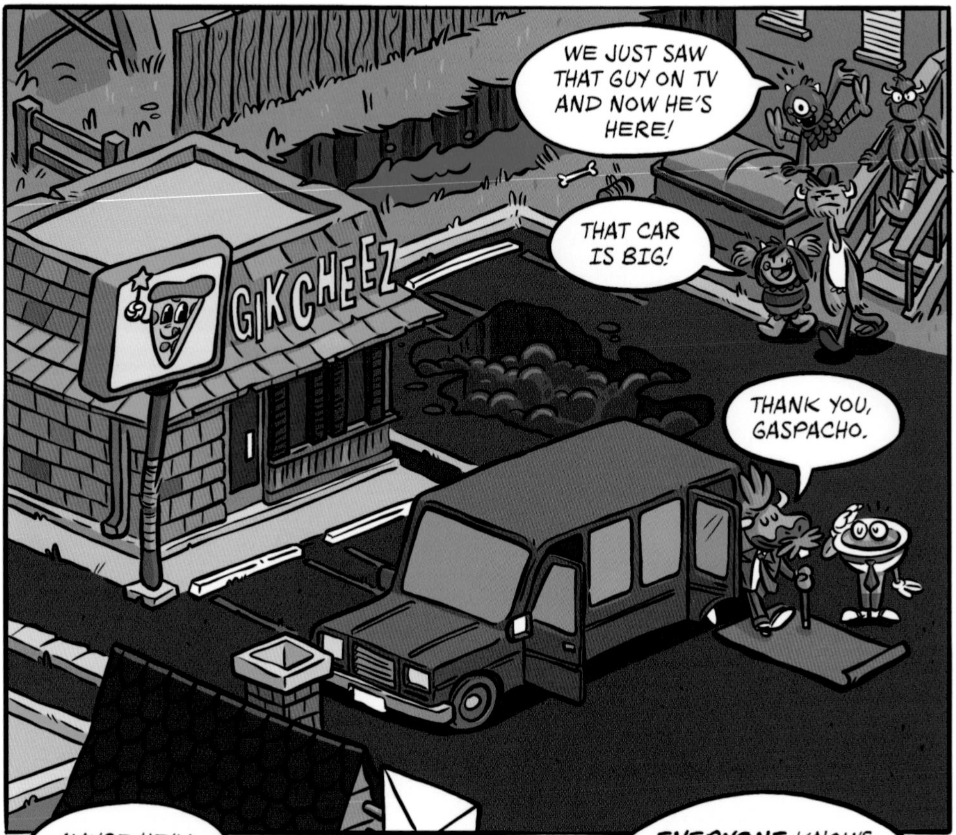

GIKCHEEZ
WE JUST SAW THAT GUY ON TV AND NOW HE'S HERE!
THAT CAR IS BIG!
THANK YOU, GASPACHO.

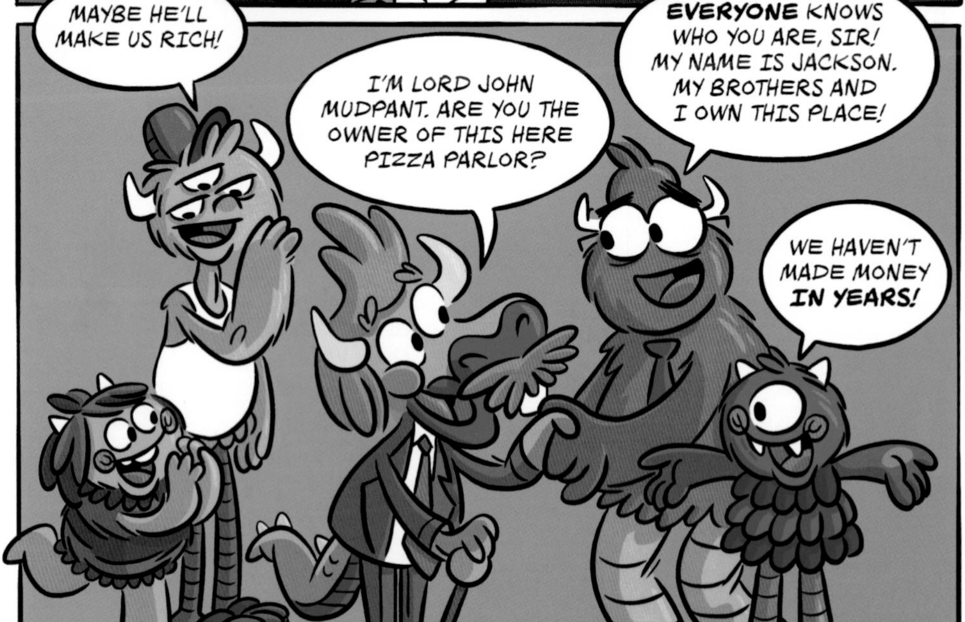

MAYBE HE'LL MAKE US RICH!
I'M LORD JOHN MUDPANT. ARE YOU THE OWNER OF THIS HERE PIZZA PARLOR?
EVERYONE KNOWS WHO YOU ARE, SIR! MY NAME IS JACKSON. MY BROTHERS AND I OWN THIS PLACE!
WE HAVEN'T MADE MONEY **IN YEARS!**

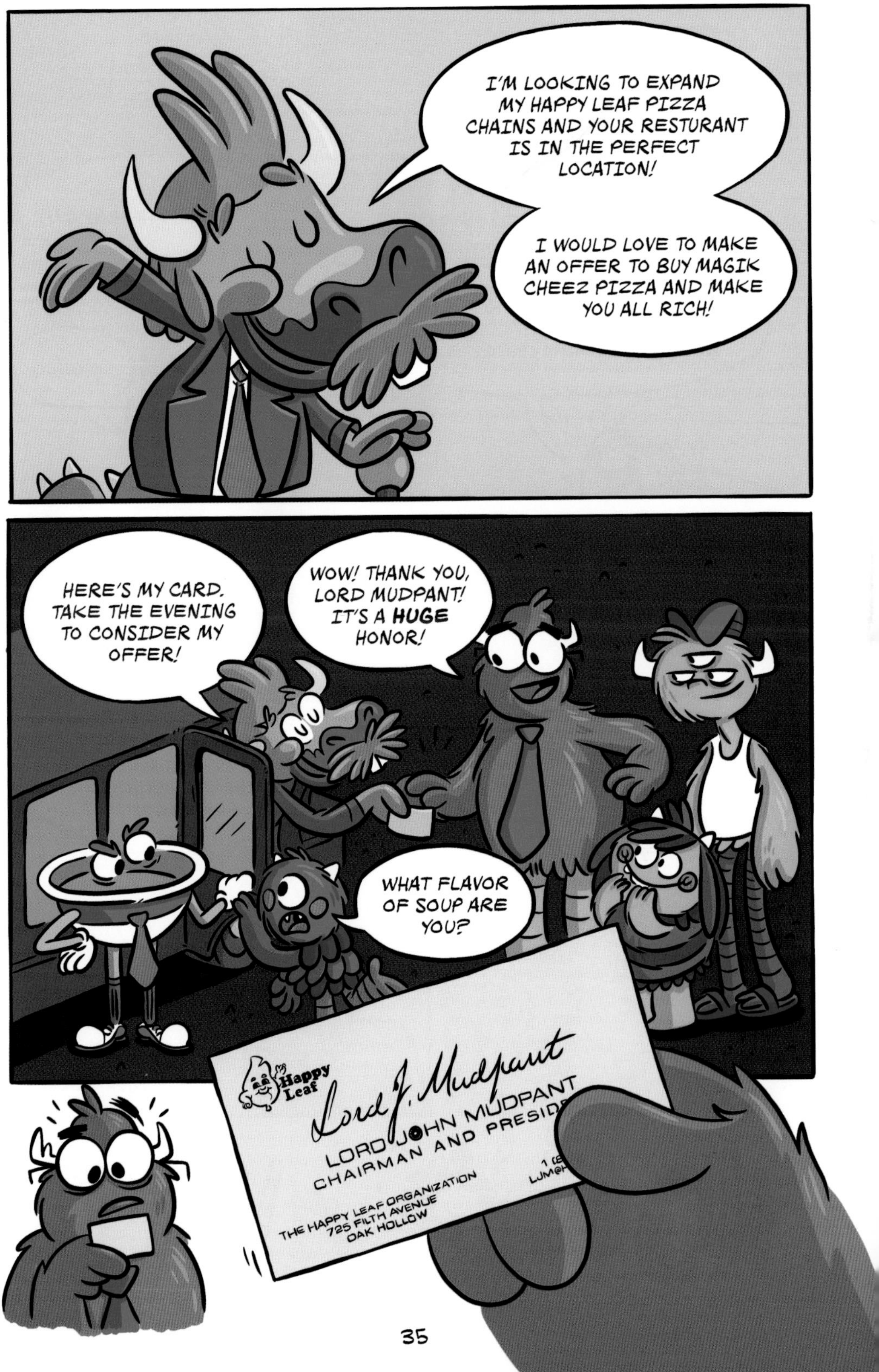
I'M LOOKING TO EXPAND MY HAPPY LEAF PIZZA CHAINS AND YOUR RESTURANT IS IN THE PERFECT LOCATION!
I WOULD LOVE TO MAKE AN OFFER TO BUY MAGIK CHEEZ PIZZA AND MAKE YOU ALL RICH!
HERE'S MY CARD. TAKE THE EVENING TO CONSIDER MY OFFER!
WOW! THANK YOU, LORD MUDPANT! IT'S A **HUGE** HONOR!
WHAT FLAVOR OF SOUP ARE YOU?
Happy Leaf
Lord J. Mudpant
LORD JOHN MUDPANT
CHAIRMAN AND PRESID
THE HAPPY LEAF ORGANIZATION
725 FILTH AVENUE
OAK HOLLOW

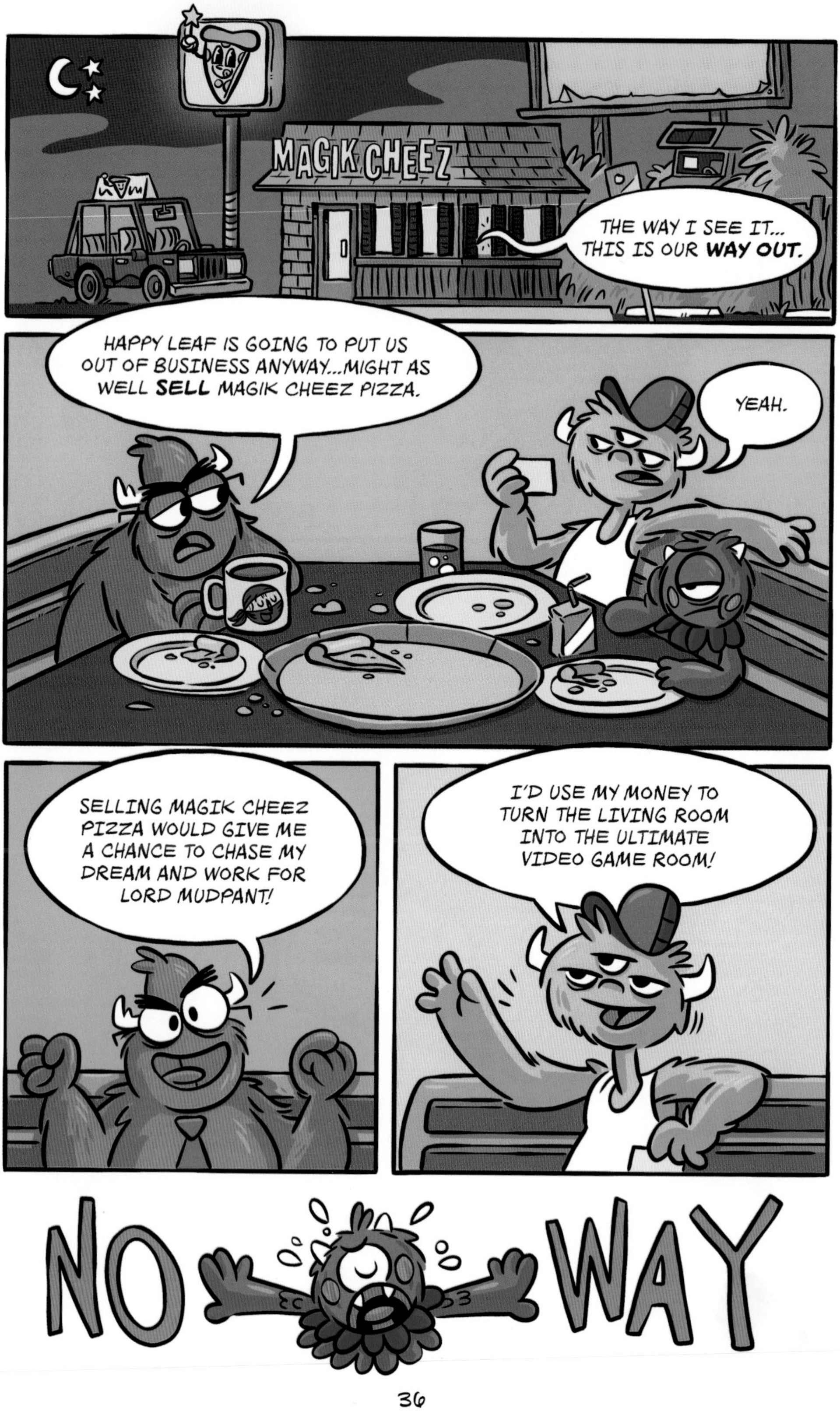
MAGIK CHEEZ
THE WAY I SEE IT... THIS IS OUR **WAY OUT.**
HAPPY LEAF IS GOING TO PUT US OUT OF BUSINESS ANYWAY...MIGHT AS WELL **SELL** MAGIK CHEEZ PIZZA.
YEAH.
SELLING MAGIK CHEEZ PIZZA WOULD GIVE ME A CHANCE TO CHASE MY DREAM AND WORK FOR LORD MUDPANT!
I'D USE MY MONEY TO TURN THE LIVING ROOM INTO THE ULTIMATE VIDEO GAME ROOM!
NO WAY

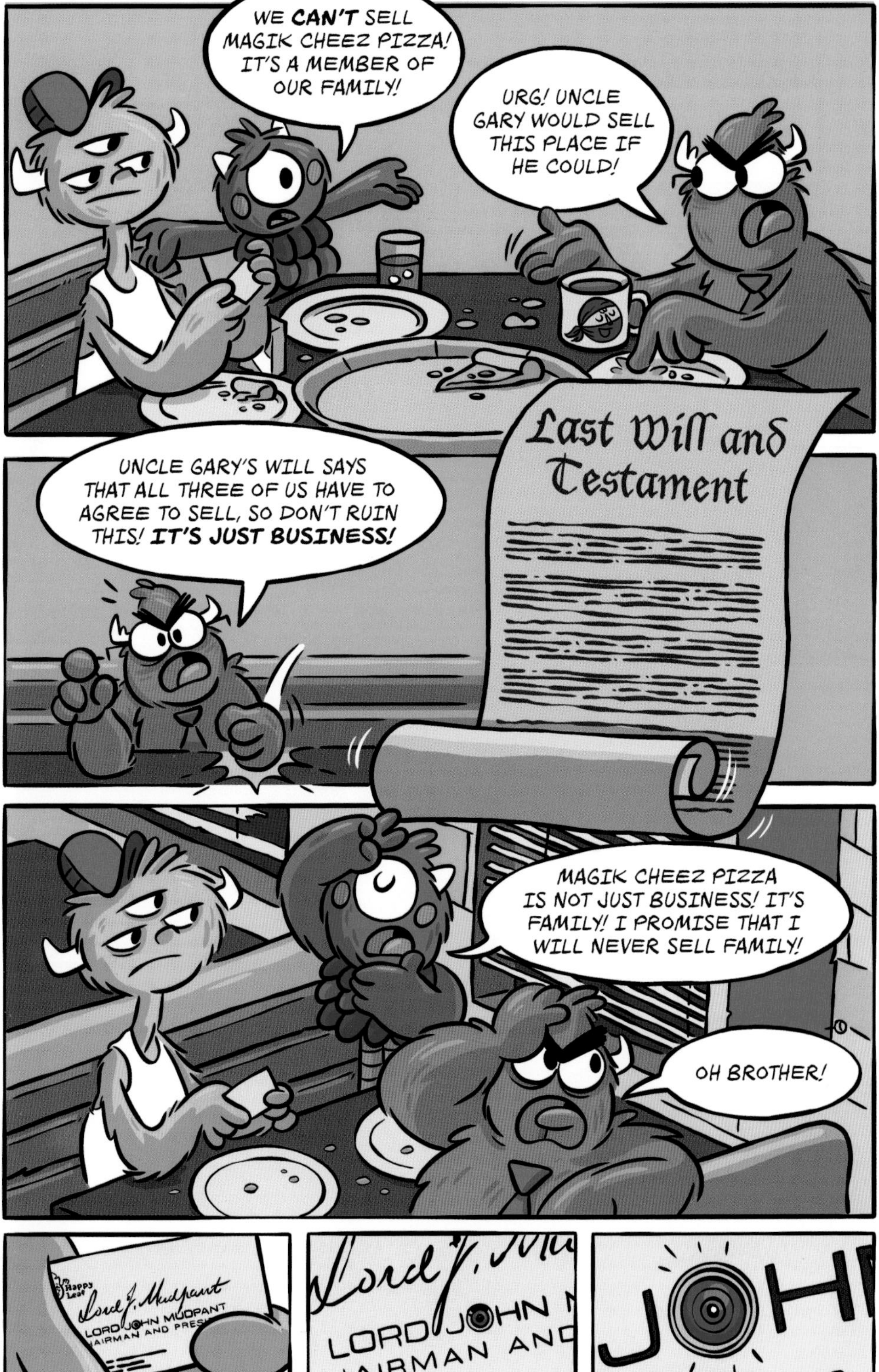
WE **CAN'T** SELL MAGIK CHEEZ PIZZA! IT'S A MEMBER OF OUR FAMILY!
URG! UNCLE GARY WOULD SELL THIS PLACE IF HE COULD!
Last Will and Testament
UNCLE GARY'S WILL SAYS THAT ALL THREE OF US HAVE TO AGREE TO SELL, SO DON'T RUIN THIS! **IT'S JUST BUSINESS!**
MAGIK CHEEZ PIZZA IS NOT JUST BUSINESS! IT'S FAMILY! I PROMISE THAT I WILL NEVER SELL FAMILY!
OH BROTHER!
LORD JOHN MUDPANT
CHAIRMAN AND

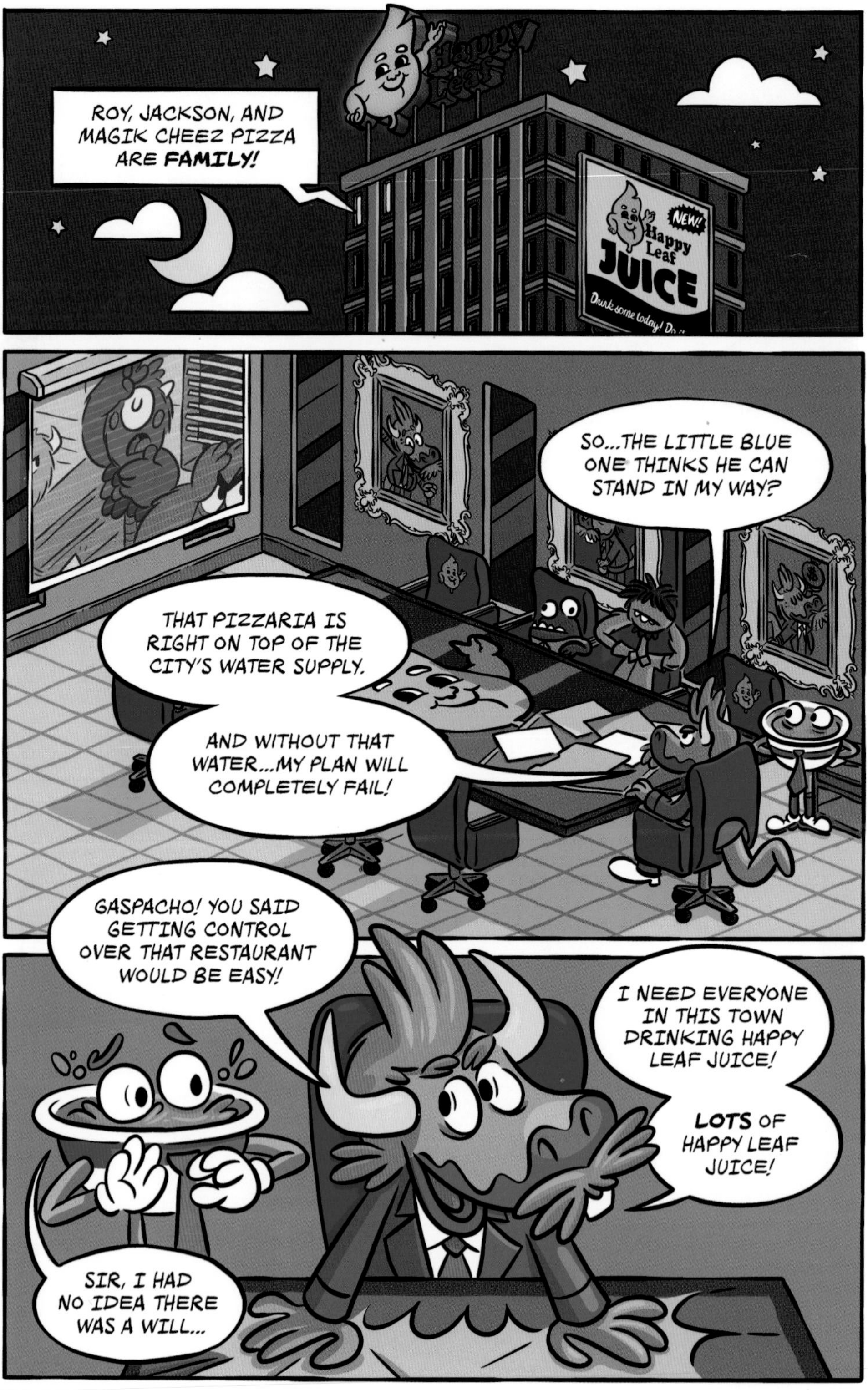
ROY, JACKSON, AND MAGIK CHEEZ PIZZA ARE **FAMILY!**
NEW!
Happy Leaf
JUICE
Happy Leaf
SO...THE LITTLE BLUE ONE THINKS HE CAN STAND IN MY WAY?
THAT PIZZARIA IS RIGHT ON TOP OF THE CITY'S WATER SUPPLY.
AND WITHOUT THAT WATER...MY PLAN WILL COMPLETELY FAIL!
GASPACHO! YOU SAID GETTING CONTROL OVER THAT RESTAURANT WOULD BE EASY!
SIR, I HAD NO IDEA THERE WAS A WILL...
I NEED EVERYONE IN THIS TOWN DRINKING HAPPY LEAF JUICE!
LOTS OF HAPPY LEAF JUICE!

DRINKING HAPPY LEAF JUICE TURNS FOLKS INTO ZOMBIES...MY ZOMBIES!

IF I CAN'T GROW MY OWN ARMY OF LOYAL ZOMBIES, I CAN'T CONTROL THE CITY!

BOSS, WHY DO YOU WANT TO CONTROL THE CITY?

I DON'T WANT CONTROL OF THE CITY...

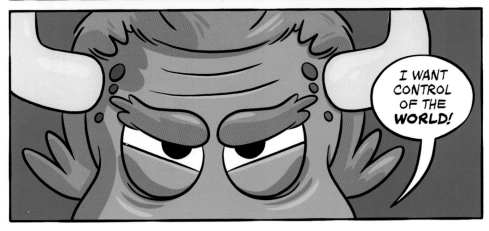

I WANT CONTROL OF THE WORLD!

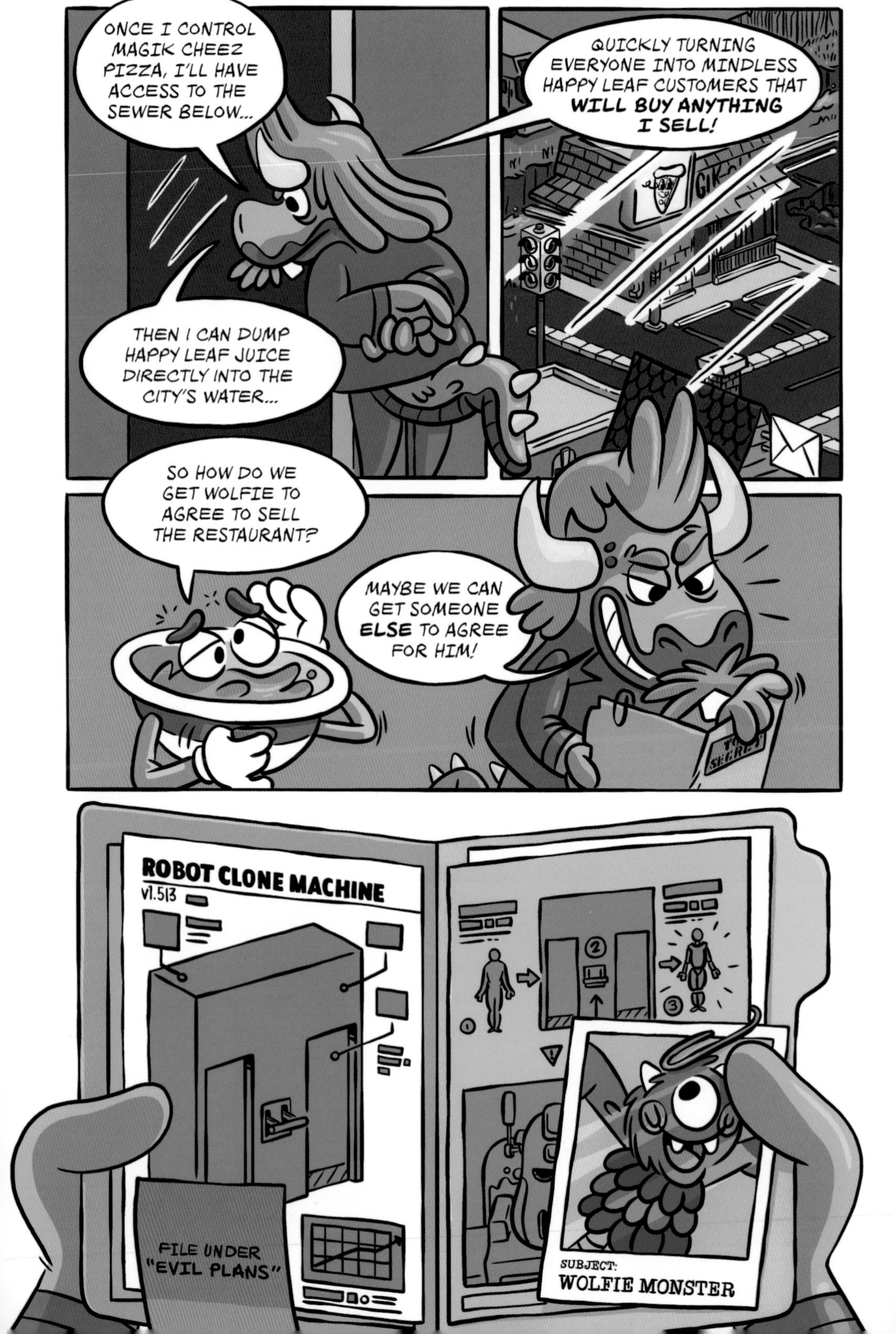
ONCE I CONTROL MAGIK CHEEZ PIZZA, I'LL HAVE ACCESS TO THE SEWER BELOW...
QUICKLY TURNING EVERYONE INTO MINDLESS HAPPY LEAF CUSTOMERS THAT **WILL BUY ANYTHING I SELL!**
THEN I CAN DUMP HAPPY LEAF JUICE DIRECTLY INTO THE CITY'S WATER...
SO HOW DO WE GET WOLFIE TO AGREE TO SELL THE RESTAURANT?
MAYBE WE CAN GET SOMEONE **ELSE** TO AGREE FOR HIM!
ROBOT CLONE MACHINE
v1.513
FILE UNDER "EVIL PLANS"
SUBJECT:
WOLFIE MONSTER

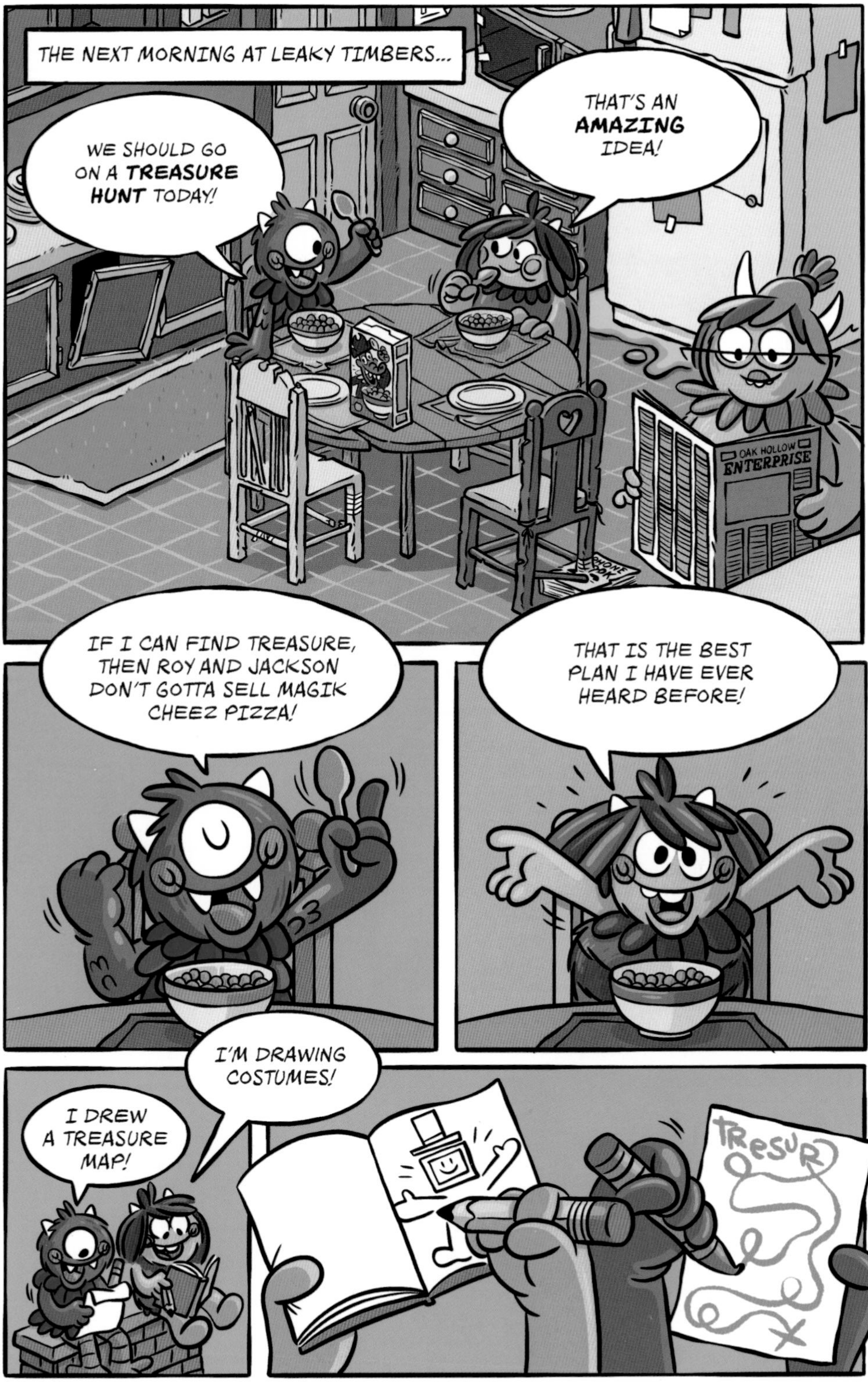
THE NEXT MORNING AT LEAKY TIMBERS...
WE SHOULD GO ON A **TREASURE HUNT** TODAY!
THAT'S AN **AMAZING** IDEA!
OAK HOLLOW ENTERPRISE
IF I CAN FIND TREASURE, THEN ROY AND JACKSON DON'T GOTTA SELL MAGIK CHEEZ PIZZA!
THAT IS THE BEST PLAN I HAVE EVER HEARD BEFORE!
I DREW A TREASURE MAP!
I'M DRAWING COSTUMES!
TRESUR

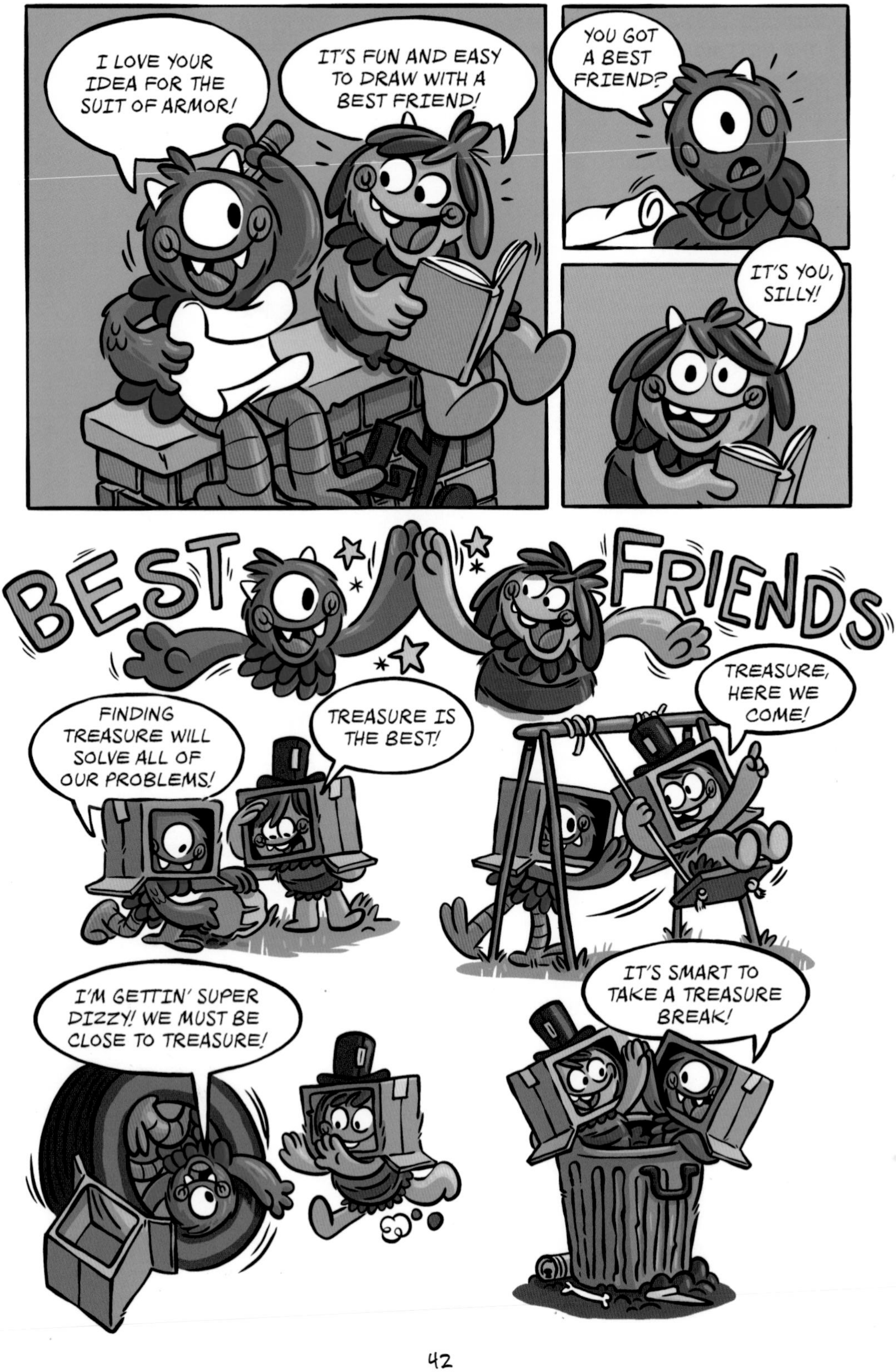
I LOVE YOUR IDEA FOR THE SUIT OF ARMOR!
IT'S FUN AND EASY TO DRAW WITH A BEST FRIEND!
YOU GOT A BEST FRIEND?
IT'S YOU, SILLY!
BEST FRIENDS
FINDING TREASURE WILL SOLVE ALL OF OUR PROBLEMS!
TREASURE IS THE BEST!
TREASURE, HERE WE COME!
I'M GETTIN' SUPER DIZZY! WE MUST BE CLOSE TO TREASURE!
IT'S SMART TO TAKE A TREASURE BREAK!

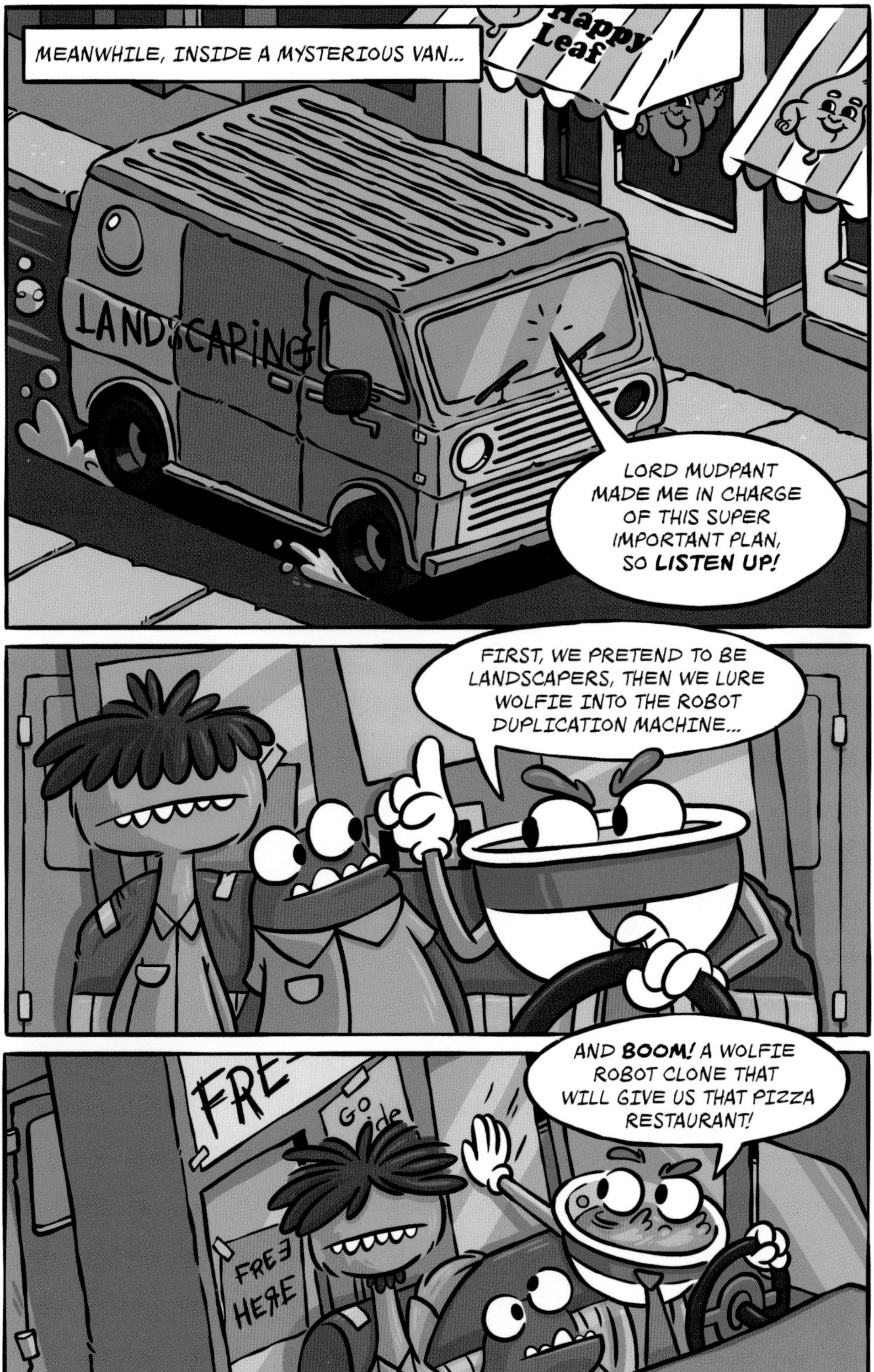
MEANWHILE, INSIDE A MYSTERIOUS VAN...
Happy Leaf
LANDSCAPING
LORD MUDPANT MADE ME IN CHARGE OF THIS SUPER IMPORTANT PLAN, SO **LISTEN UP!**
FIRST, WE PRETEND TO BE LANDSCAPERS, THEN WE LURE WOLFIE INTO THE ROBOT DUPLICATION MACHINE...
AND **BOOM!** A WOLFIE ROBOT CLONE THAT WILL GIVE US THAT PIZZA RESTAURANT!
FRE
FREE HERE

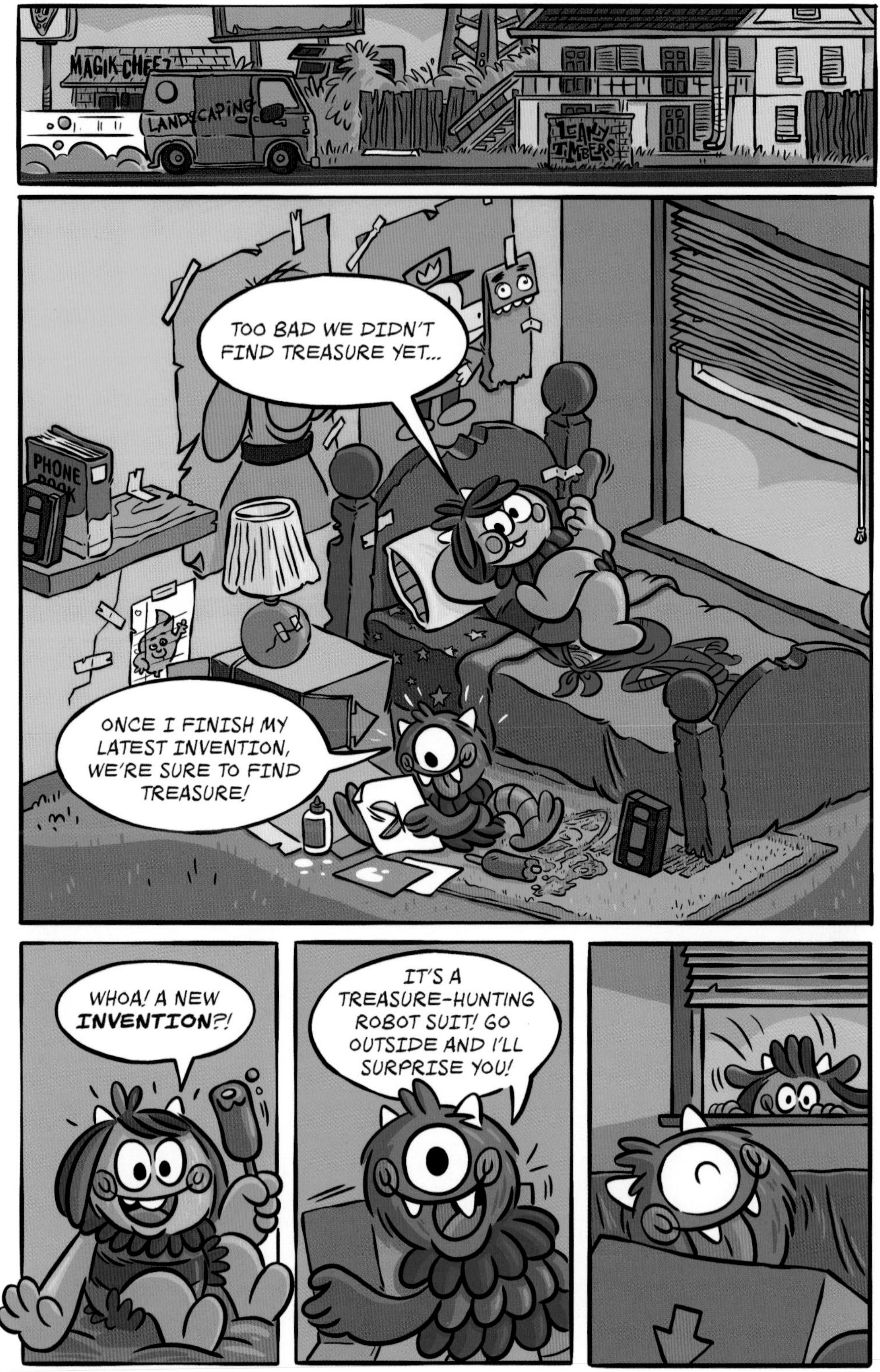
LANDSCAPING
PHONE BOOK
TOO BAD WE DIDN'T FIND TREASURE YET...
ONCE I FINISH MY LATEST INVENTION, WE'RE SURE TO FIND TREASURE!
WHOA! A NEW **INVENTION**?!
IT'S A TREASURE-HUNTING ROBOT SUIT! GO OUTSIDE AND I'LL SURPRISE YOU!

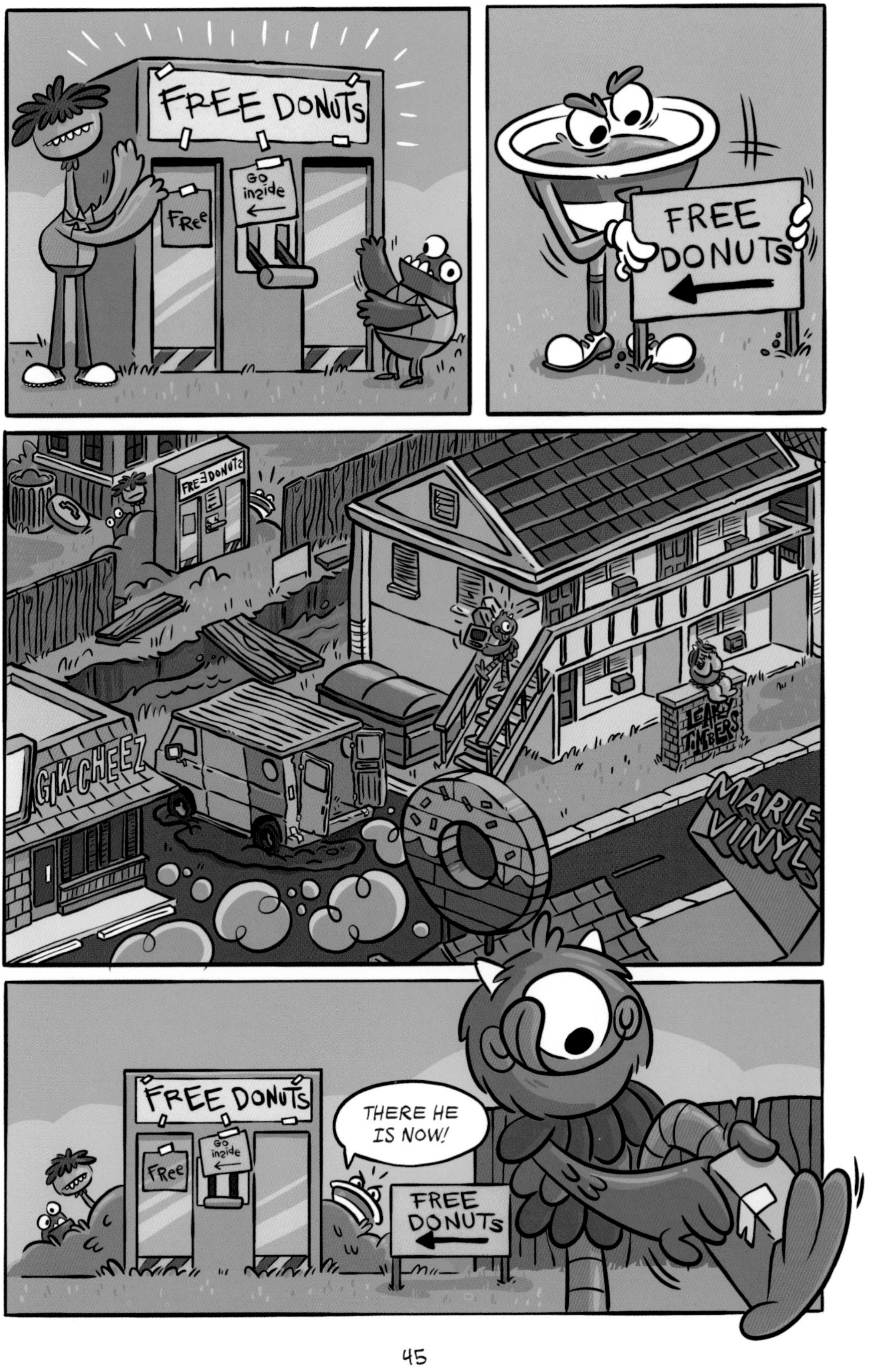
FREE DONUTS
Go inside
Free
FREE DONUTS
FREE DONUTS
LEAKY TIMBERS
MARIE VINYL
FREE DONUTS
Go inside
Free
THERE HE IS NOW!
FREE DONUTS

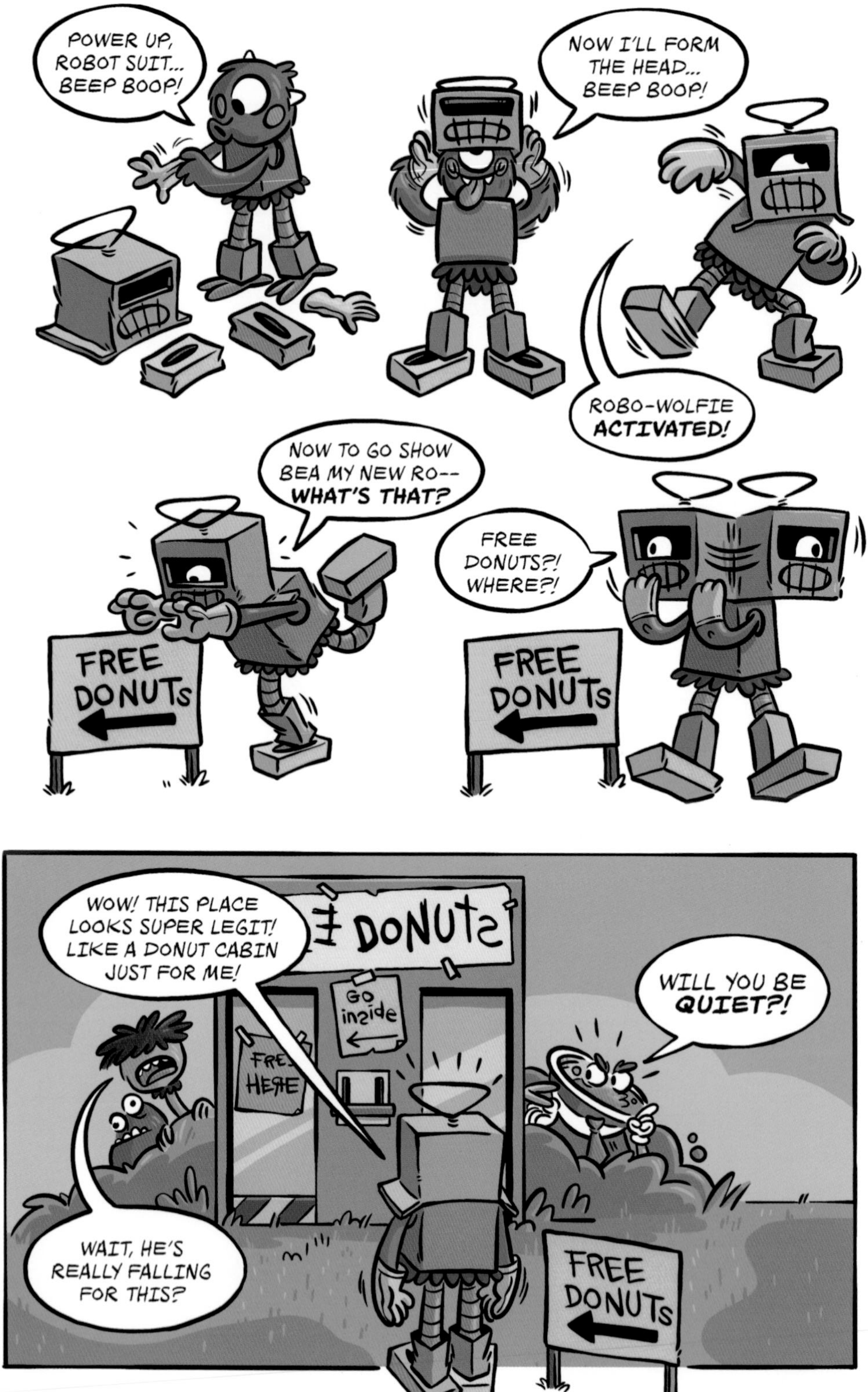
POWER UP, ROBOT SUIT... BEEP BOOP!
NOW I'LL FORM THE HEAD... BEEP BOOP!
ROBO-WOLFIE **ACTIVATED!**
NOW TO GO SHOW BEA MY NEW RO-- **WHAT'S THAT?**
FREE DONUTS
FREE DONUTS?! WHERE?!
FREE DONUTS
DONUTS
WOW! THIS PLACE LOOKS SUPER LEGIT! LIKE A DONUT CABIN JUST FOR ME!
Go inside
WILL YOU BE **QUIET?!**
WAIT, HE'S REALLY FALLING FOR THIS?
FREE DONUTS

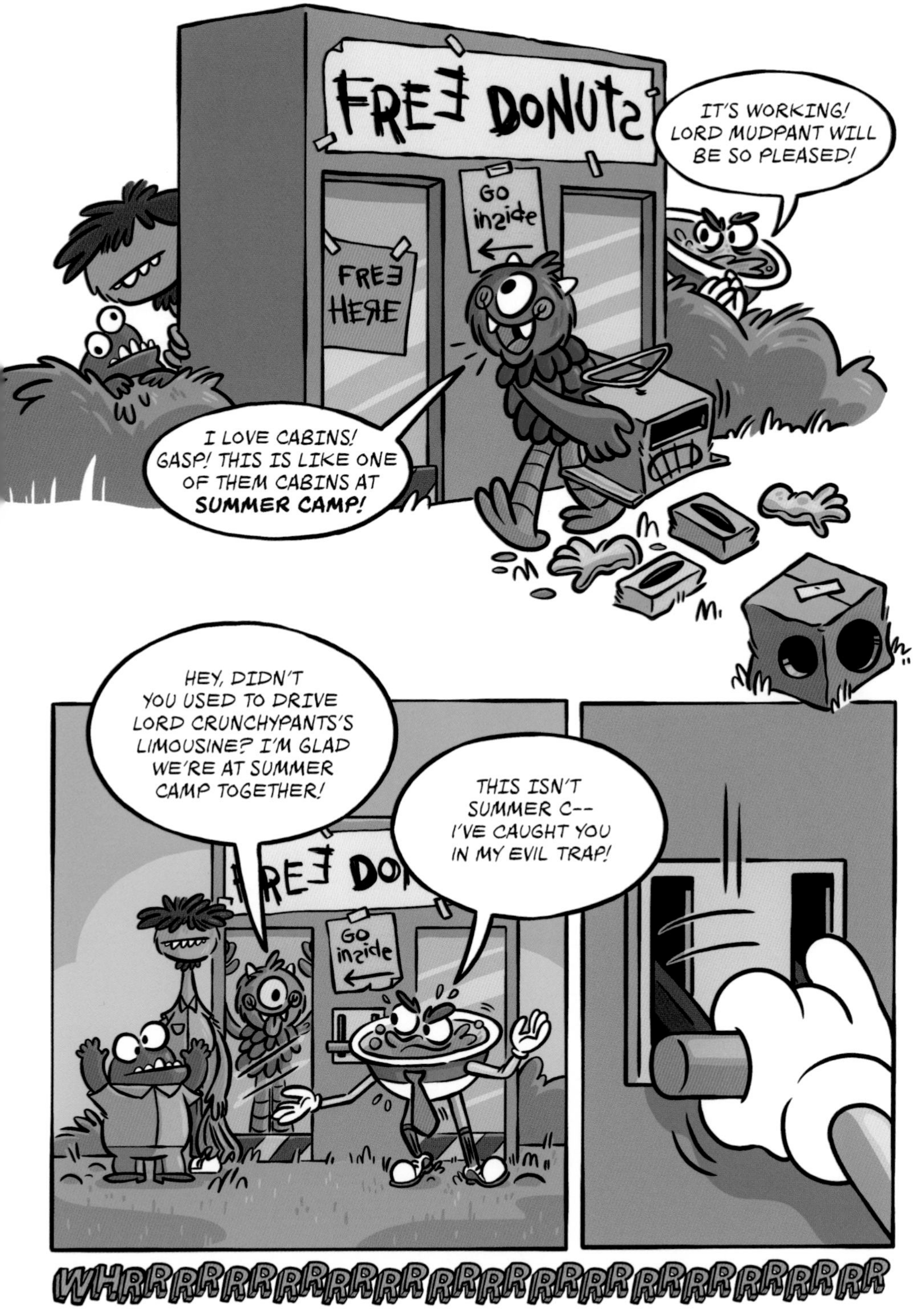

FREƎ DONUTƧ
GO inƨide
FREƎ HEЯE
IT'S WORKING! LORD MUDPANT WILL BE SO PLEASED!
I LOVE CABINS! GASP! THIS IS LIKE ONE OF THEM CABINS AT SUMMER CAMP!
HEY, DIDN'T YOU USED TO DRIVE LORD CRUNCHYPANTS'S LIMOUSINE? I'M GLAD WE'RE AT SUMMER CAMP TOGETHER!
THIS ISN'T SUMMER C-- I'VE CAUGHT YOU IN MY EVIL TRAP!
WHRRRRRRRRRRRRRRRRRRRRRRRRRRRRRRRRR

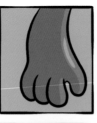
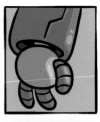

WHRRRRRRRRRRRRRRRRRRRRRRRRRRRRRRRRRRRR

IT'S **WORKING!** SOON, LORD MUDPANT WILL SEE WHAT AN **EVIL GENIUS** I CAN BE!

HE WILL LET ME, **GASPACHO**, SIT AT THE **BIG TABLE**, AND BE HIS **RIGHT-HAND MAN.**

WHRRRRRRRRRRRRRRRRRRR RRRRRRRRRR

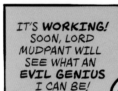

GO inside ←

WOW! MY FIRST SUMMER CAMP PROJECT IS ME! HELLO, ROBOT ME!

I AM IN SEARCH OF A BEST FRIEND. I ALSO REQUIRE CHEAP AND BAD PIZZA FOR MY BONES.

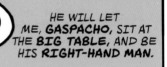

48

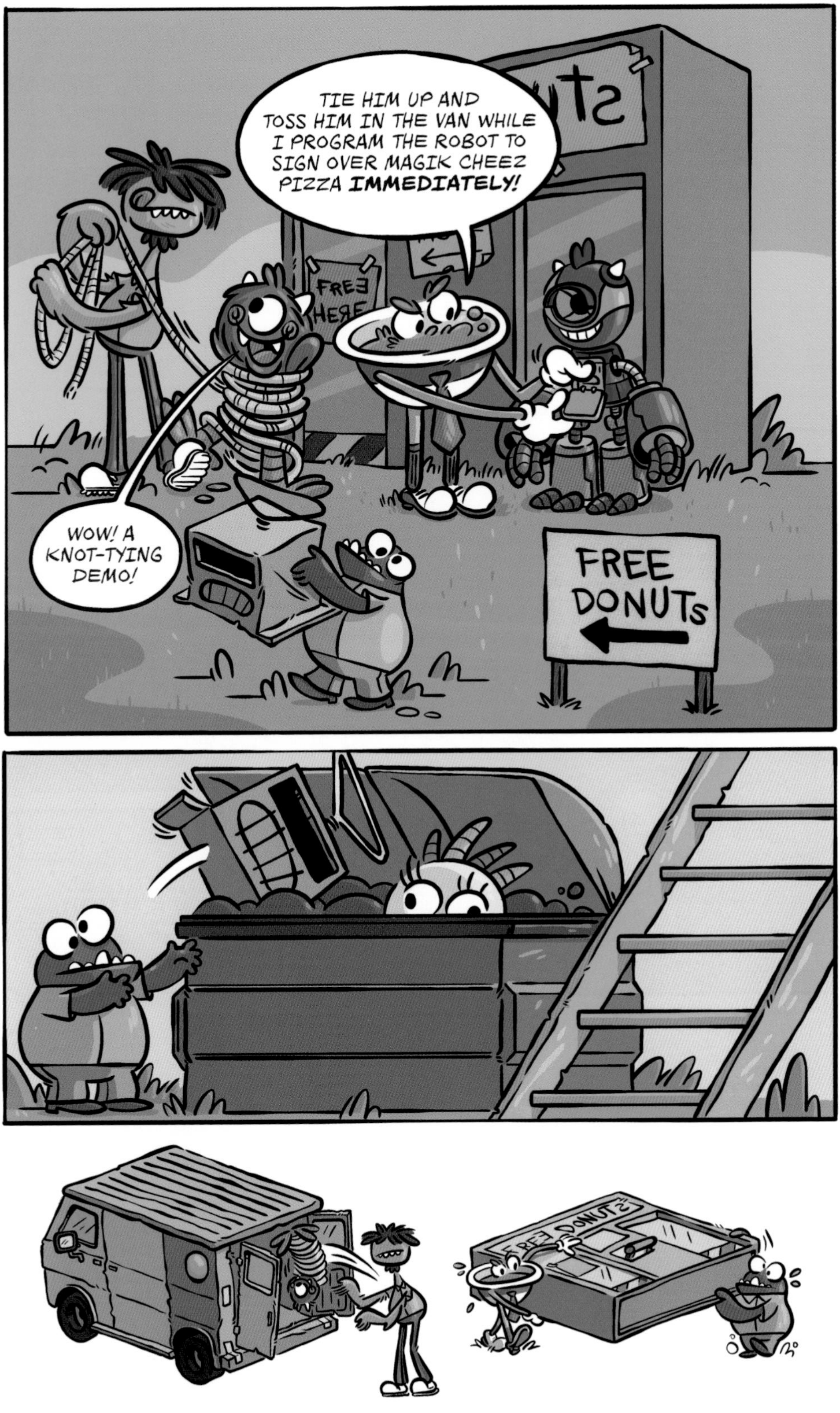
TIE HIM UP AND TOSS HIM IN THE VAN WHILE I PROGRAM THE ROBOT TO SIGN OVER MAGIK CHEEZ PIZZA **IMMEDIATELY!**
WOW! A KNOT-TYING DEMO!
FREE HERE
FREE DONUTs
FREE DONUTS

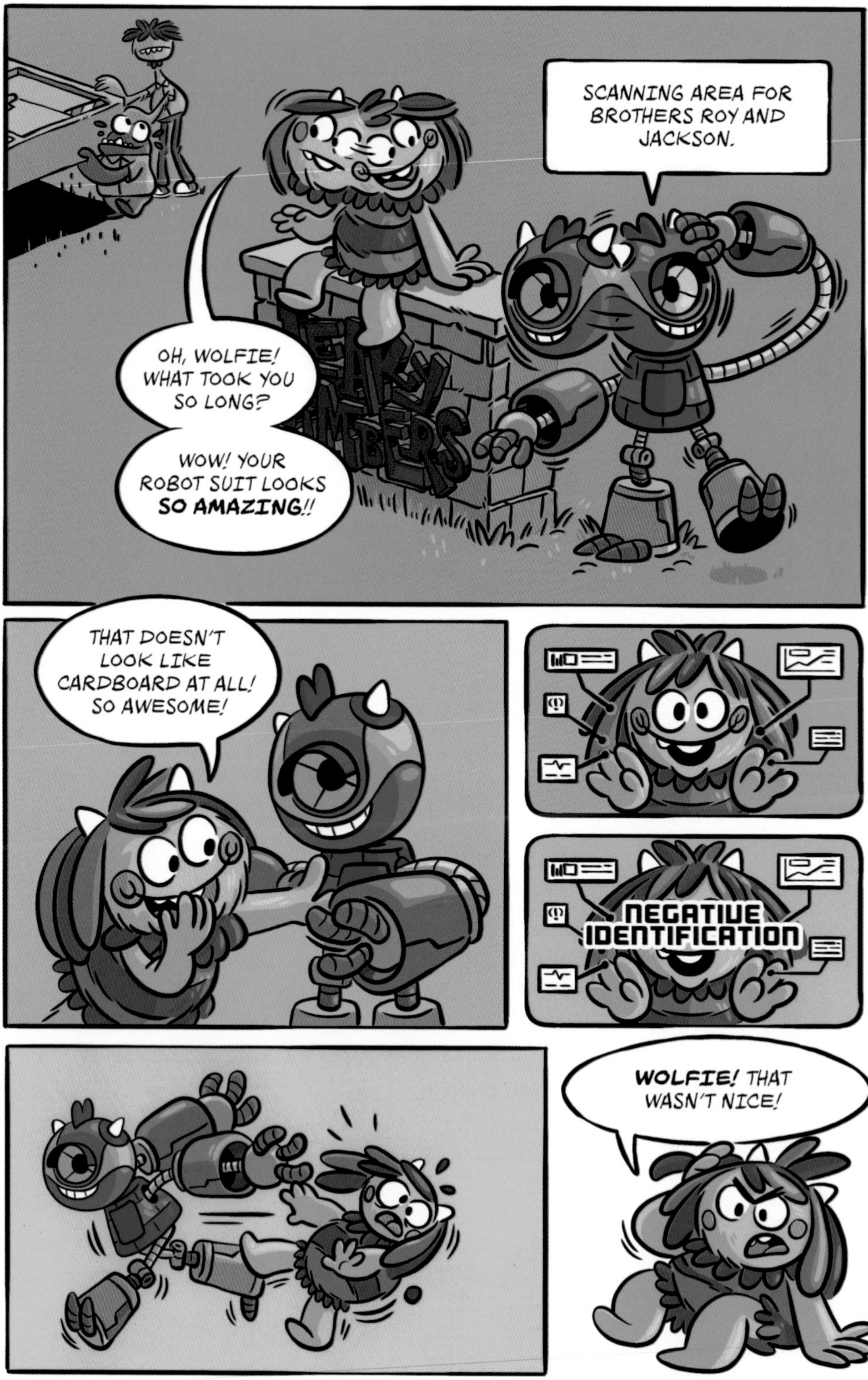
SCANNING AREA FOR BROTHERS ROY AND JACKSON.
OH, WOLFIE! WHAT TOOK YOU SO LONG?
WOW! YOUR ROBOT SUIT LOOKS **SO AMAZING!!**
THAT DOESN'T LOOK LIKE CARDBOARD AT ALL! SO AWESOME!
NEGATIVE IDENTIFICATION
WOLFIE! THAT WASN'T NICE!

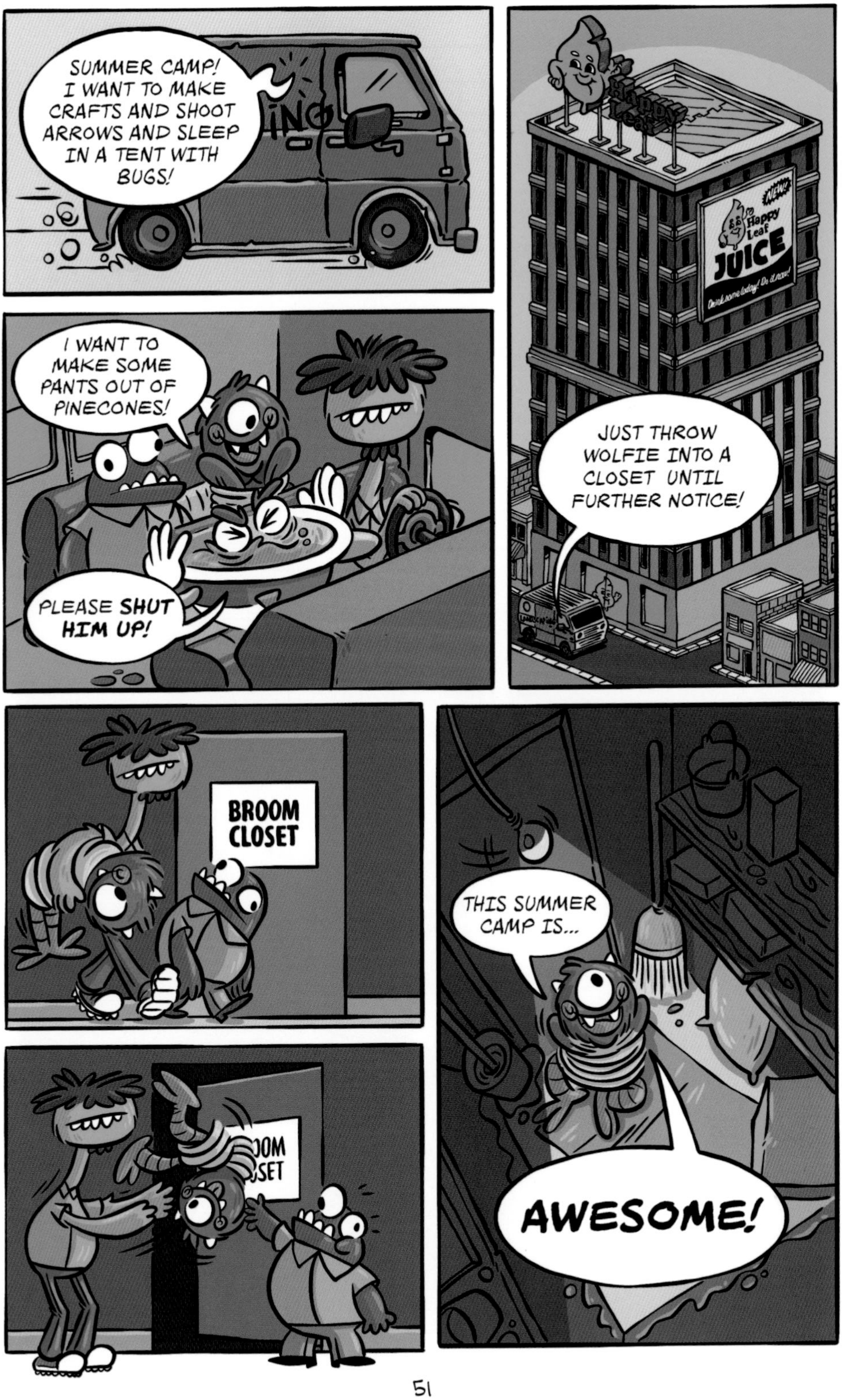
SUMMER CAMP! I WANT TO MAKE CRAFTS AND SHOOT ARROWS AND SLEEP IN A TENT WITH BUGS!
Happy Leaf
NEW!
Happy Leaf
JUICE
I WANT TO MAKE SOME PANTS OUT OF PINECONES!
PLEASE **SHUT HIM UP!**
JUST THROW WOLFIE INTO A CLOSET UNTIL FURTHER NOTICE!
BROOM CLOSET
THIS SUMMER CAMP IS...
AWESOME!

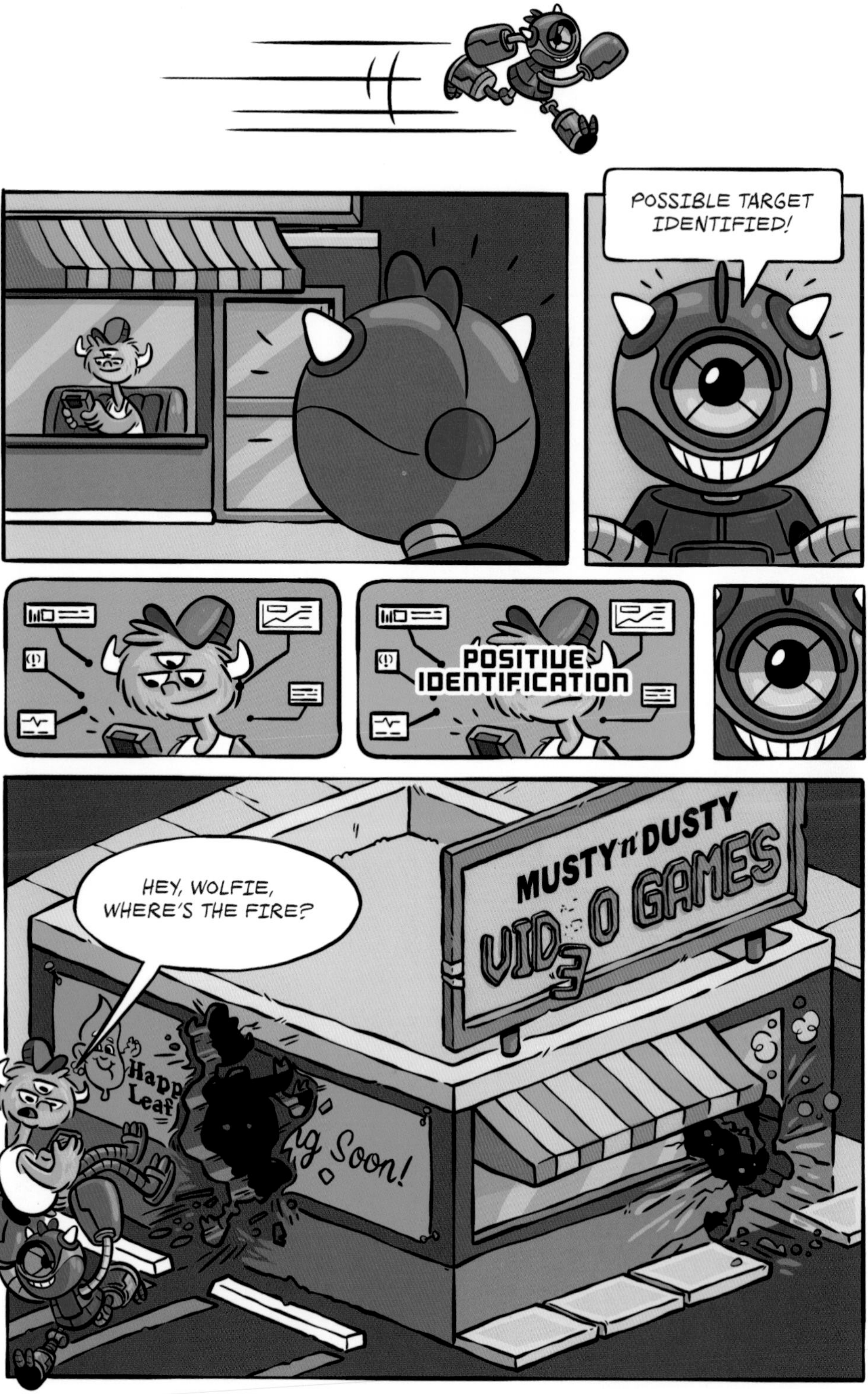
POSSIBLE TARGET IDENTIFIED!
POSITIVE IDENTIFICATION
MUSTY 'n' DUSTY
VID 3 O GAMES
HEY, WOLFIE, WHERE'S THE FIRE?
Happy Leaf
g Soon!

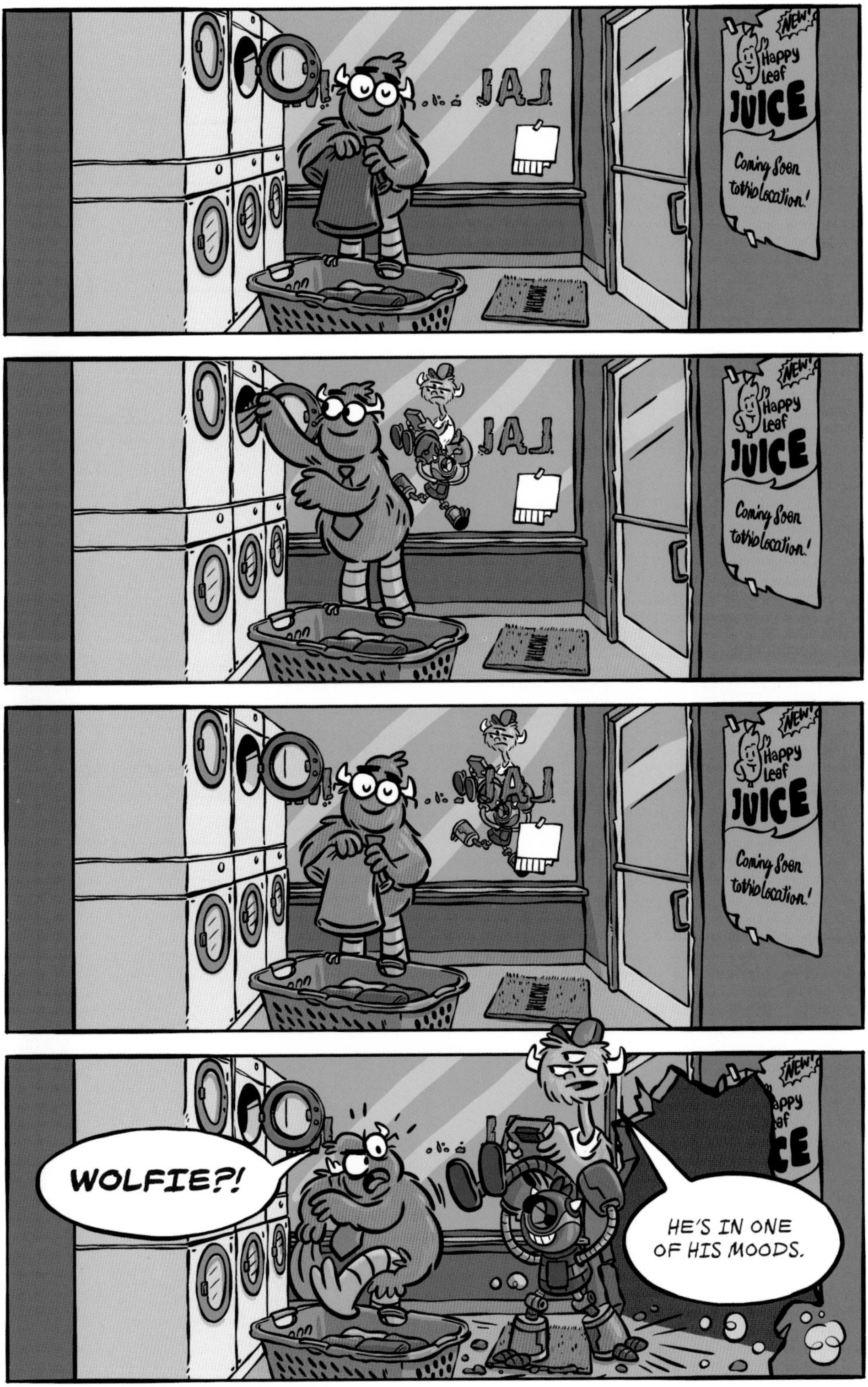
NEW!
Happy Leaf
JUICE
Coming Soon to this location!
WOLFIE?!
HE'S IN ONE OF HIS MOODS.

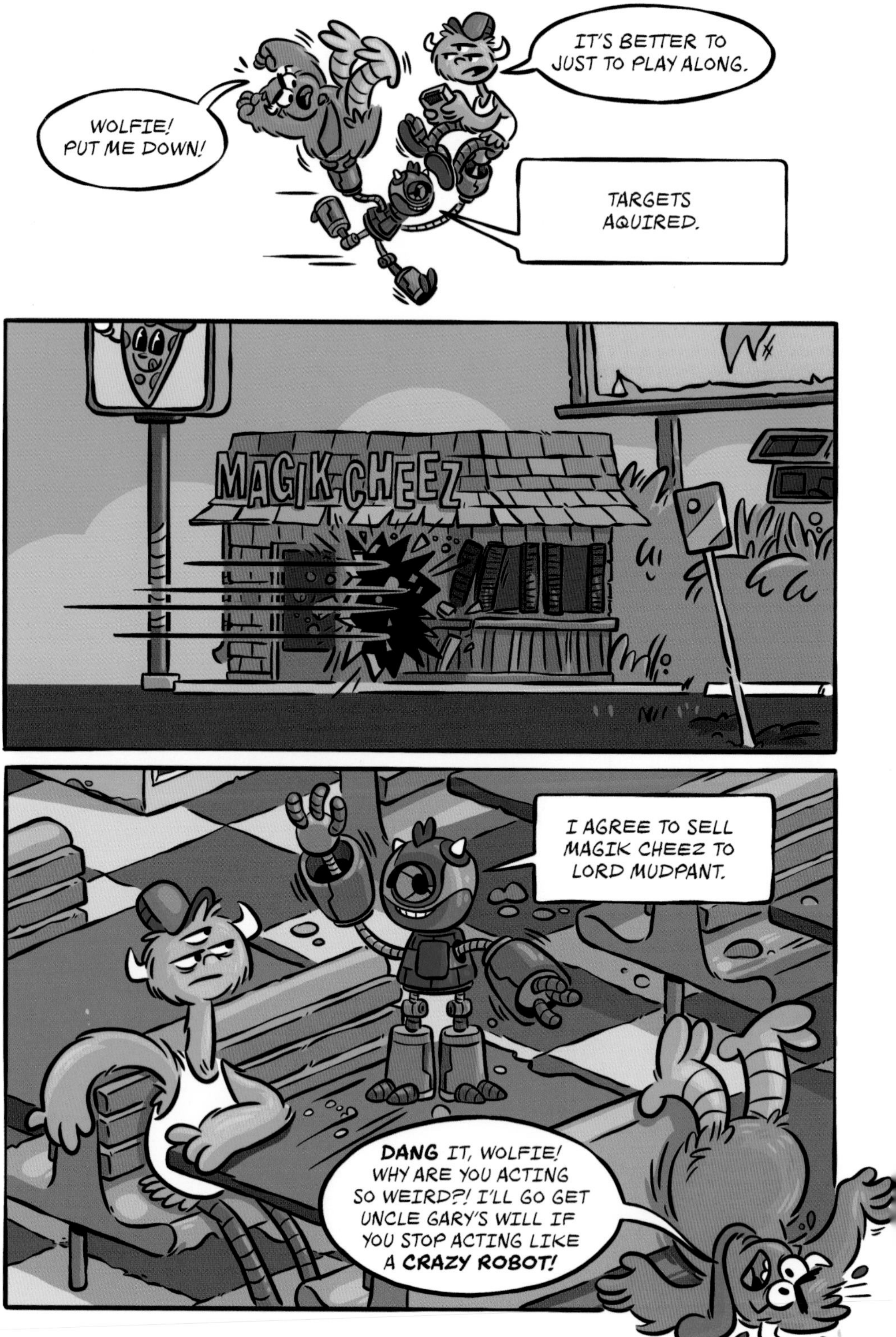

WOLFIE! PUT ME DOWN!
IT'S BETTER TO JUST TO PLAY ALONG.
TARGETS AQUIRED.
MAGIK CHEEZ
I AGREE TO SELL MAGIK CHEEZ TO LORD MUDPANT.
DANG IT, WOLFIE! WHY ARE YOU ACTING SO WEIRD?! I'LL GO GET UNCLE GARY'S WILL IF YOU STOP ACTING LIKE A **CRAZY ROBOT!**

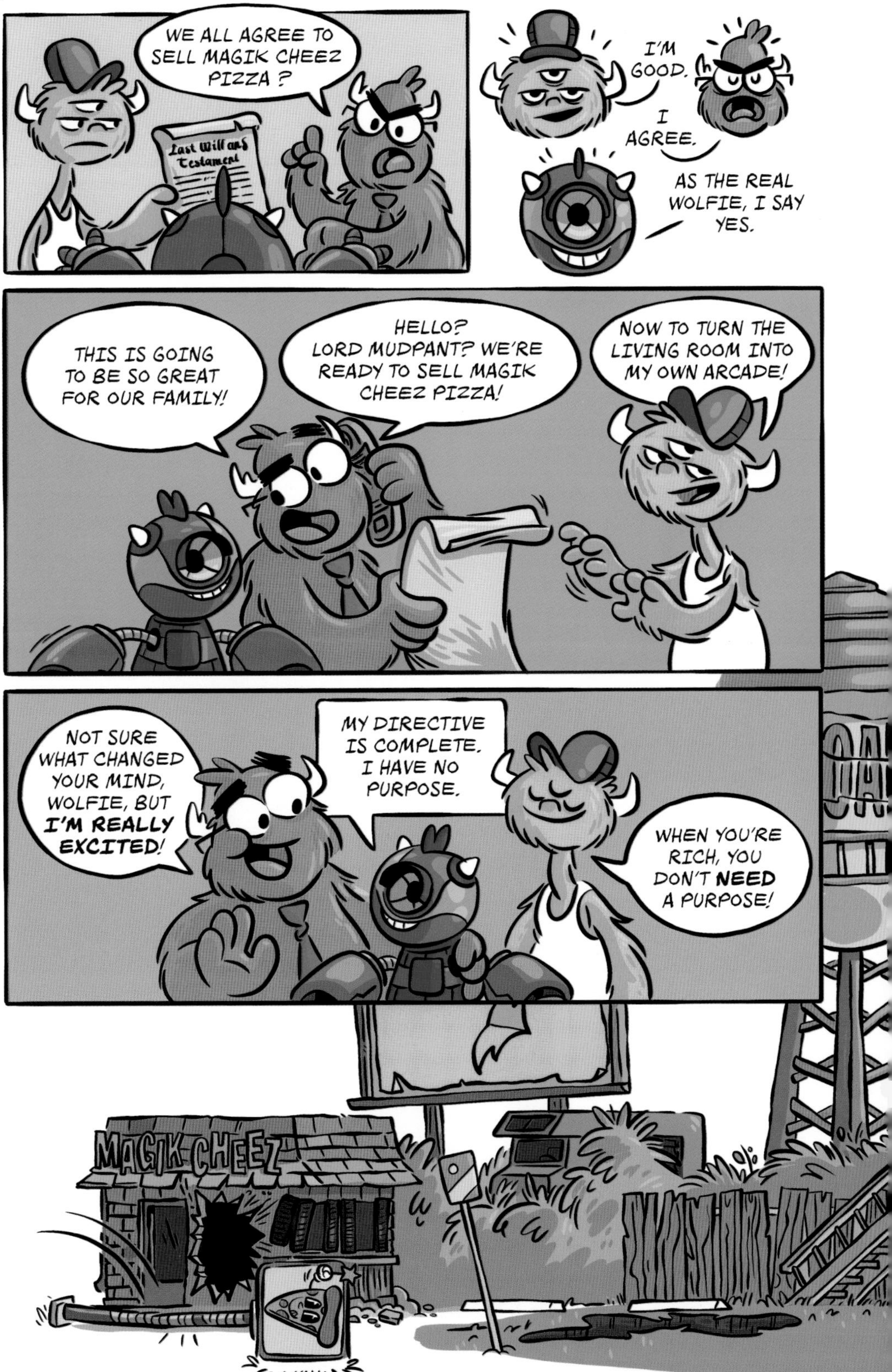
WE ALL AGREE TO SELL MAGIK CHEEZ PIZZA?
Last Will and Testament
I'M GOOD.
I AGREE.
AS THE REAL WOLFIE, I SAY YES.
THIS IS GOING TO BE SO GREAT FOR OUR FAMILY!
HELLO? LORD MUDPANT? WE'RE READY TO SELL MAGIK CHEEZ PIZZA!
NOW TO TURN THE LIVING ROOM INTO MY OWN ARCADE!
NOT SURE WHAT CHANGED YOUR MIND, WOLFIE, BUT **I'M REALLY EXCITED**!
MY DIRECTIVE IS COMPLETE. I HAVE NO PURPOSE.
WHEN YOU'RE RICH, YOU DON'T **NEED** A PURPOSE!
MAGIK CHEEZ

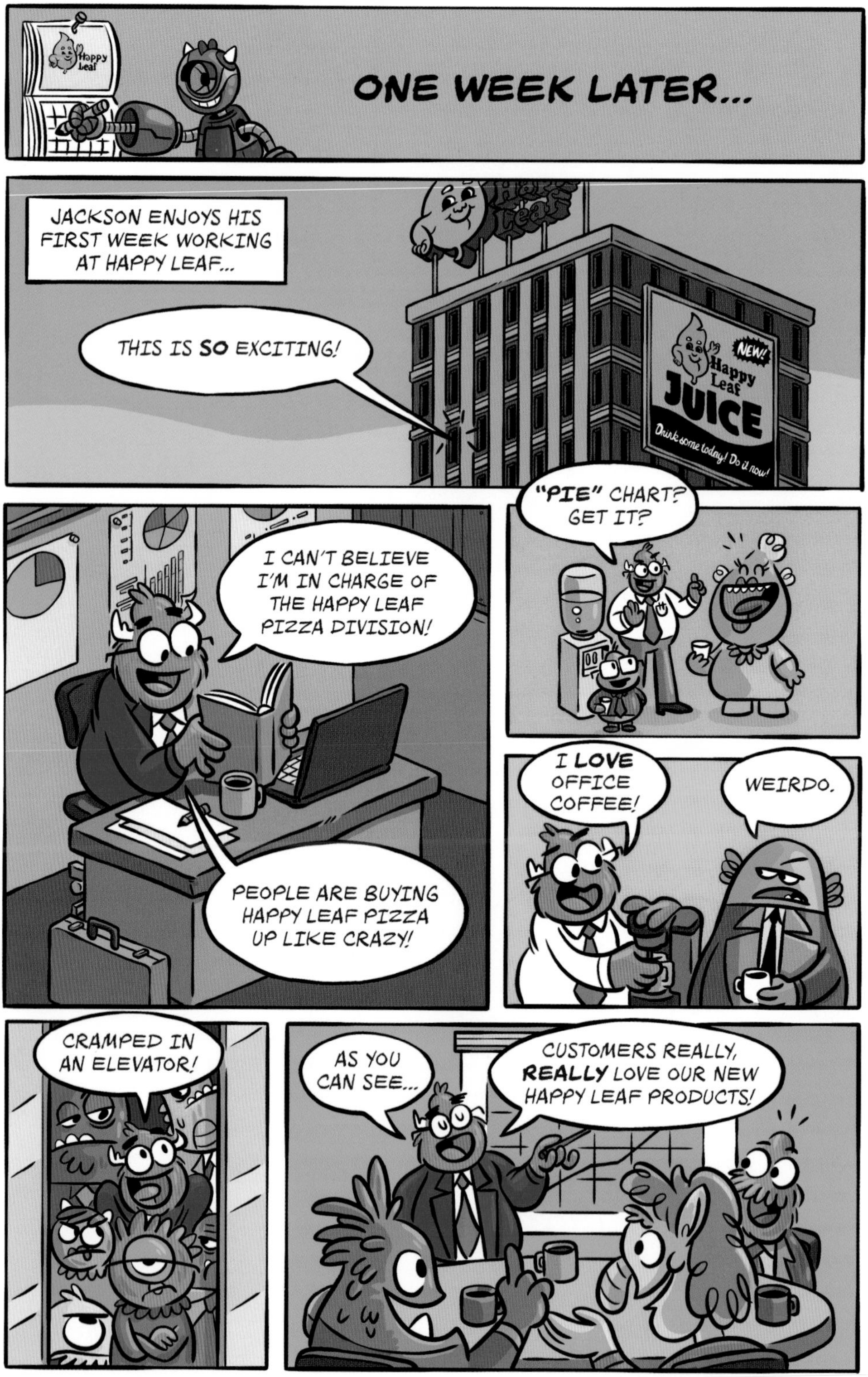
Happy Leaf
ONE WEEK LATER...
JACKSON ENJOYS HIS FIRST WEEK WORKING AT HAPPY LEAF...
THIS IS SO EXCITING!
NEW!
Happy Leaf
JUICE
Drink some today! Do it now!
I CAN'T BELIEVE I'M IN CHARGE OF THE HAPPY LEAF PIZZA DIVISION!
PEOPLE ARE BUYING HAPPY LEAF PIZZA UP LIKE CRAZY!
"PIE" CHART? GET IT?
I LOVE OFFICE COFFEE!
WEIRDO.
CRAMPED IN AN ELEVATOR!
AS YOU CAN SEE...
CUSTOMERS REALLY, REALLY LOVE OUR NEW HAPPY LEAF PRODUCTS!

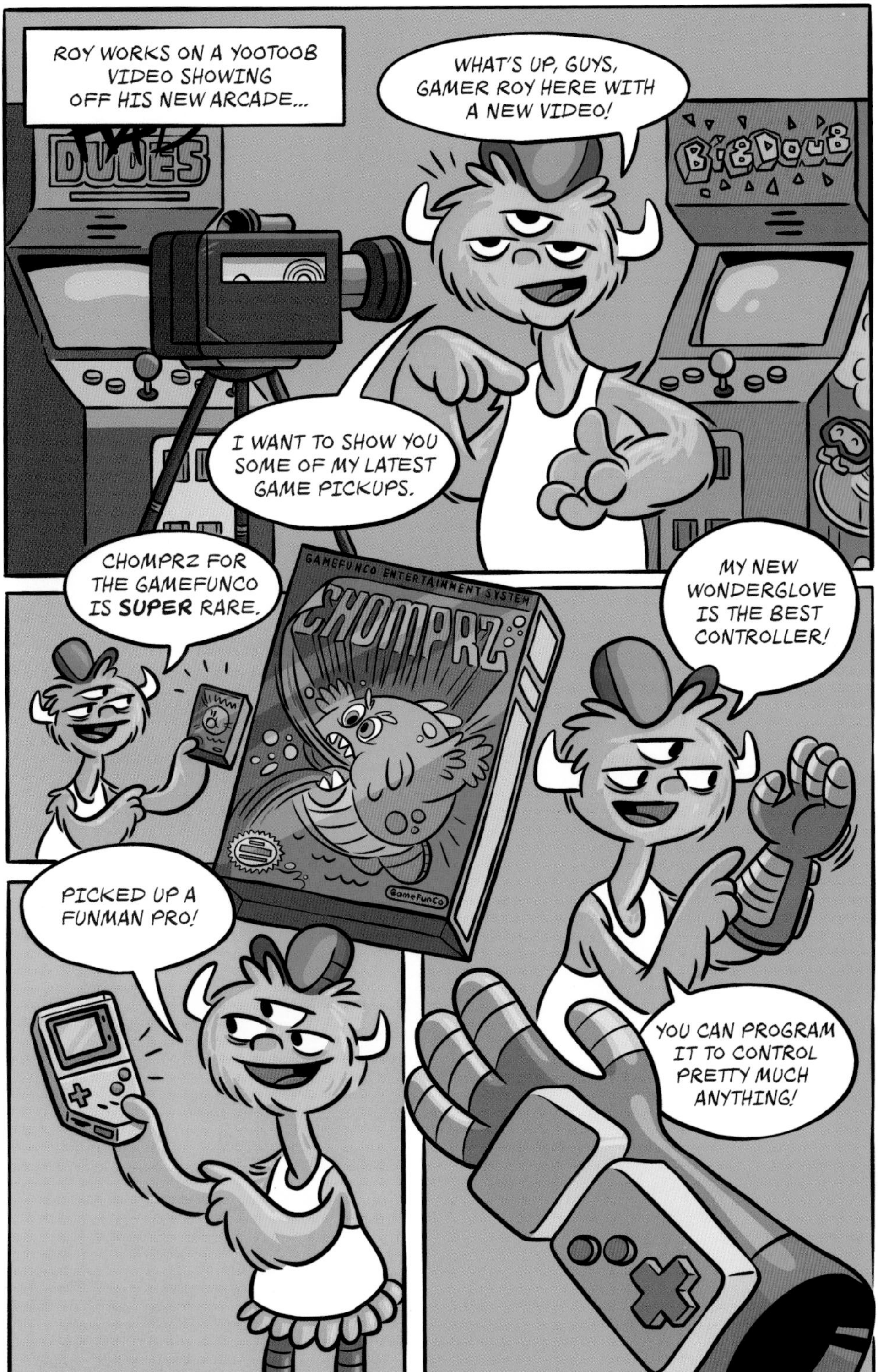
ROY WORKS ON A YOOTOOB VIDEO SHOWING OFF HIS NEW ARCADE...
WHAT'S UP, GUYS, GAMER ROY HERE WITH A NEW VIDEO!
I WANT TO SHOW YOU SOME OF MY LATEST GAME PICKUPS.
DUDES
CHOMPRZ FOR THE GAMEFUNCO IS **SUPER** RARE.
GAMEFUNCO ENTERTAINMENT SYSTEM
CHOMPRZ
GameFunCo
MY NEW WONDERGLOVE IS THE BEST CONTROLLER!
PICKED UP A FUNMAN PRO!
YOU CAN PROGRAM IT TO CONTROL PRETTY MUCH ANYTHING!

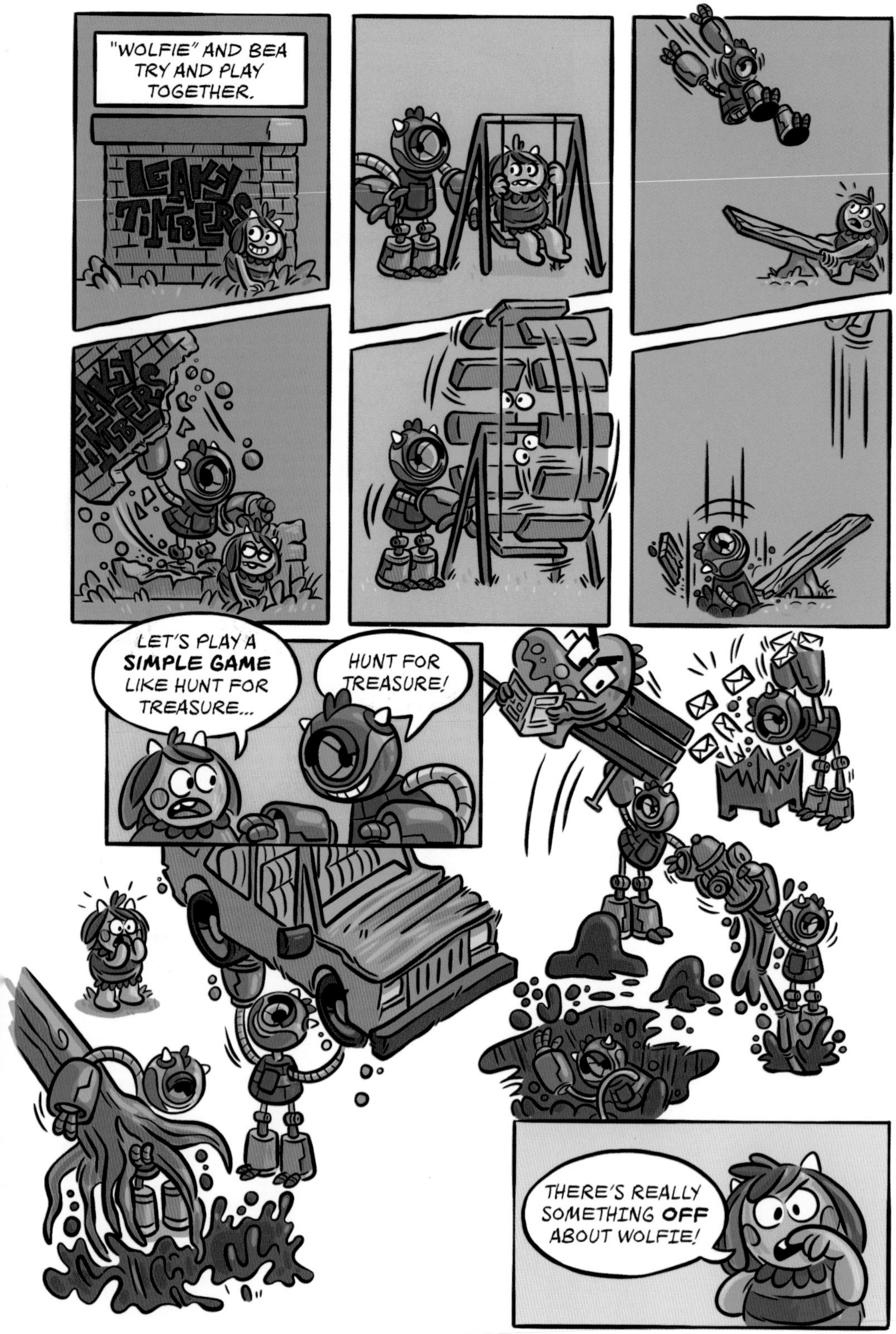
"WOLFIE" AND BEA TRY AND PLAY TOGETHER.
LEAKY TIMBERS
LET'S PLAY A **SIMPLE GAME** LIKE HUNT FOR TREASURE...
HUNT FOR TREASURE!
THERE'S REALLY SOMETHING **OFF** ABOUT WOLFIE!

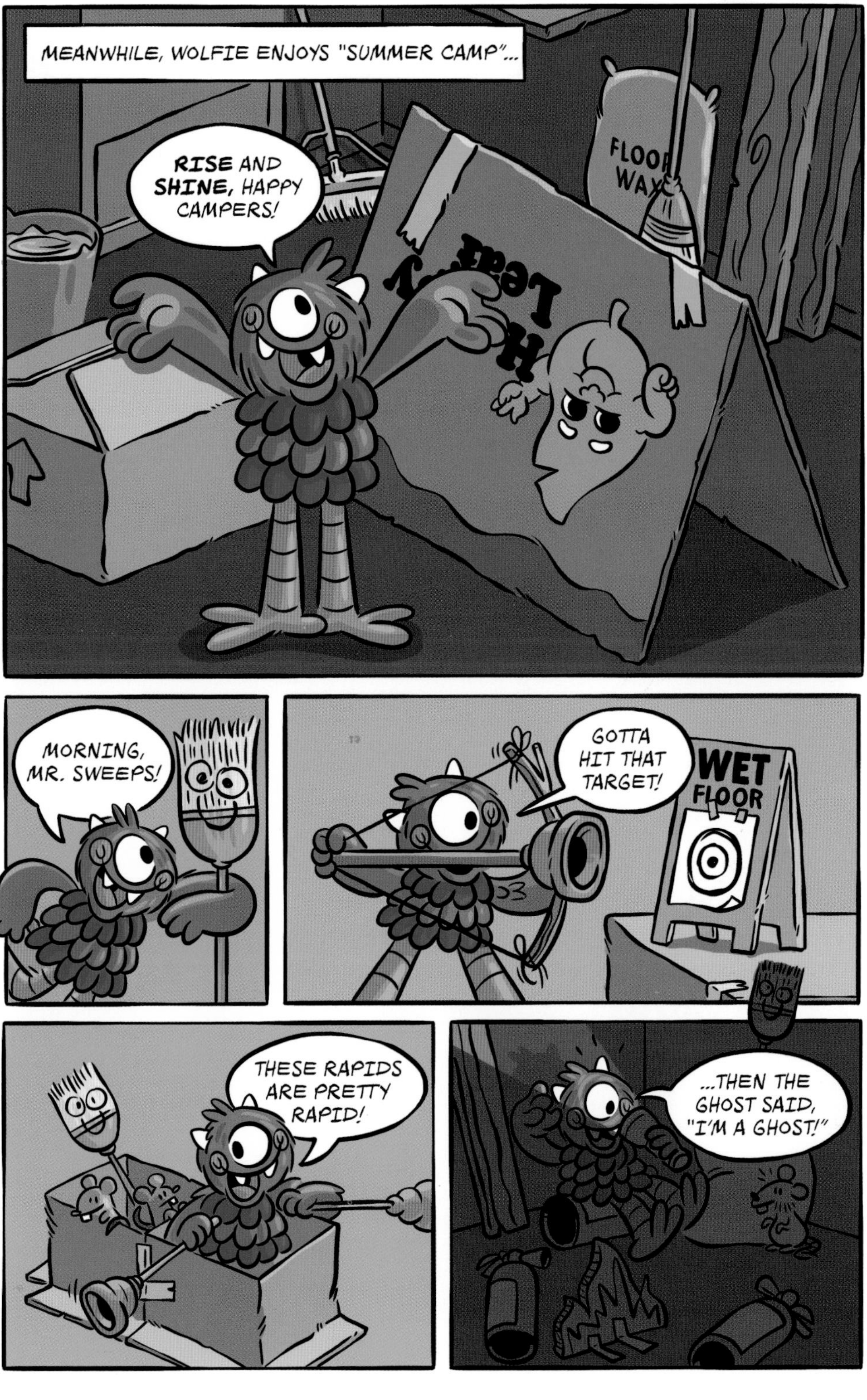
MEANWHILE, WOLFIE ENJOYS "SUMMER CAMP"...
RISE AND SHINE, HAPPY CAMPERS!
FLOOR WAX
MORNING, MR. SWEEPS!
GOTTA HIT THAT TARGET!
WET FLOOR
THESE RAPIDS ARE PRETTY RAPID!
...THEN THE GHOST SAID, "I'M A GHOST!"

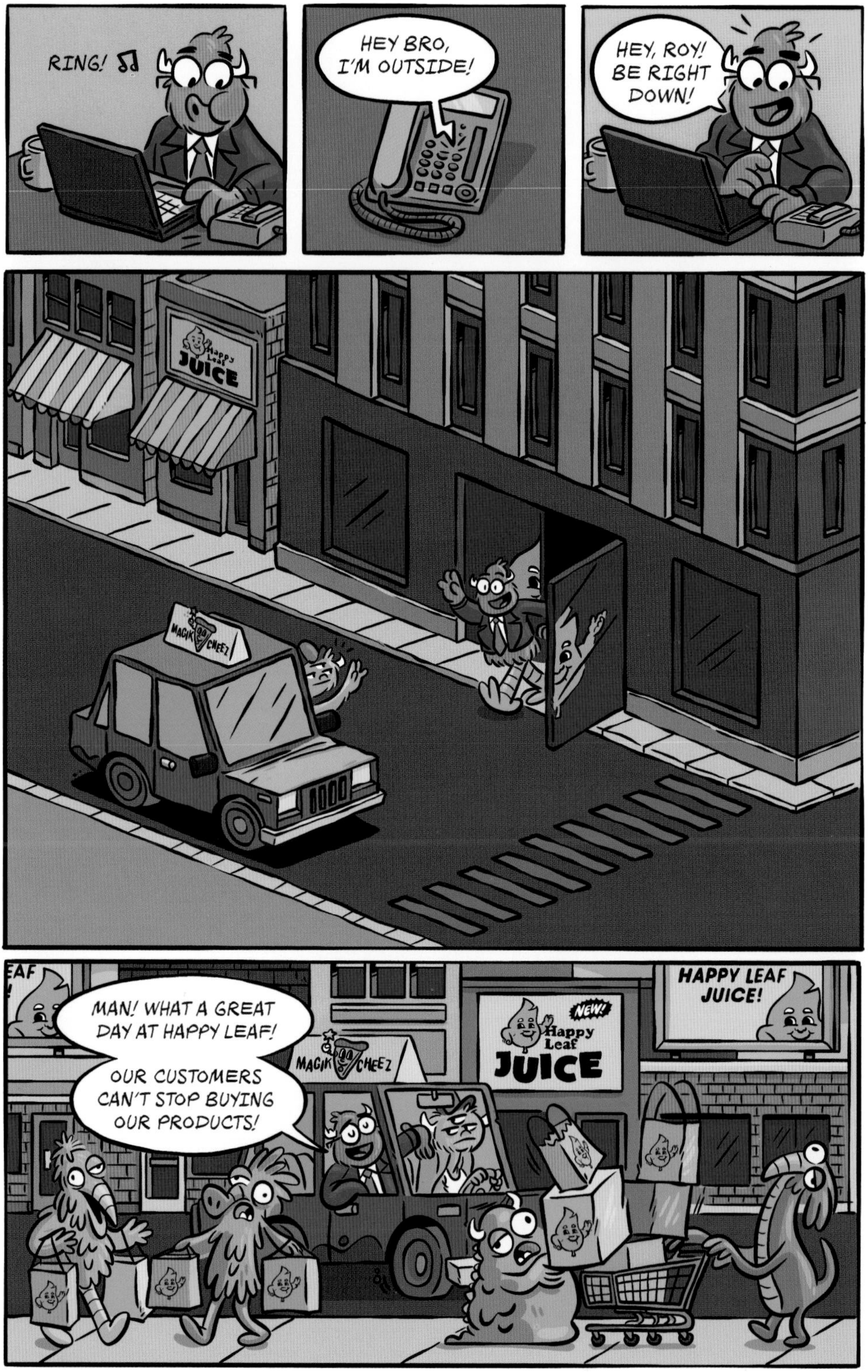
RING!
HEY BRO, I'M OUTSIDE!
HEY, ROY! BE RIGHT DOWN!
Happy Leaf JUICE
MAGIK CHEEZ
HAPPY LEAF JUICE!
NEW! Happy Leaf JUICE
MAGIK CHEEZ
MAN! WHAT A GREAT DAY AT HAPPY LEAF!
OUR CUSTOMERS CAN'T STOP BUYING OUR PRODUCTS!

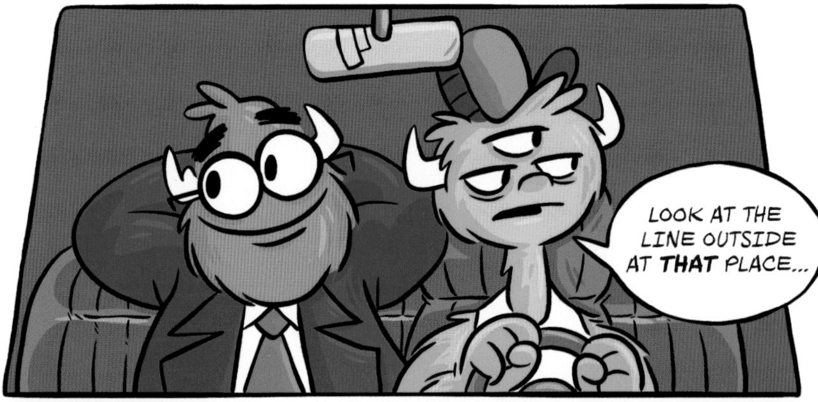
LOOK AT THE LINE OUTSIDE AT **THAT** PLACE...

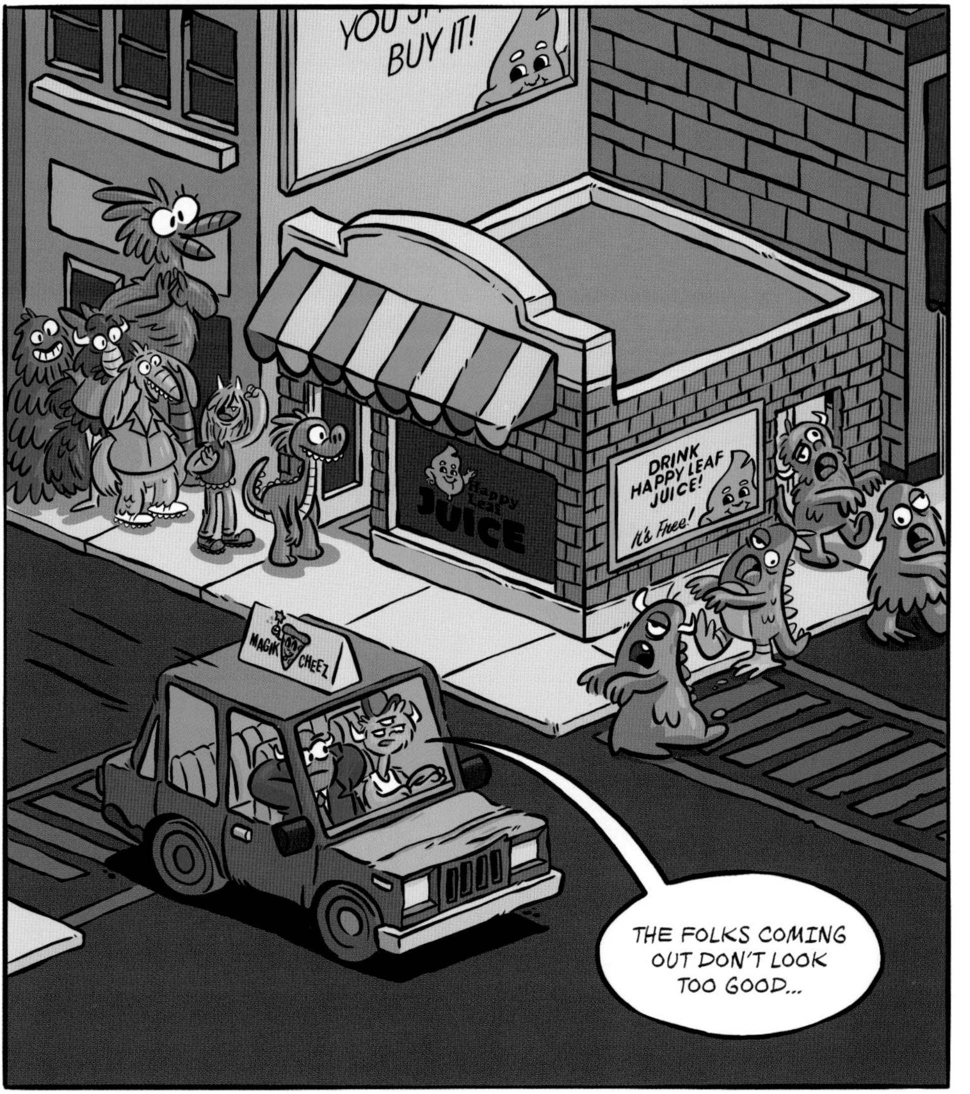
BUY IT!
Happy Leaf JUICE
DRINK HAPPY LEAF JUICE!
It's Free!
MAGIK CHEEZ
THE FOLKS COMING OUT DON'T LOOK TOO GOOD...

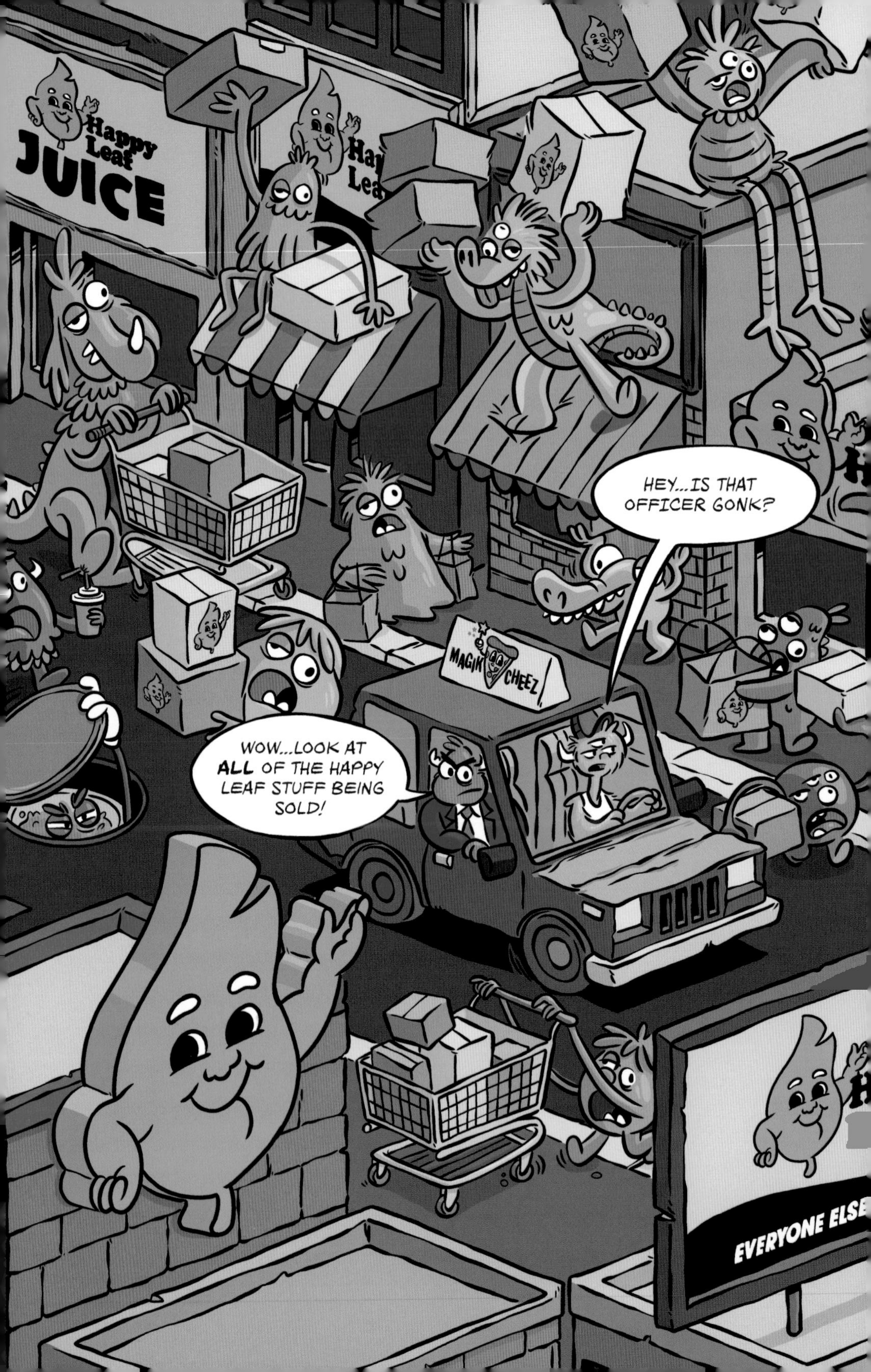
HEY...IS THAT OFFICER GONK?
WOW...LOOK AT ALL OF THE HAPPY LEAF STUFF BEING SOLD!
Happy Leaf JUICE
MAGIK CHEEZ
EVERYONE ELSE

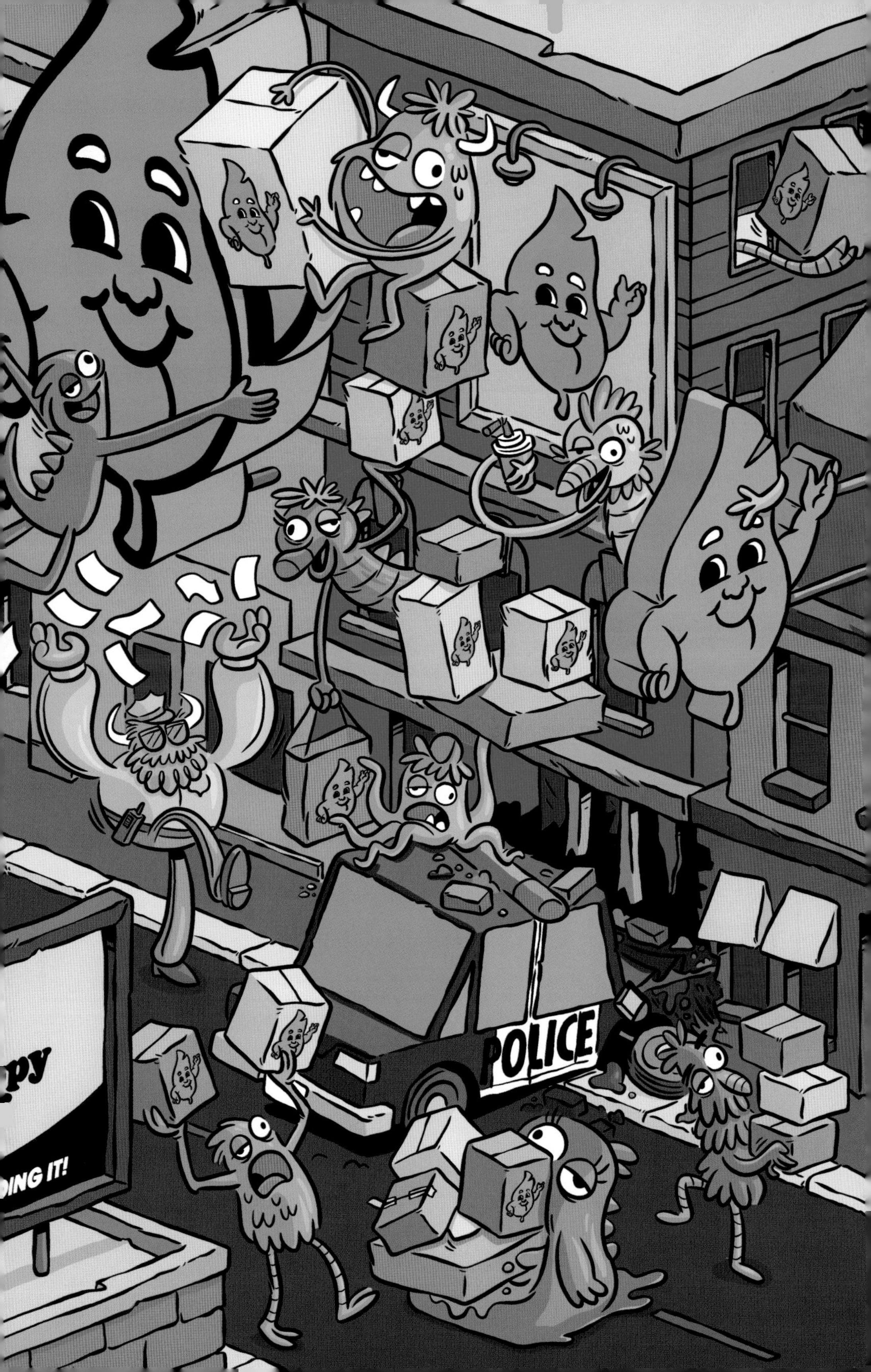
POLICE
py
OING IT!

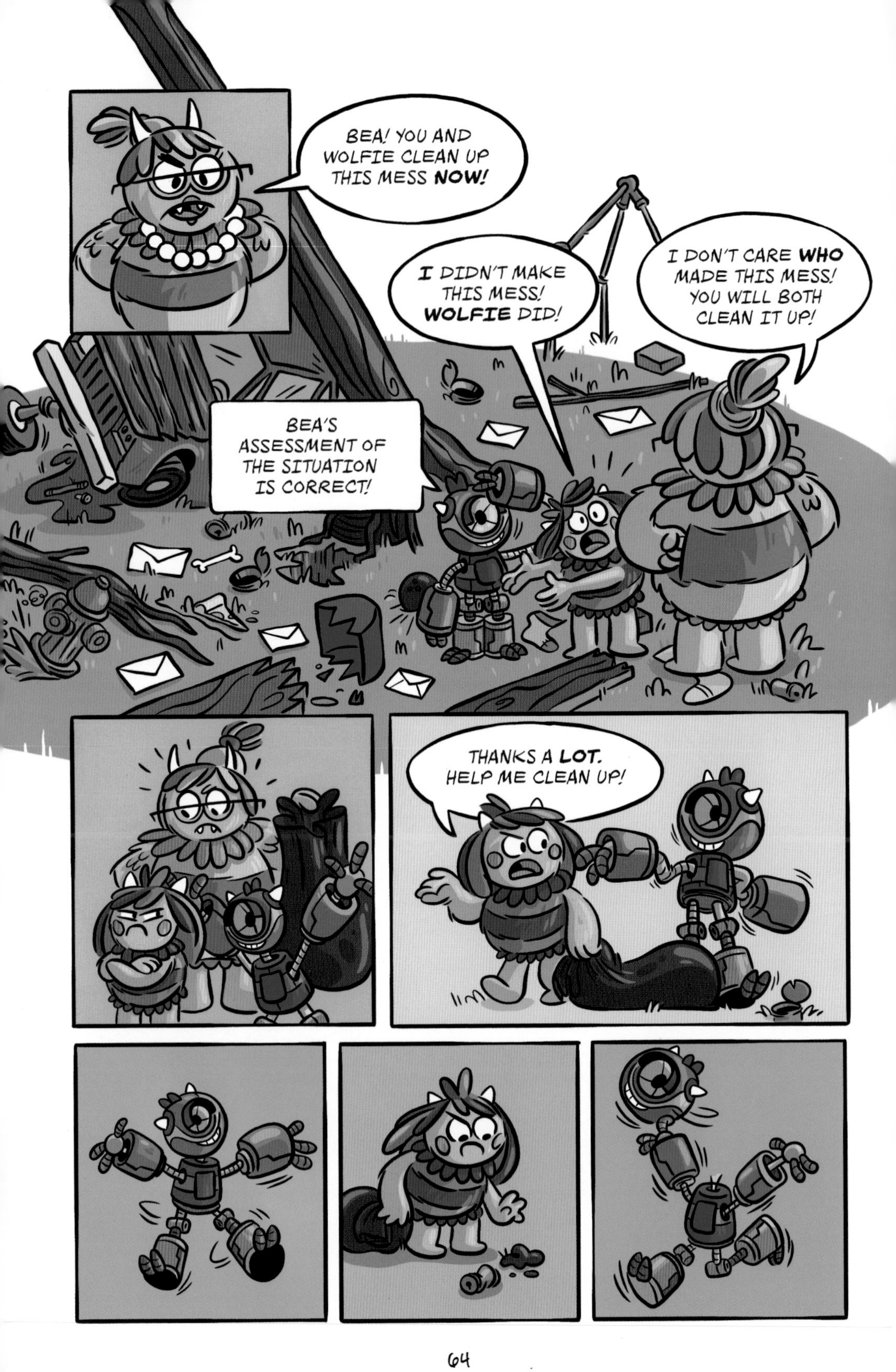
BEA! YOU AND WOLFIE CLEAN UP THIS MESS **NOW!**
I DIDN'T MAKE THIS MESS! **WOLFIE** DID!
I DON'T CARE **WHO** MADE THIS MESS! YOU WILL BOTH CLEAN IT UP!
BEA'S ASSESSMENT OF THE SITUATION IS CORRECT!
THANKS A **LOT.** HELP ME CLEAN UP!

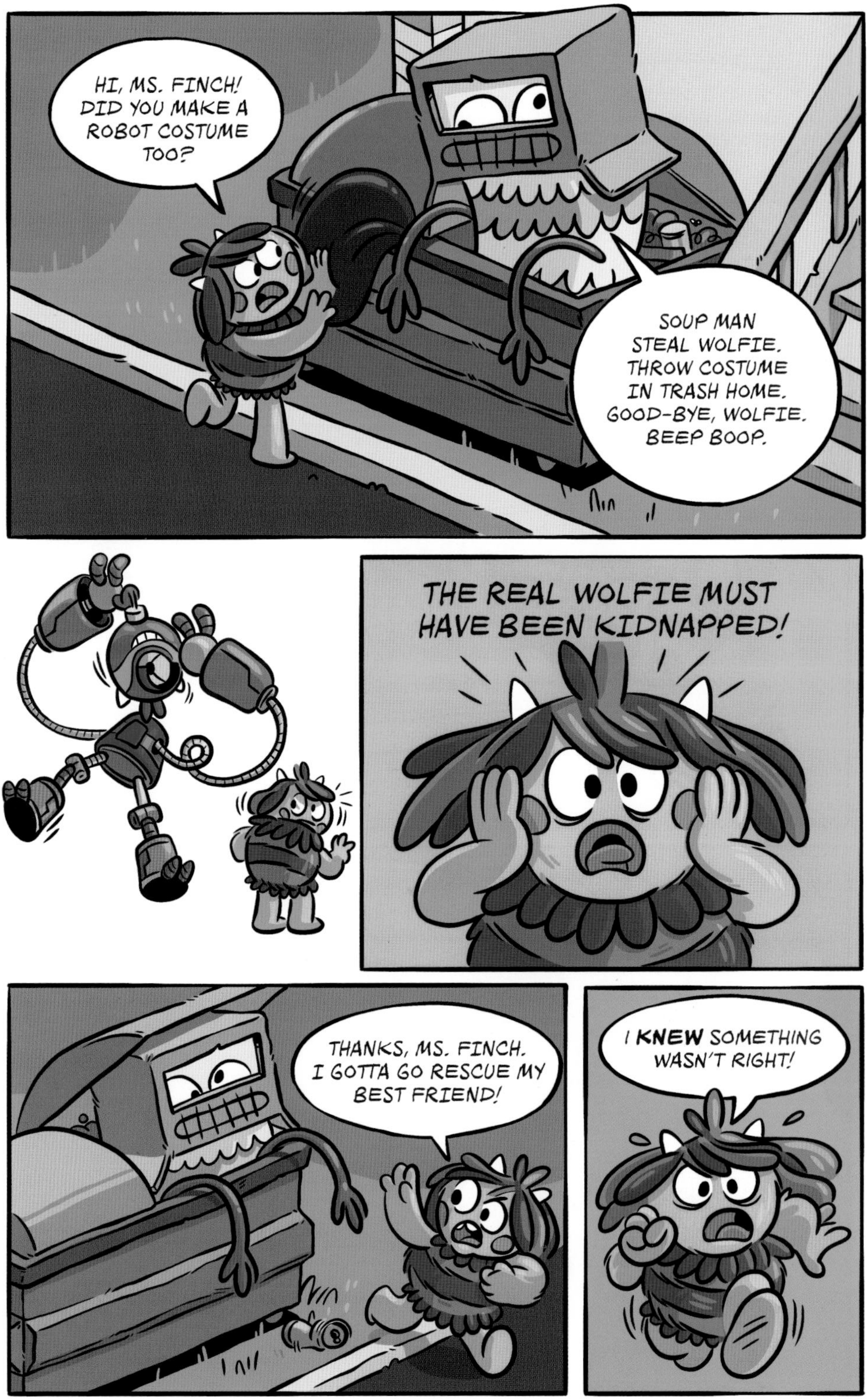
HI, MS. FINCH! DID YOU MAKE A ROBOT COSTUME TOO?
SOUP MAN STEAL WOLFIE. THROW COSTUME IN TRASH HOME. GOOD-BYE, WOLFIE. BEEP BOOP.
THE REAL WOLFIE MUST HAVE BEEN KIDNAPPED!
THANKS, MS. FINCH. I GOTTA GO RESCUE MY BEST FRIEND!
I **KNEW** SOMETHING WASN'T RIGHT!

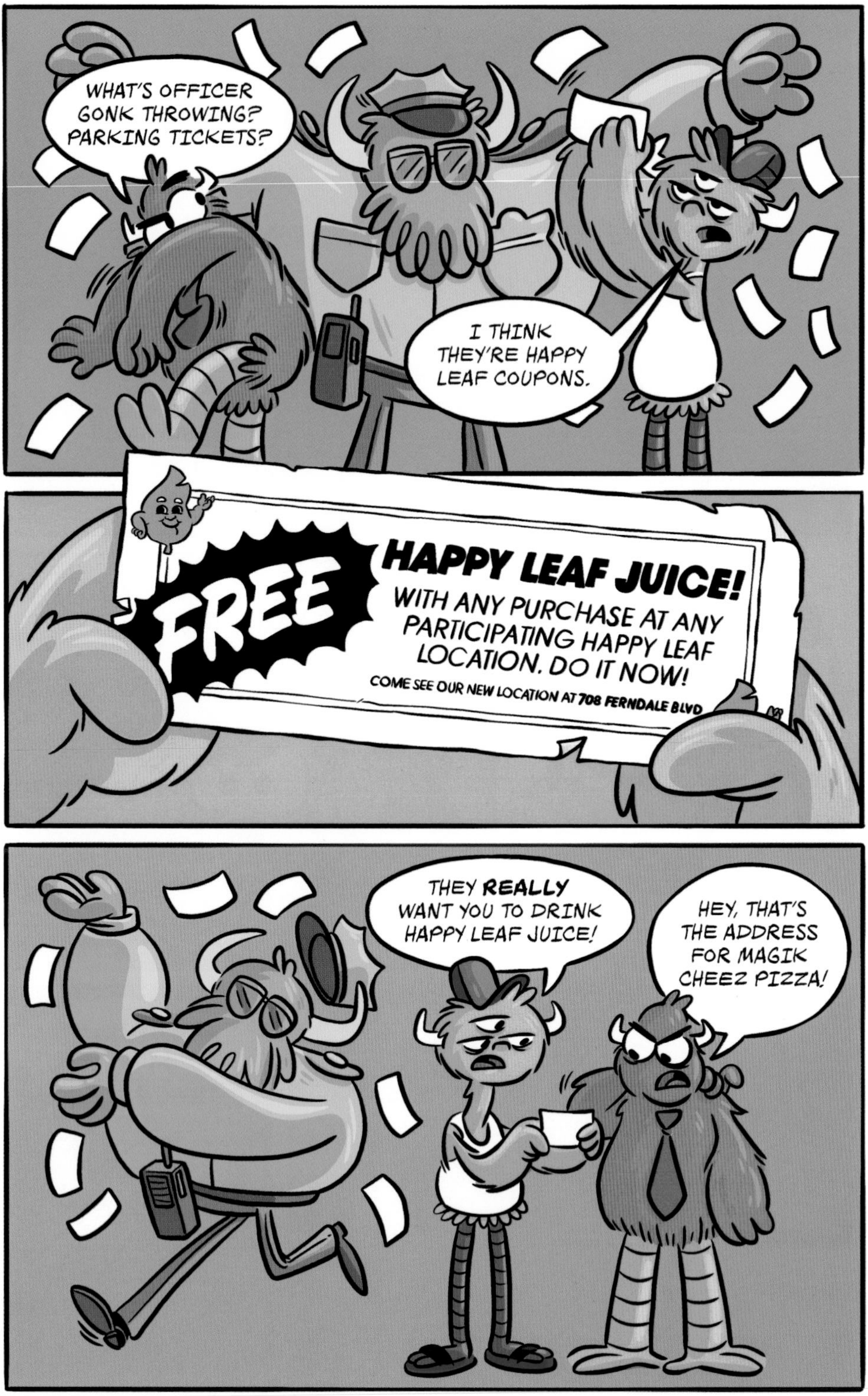
WHAT'S OFFICER GONK THROWING? PARKING TICKETS?
I THINK THEY'RE HAPPY LEAF COUPONS.
FREE
HAPPY LEAF JUICE!
WITH ANY PURCHASE AT ANY PARTICIPATING HAPPY LEAF LOCATION. DO IT NOW!
COME SEE OUR NEW LOCATION AT 708 FERNDALE BLVD
THEY **REALLY** WANT YOU TO DRINK HAPPY LEAF JUICE!
HEY, THAT'S THE ADDRESS FOR MAGIK CHEEZ PIZZA!

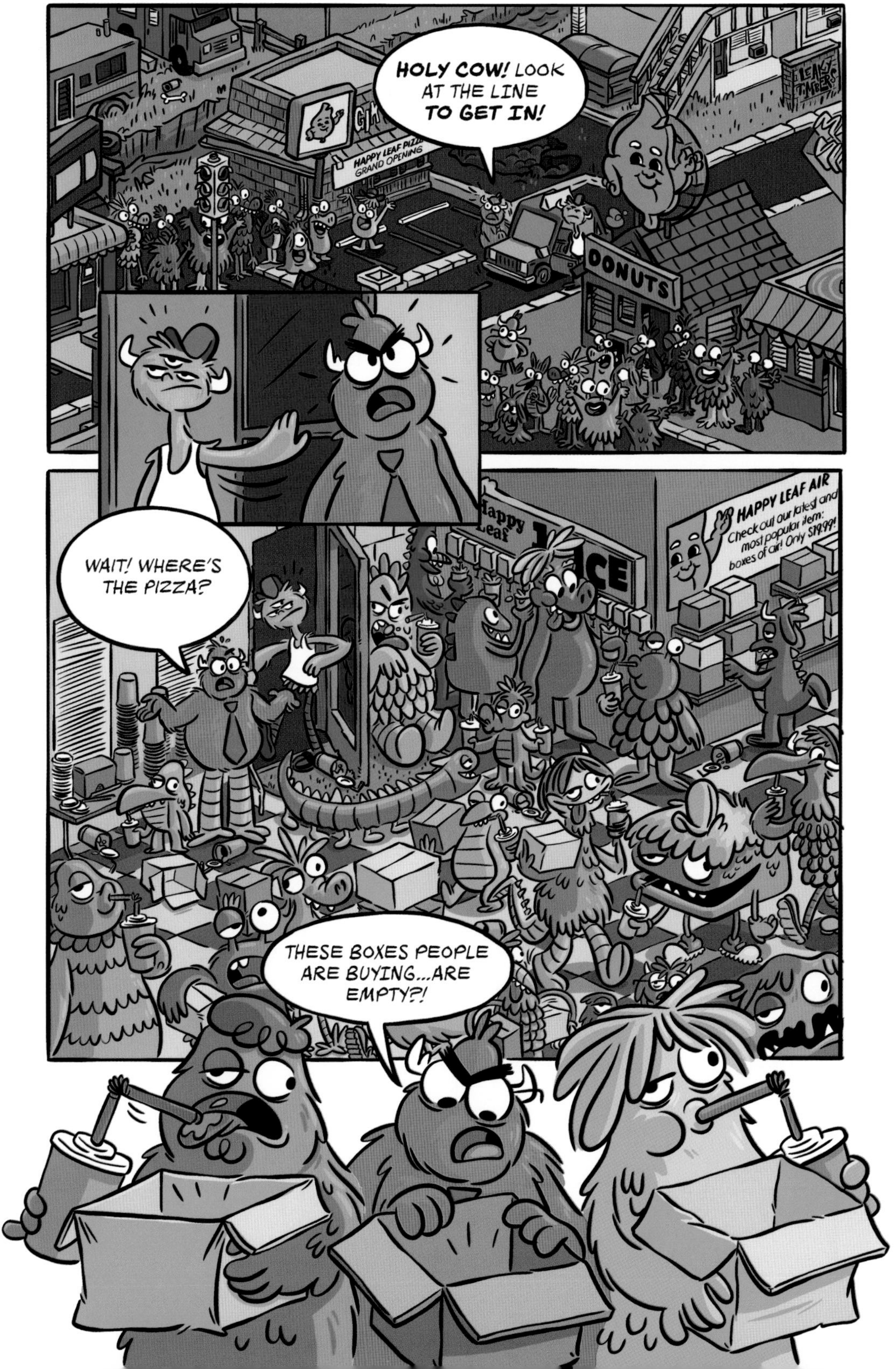
HOLY COW! LOOK AT THE LINE TO GET IN!
HAPPY LEAF
GRAND OPENING
LEAKY TIMBERS
DONUTS
WAIT! WHERE'S THE PIZZA?
Happy Leaf
HAPPY LEAF AIR
Check out our latest and most popular item: boxes of air! Only $19.99!
THESE BOXES PEOPLE ARE BUYING...ARE EMPTY?!

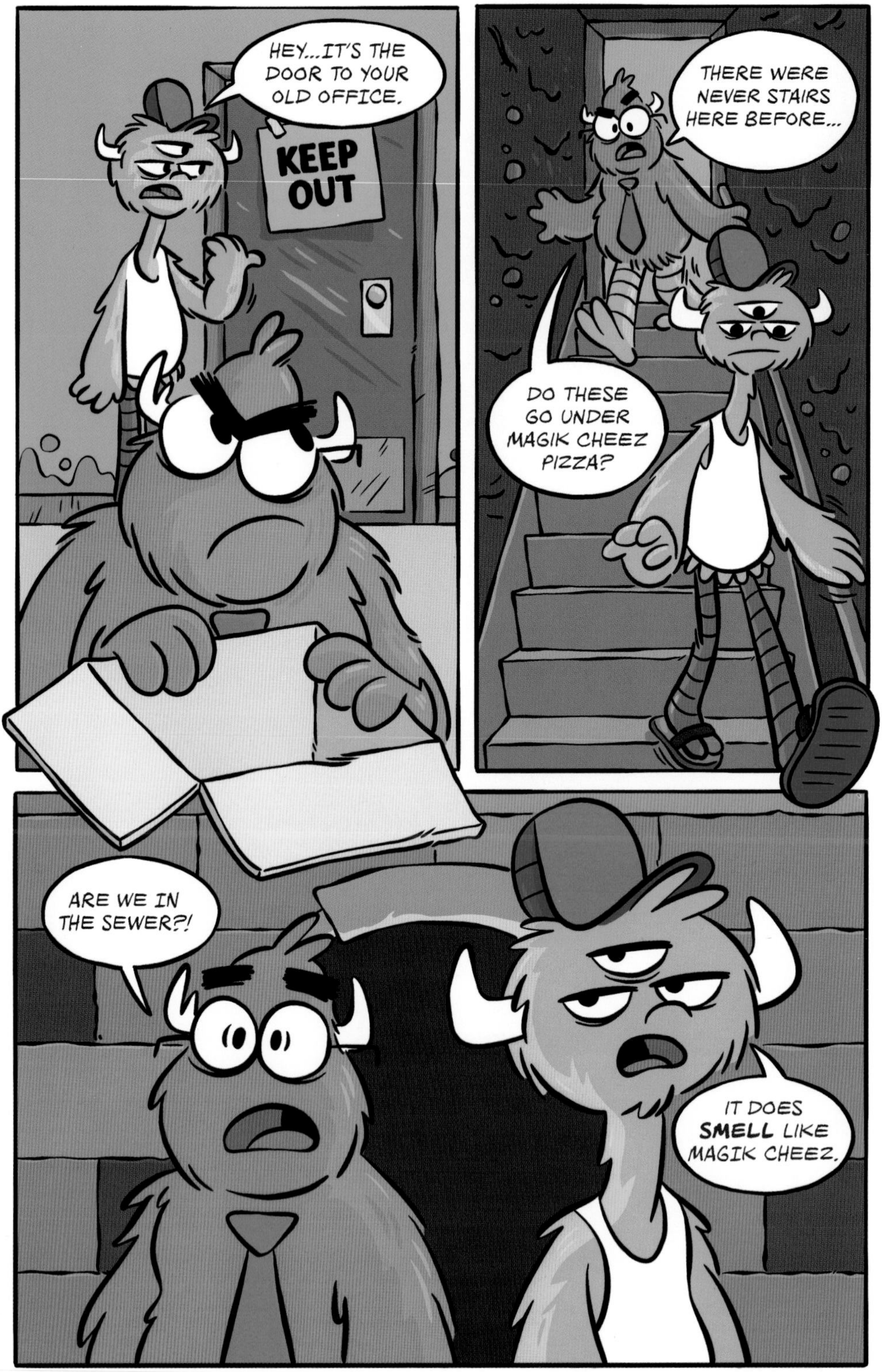
HEY...IT'S THE DOOR TO YOUR OLD OFFICE.
KEEP OUT
THERE WERE NEVER STAIRS HERE BEFORE...
DO THESE GO UNDER MAGIK CHEEZ PIZZA?
ARE WE IN THE SEWER?!
IT DOES **SMELL** LIKE MAGIK CHEEZ.

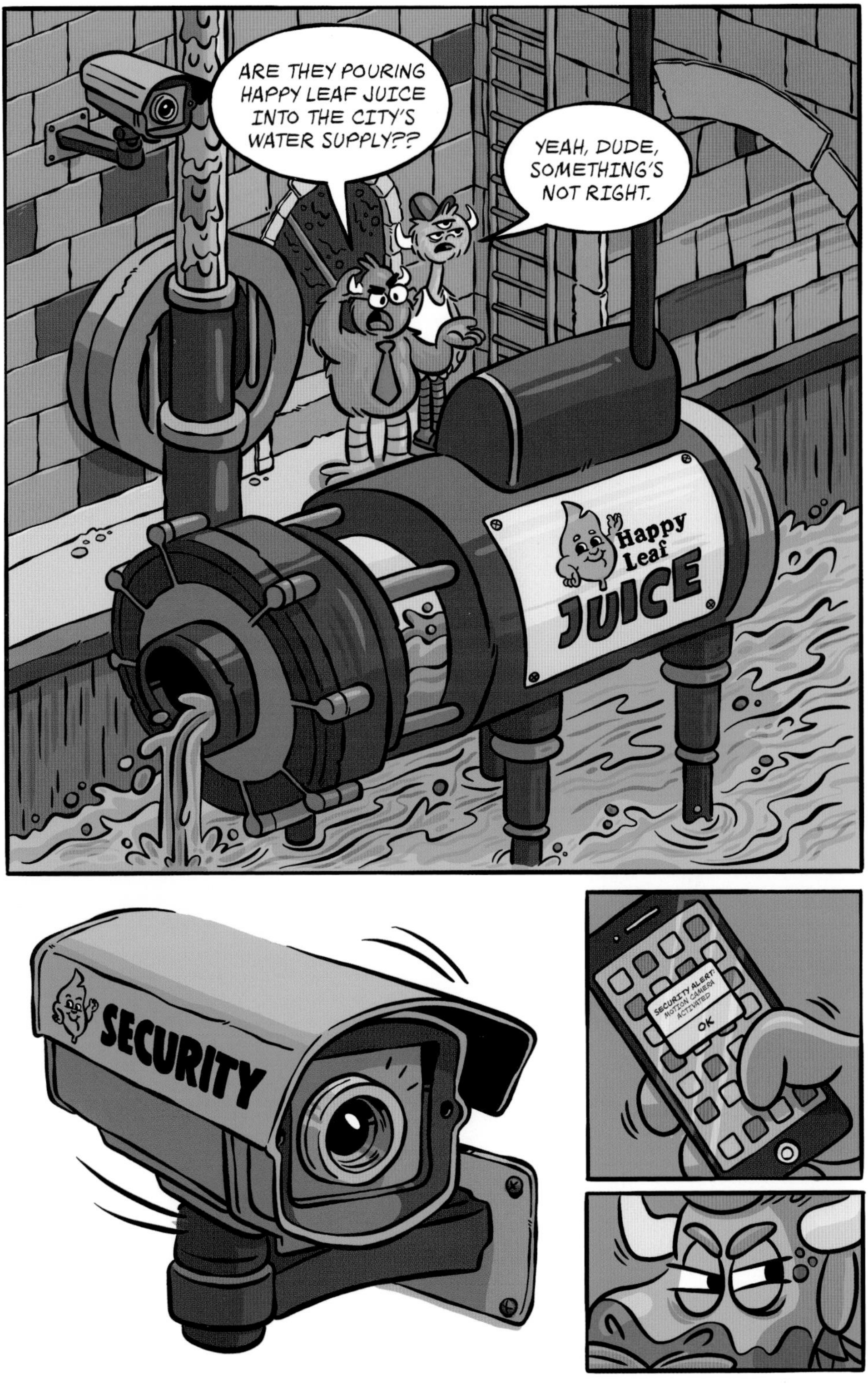
ARE THEY POURING HAPPY LEAF JUICE INTO THE CITY'S WATER SUPPLY??
YEAH, DUDE, SOMETHING'S NOT RIGHT.
Happy Leaf JUICE
SECURITY
SECURITY ALERT: MOTION CAMERA ACTIVATED
OK

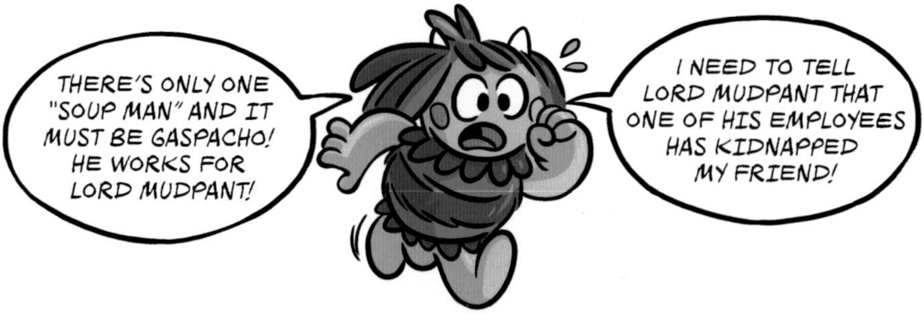
THERE'S ONLY ONE "SOUP MAN" AND IT MUST BE GASPACHO! HE WORKS FOR LORD MUDPANT!
I NEED TO TELL LORD MUDPANT THAT ONE OF HIS EMPLOYEES HAS KIDNAPPED MY FRIEND!

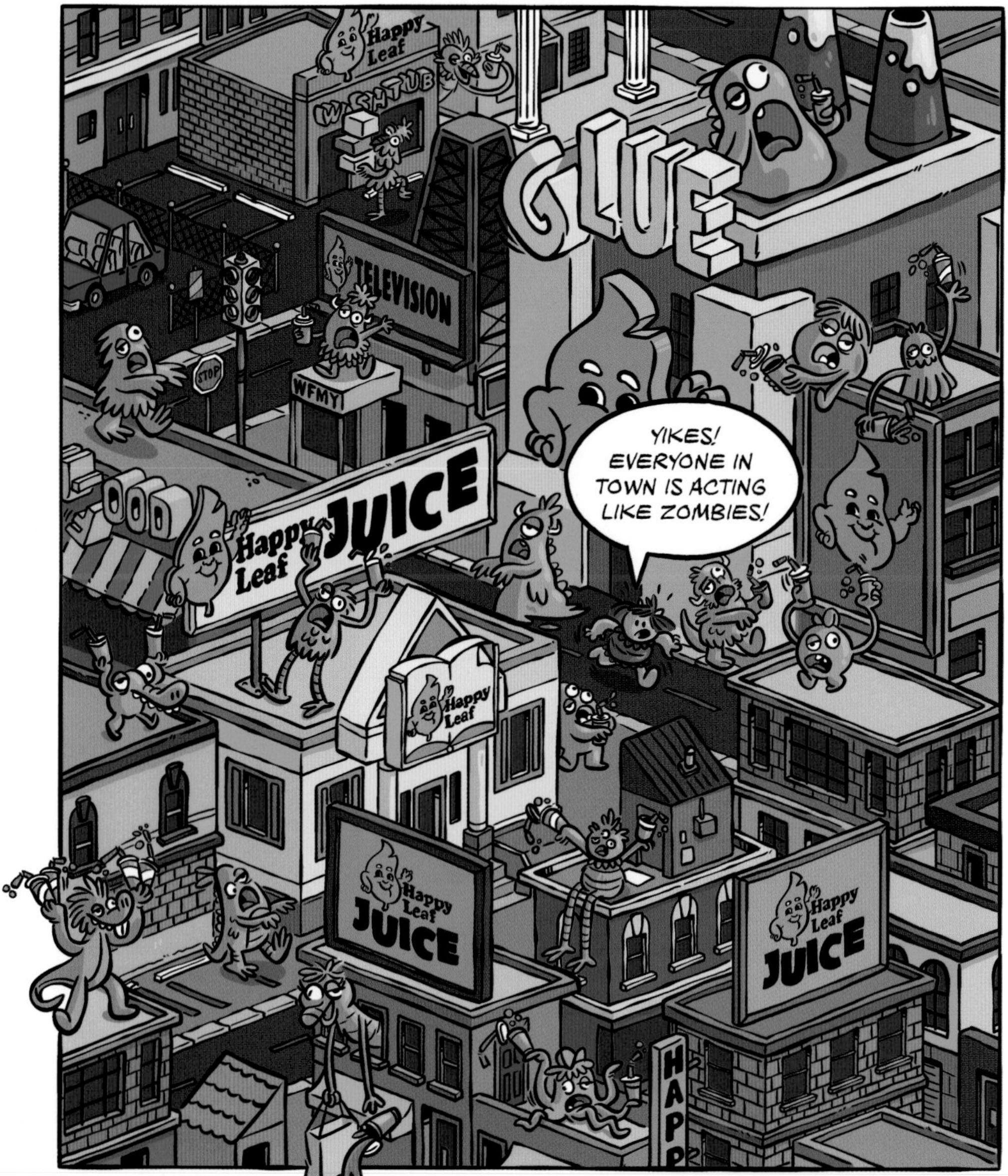
Happy Leaf
GLUE
TELEVISION
STOP
WFMY
Happy Leaf JUICE
YIKES! EVERYONE IN TOWN IS ACTING LIKE ZOMBIES!
Happy Leaf
Happy Leaf JUICE
Happy Leaf JUICE
HAPP

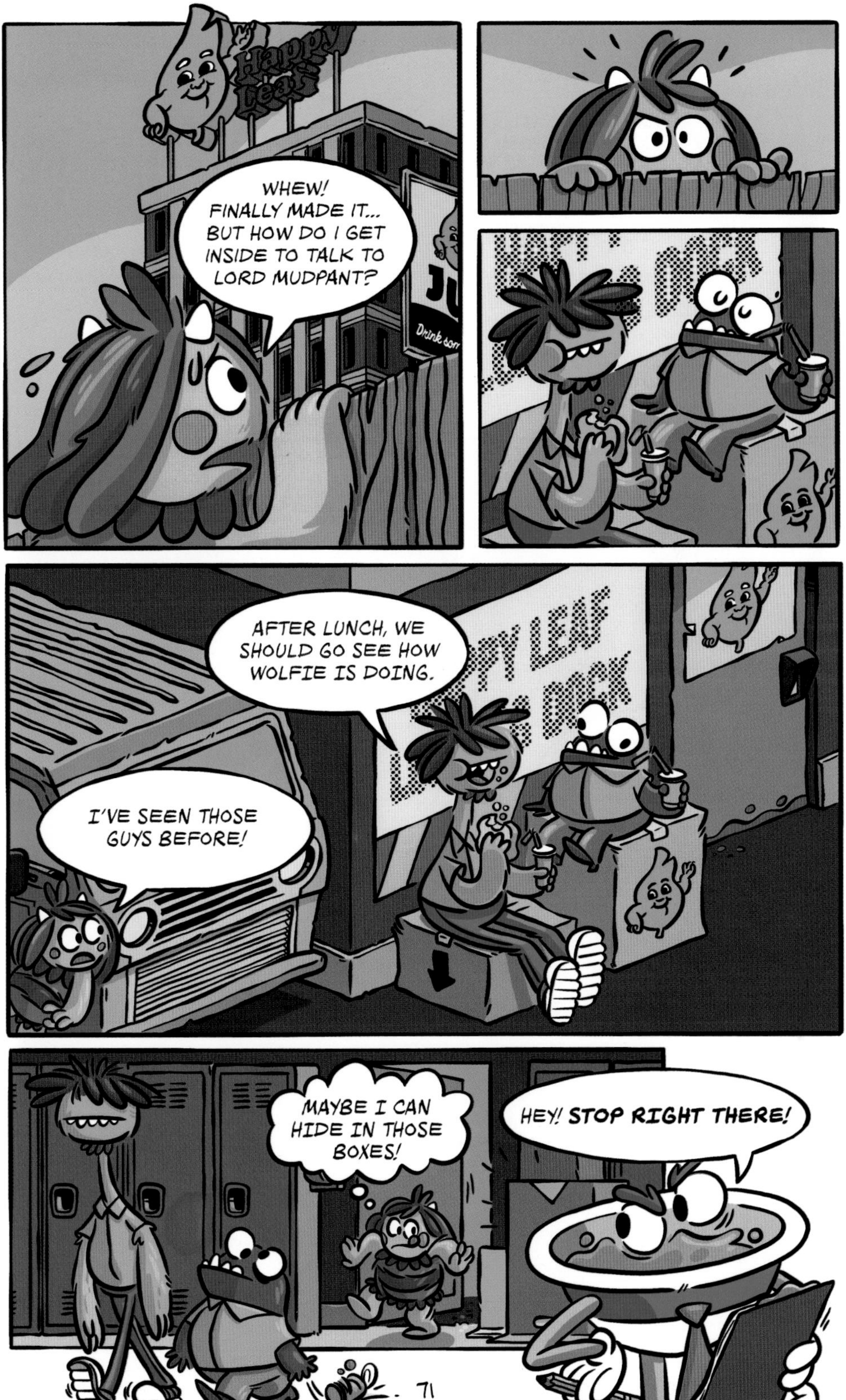

WHEW! FINALLY MADE IT... BUT HOW DO I GET INSIDE TO TALK TO LORD MUDPANT?
AFTER LUNCH, WE SHOULD GO SEE HOW WOLFIE IS DOING.
I'VE SEEN THOSE GUYS BEFORE!
MAYBE I CAN HIDE IN THOSE BOXES!
HEY! STOP RIGHT THERE!

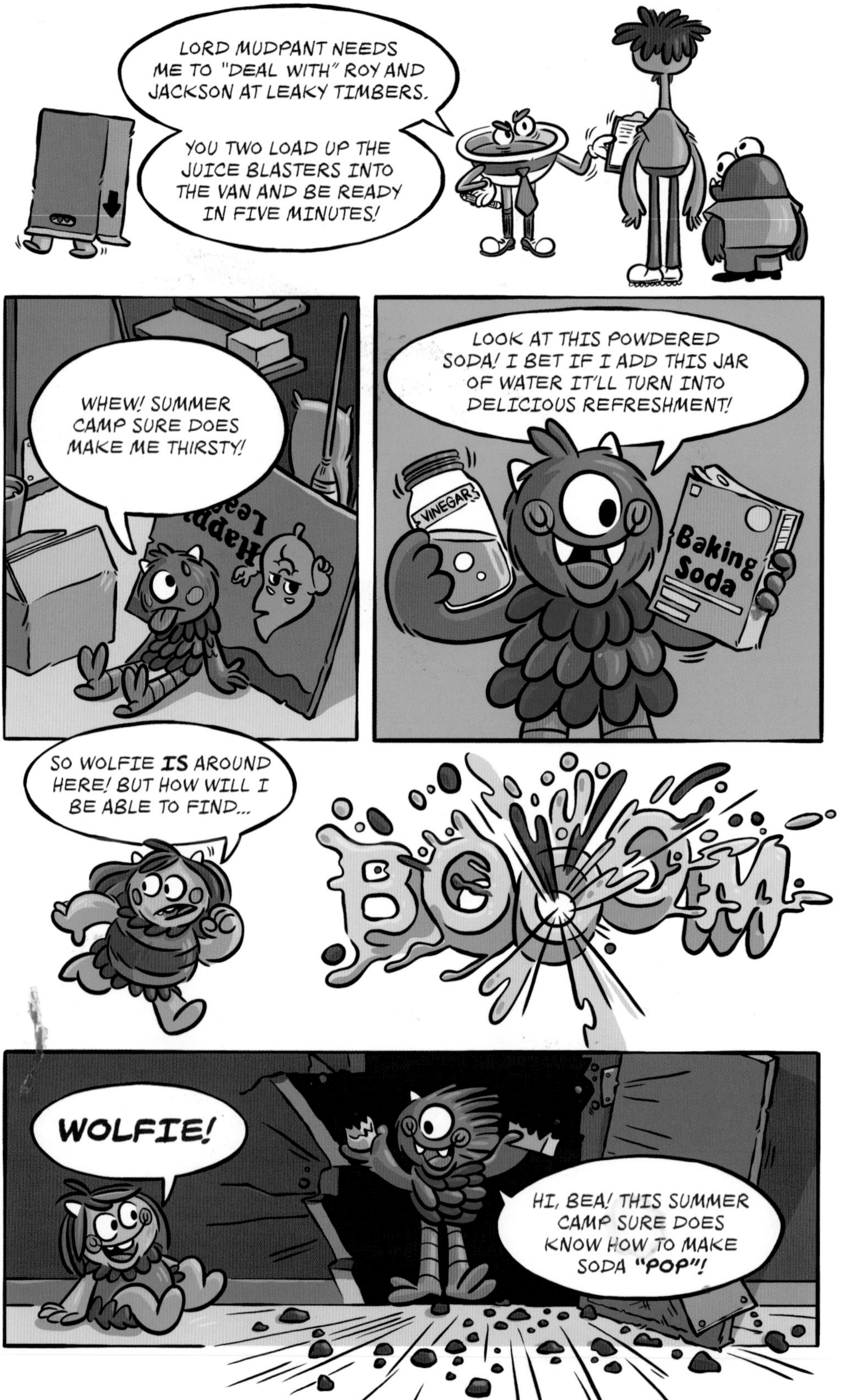
LORD MUDPANT NEEDS ME TO "DEAL WITH" ROY AND JACKSON AT LEAKY TIMBERS.
YOU TWO LOAD UP THE JUICE BLASTERS INTO THE VAN AND BE READY IN FIVE MINUTES!
WHEW! SUMMER CAMP SURE DOES MAKE ME THIRSTY!
LOOK AT THIS POWDERED SODA! I BET IF I ADD THIS JAR OF WATER IT'LL TURN INTO DELICIOUS REFRESHMENT!
VINEGAR
Baking Soda
SO WOLFIE **IS** AROUND HERE! BUT HOW WILL I BE ABLE TO FIND...
BOOOM
WOLFIE!
HI, BEA! THIS SUMMER CAMP SURE DOES KNOW HOW TO MAKE SODA **"POP"**!

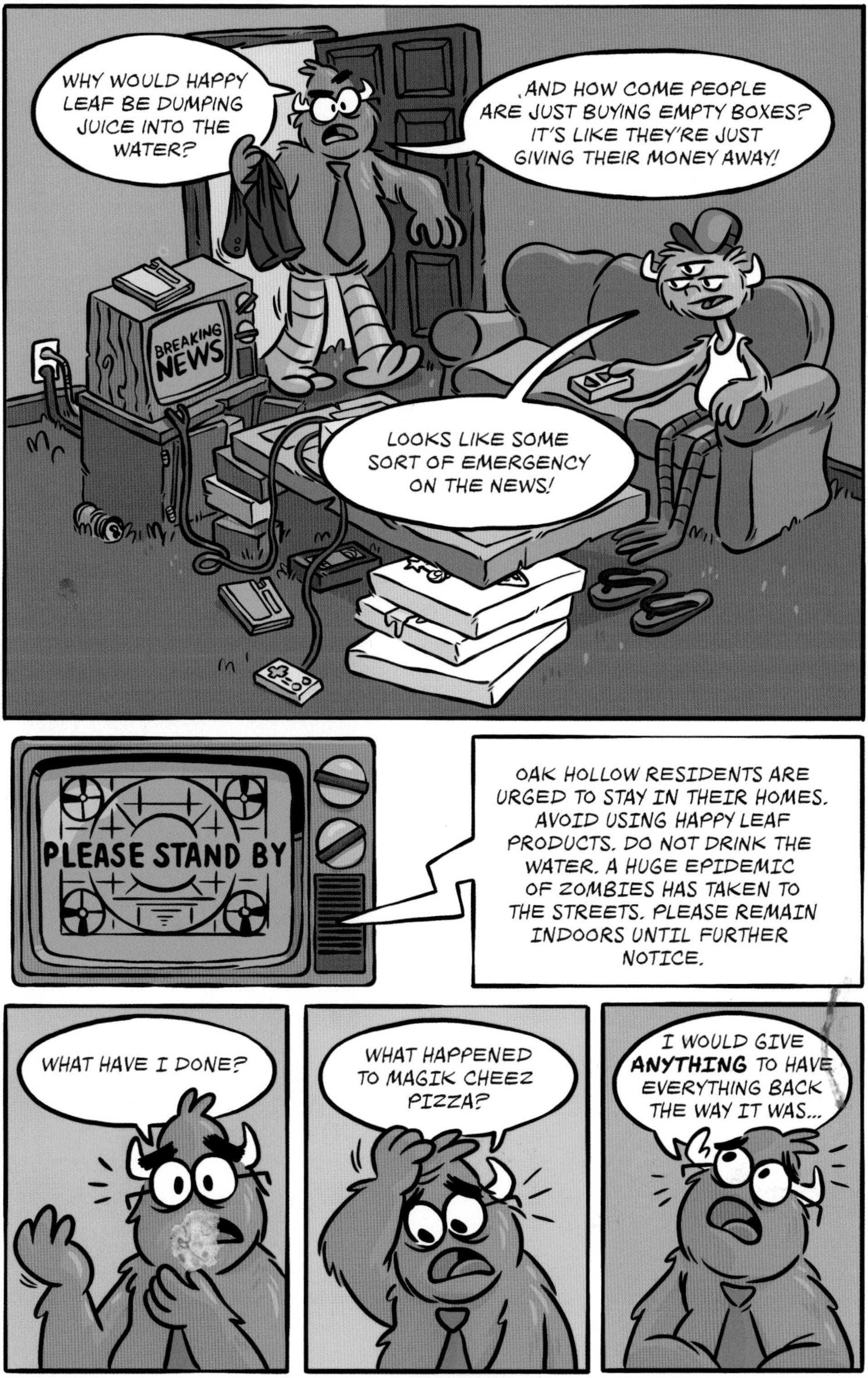
WHY WOULD HAPPY LEAF BE DUMPING JUICE INTO THE WATER?
AND HOW COME PEOPLE ARE JUST BUYING EMPTY BOXES? IT'S LIKE THEY'RE JUST GIVING THEIR MONEY AWAY!
BREAKING NEWS
LOOKS LIKE SOME SORT OF EMERGENCY ON THE NEWS!
PLEASE STAND BY
OAK HOLLOW RESIDENTS ARE URGED TO STAY IN THEIR HOMES. AVOID USING HAPPY LEAF PRODUCTS. DO NOT DRINK THE WATER. A HUGE EPIDEMIC OF ZOMBIES HAS TAKEN TO THE STREETS. PLEASE REMAIN INDOORS UNTIL FURTHER NOTICE.
WHAT HAVE I DONE?
WHAT HAPPENED TO MAGIK CHEEZ PIZZA?
I WOULD GIVE **ANYTHING** TO HAVE EVERYTHING BACK THE WAY IT WAS...

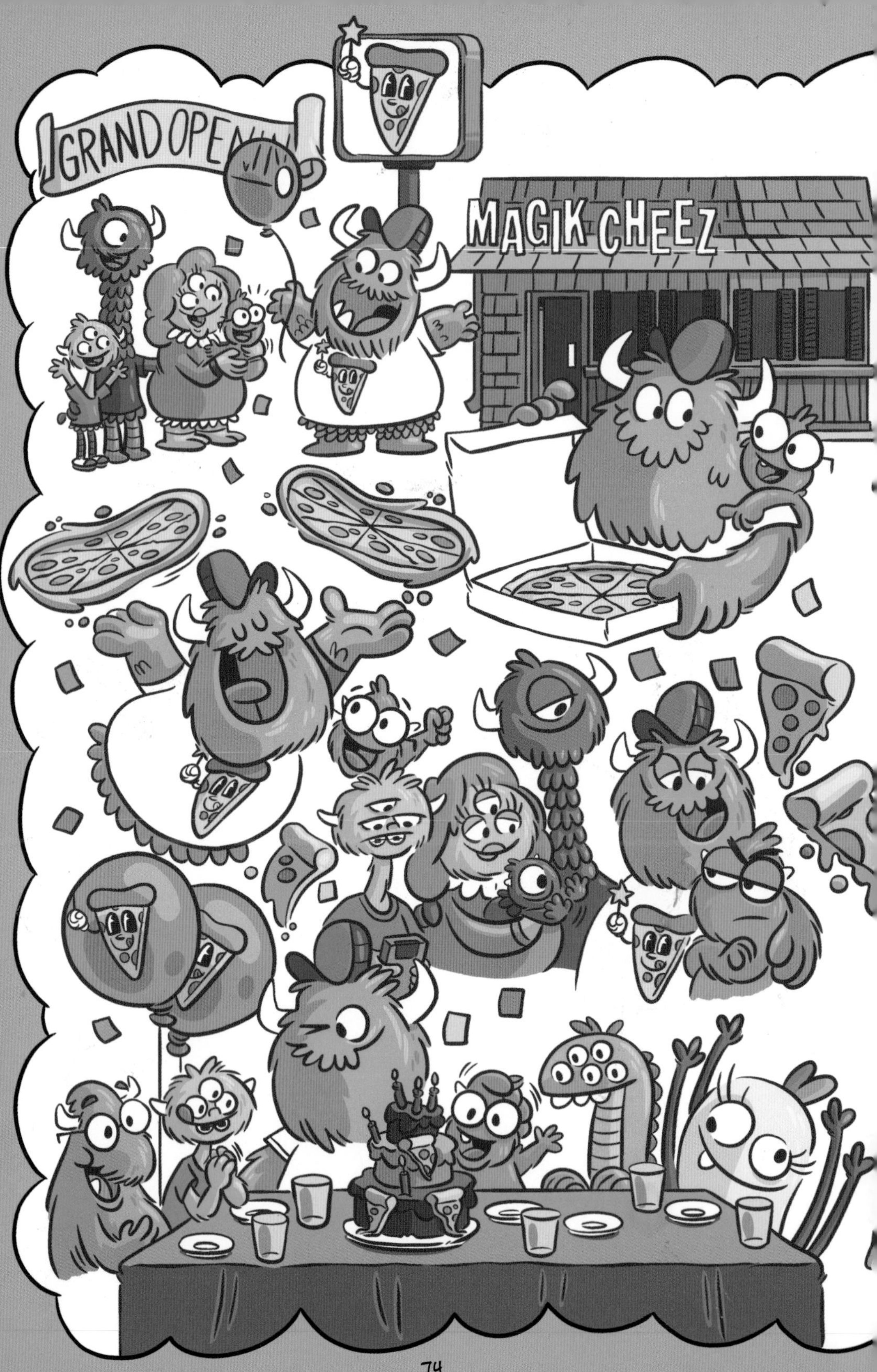
GRAND OPEN
MAGIK CHEEZ

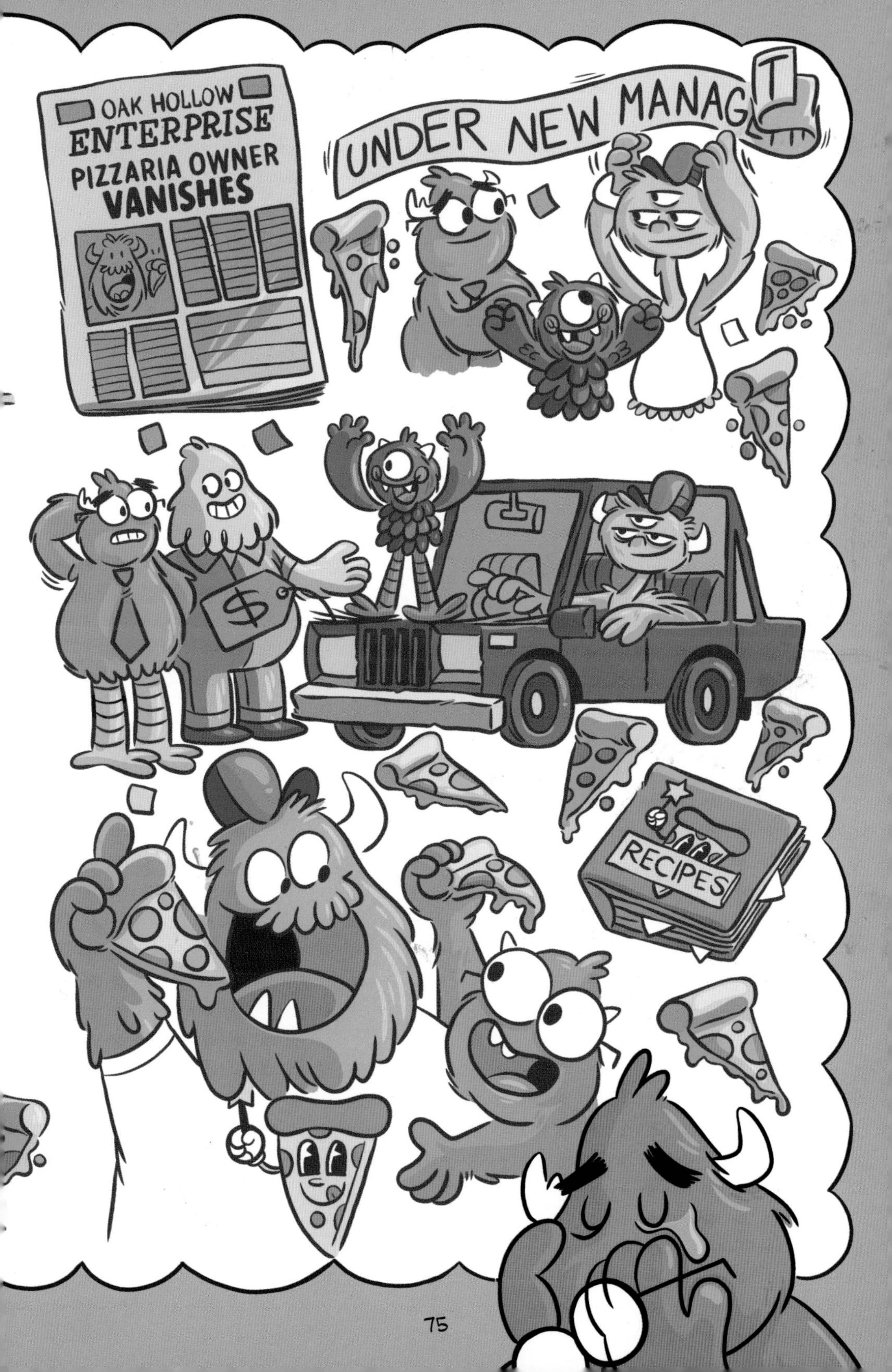

OAK HOLLOW
ENTERPRISE
PIZZARIA OWNER
VANISHES
UNDER NEW MANAG
T
RECIPES

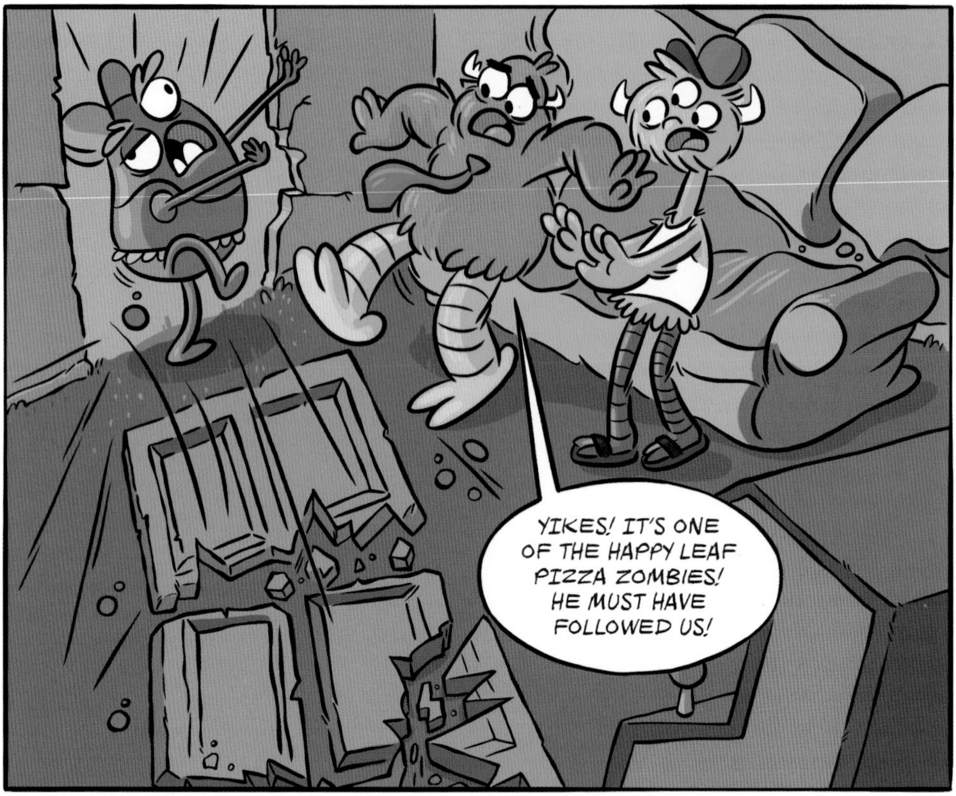
YIKES! IT'S ONE OF THE HAPPY LEAF PIZZA ZOMBIES! HE MUST HAVE FOLLOWED US!

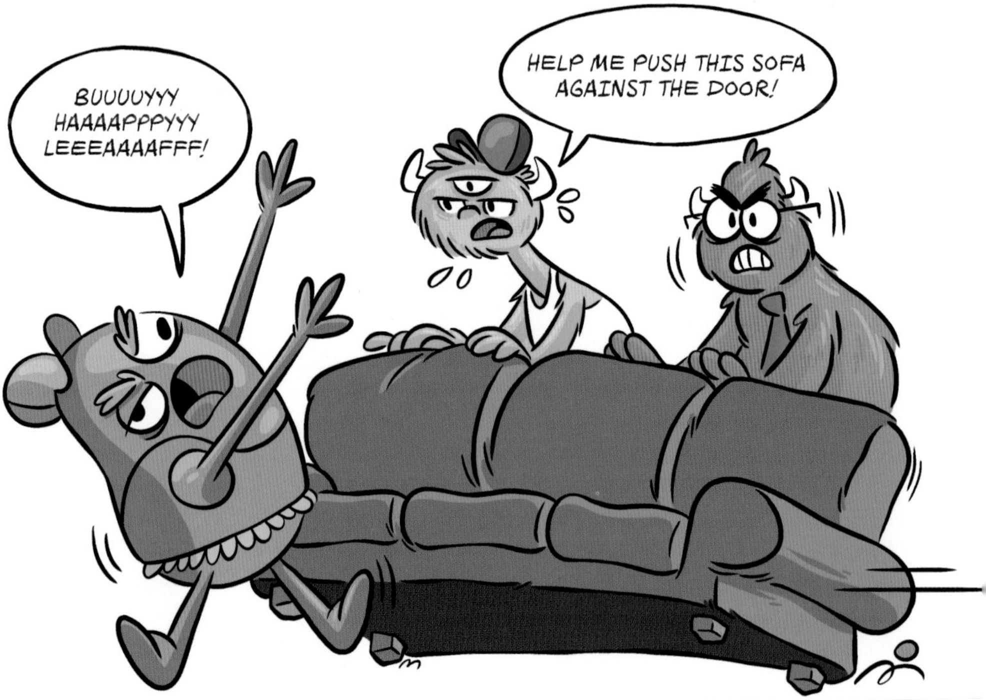
BUUUUYYY HAAAAPPPYYY LEEEAAAAFFF!
HELP ME PUSH THIS SOFA AGAINST THE DOOR!

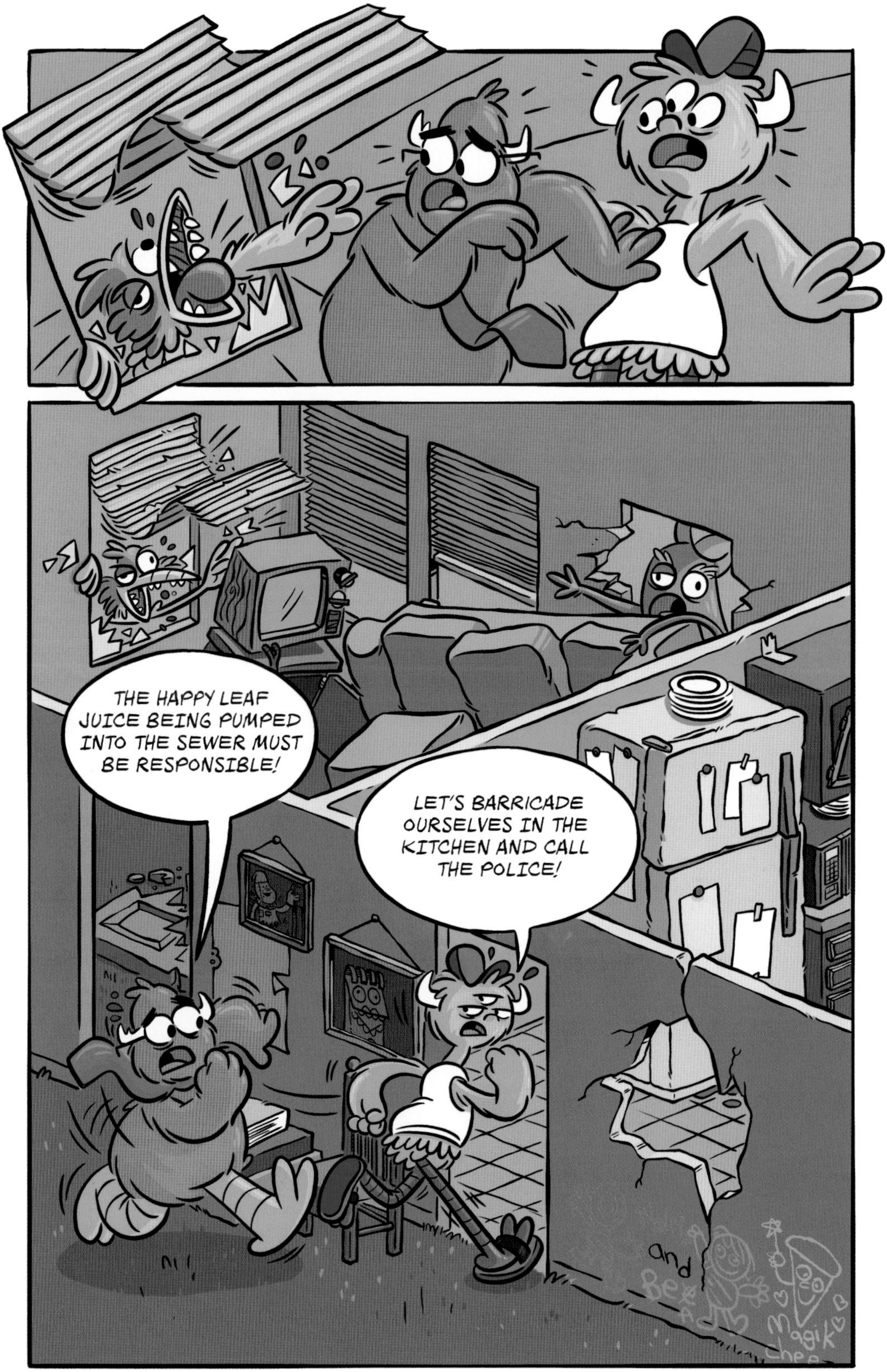
THE HAPPY LEAF JUICE BEING PUMPED INTO THE SEWER MUST BE RESPONSIBLE!
LET'S BARRICADE OURSELVES IN THE KITCHEN AND CALL THE POLICE!

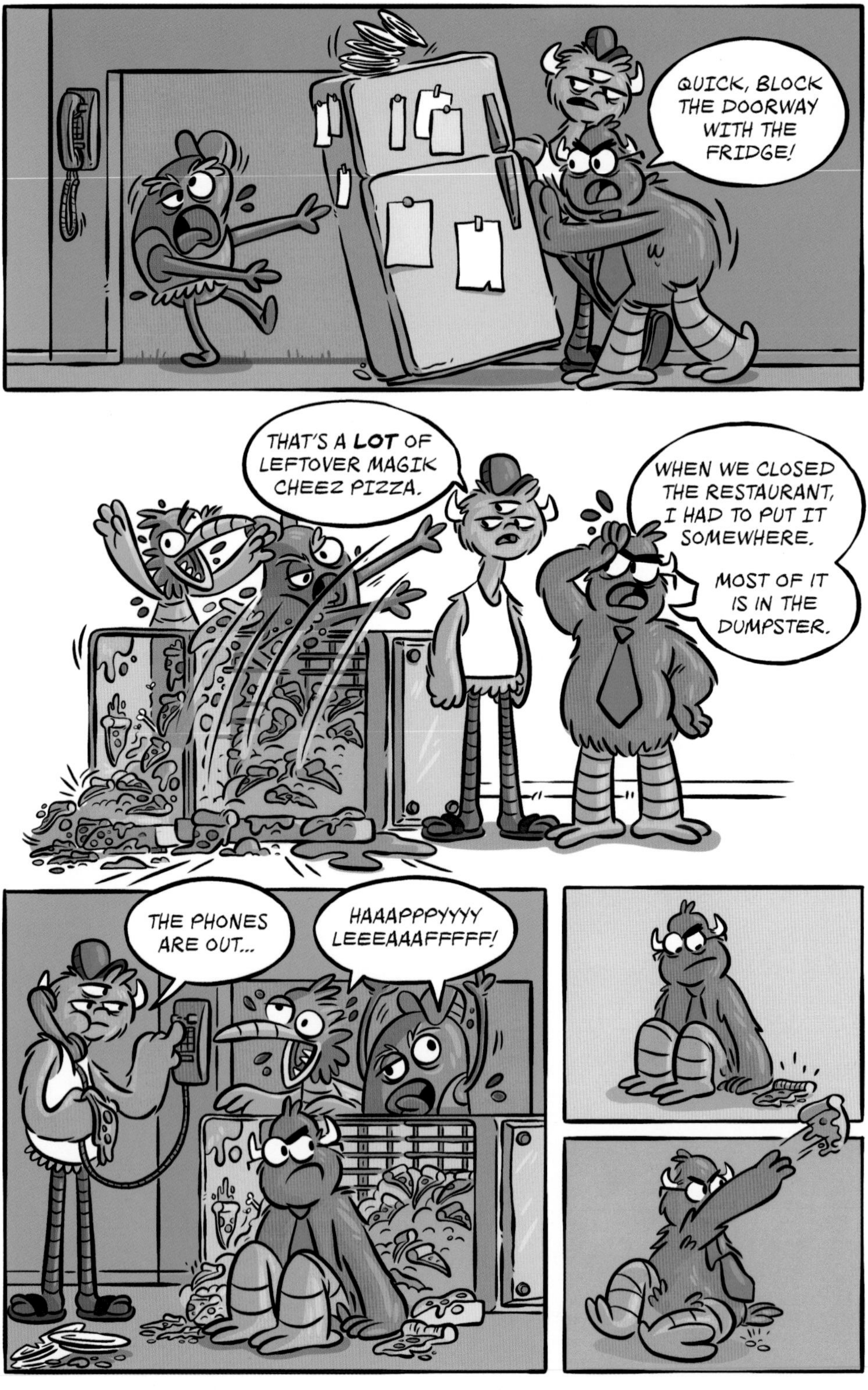
QUICK, BLOCK THE DOORWAY WITH THE FRIDGE!
THAT'S A LOT OF LEFTOVER MAGIK CHEEZ PIZZA.
WHEN WE CLOSED THE RESTAURANT, I HAD TO PUT IT SOMEWHERE.
MOST OF IT IS IN THE DUMPSTER.
THE PHONES ARE OUT...
HAAAPPPYYYY LEEEAAAFFFFF!

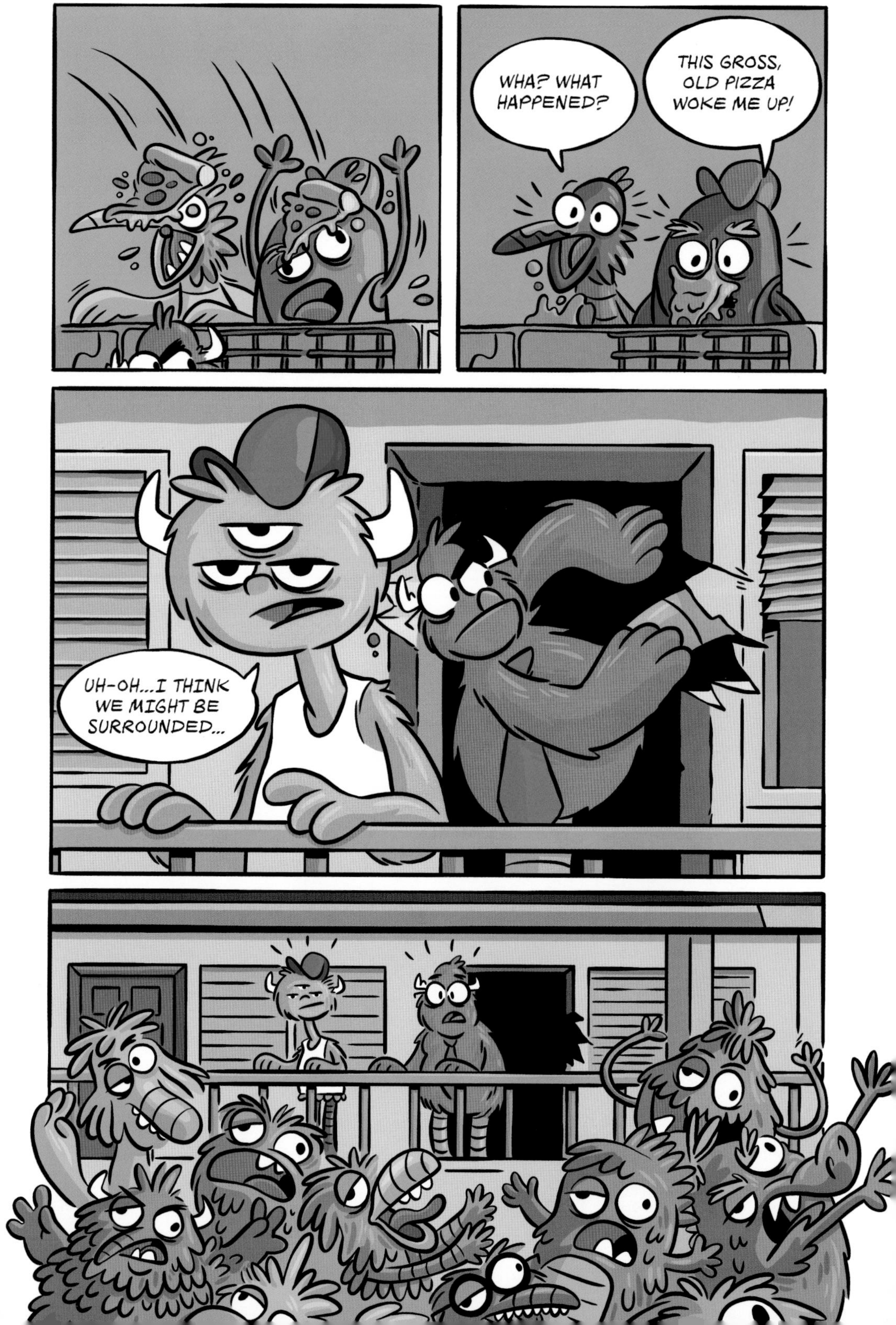
WHA? WHAT HAPPENED?
THIS GROSS, OLD PIZZA WOKE ME UP!
UH-OH...I THINK WE MIGHT BE SURROUNDED...

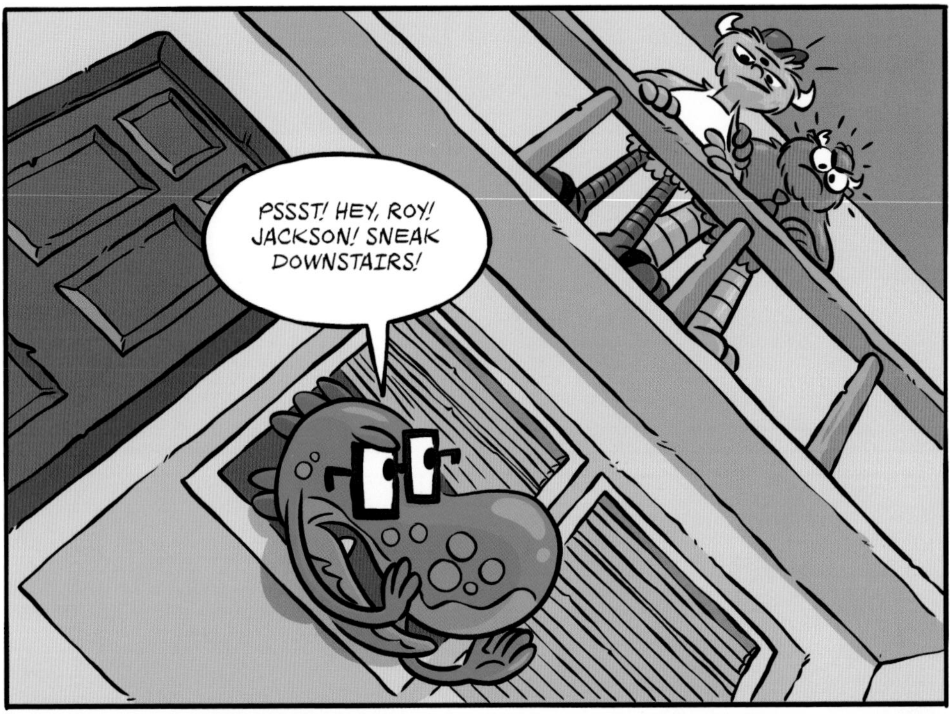
PSSST! HEY, ROY! JACKSON! SNEAK DOWNSTAIRS!

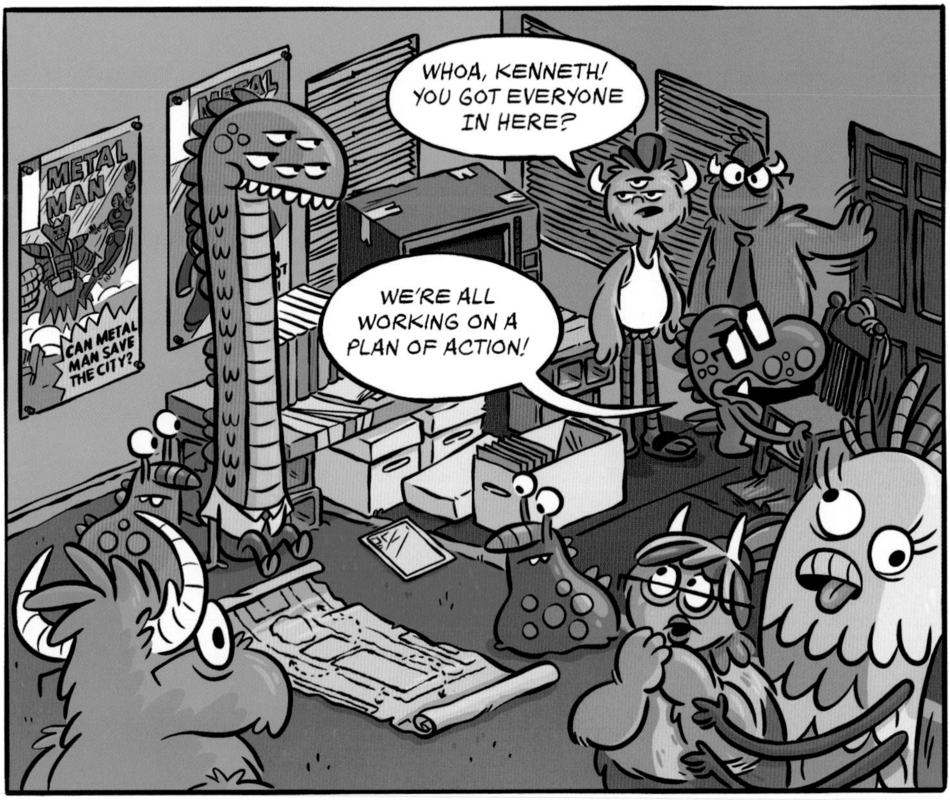
METAL MAN
CAN METAL MAN SAVE THE CITY?
WHOA, KENNETH! YOU GOT EVERYONE IN HERE?
WE'RE ALL WORKING ON A PLAN OF ACTION!

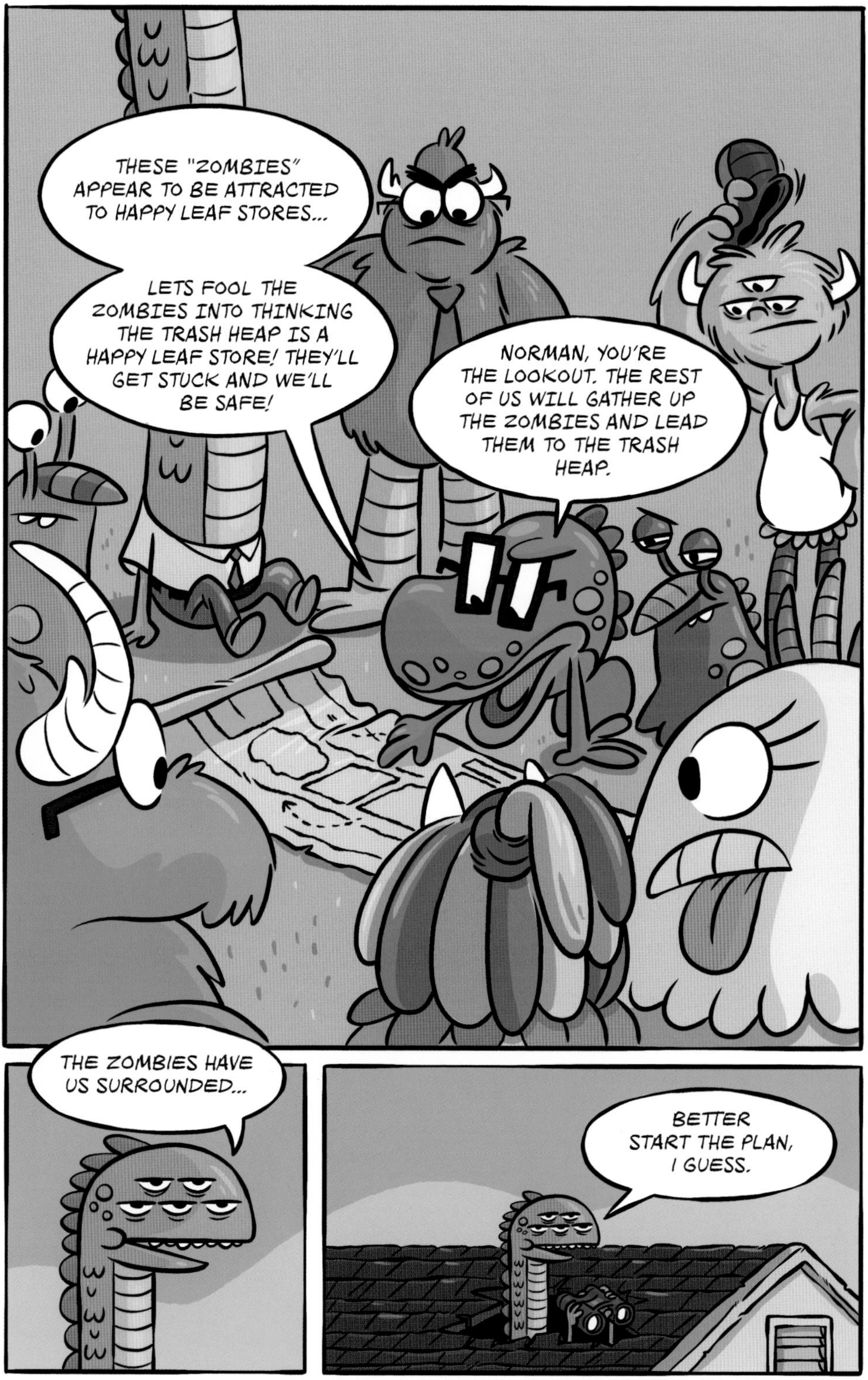
THESE "ZOMBIES" APPEAR TO BE ATTRACTED TO HAPPY LEAF STORES...
LETS FOOL THE ZOMBIES INTO THINKING THE TRASH HEAP IS A HAPPY LEAF STORE! THEY'LL GET STUCK AND WE'LL BE SAFE!
NORMAN, YOU'RE THE LOOKOUT. THE REST OF US WILL GATHER UP THE ZOMBIES AND LEAD THEM TO THE TRASH HEAP.
THE ZOMBIES HAVE US SURROUNDED...
BETTER START THE PLAN, I GUESS.

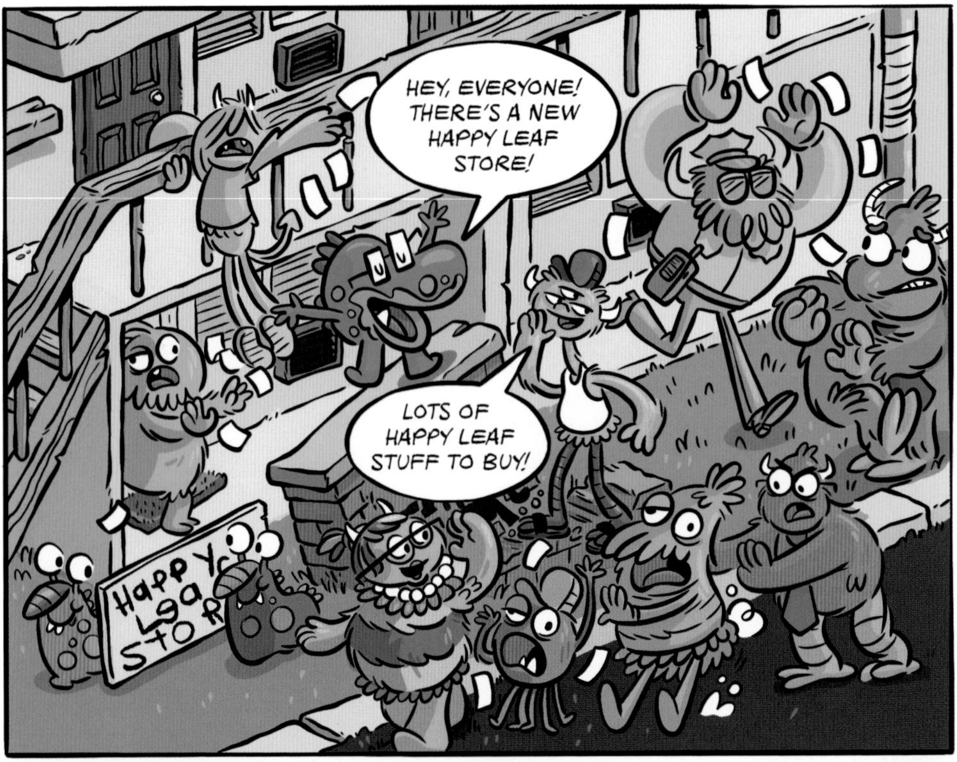
HEY, EVERYONE! THERE'S A NEW HAPPY LEAF STORE!
LOTS OF HAPPY LEAF STUFF TO BUY!
Happy Leaf StoRe

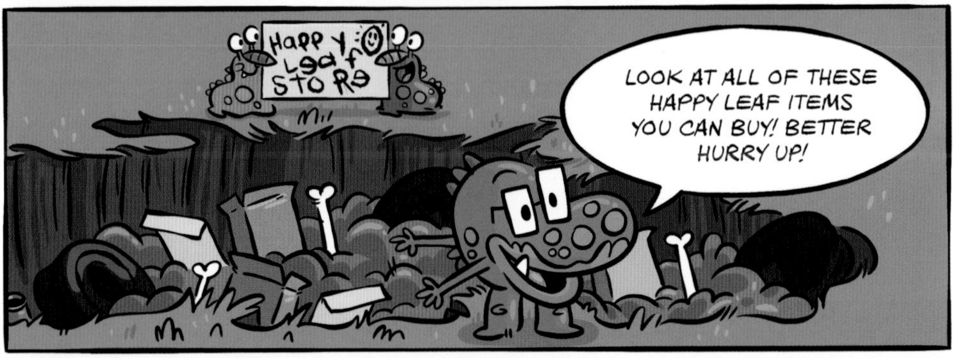
Happy Leaf StoRe
LOOK AT ALL OF THESE HAPPY LEAF ITEMS YOU CAN BUY! BETTER HURRY UP!

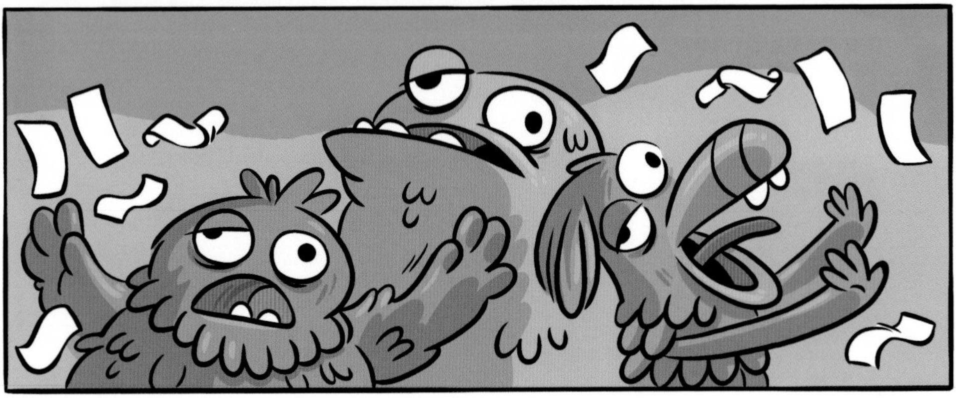

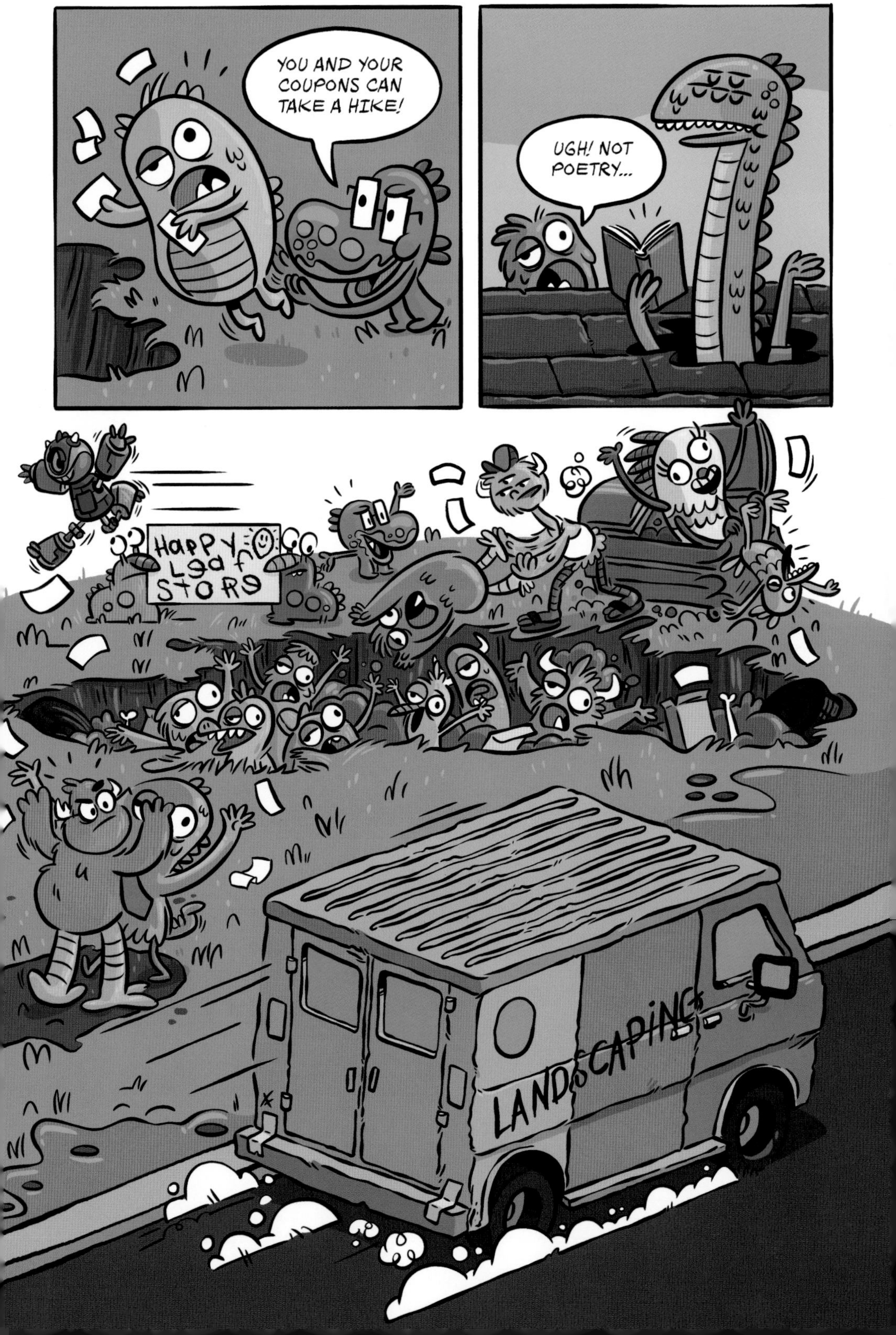
YOU AND YOUR COUPONS CAN TAKE A HIKE!
UGH! NOT POETRY...
Happy Leaf Store
LANDSCAPING

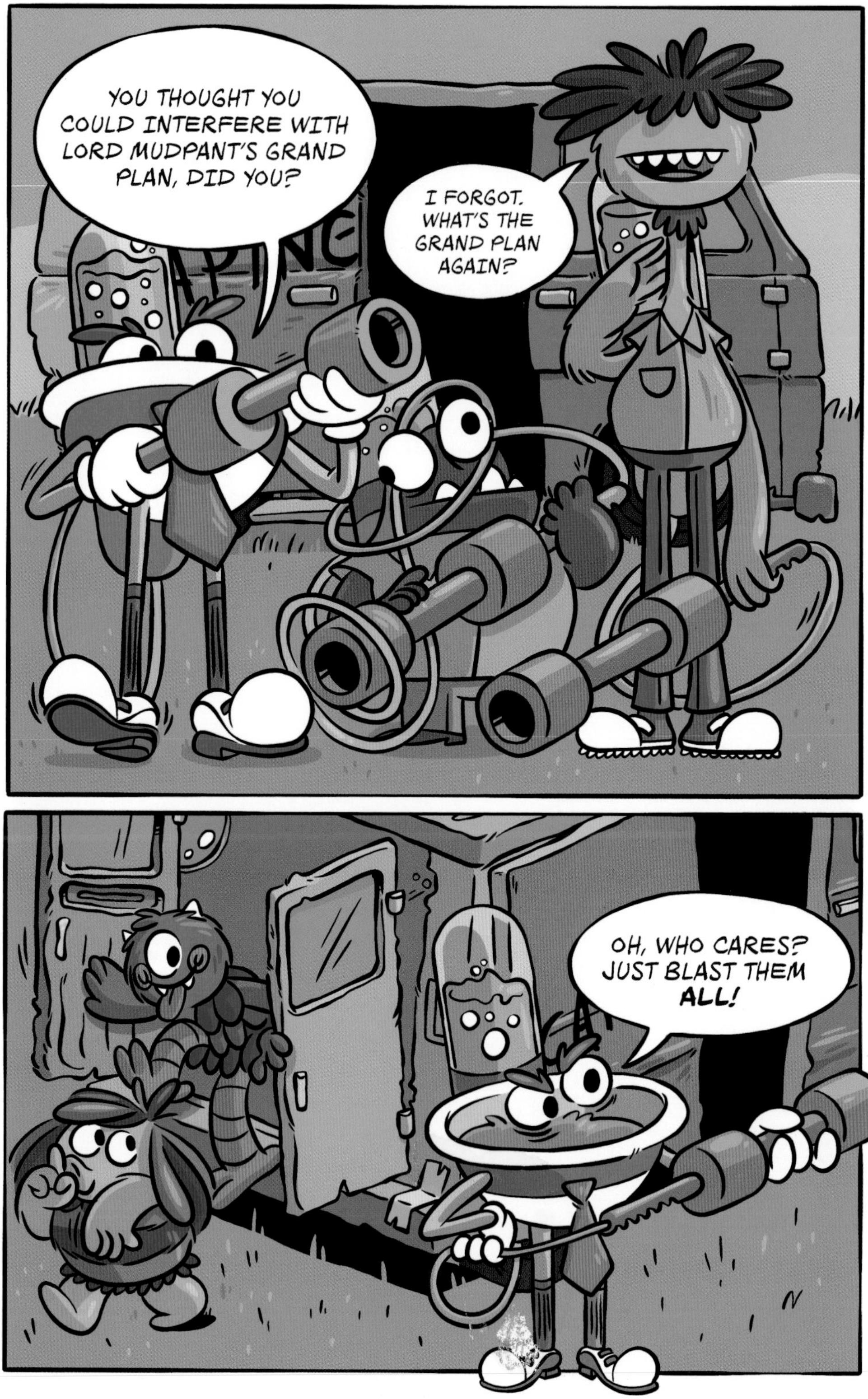
YOU THOUGHT YOU COULD INTERFERE WITH LORD MUDPANT'S GRAND PLAN, DID YOU?
I FORGOT. WHAT'S THE GRAND PLAN AGAIN?
OH, WHO CARES? JUST BLAST THEM **ALL!**

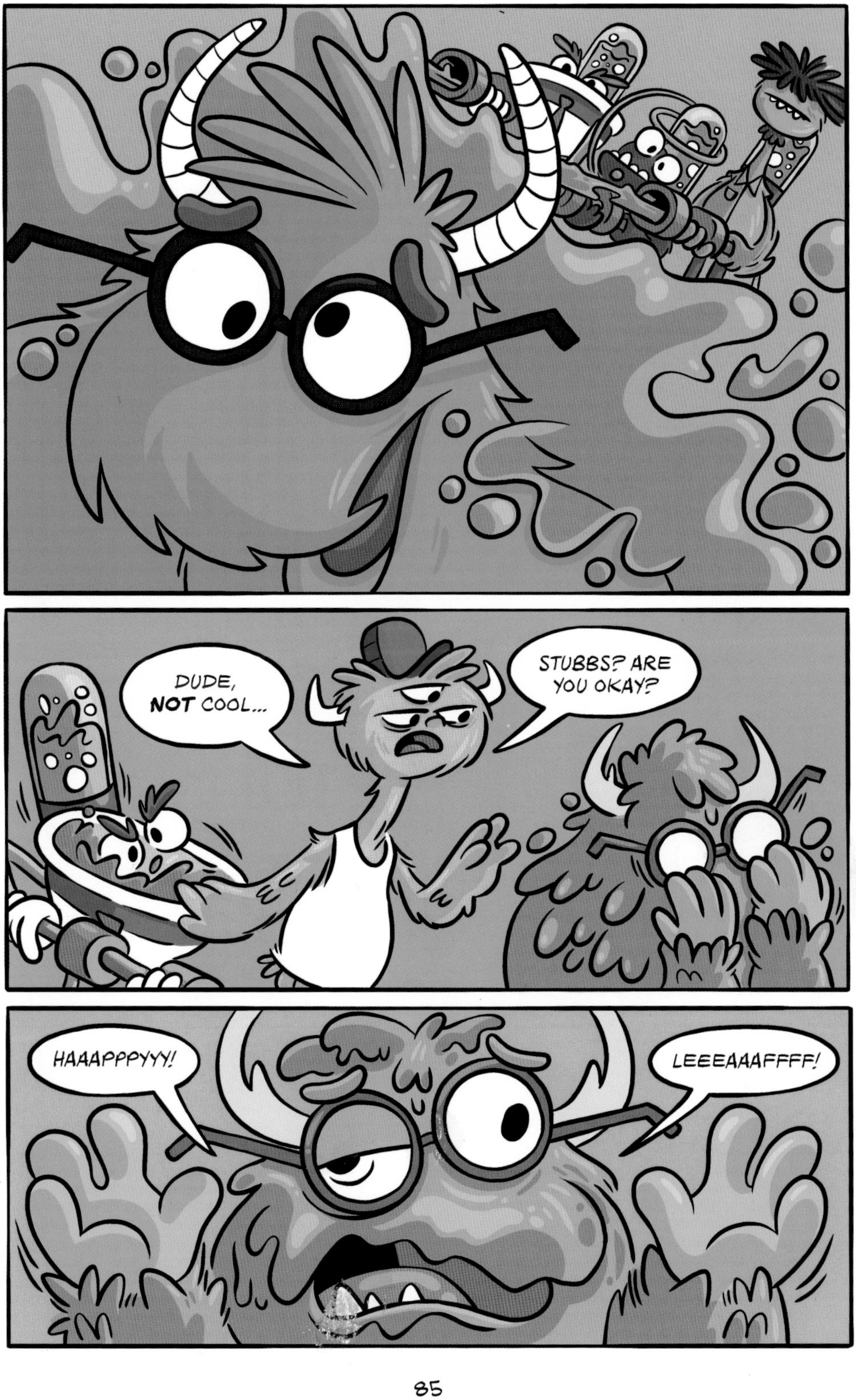
DUDE, **NOT** COOL...
STUBBS? ARE YOU OKAY?
HAAAPPPYYY!
LEEEAAAFFFF!

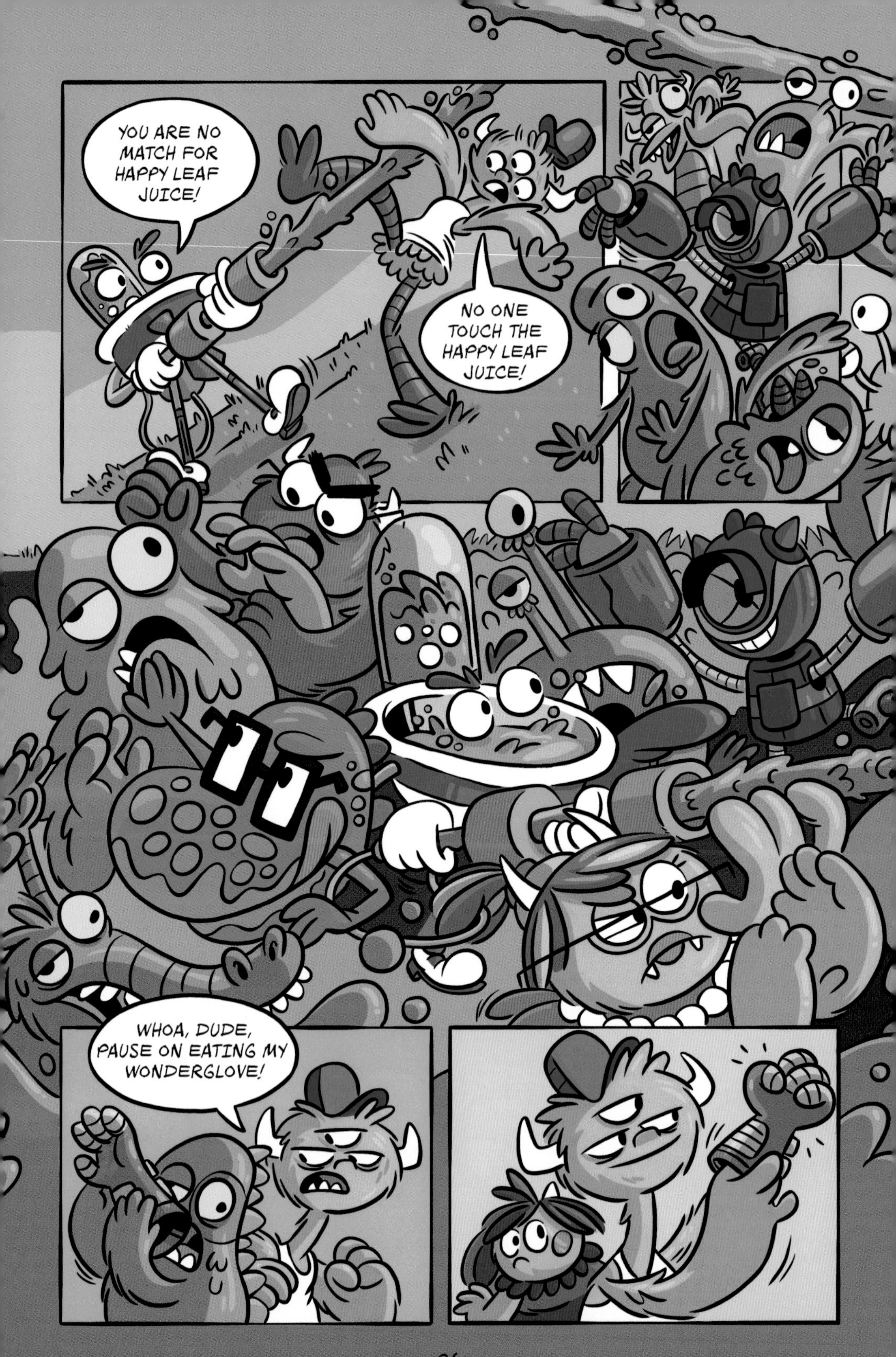
YOU ARE NO MATCH FOR HAPPY LEAF JUICE!
NO ONE TOUCH THE HAPPY LEAF JUICE!
WHOA, DUDE, PAUSE ON EATING MY WONDERGLOVE!

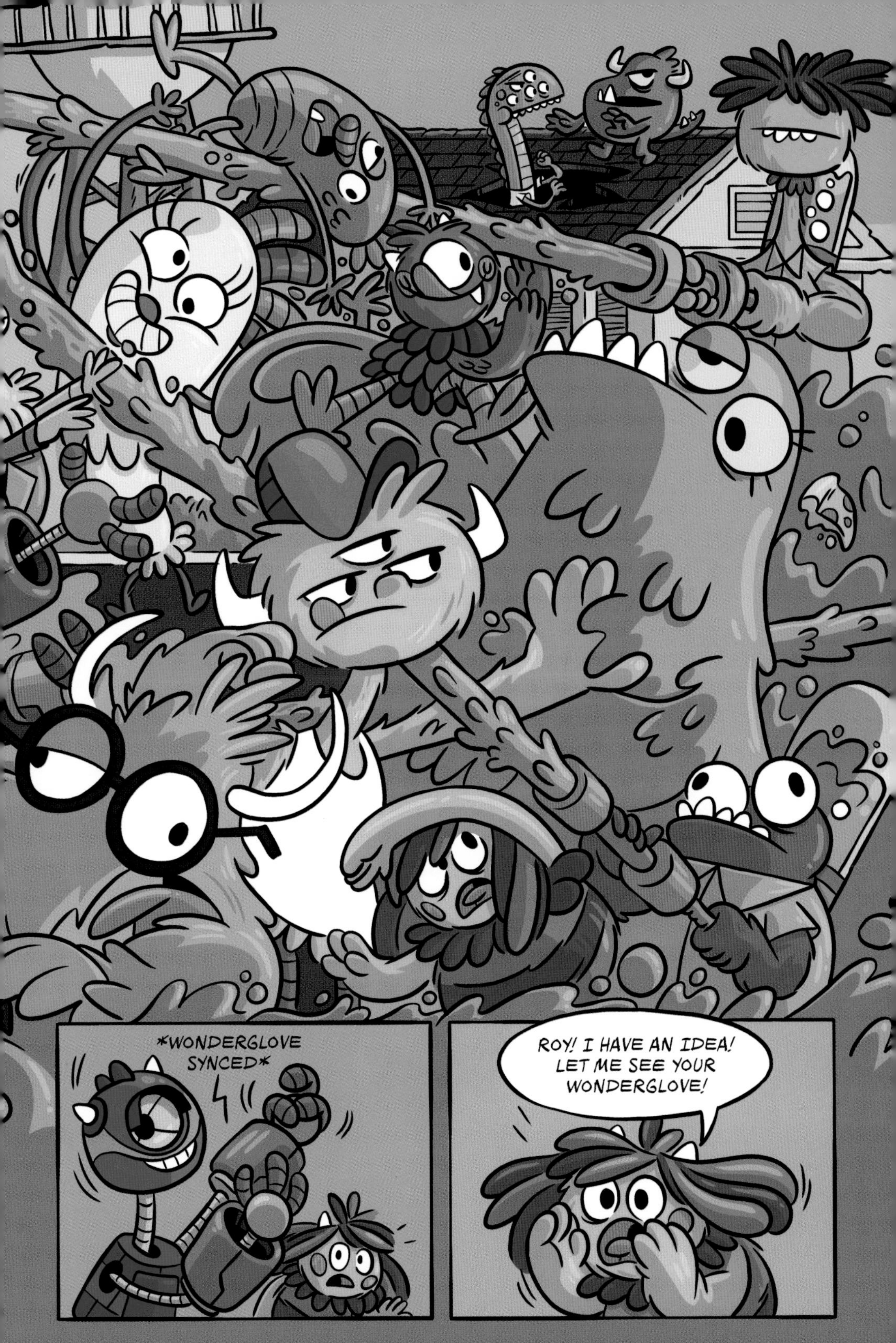
WONDERGLOVE SYNCED
ROY! I HAVE AN IDEA! LET ME SEE YOUR WONDERGLOVE!

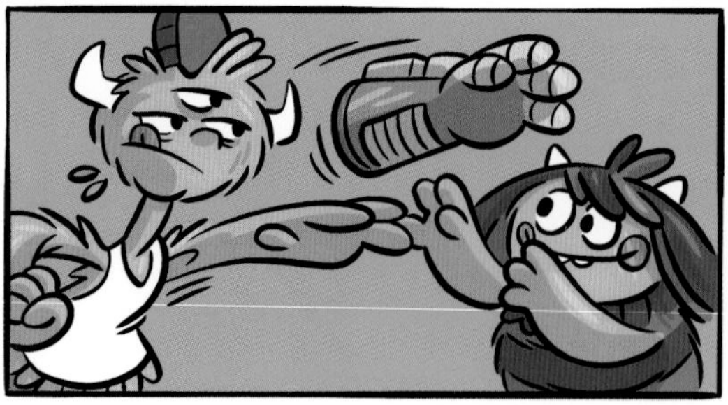

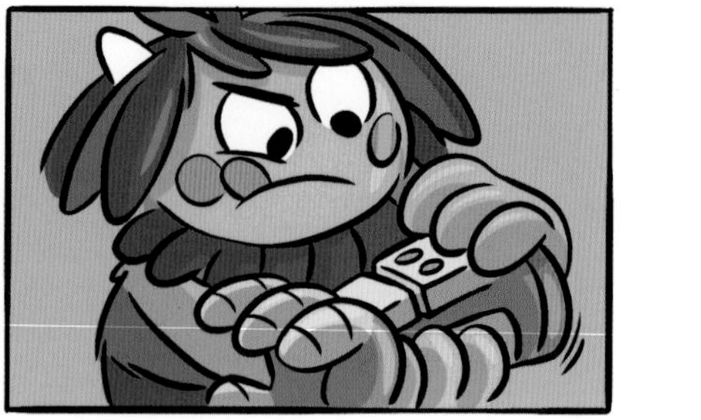

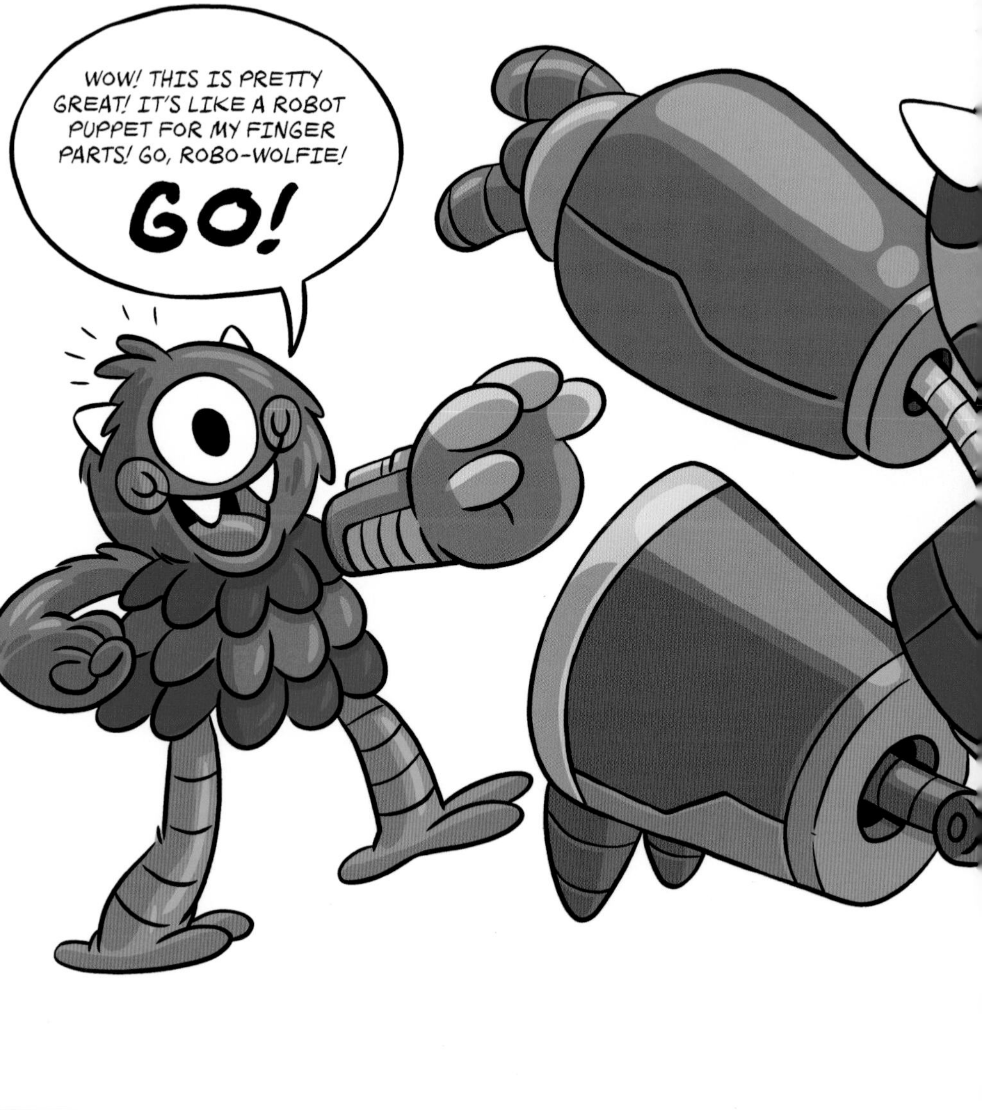
WOW! THIS IS PRETTY GREAT! IT'S LIKE A ROBOT PUPPET FOR MY FINGER PARTS! GO, ROBO-WOLFIE!
GO!

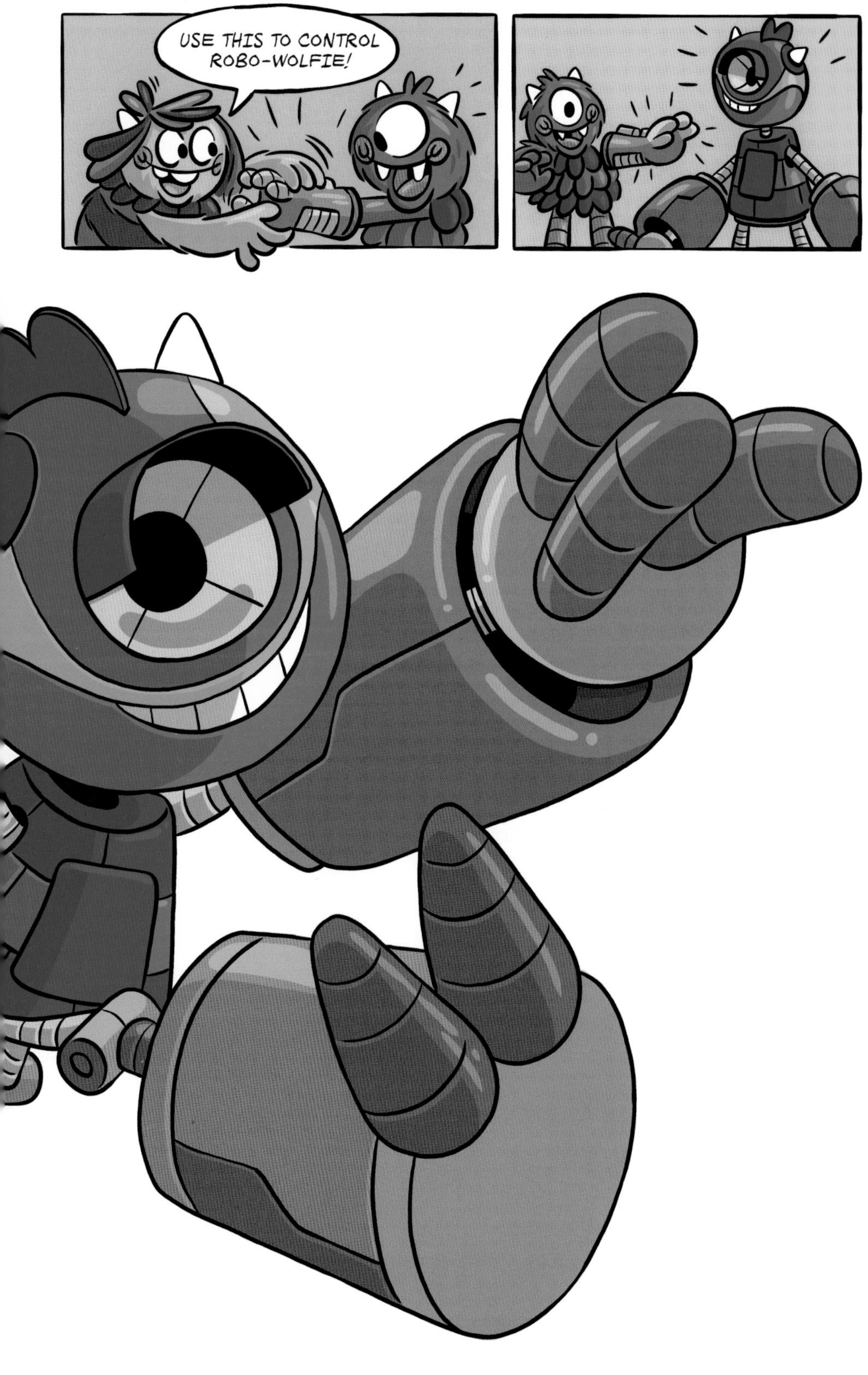
USE THIS TO CONTROL ROBO-WOLFIE!

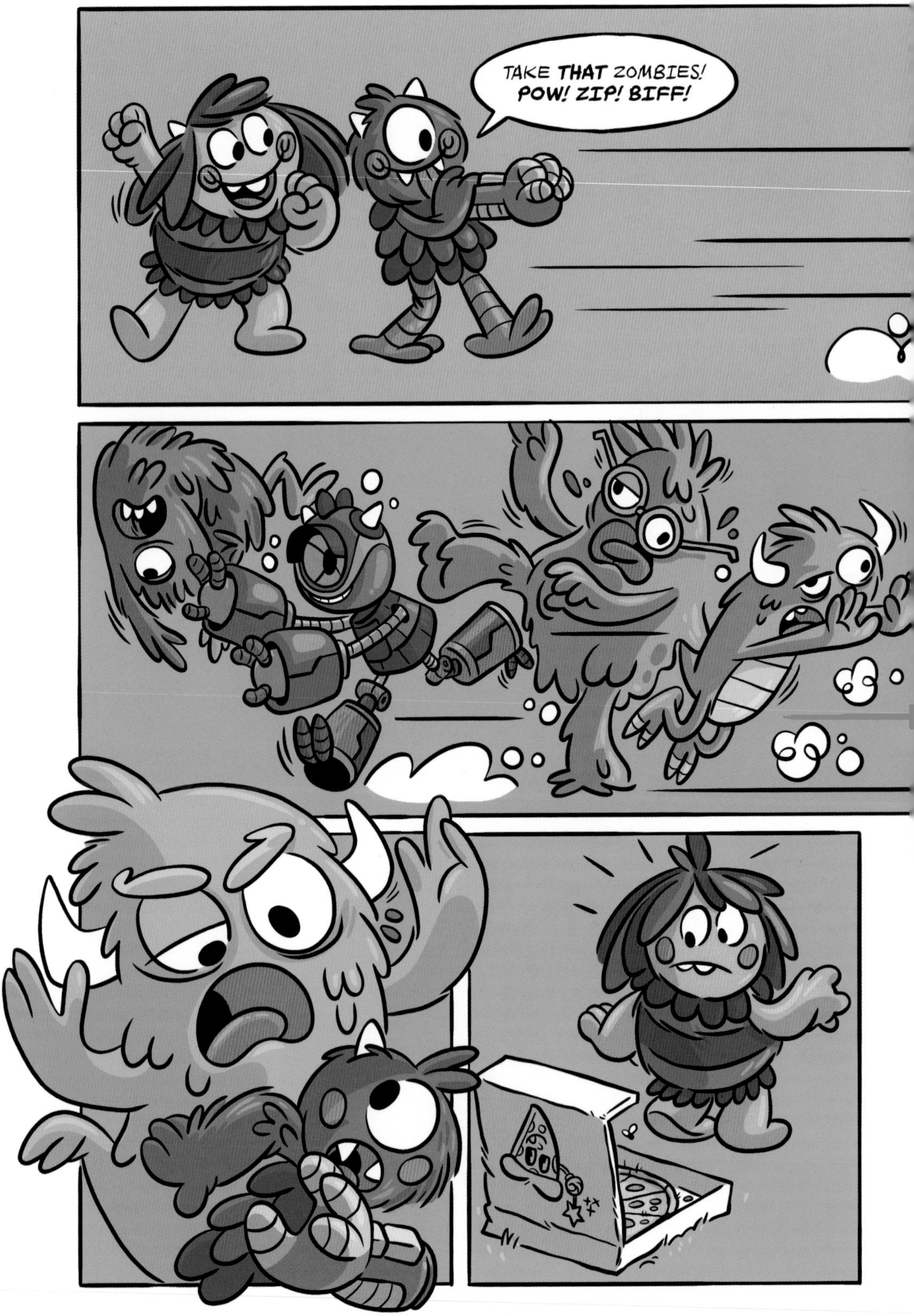
TAKE THAT ZOMBIES!
POW! ZIP! BIFF!

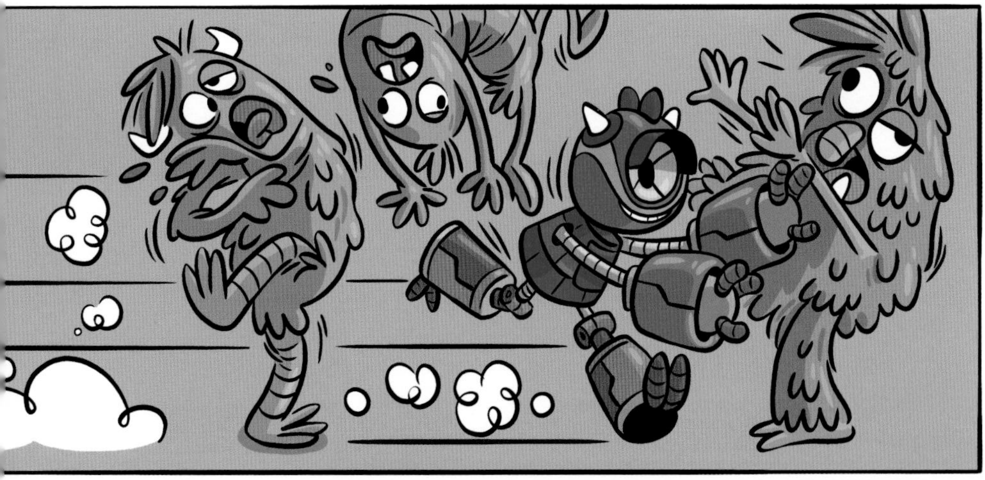

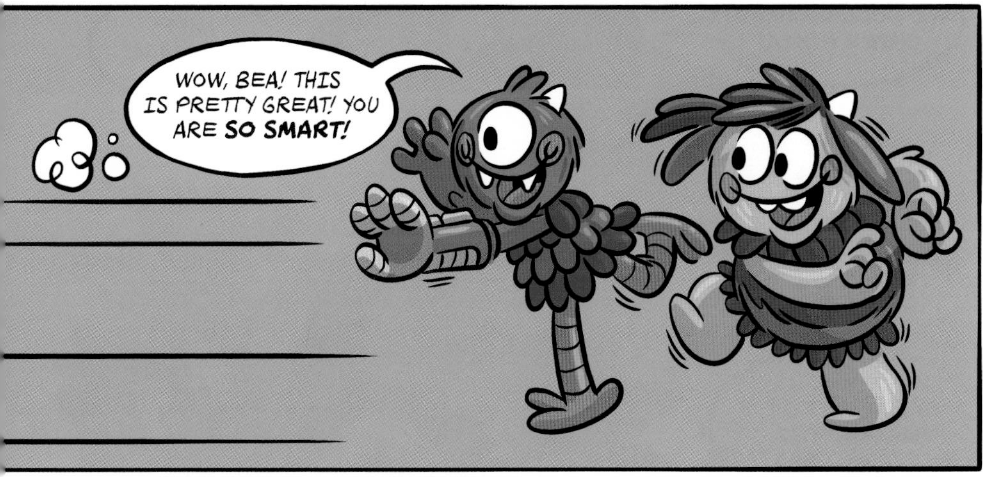
WOW, BEA! THIS IS PRETTY GREAT! YOU ARE **SO SMART!**

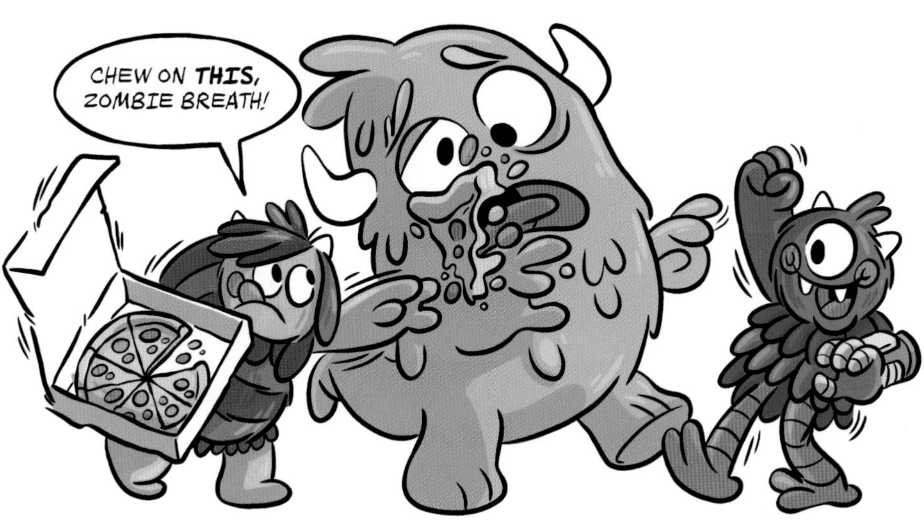
CHEW ON **THIS,** ZOMBIE BREATH!

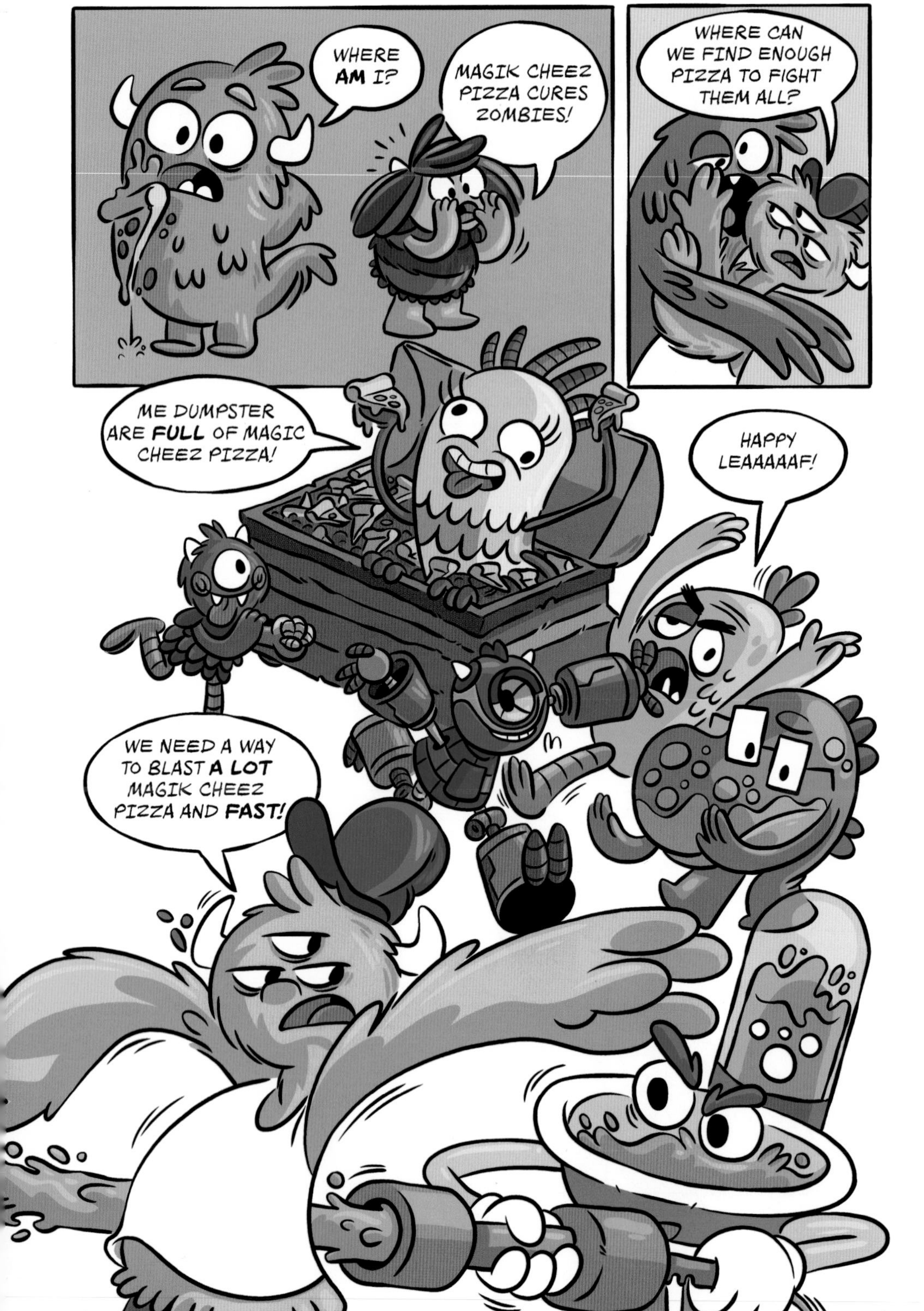
WHERE AM I?
MAGIK CHEEZ PIZZA CURES ZOMBIES!
WHERE CAN WE FIND ENOUGH PIZZA TO FIGHT THEM ALL?
ME DUMPSTER ARE FULL OF MAGIC CHEEZ PIZZA!
HAPPY LEAAAAAF!
WE NEED A WAY TO BLAST A LOT MAGIK CHEEZ PIZZA AND FAST!

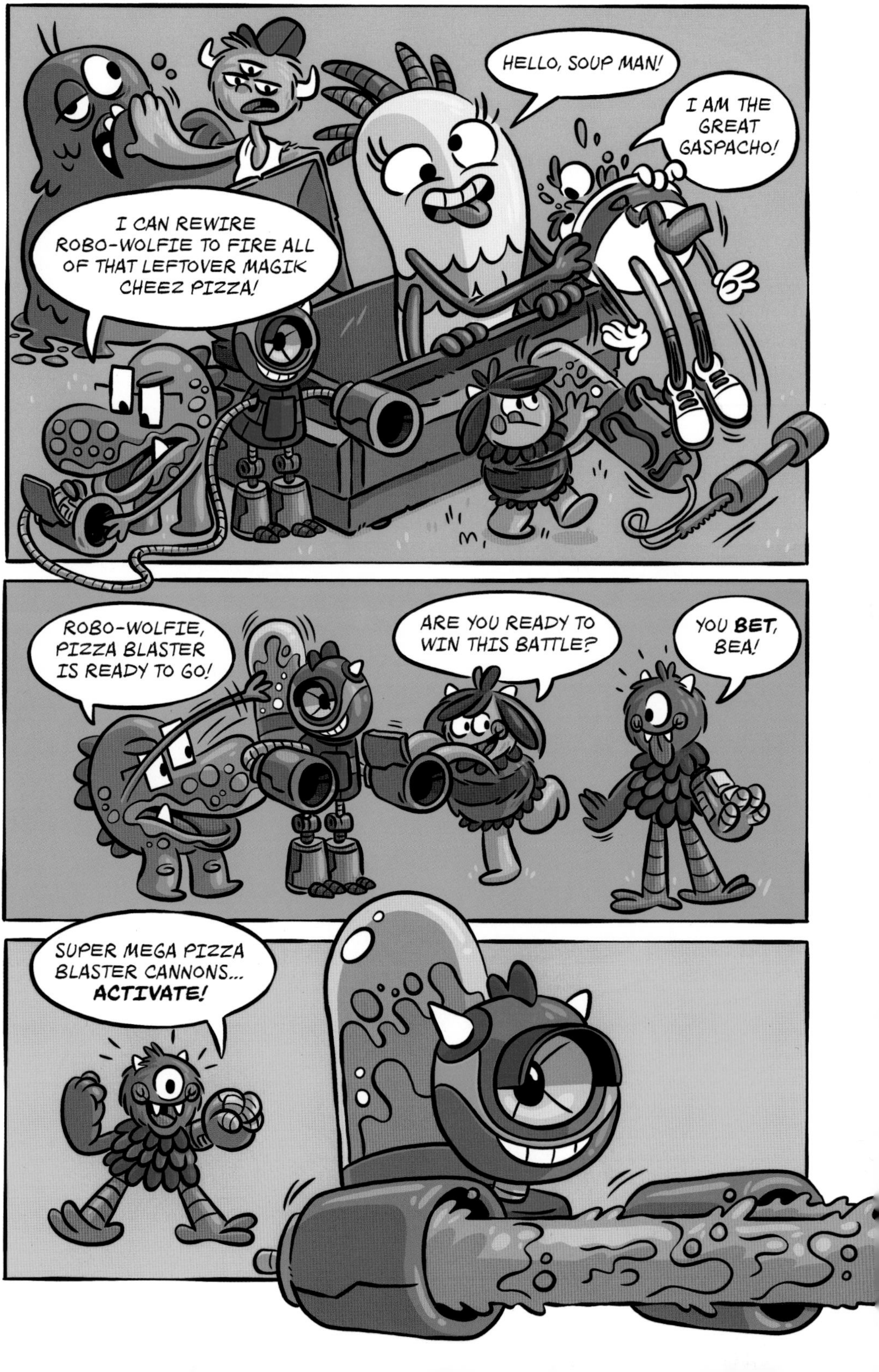
HELLO, SOUP MAN!
I AM THE GREAT GASPACHO!
I CAN REWIRE ROBO-WOLFIE TO FIRE ALL OF THAT LEFTOVER MAGIK CHEEZ PIZZA!
ROBO-WOLFIE, PIZZA BLASTER IS READY TO GO!
ARE YOU READY TO WIN THIS BATTLE?
YOU BET, BEA!
SUPER MEGA PIZZA BLASTER CANNONS... ACTIVATE!

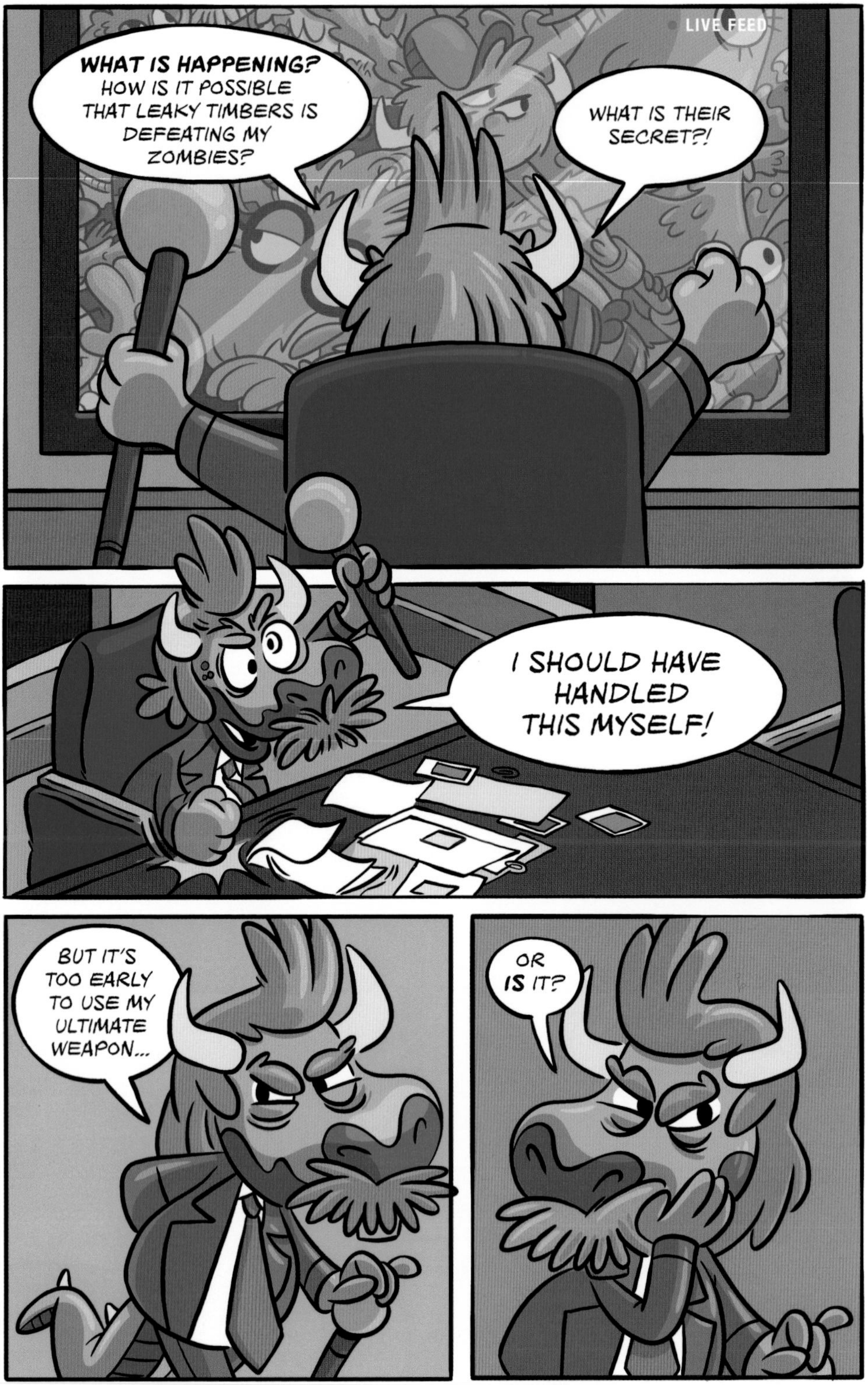
LIVE FEED
WHAT IS HAPPENING? HOW IS IT POSSIBLE THAT LEAKY TIMBERS IS DEFEATING MY ZOMBIES?
WHAT IS THEIR SECRET?!
I SHOULD HAVE HANDLED THIS MYSELF!
BUT IT'S TOO EARLY TO USE MY ULTIMATE WEAPON...
OR IS IT?

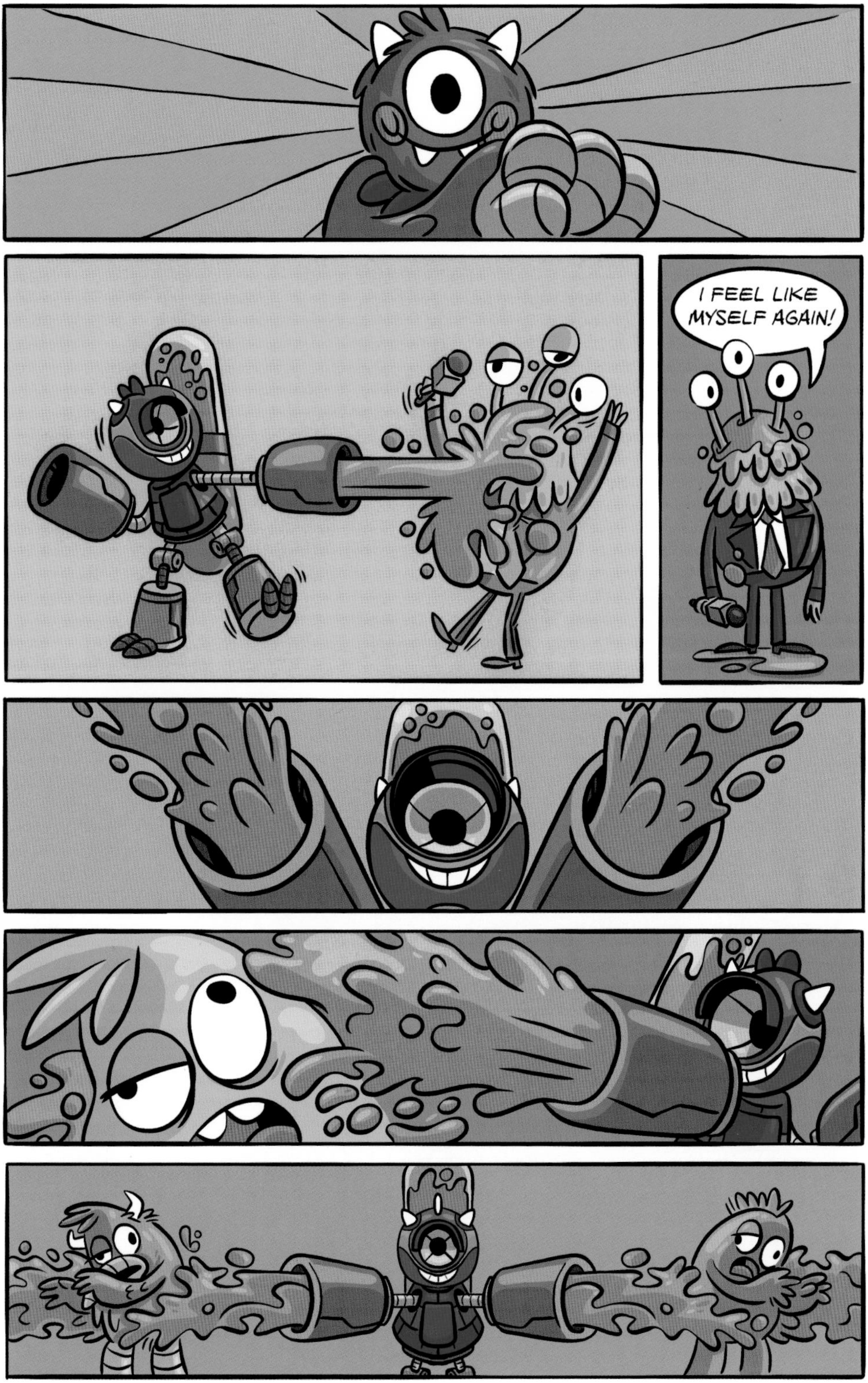
I FEEL LIKE MYSELF AGAIN!

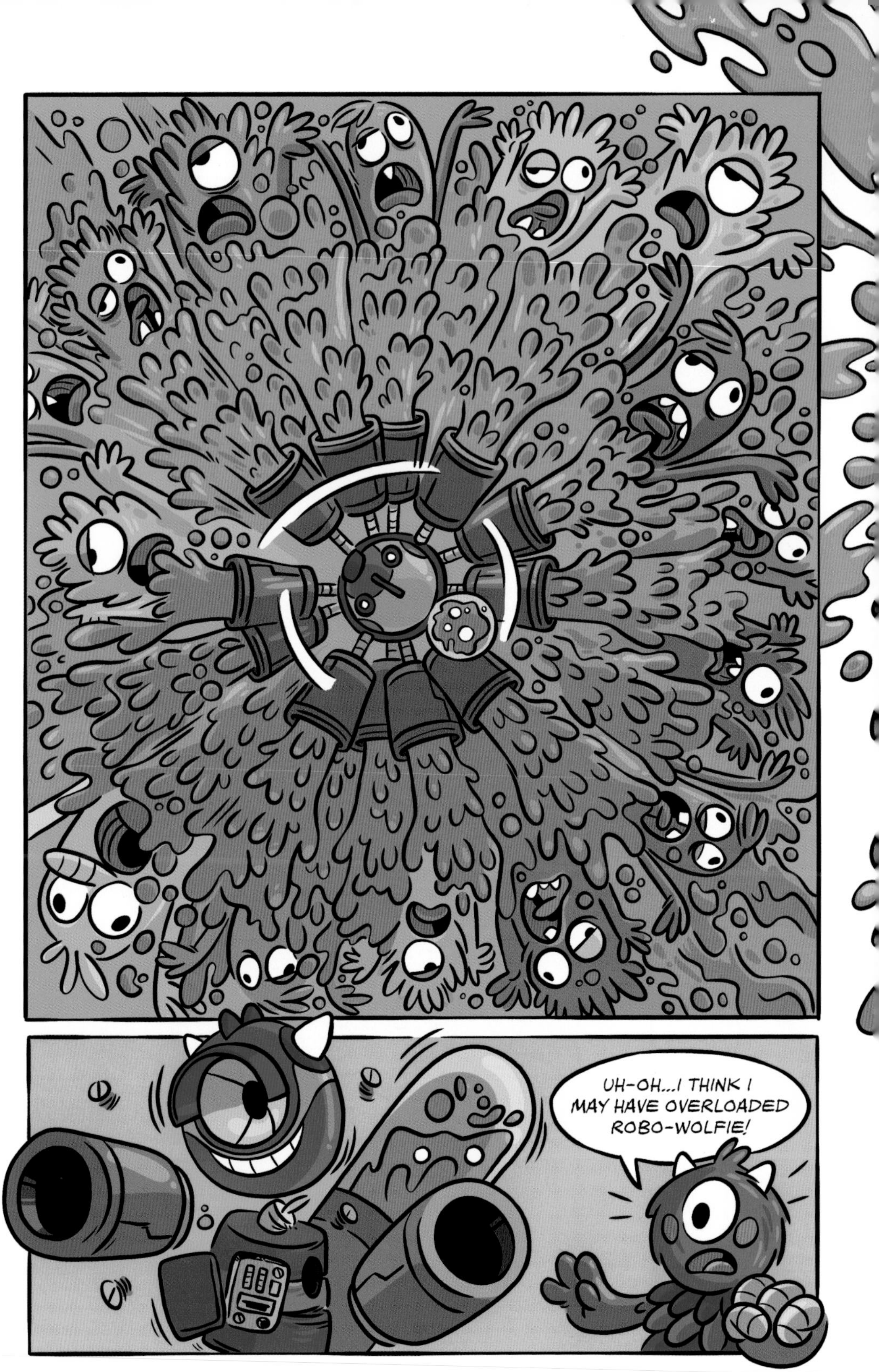
UH-OH...I THINK I MAY HAVE OVERLOADED ROBO-WOLFIE!

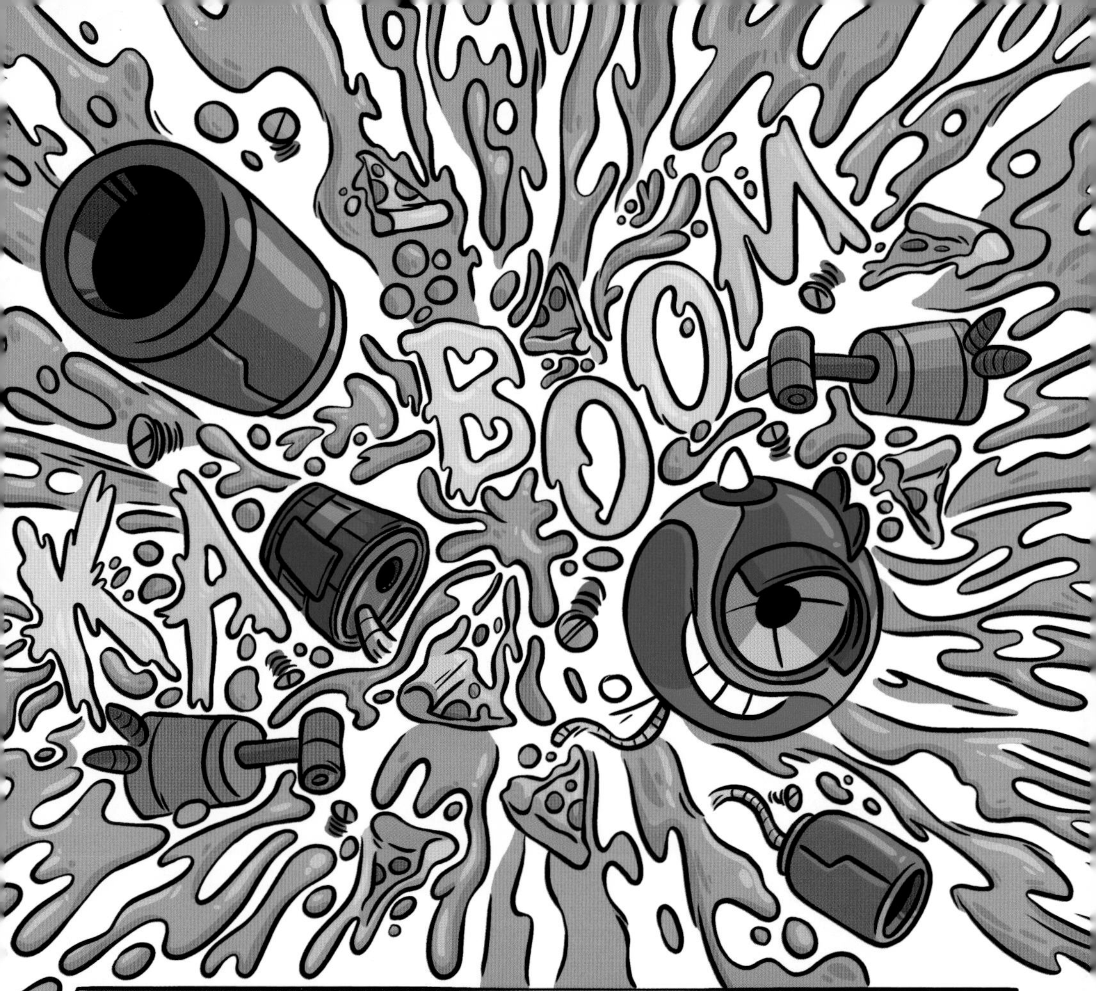
KA-BOOM!

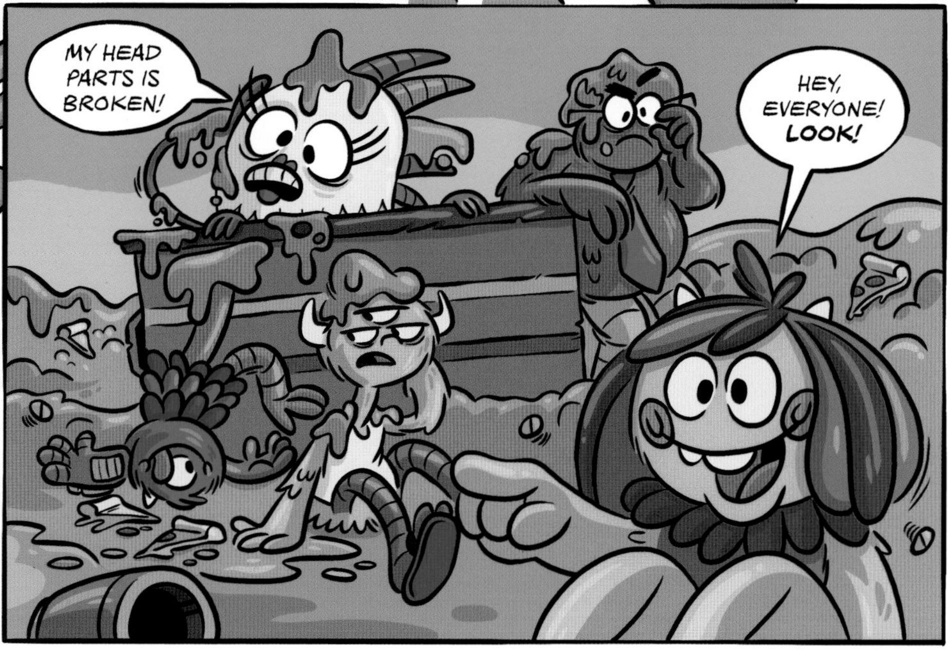
MY HEAD PARTS IS BROKEN!
HEY, EVERYONE! LOOK!

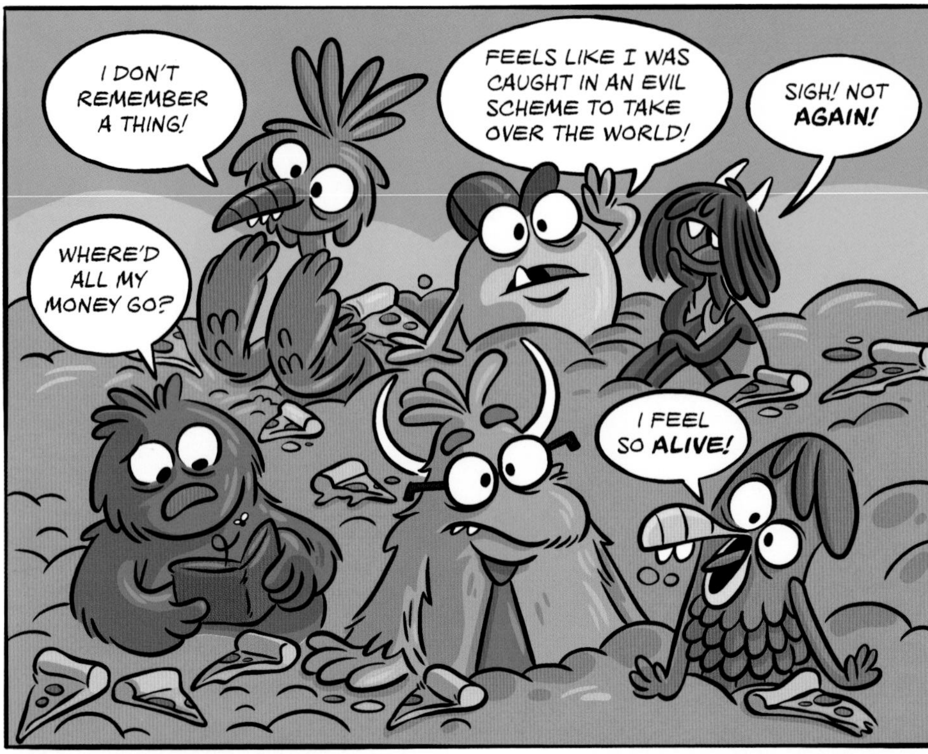
I DON'T REMEMBER A THING!
FEELS LIKE I WAS CAUGHT IN AN EVIL SCHEME TO TAKE OVER THE WORLD!
SIGH! NOT **AGAIN!**
WHERE'D ALL MY MONEY GO?
I FEEL SO **ALIVE!**

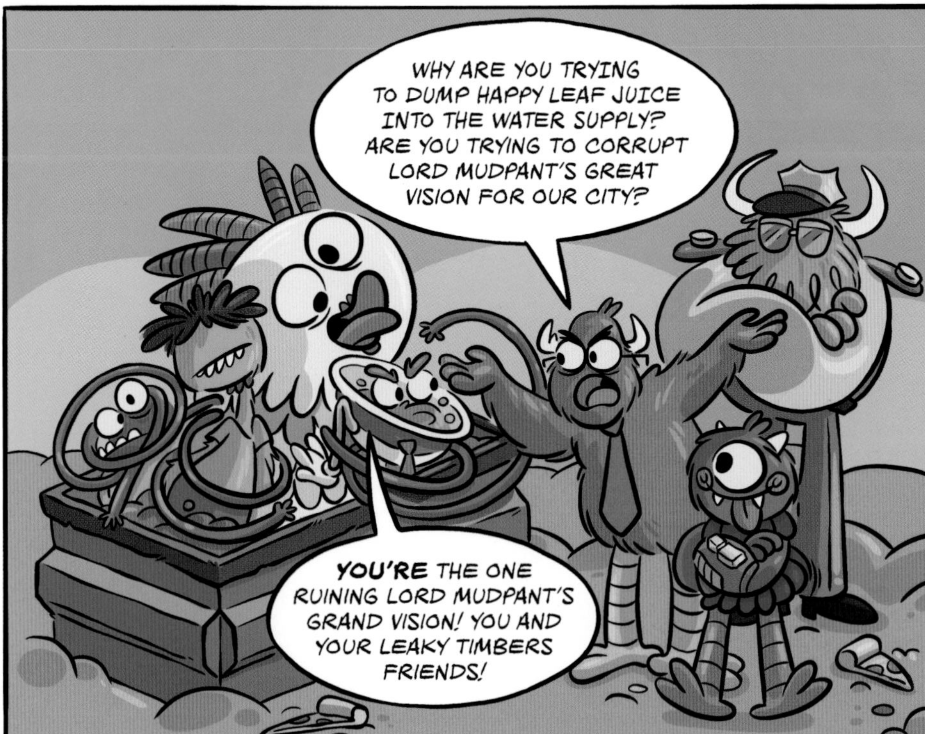
WHY ARE YOU TRYING TO DUMP HAPPY LEAF JUICE INTO THE WATER SUPPLY? ARE YOU TRYING TO CORRUPT LORD MUDPANT'S GREAT VISION FOR OUR CITY?
YOU'RE THE ONE RUINING LORD MUDPANT'S GRAND VISION! YOU AND YOUR LEAKY TIMBERS FRIENDS!

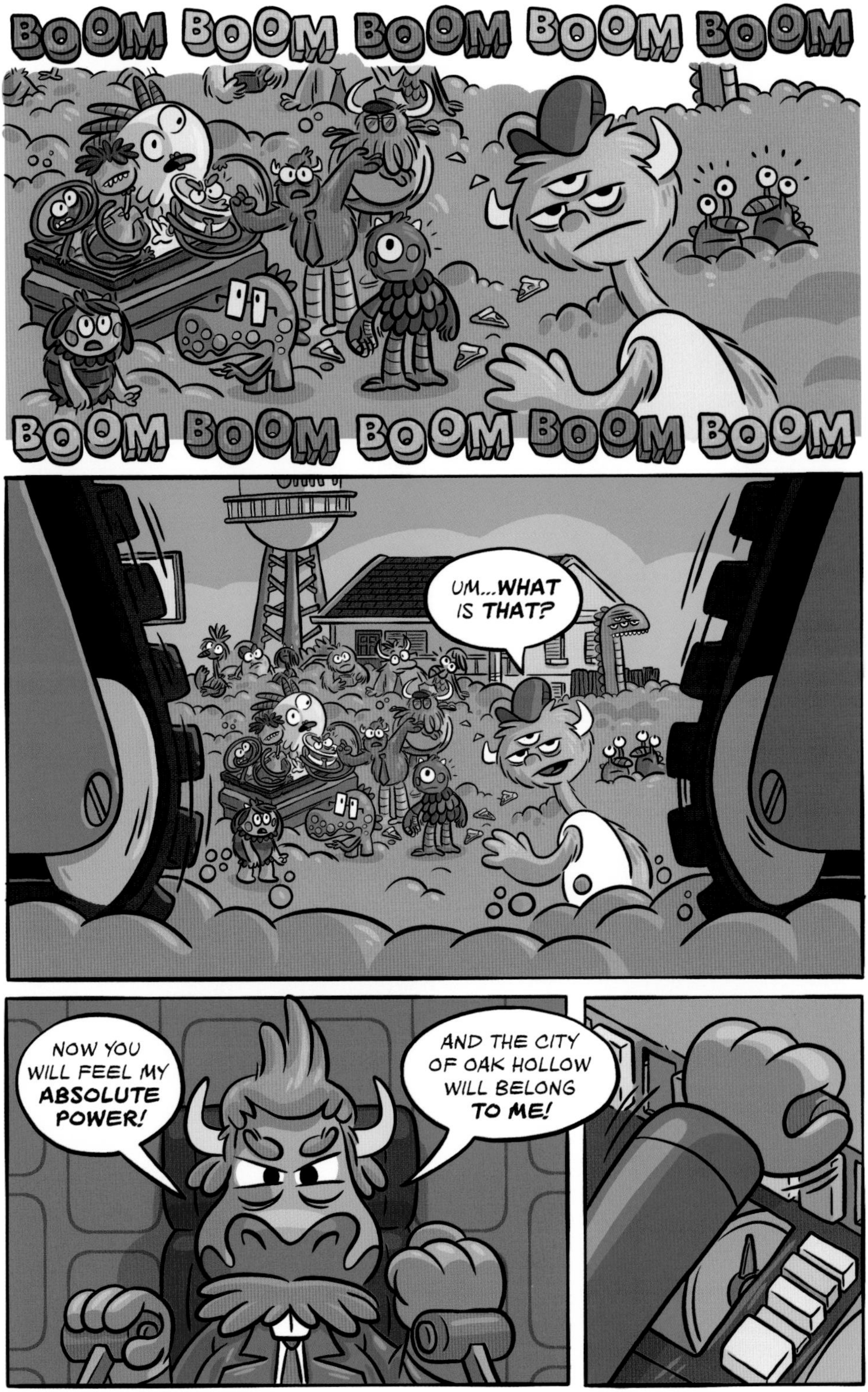
BOOM BOOM BOOM BOOM BOOM
BOOM BOOM BOOM BOOM BOOM
UM...WHAT IS THAT?
NOW YOU WILL FEEL MY ABSOLUTE POWER!
AND THE CITY OF OAK HOLLOW WILL BELONG TO ME!

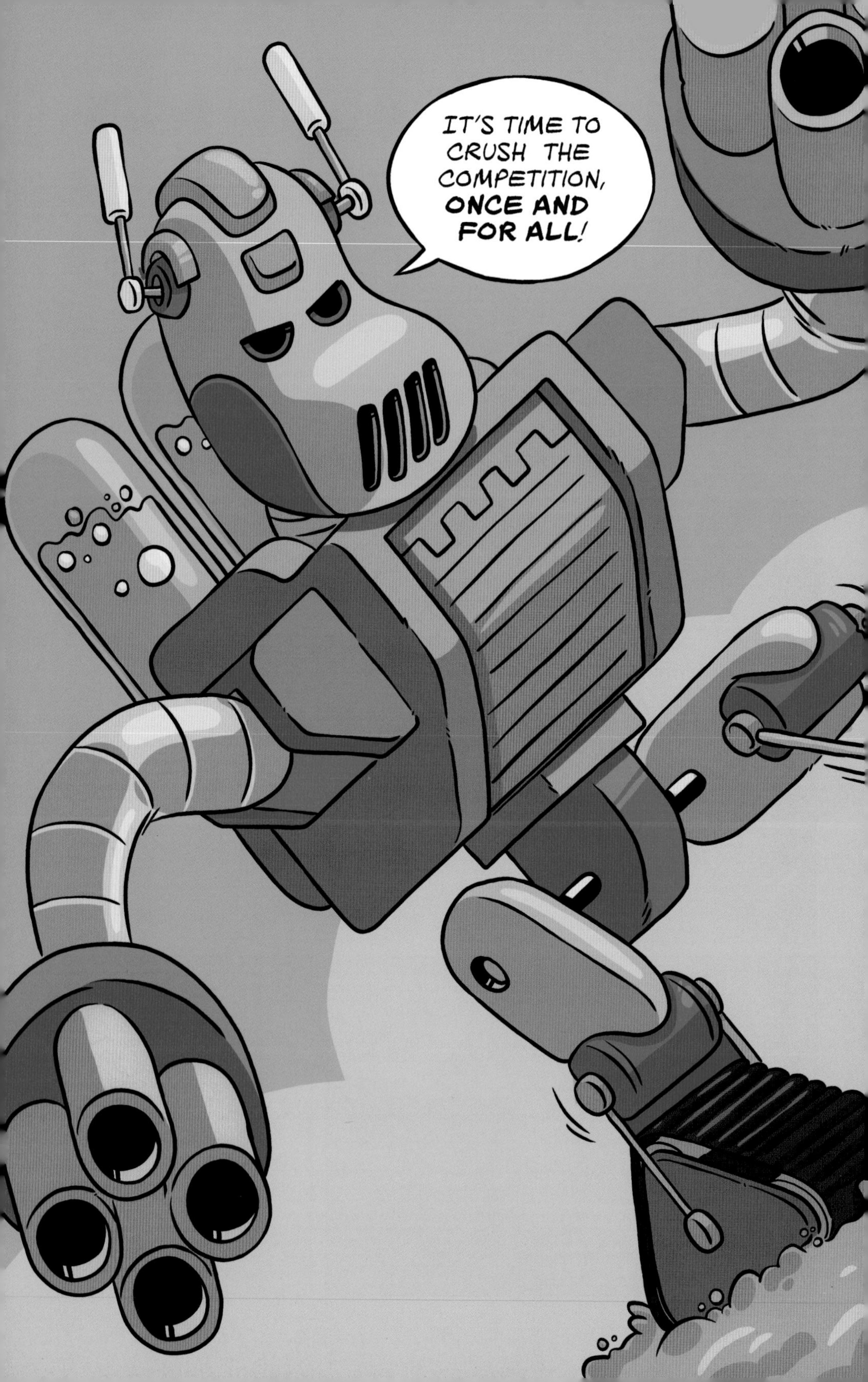
IT'S TIME TO CRUSH THE COMPETITION, **ONCE AND FOR ALL!**

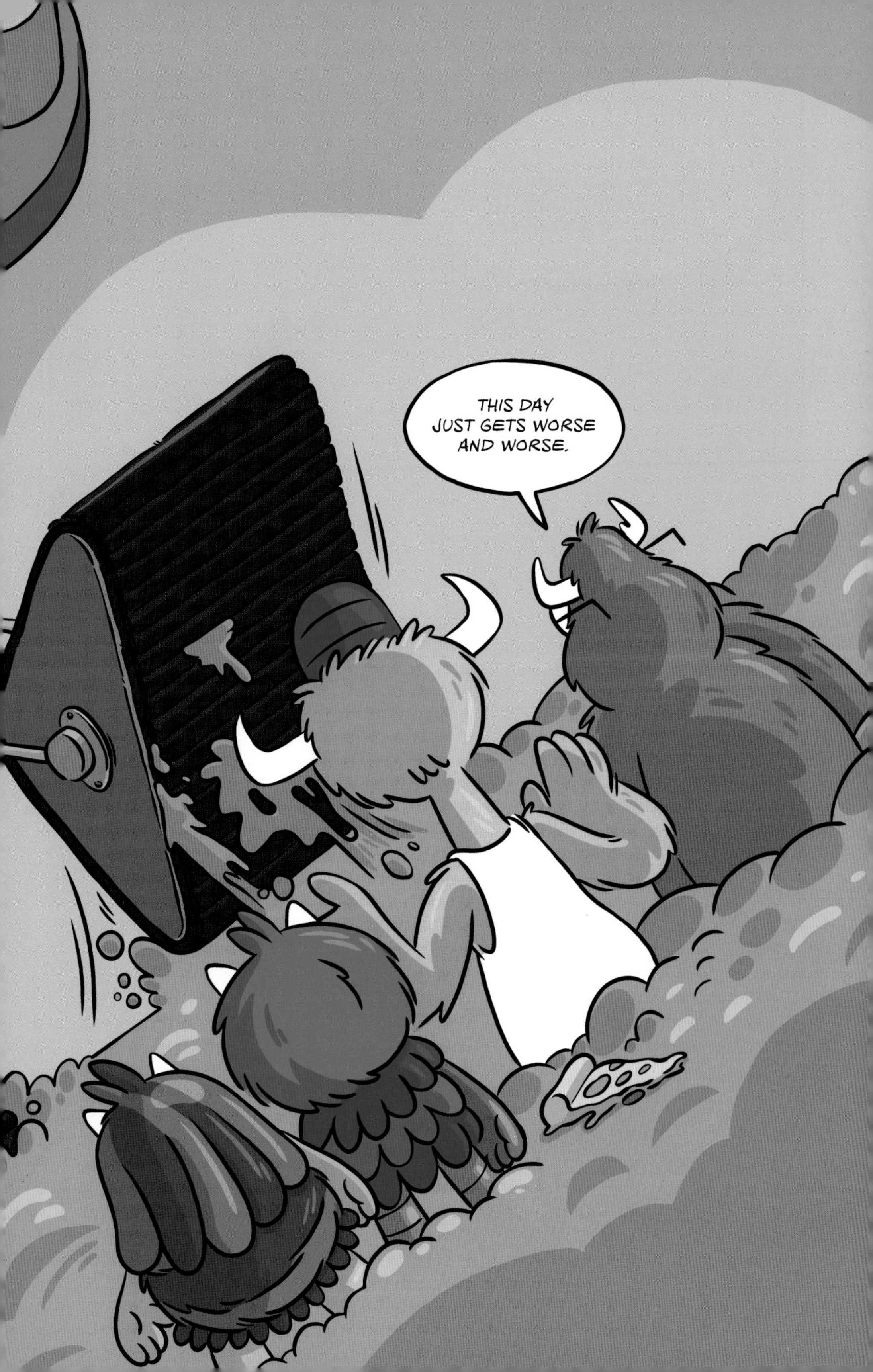
THIS DAY JUST GETS WORSE AND WORSE.

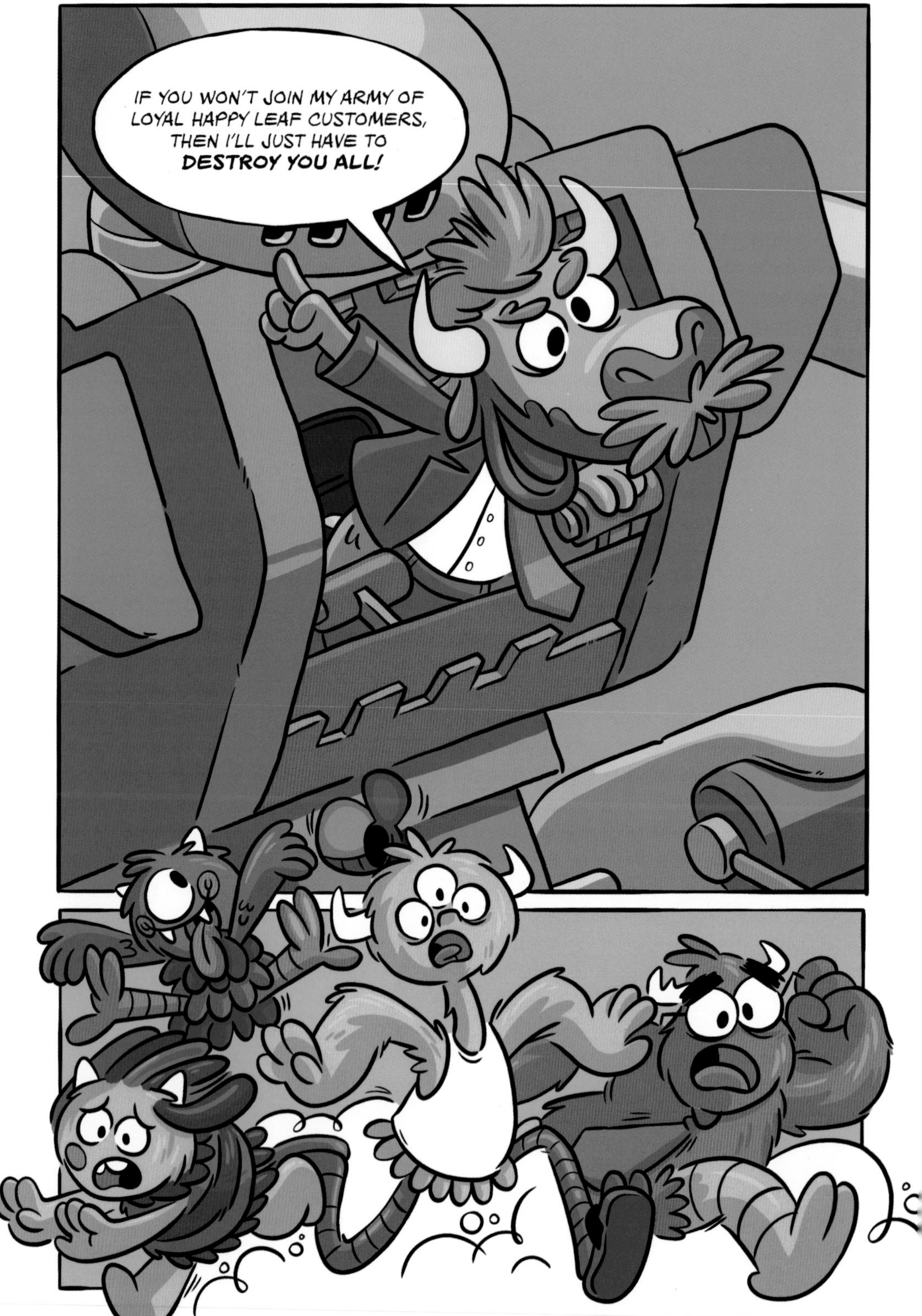
IF YOU WON'T JOIN MY ARMY OF LOYAL HAPPY LEAF CUSTOMERS, THEN I'LL JUST HAVE TO **DESTROY YOU ALL!**

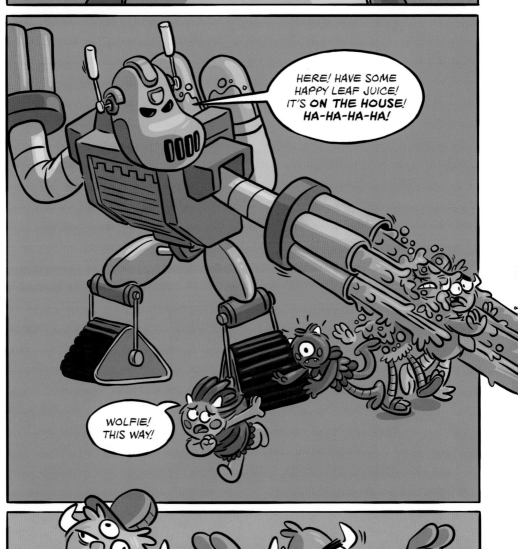

HERE! HAVE SOME HAPPY LEAF JUICE! IT'S **ON THE HOUSE!** HA-HA-HA-HA!

WOLFIE! THIS WAY!

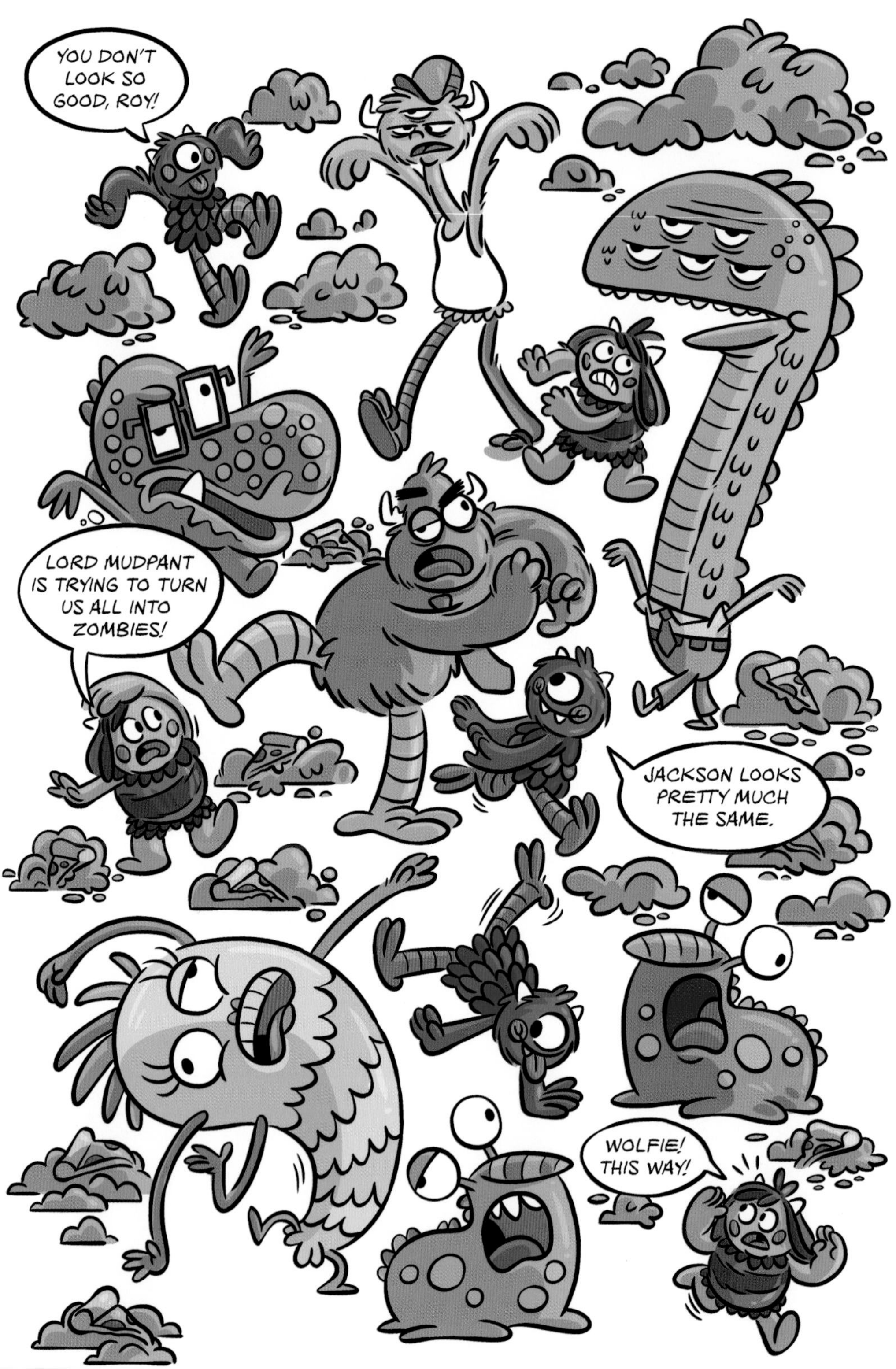
YOU DON'T LOOK SO GOOD, ROY!
LORD MUDPANT IS TRYING TO TURN US ALL INTO ZOMBIES!
JACKSON LOOKS PRETTY MUCH THE SAME.
WOLFIE! THIS WAY!

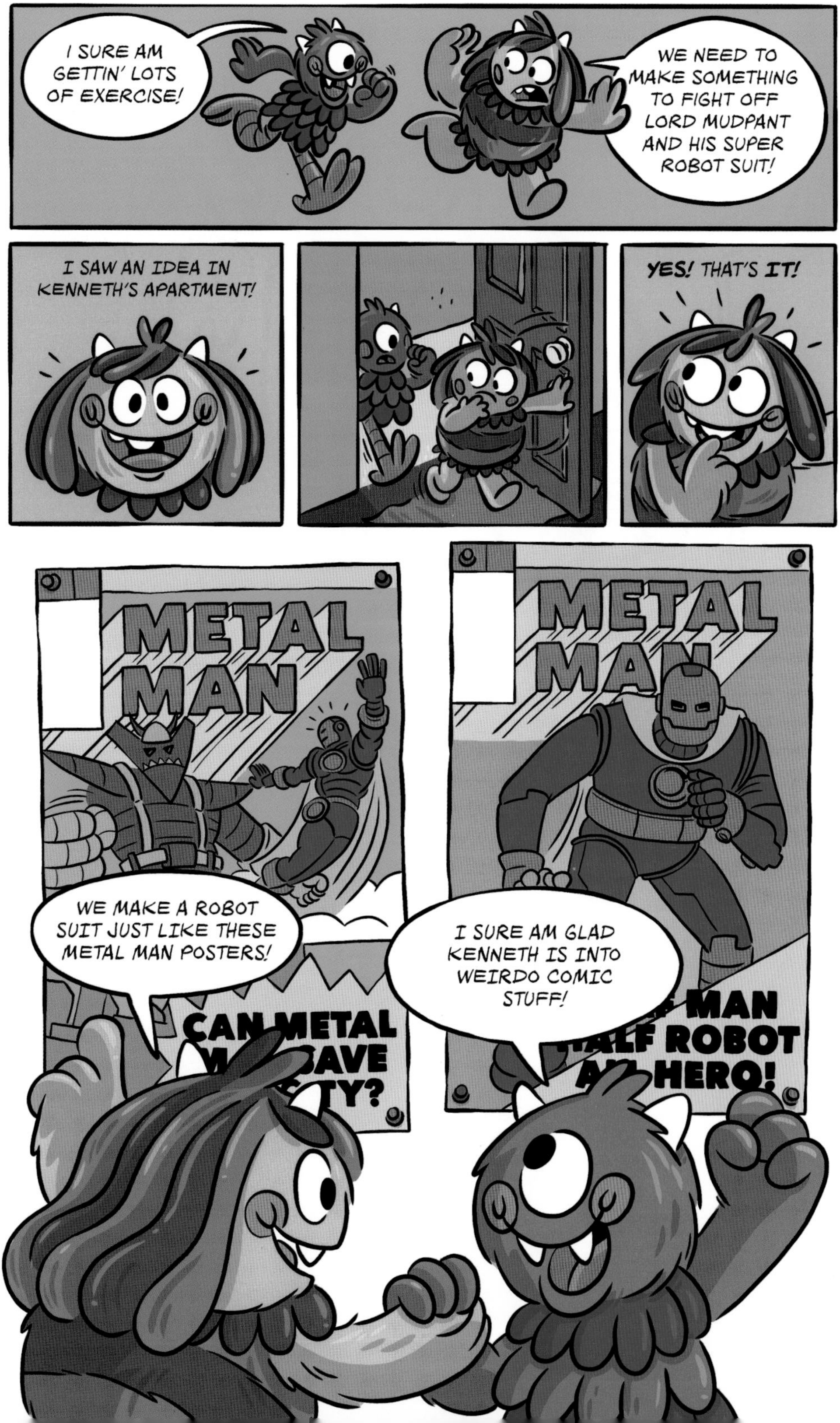
I SURE AM GETTIN' LOTS OF EXERCISE!
WE NEED TO MAKE SOMETHING TO FIGHT OFF LORD MUDPANT AND HIS SUPER ROBOT SUIT!
I SAW AN IDEA IN KENNETH'S APARTMENT!
YES! THAT'S IT!
METAL MAN
METAL MAN
WE MAKE A ROBOT SUIT JUST LIKE THESE METAL MAN POSTERS!
I SURE AM GLAD KENNETH IS INTO WEIRDO COMIC STUFF!

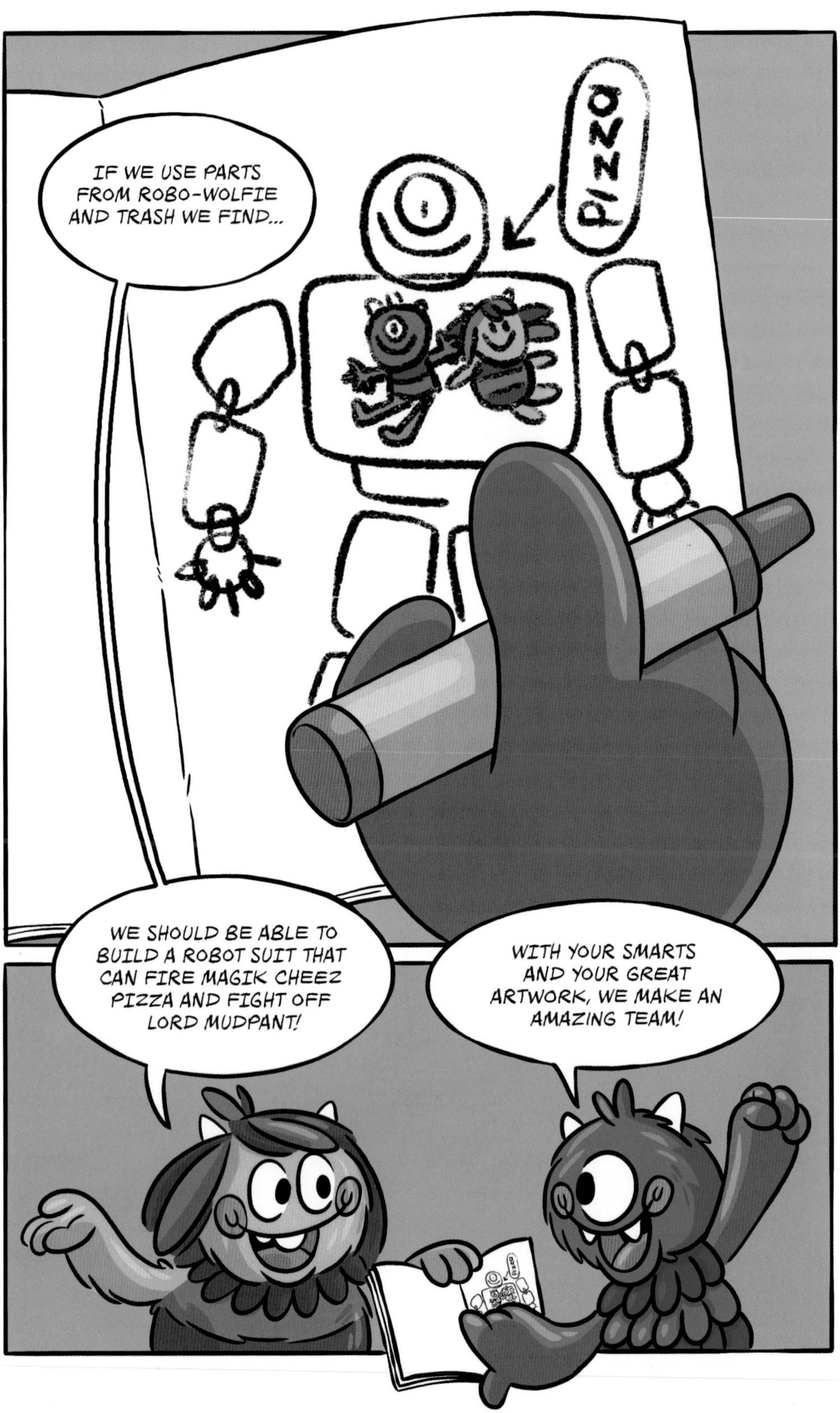
IF WE USE PARTS FROM ROBO-WOLFIE AND TRASH WE FIND...
WE SHOULD BE ABLE TO BUILD A ROBOT SUIT THAT CAN FIRE MAGIK CHEEZ PIZZA AND FIGHT OFF LORD MUDPANT!
WITH YOUR SMARTS AND YOUR GREAT ARTWORK, WE MAKE AN AMAZING TEAM!

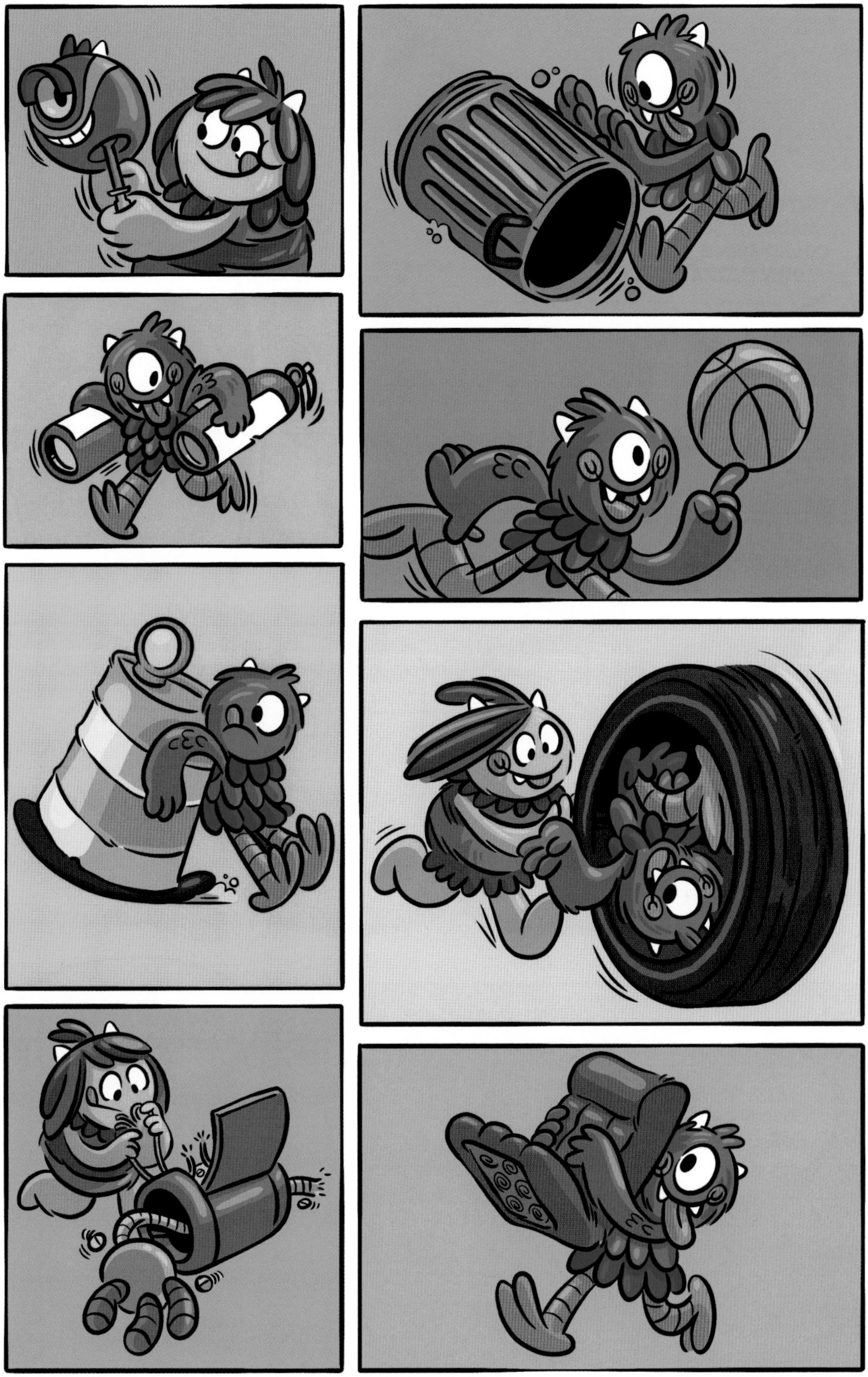

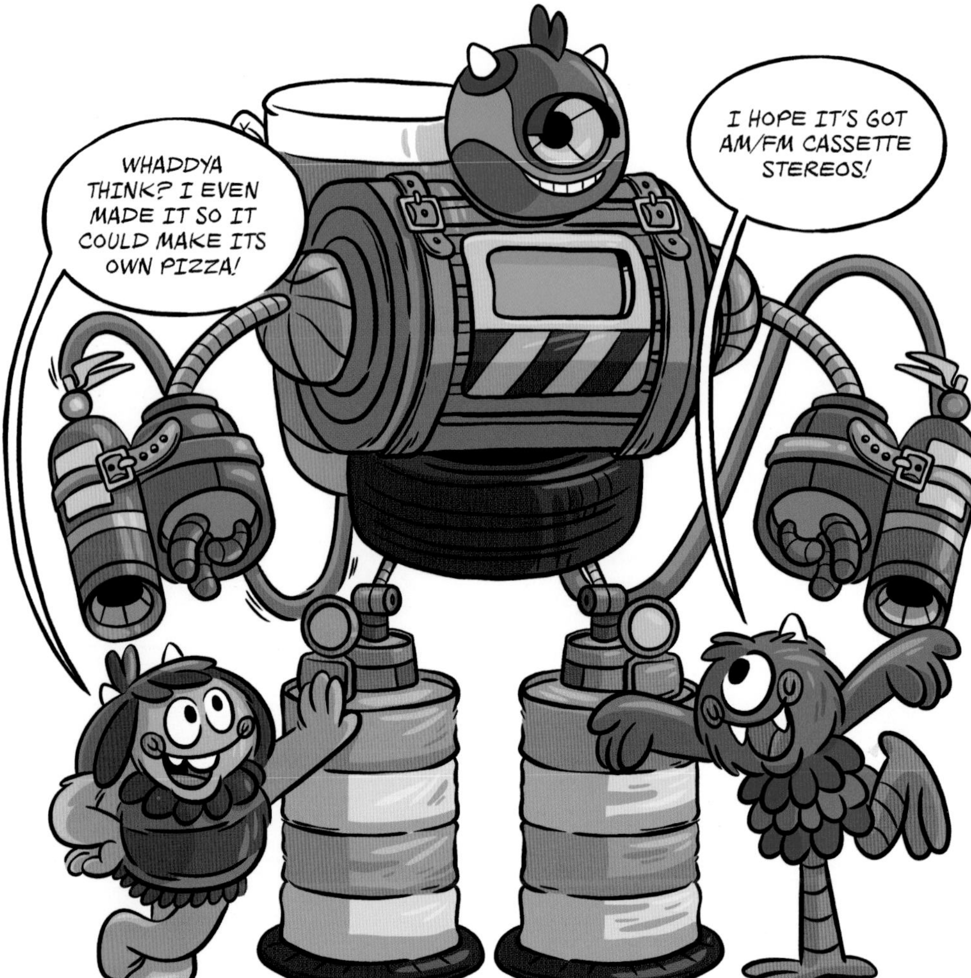
WHADDYA THINK? I EVEN MADE IT SO IT COULD MAKE ITS OWN PIZZA!
I HOPE IT'S GOT AM/FM CASSETTE STEREOS!

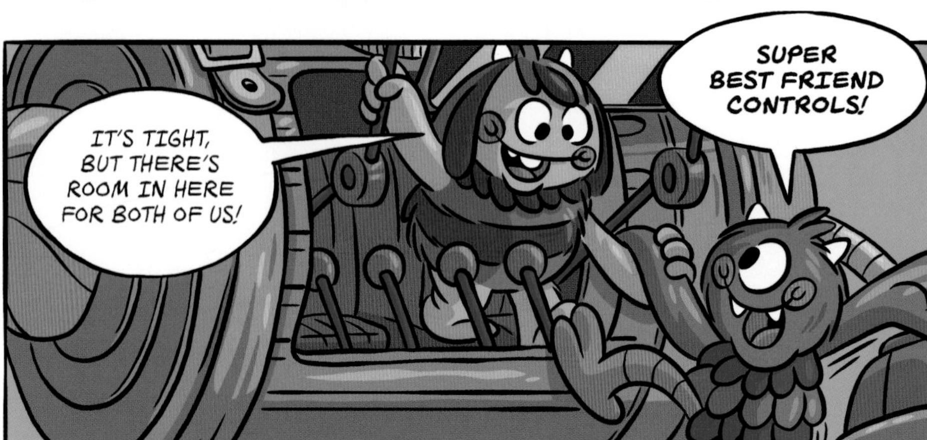
IT'S TIGHT, BUT THERE'S ROOM IN HERE FOR BOTH OF US!
SUPER BEST FRIEND CONTROLS!

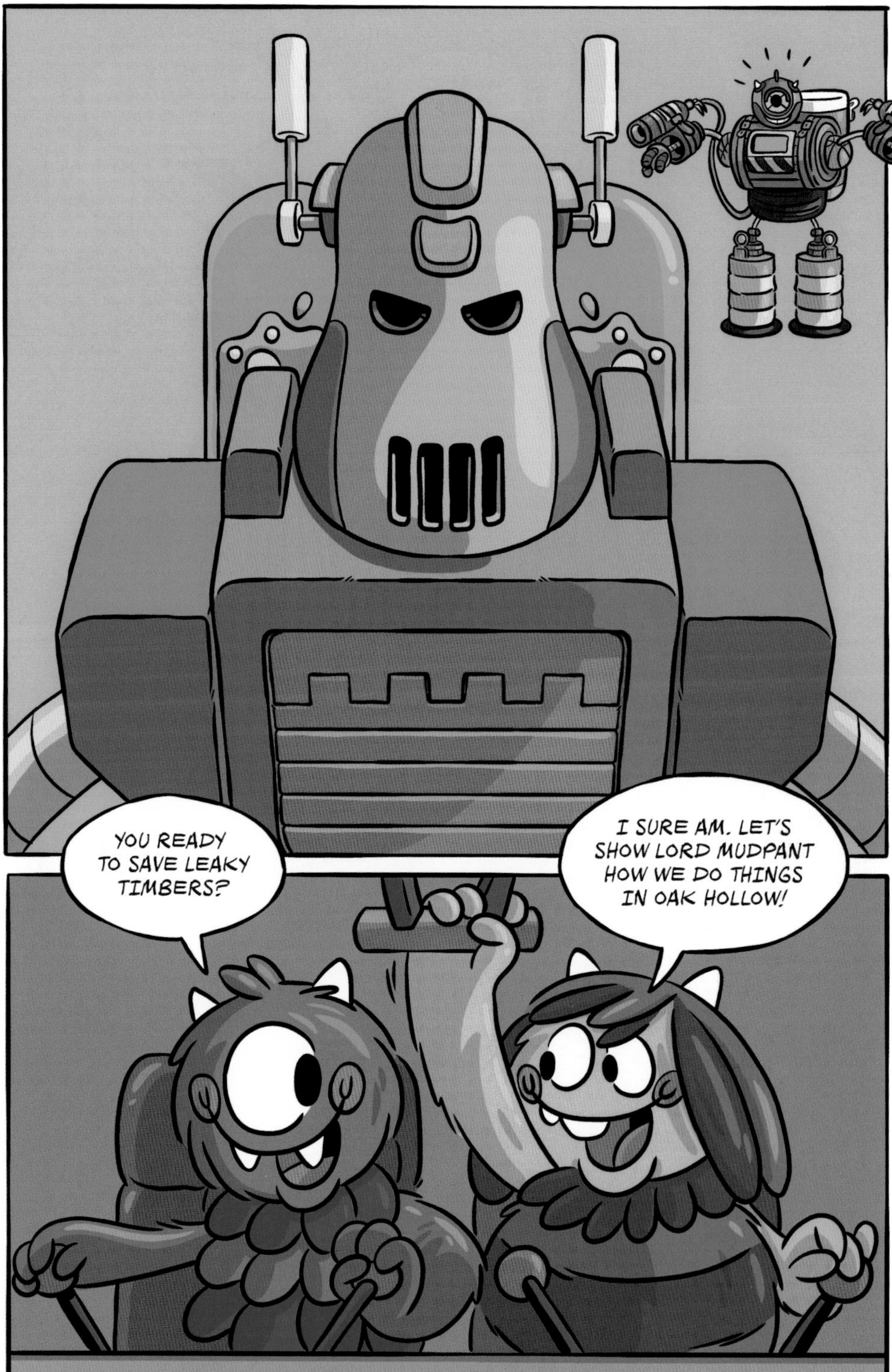
YOU READY TO SAVE LEAKY TIMBERS?
I SURE AM. LET'S SHOW LORD MUDPANT HOW WE DO THINGS IN OAK HOLLOW!

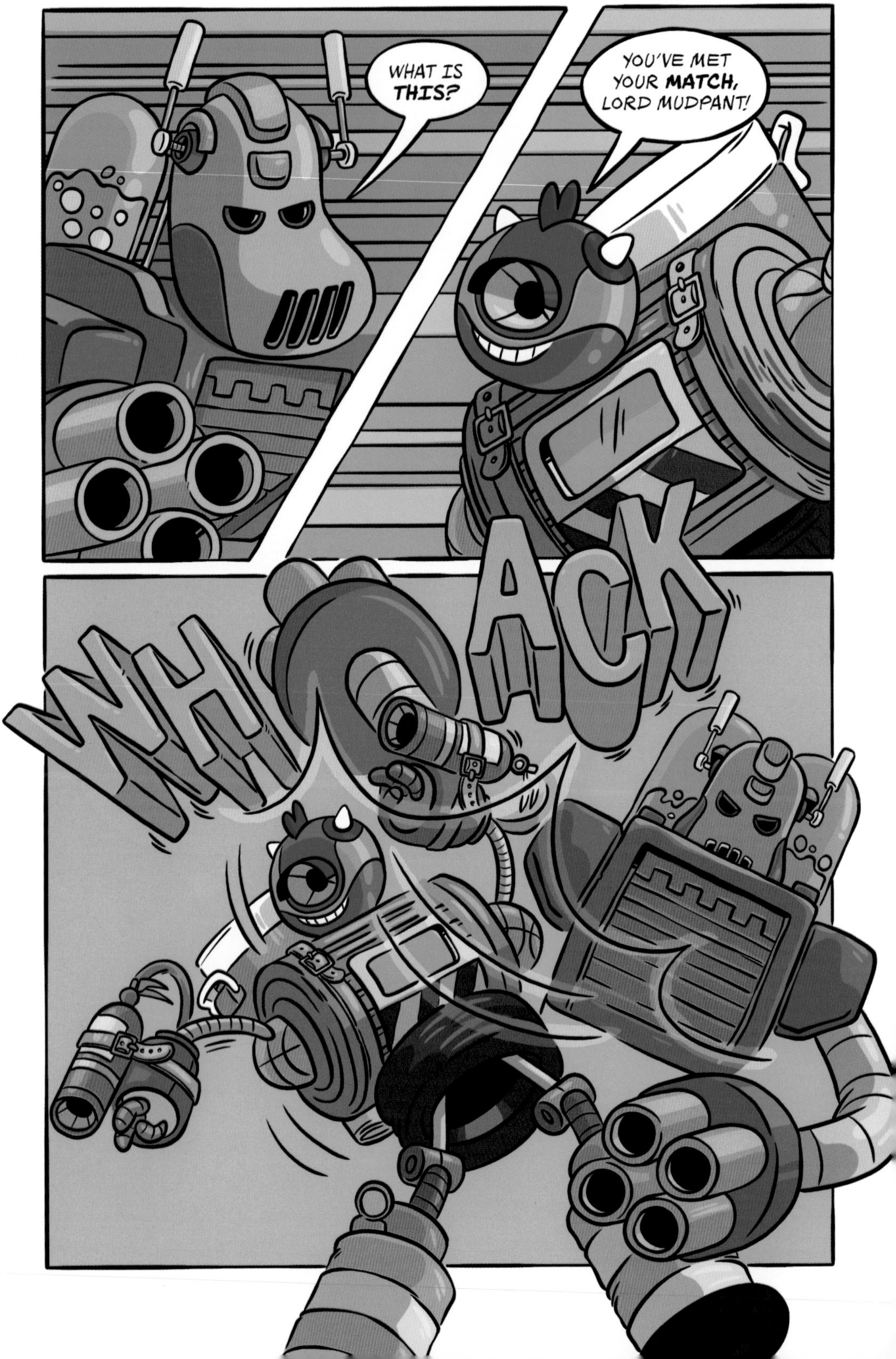
WHAT IS THIS?
YOU'VE MET YOUR MATCH, LORD MUDPANT!
WHACK

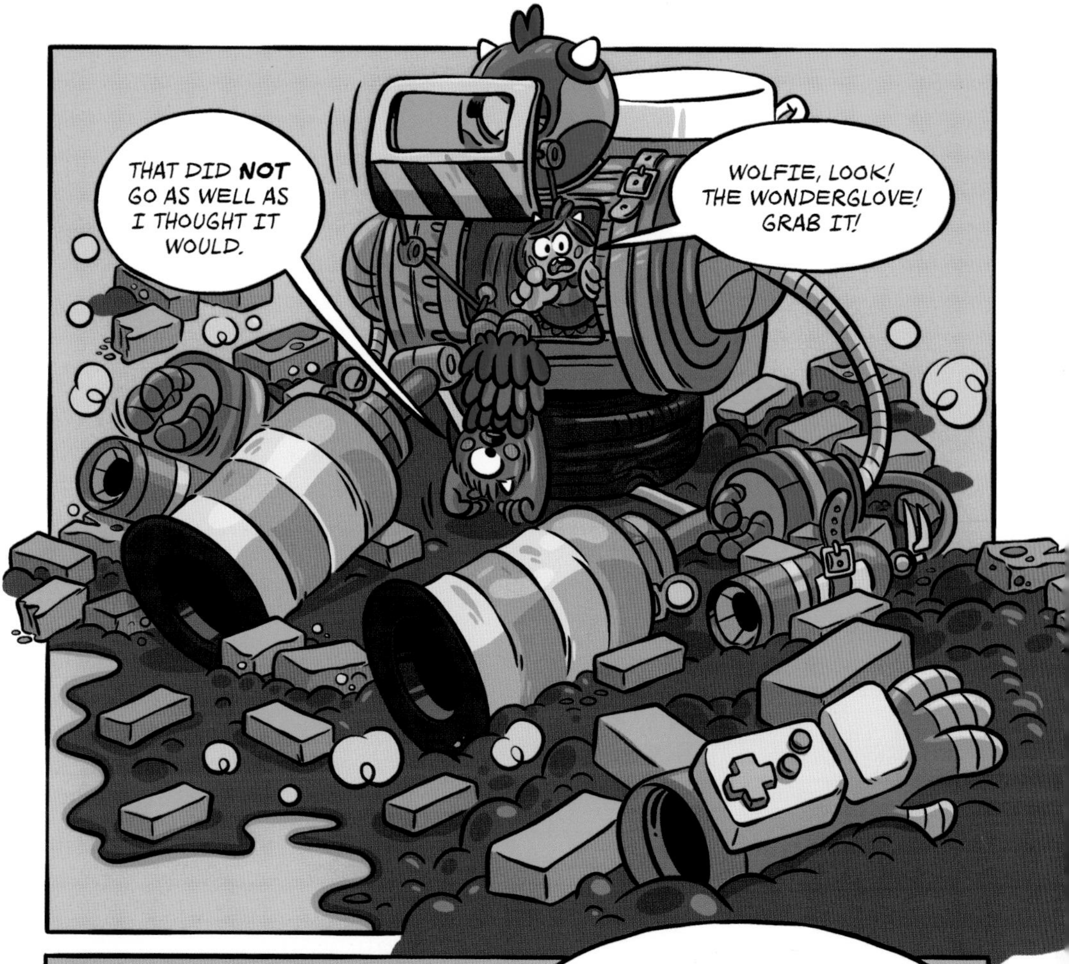
THAT DID **NOT** GO AS WELL AS I THOUGHT IT WOULD.
WOLFIE, LOOK! THE WONDERGLOVE! GRAB IT!

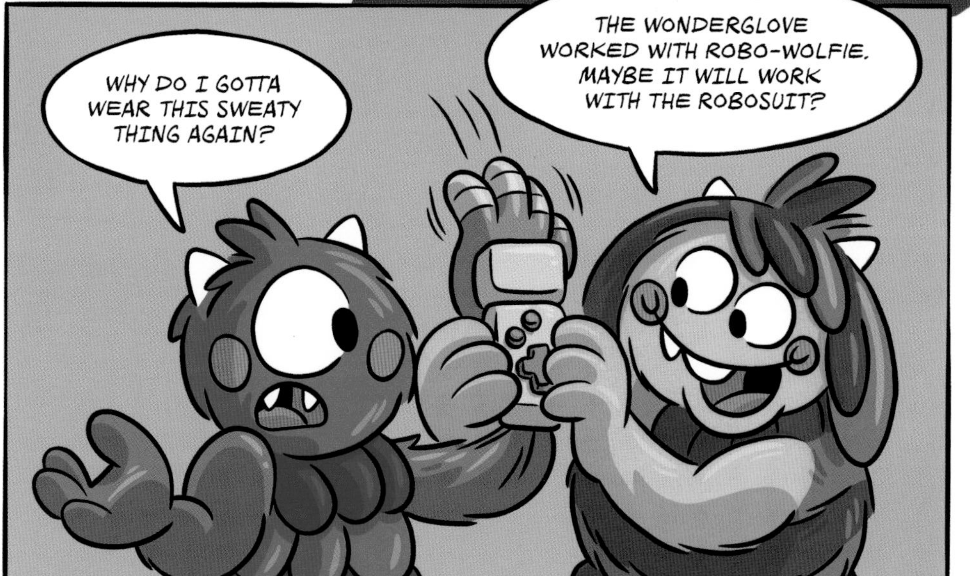
WHY DO I GOTTA WEAR THIS SWEATY THING AGAIN?
THE WONDERGLOVE WORKED WITH ROBO-WOLFIE. MAYBE IT WILL WORK WITH THE ROBOSUIT?

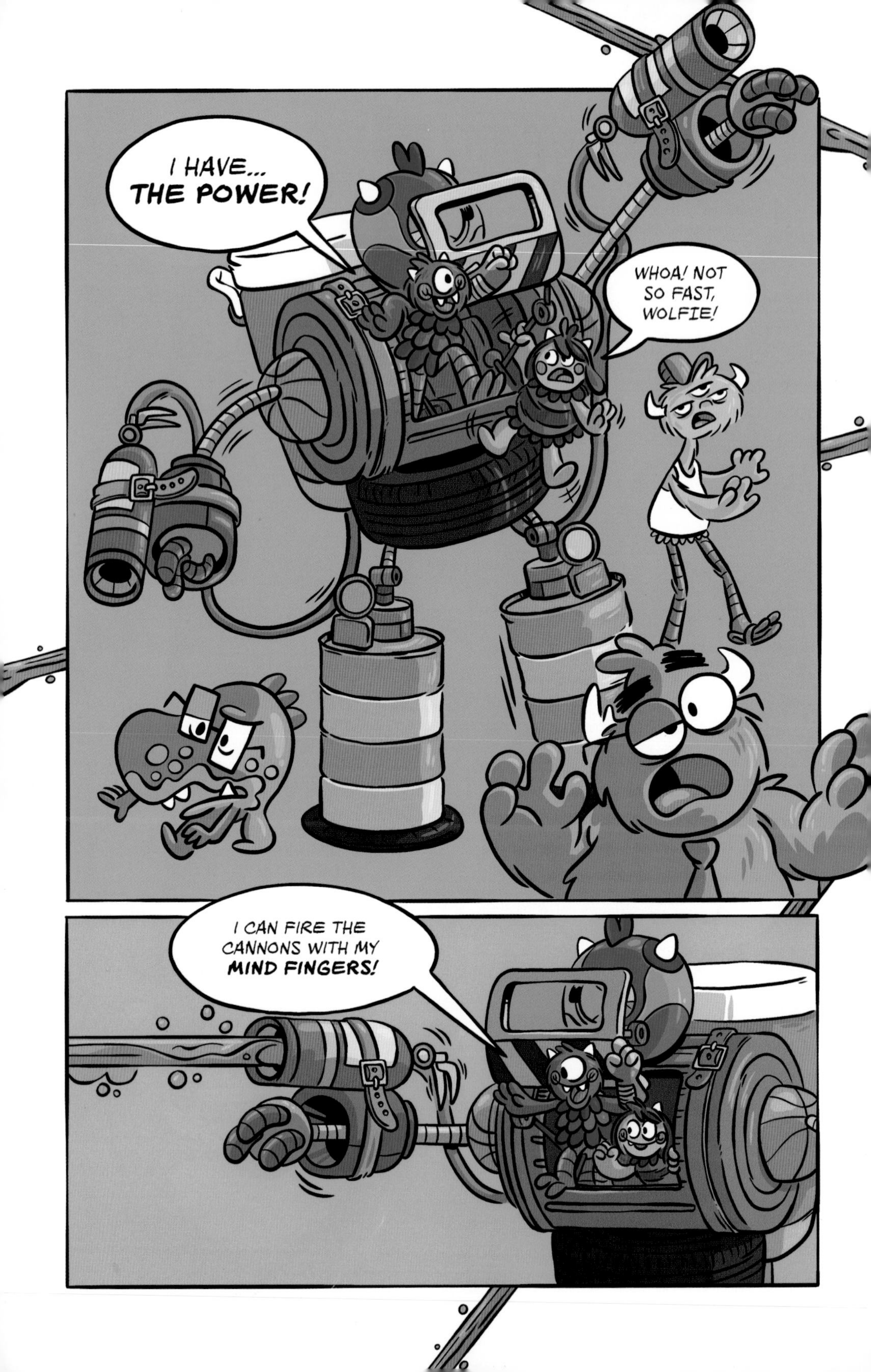
I HAVE... THE POWER!
WHOA! NOT SO FAST, WOLFIE!
I CAN FIRE THE CANNONS WITH MY MIND FINGERS!

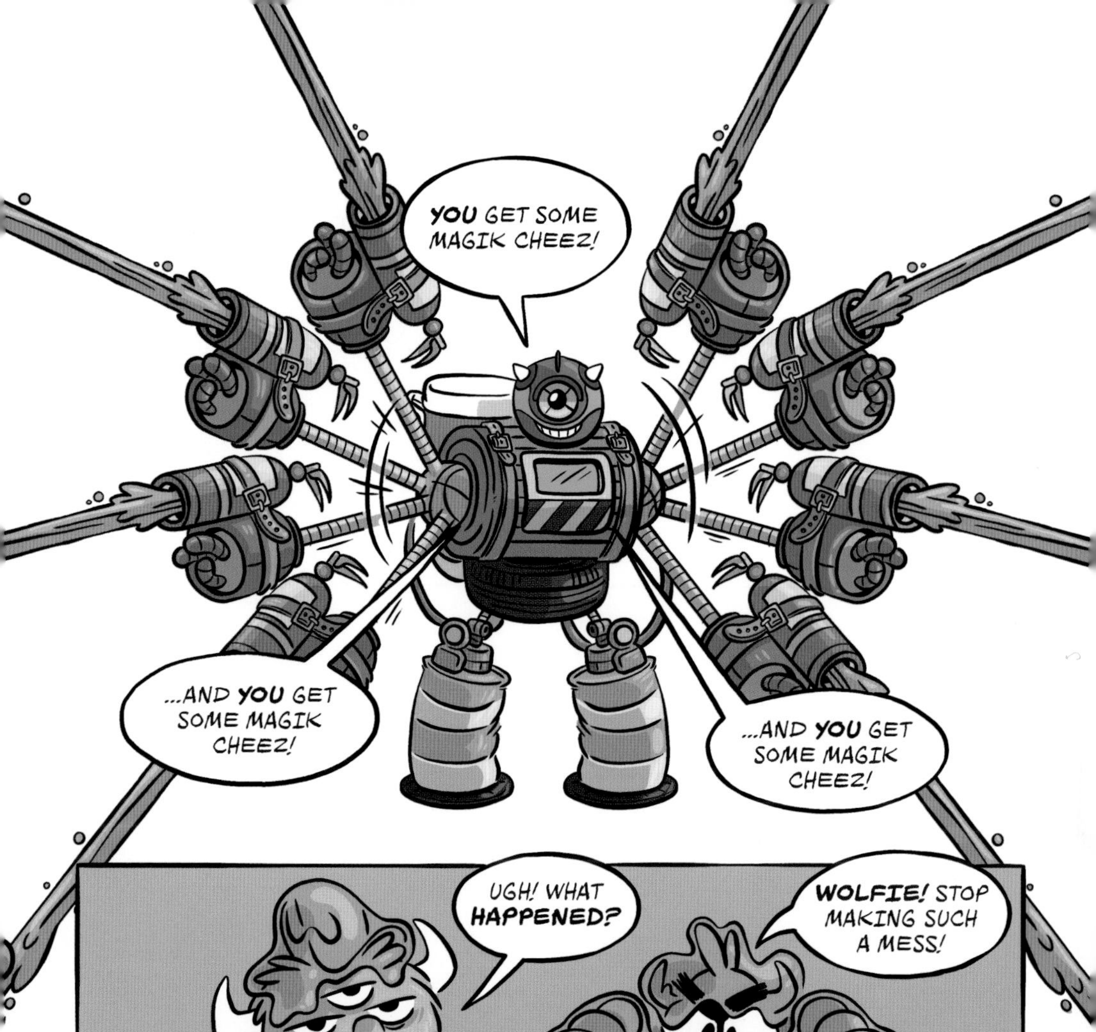
YOU GET SOME MAGIK CHEEZ!
...AND YOU GET SOME MAGIK CHEEZ!
...AND YOU GET SOME MAGIK CHEEZ!

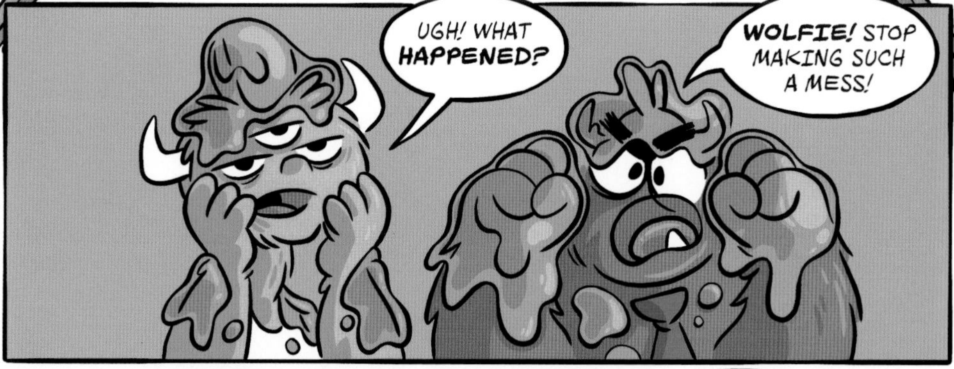
UGH! WHAT HAPPENED?
WOLFIE! STOP MAKING SUCH A MESS!

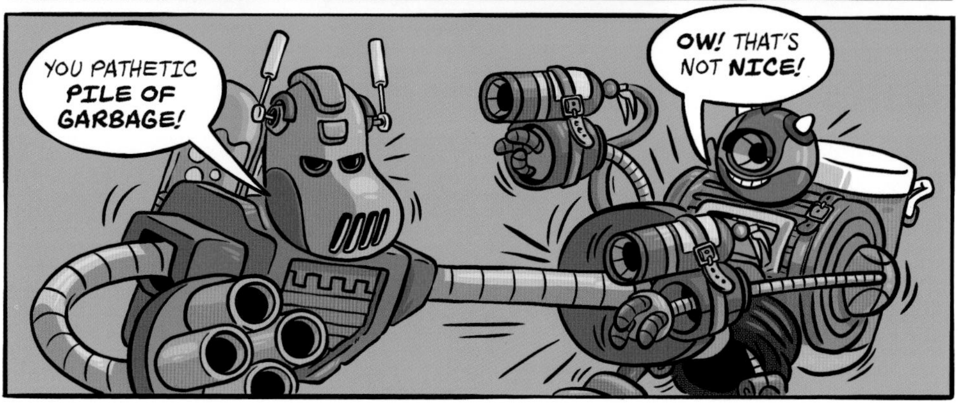
YOU PATHETIC PILE OF GARBAGE!
OW! THAT'S NOT NICE!

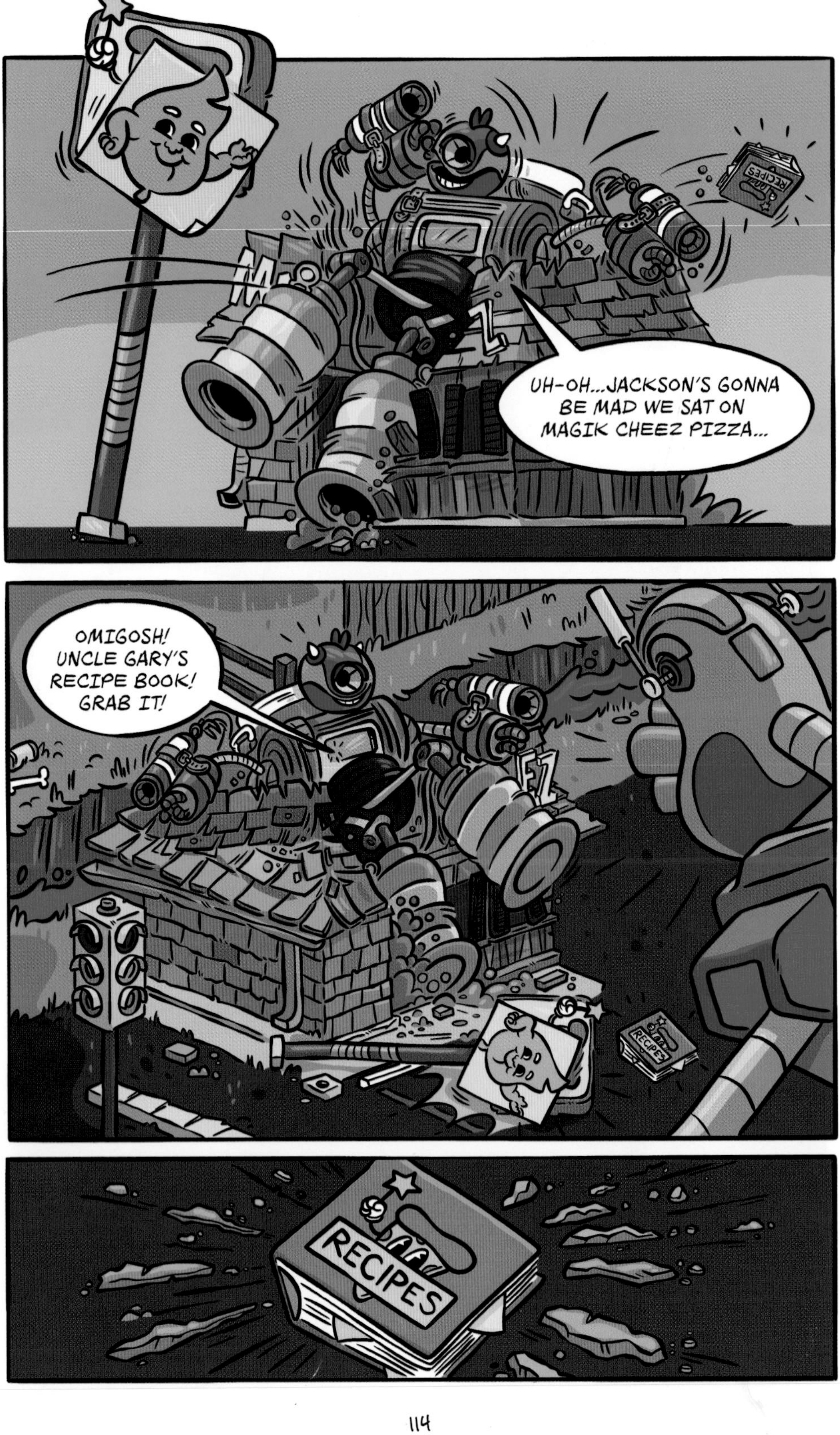
RECIPES
UH-OH...JACKSON'S GONNA BE MAD WE SAT ON MAGIK CHEEZ PIZZA...
OMIGOSH! UNCLE GARY'S RECIPE BOOK! GRAB IT!
RECIPES
RECIPES

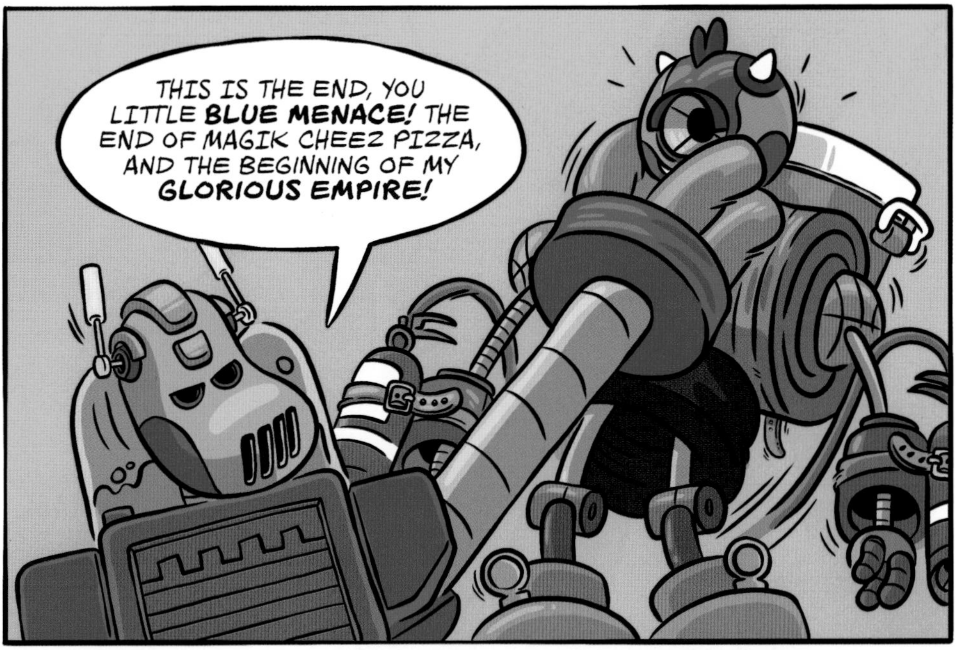
THIS IS THE END, YOU LITTLE BLUE MENACE! THE END OF MAGIK CHEEZ PIZZA, AND THE BEGINNING OF MY GLORIOUS EMPIRE!

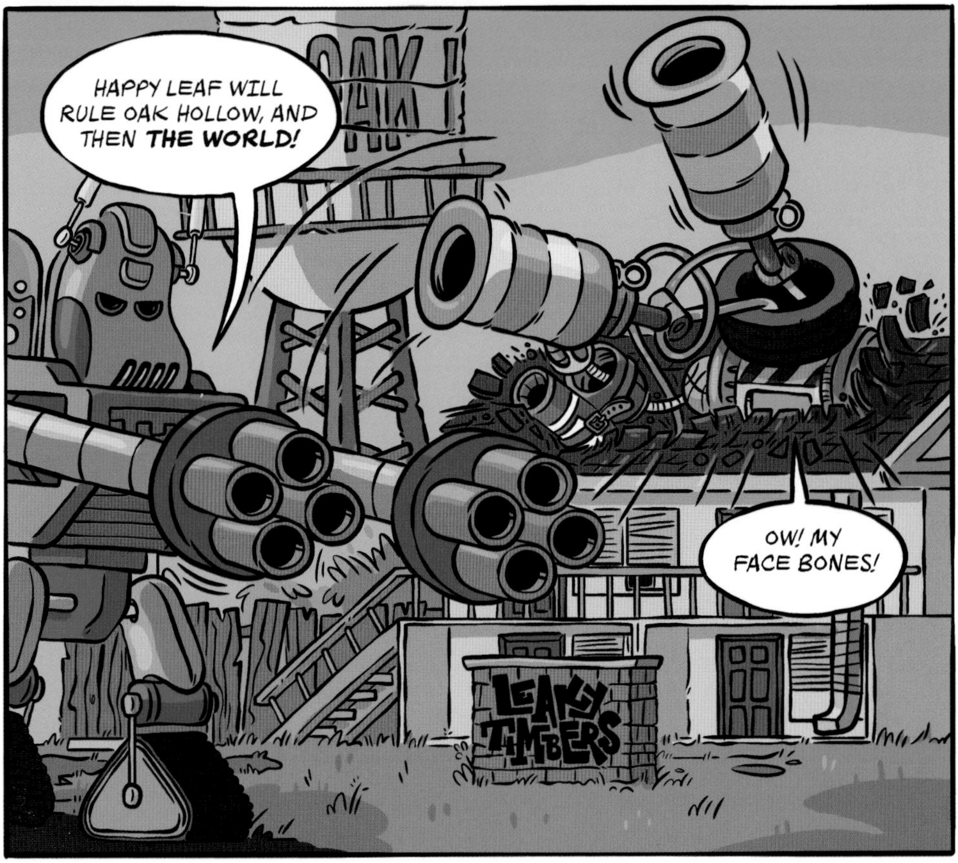
HAPPY LEAF WILL RULE OAK HOLLOW, AND THEN THE WORLD!
OW! MY FACE BONES!
LEAKY TIMBERS

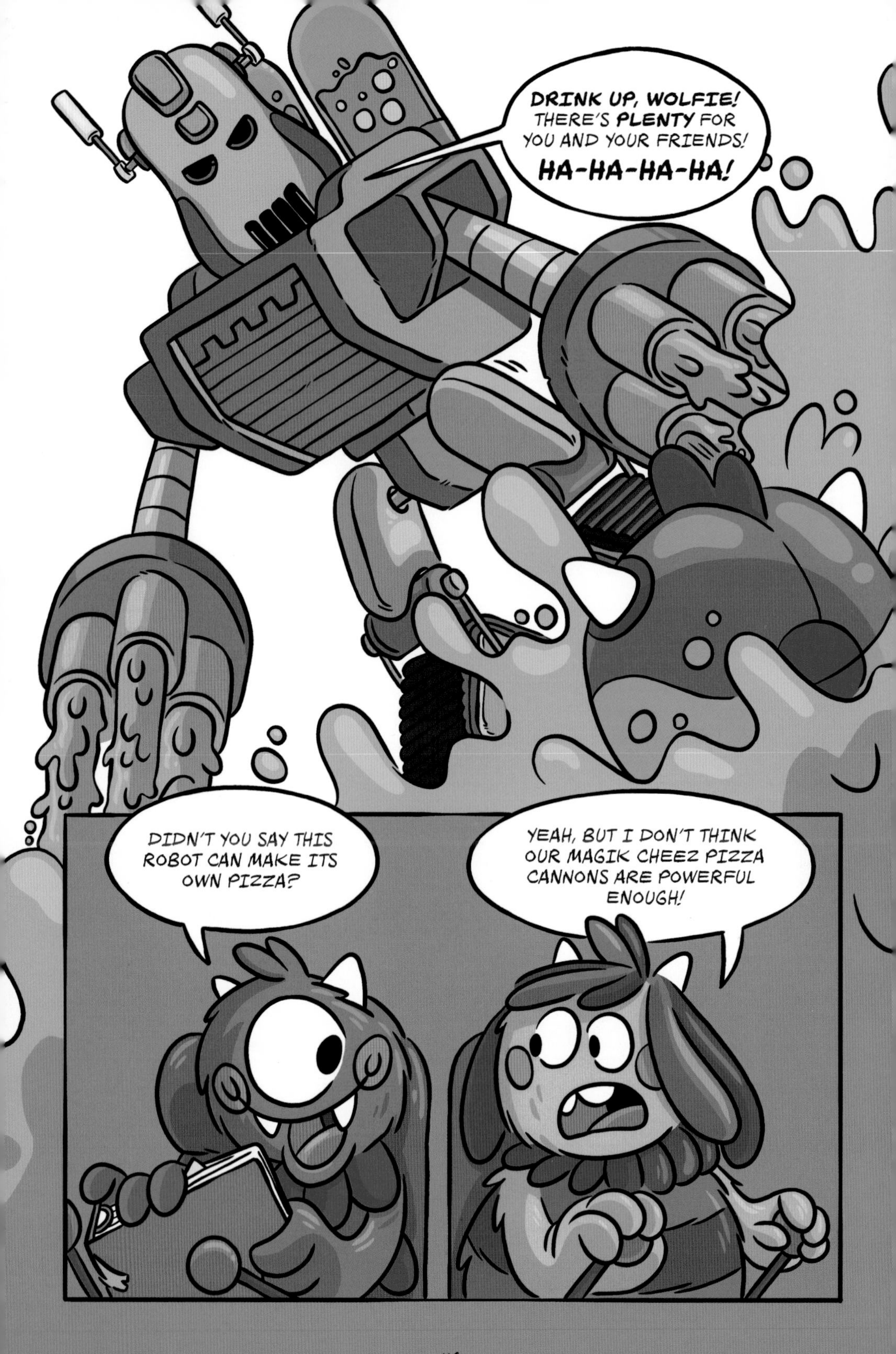
DRINK UP, WOLFIE! THERE'S PLENTY FOR YOU AND YOUR FRIENDS! HA-HA-HA-HA!
DIDN'T YOU SAY THIS ROBOT CAN MAKE ITS OWN PIZZA?
YEAH, BUT I DON'T THINK OUR MAGIK CHEEZ PIZZA CANNONS ARE POWERFUL ENOUGH!

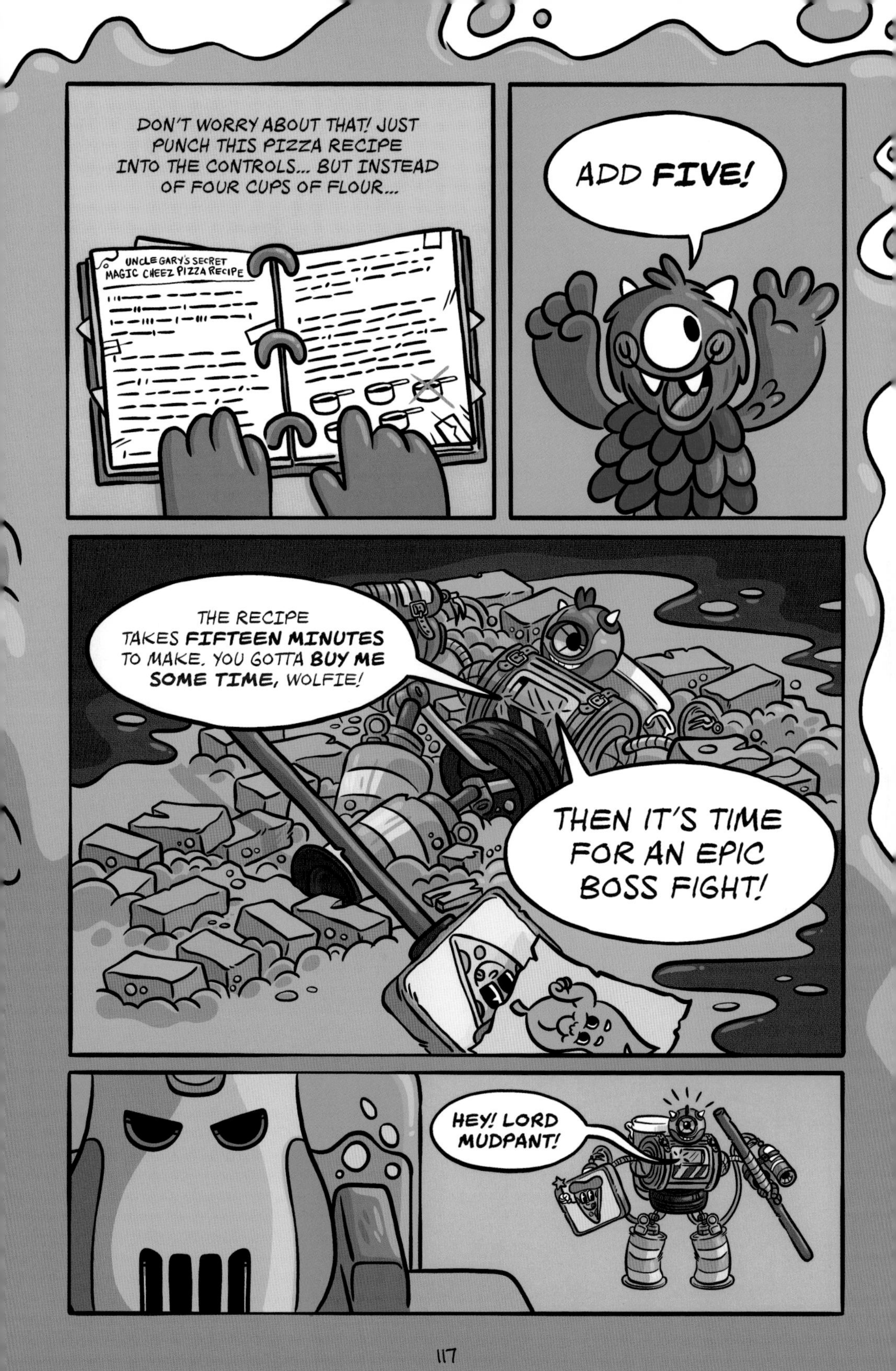
DON'T WORRY ABOUT THAT! JUST PUNCH THIS PIZZA RECIPE INTO THE CONTROLS... BUT INSTEAD OF FOUR CUPS OF FLOUR...
UNCLE GARY'S SECRET MAGIC CHEEZ PIZZA RECIPE
ADD **FIVE!**
THE RECIPE TAKES **FIFTEEN MINUTES** TO MAKE. YOU GOTTA **BUY ME SOME TIME,** WOLFIE!
THEN IT'S TIME FOR AN EPIC BOSS FIGHT!
HEY! LORD MUDPANT!

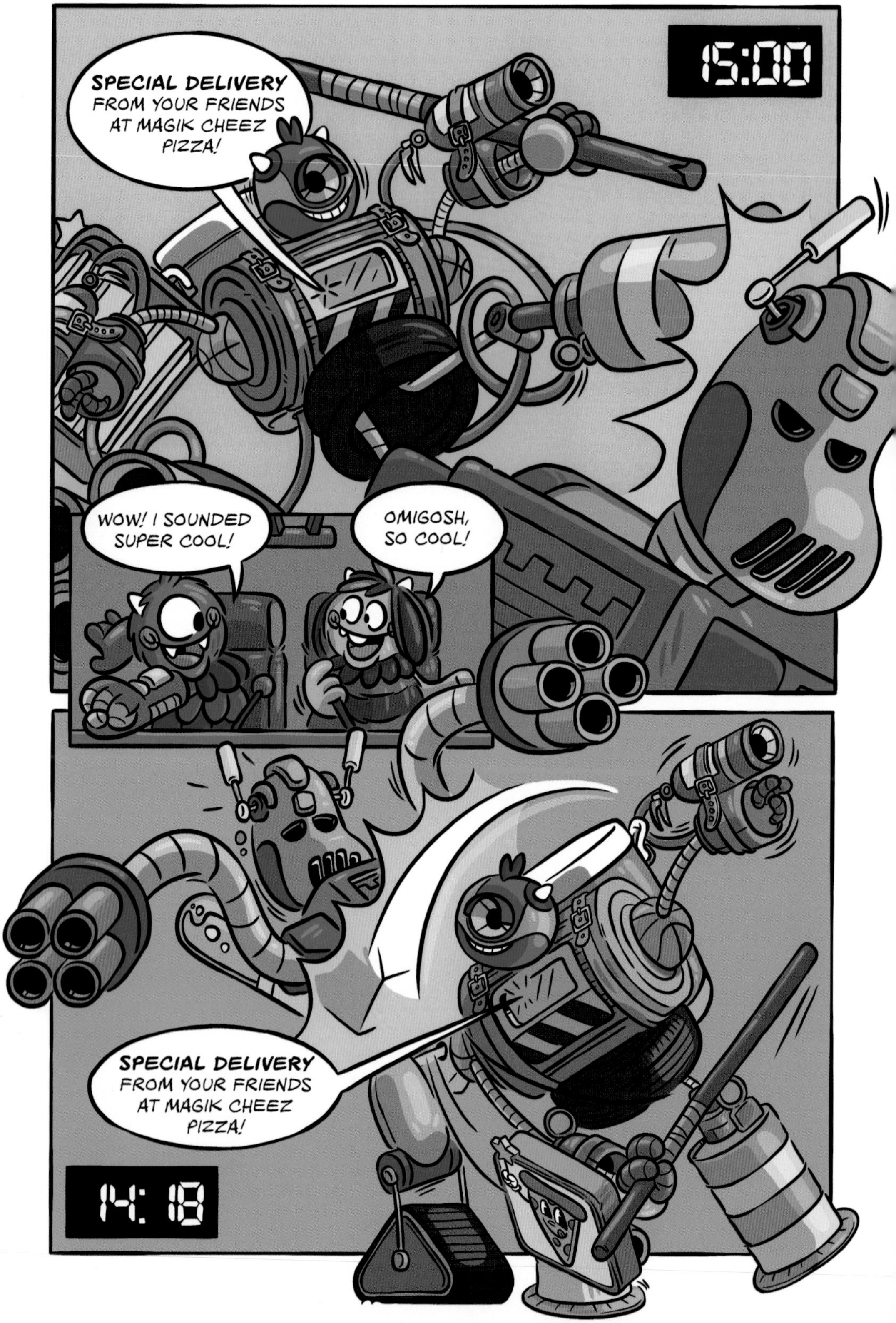
15:00
SPECIAL DELIVERY FROM YOUR FRIENDS AT MAGIK CHEEZ PIZZA!
WOW! I SOUNDED SUPER COOL!
OMIGOSH, SO COOL!
SPECIAL DELIVERY FROM YOUR FRIENDS AT MAGIK CHEEZ PIZZA!
14:18

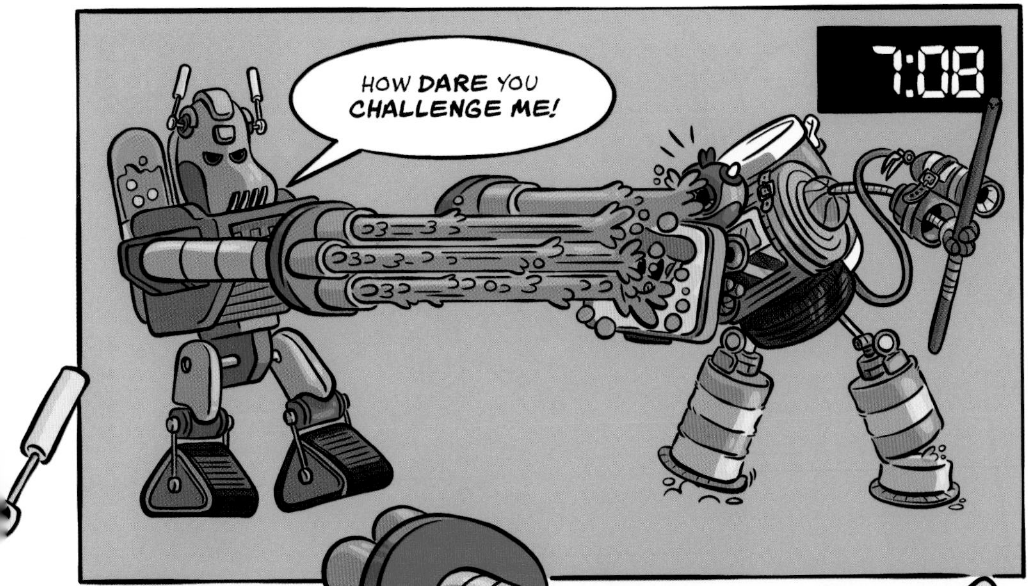
7:08
HOW **DARE** YOU **CHALLENGE ME!**

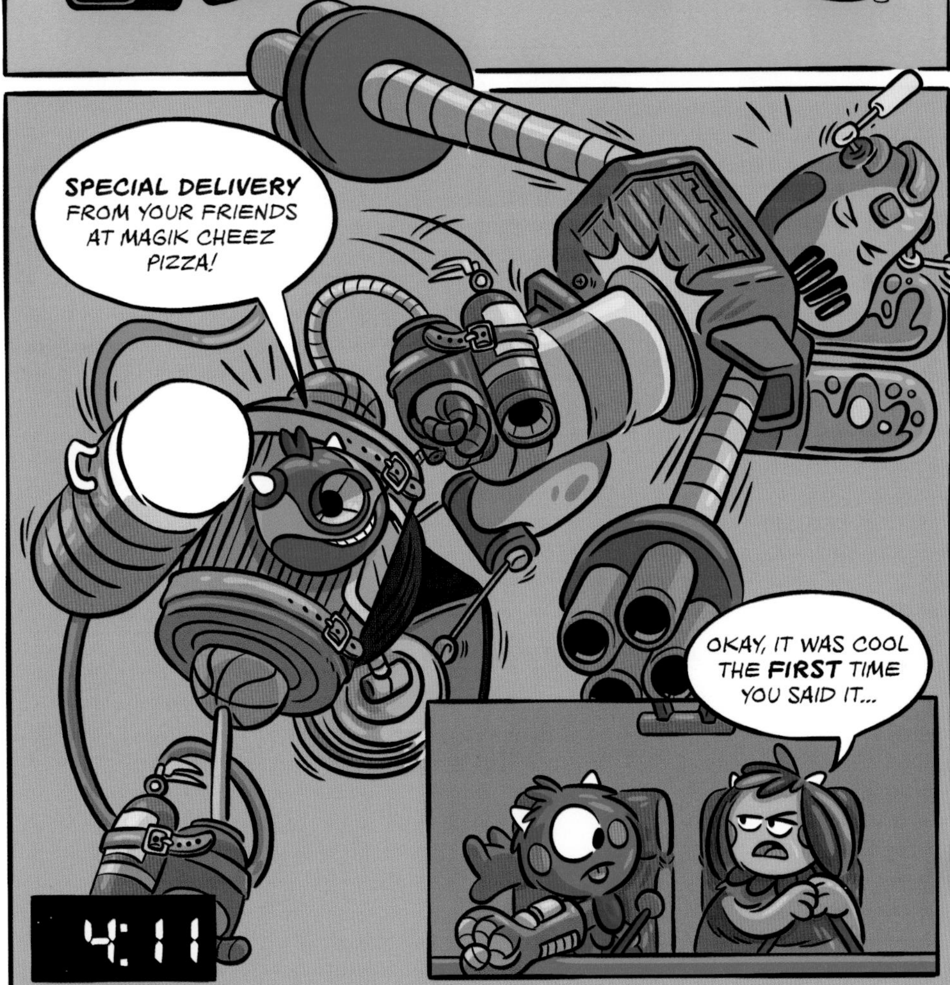
SPECIAL DELIVERY FROM YOUR FRIENDS AT MAGIK CHEEZ PIZZA!
OKAY, IT WAS COOL THE **FIRST** TIME YOU SAID IT...
4:11

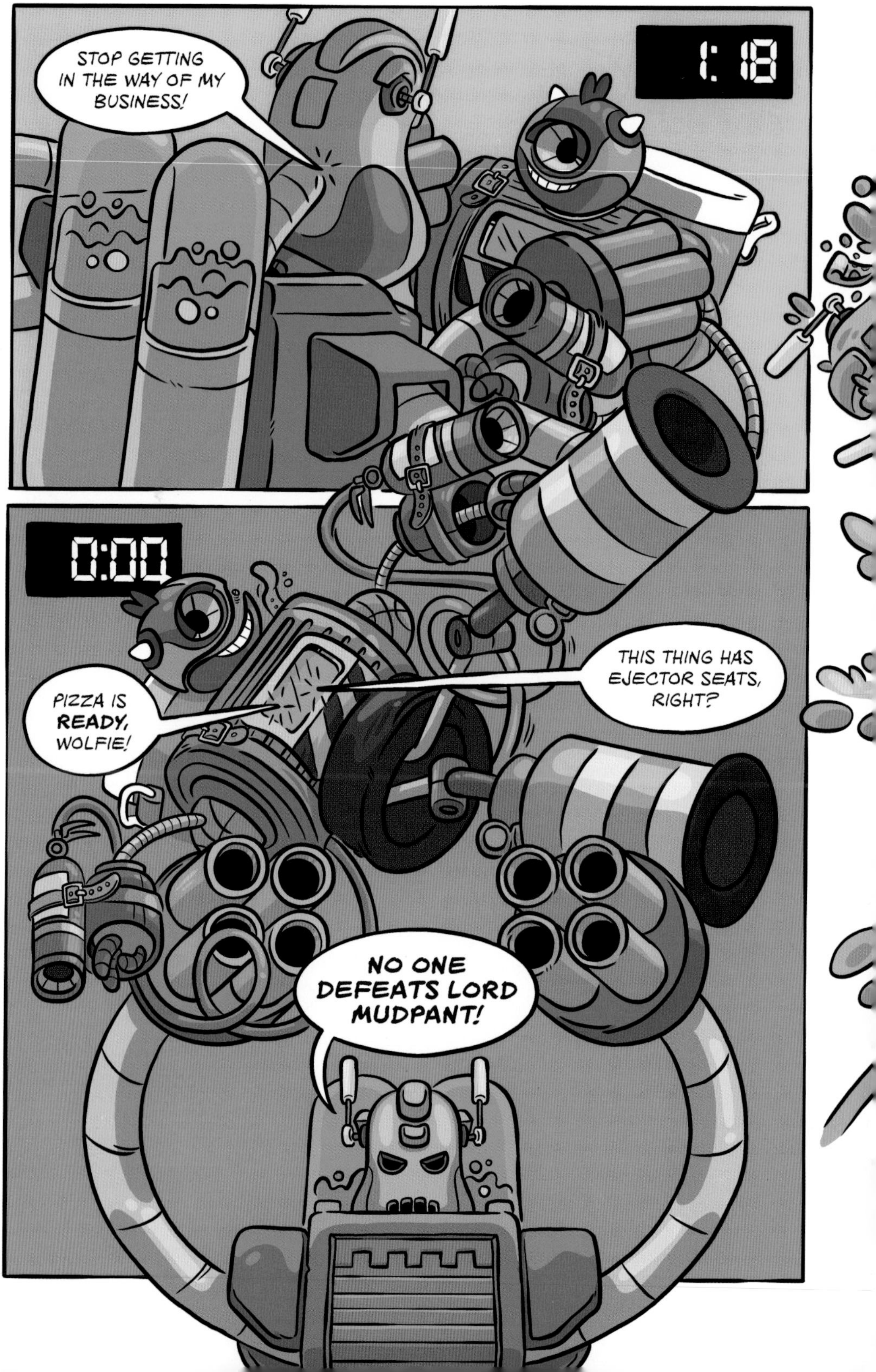
1:18
STOP GETTING IN THE WAY OF MY BUSINESS!
0:00
THIS THING HAS EJECTOR SEATS, RIGHT?
PIZZA IS READY, WOLFIE!
NO ONE DEFEATS LORD MUDPANT!

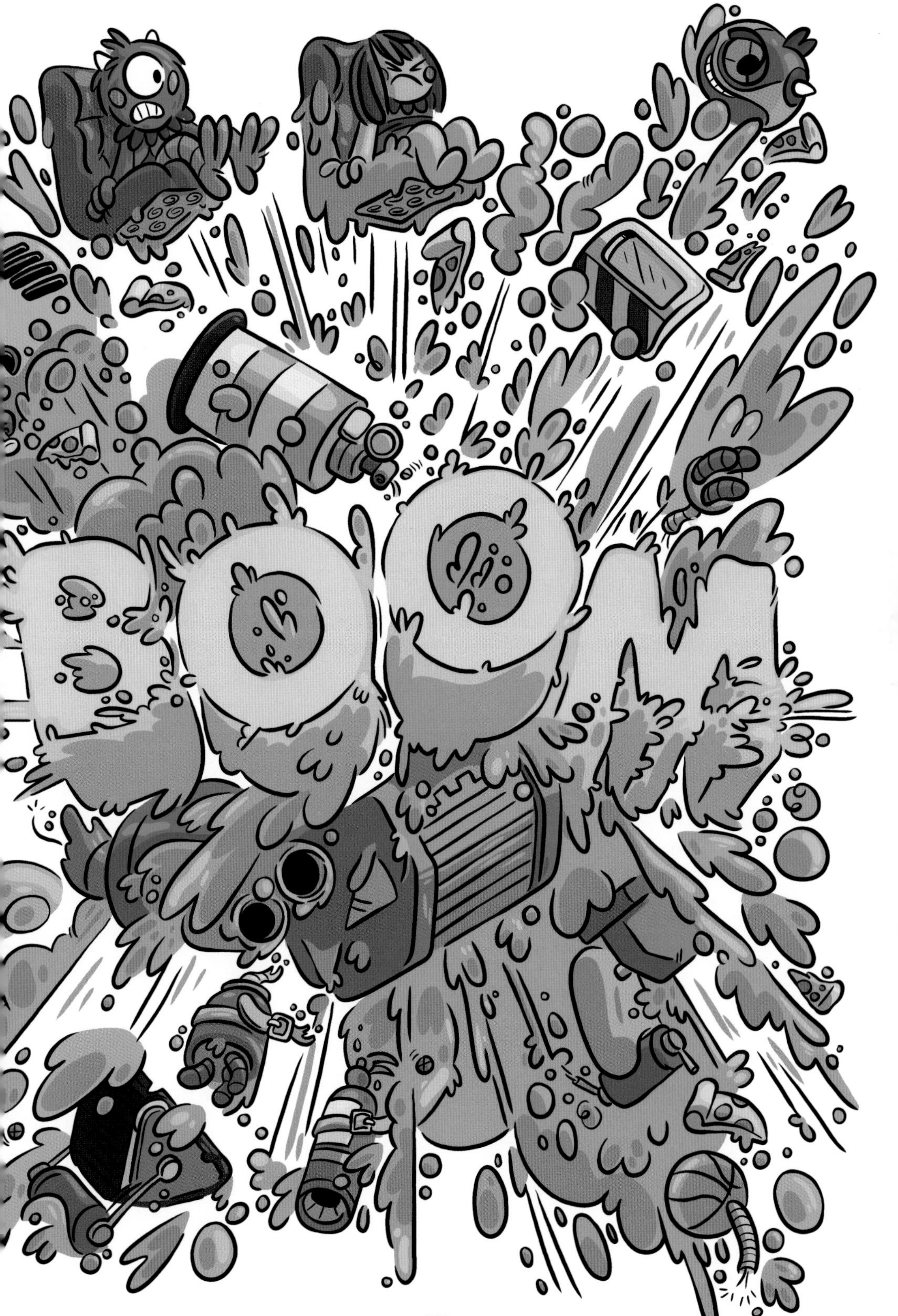
BOOM

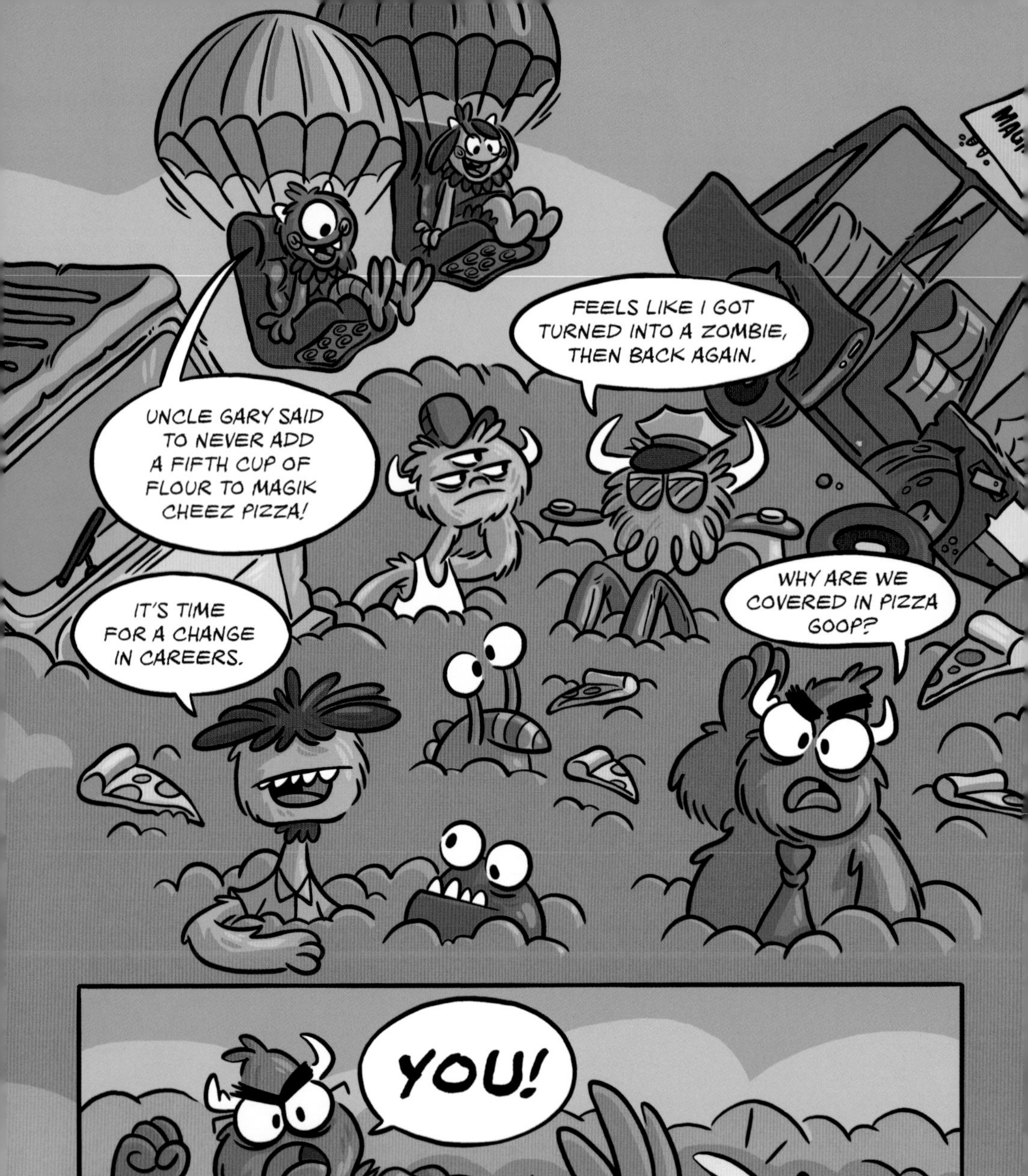
UNCLE GARY SAID TO NEVER ADD A FIFTH CUP OF FLOUR TO MAGIK CHEEZ PIZZA!
FEELS LIKE I GOT TURNED INTO A ZOMBIE, THEN BACK AGAIN.
IT'S TIME FOR A CHANGE IN CAREERS.
WHY ARE WE COVERED IN PIZZA GOOP?

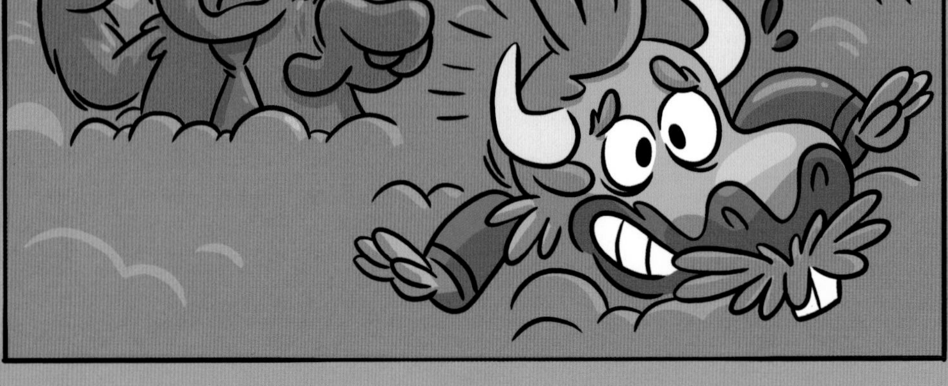
YOU!

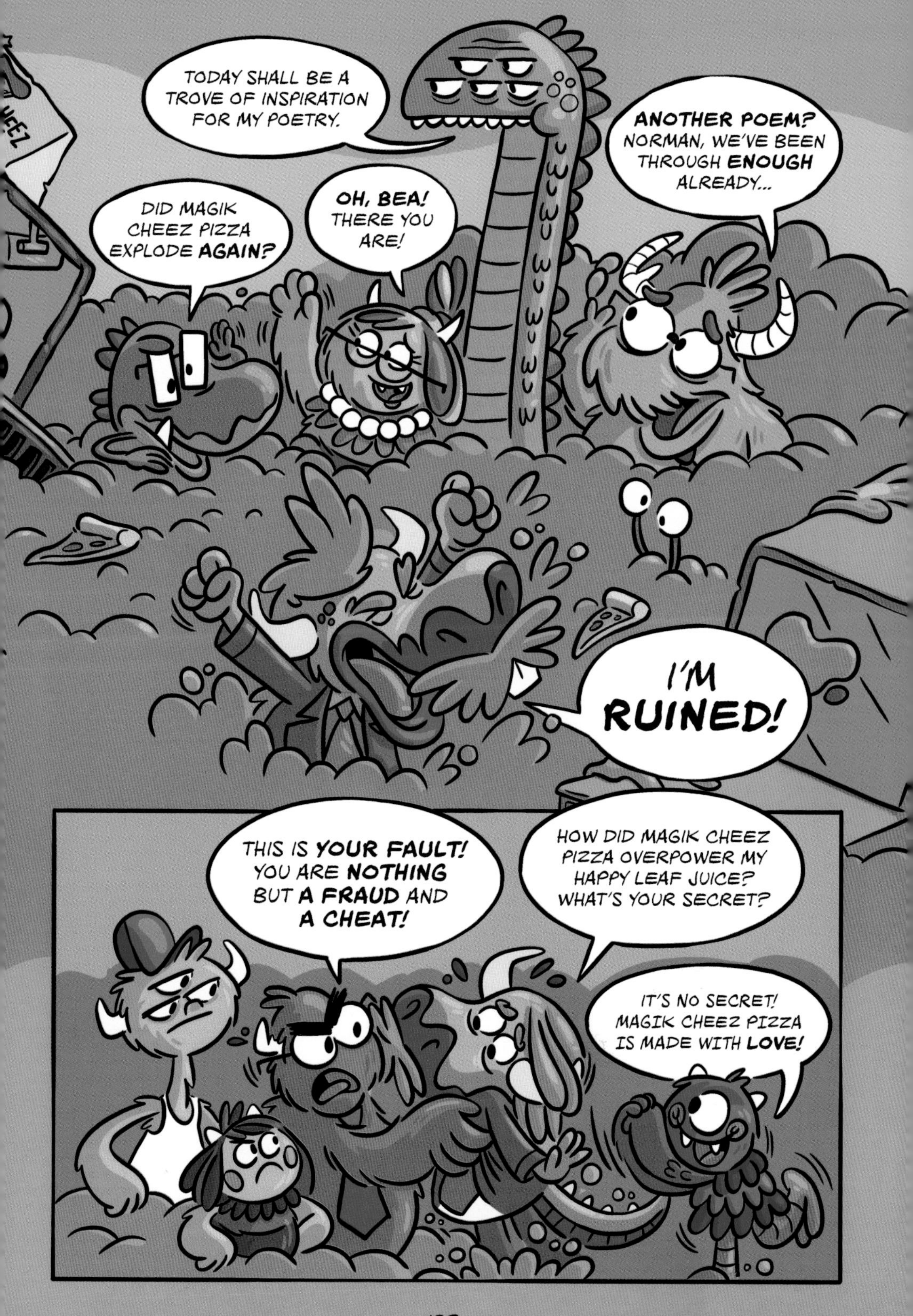
TODAY SHALL BE A TROVE OF INSPIRATION FOR MY POETRY.
ANOTHER POEM? NORMAN, WE'VE BEEN THROUGH ENOUGH ALREADY...
DID MAGIK CHEEZ PIZZA EXPLODE AGAIN?
OH, BEA! THERE YOU ARE!
I'M RUINED!
THIS IS YOUR FAULT! YOU ARE NOTHING BUT A FRAUD AND A CHEAT!
HOW DID MAGIK CHEEZ PIZZA OVERPOWER MY HAPPY LEAF JUICE? WHAT'S YOUR SECRET?
IT'S NO SECRET! MAGIK CHEEZ PIZZA IS MADE WITH LOVE!

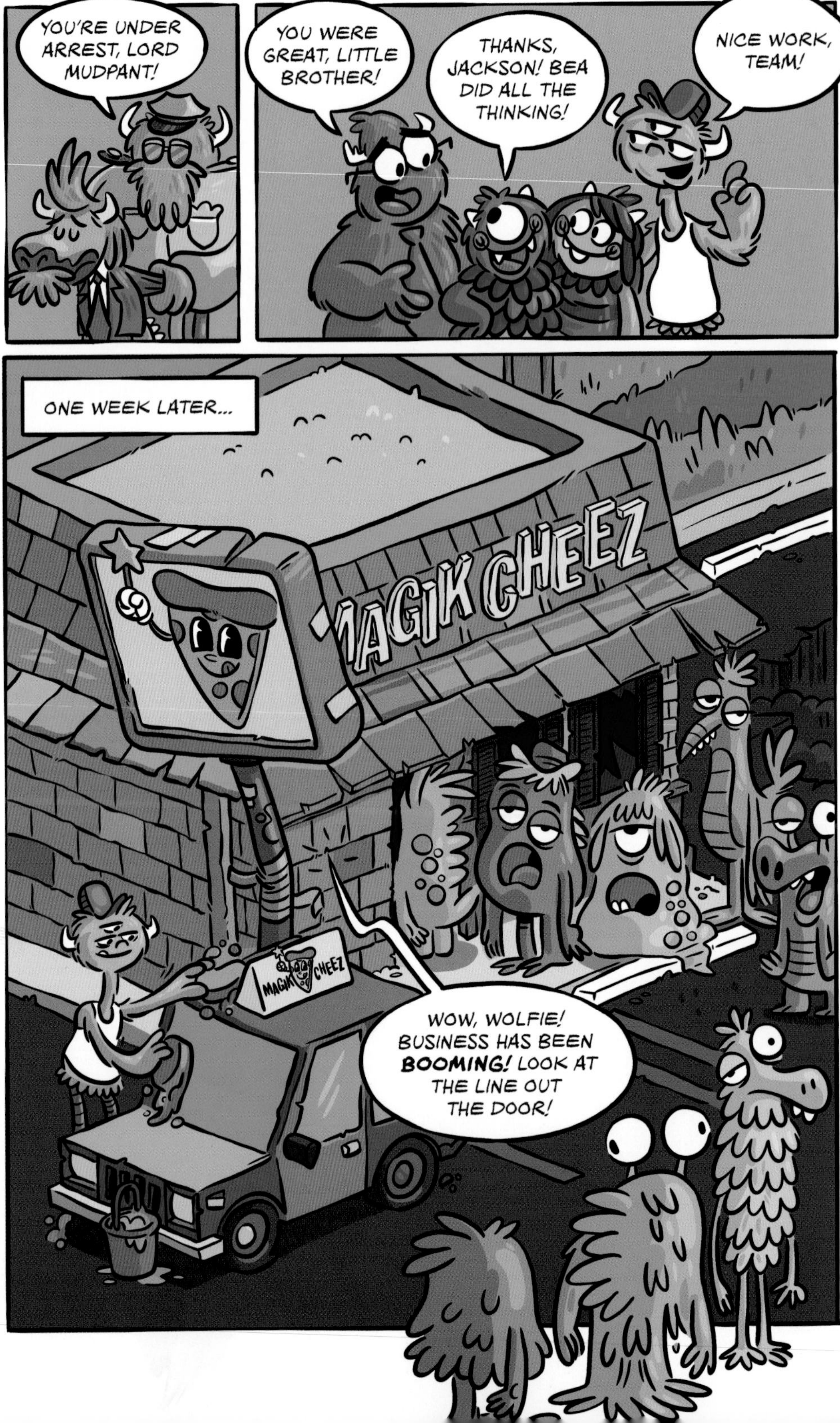
YOU'RE UNDER ARREST, LORD MUDPANT!
YOU WERE GREAT, LITTLE BROTHER!
THANKS, JACKSON! BEA DID ALL THE THINKING!
NICE WORK, TEAM!
ONE WEEK LATER...
MAGIK CHEEZ
MAGIK CHEEZ
WOW, WOLFIE! BUSINESS HAS BEEN **BOOMING!** LOOK AT THE LINE OUT THE DOOR!

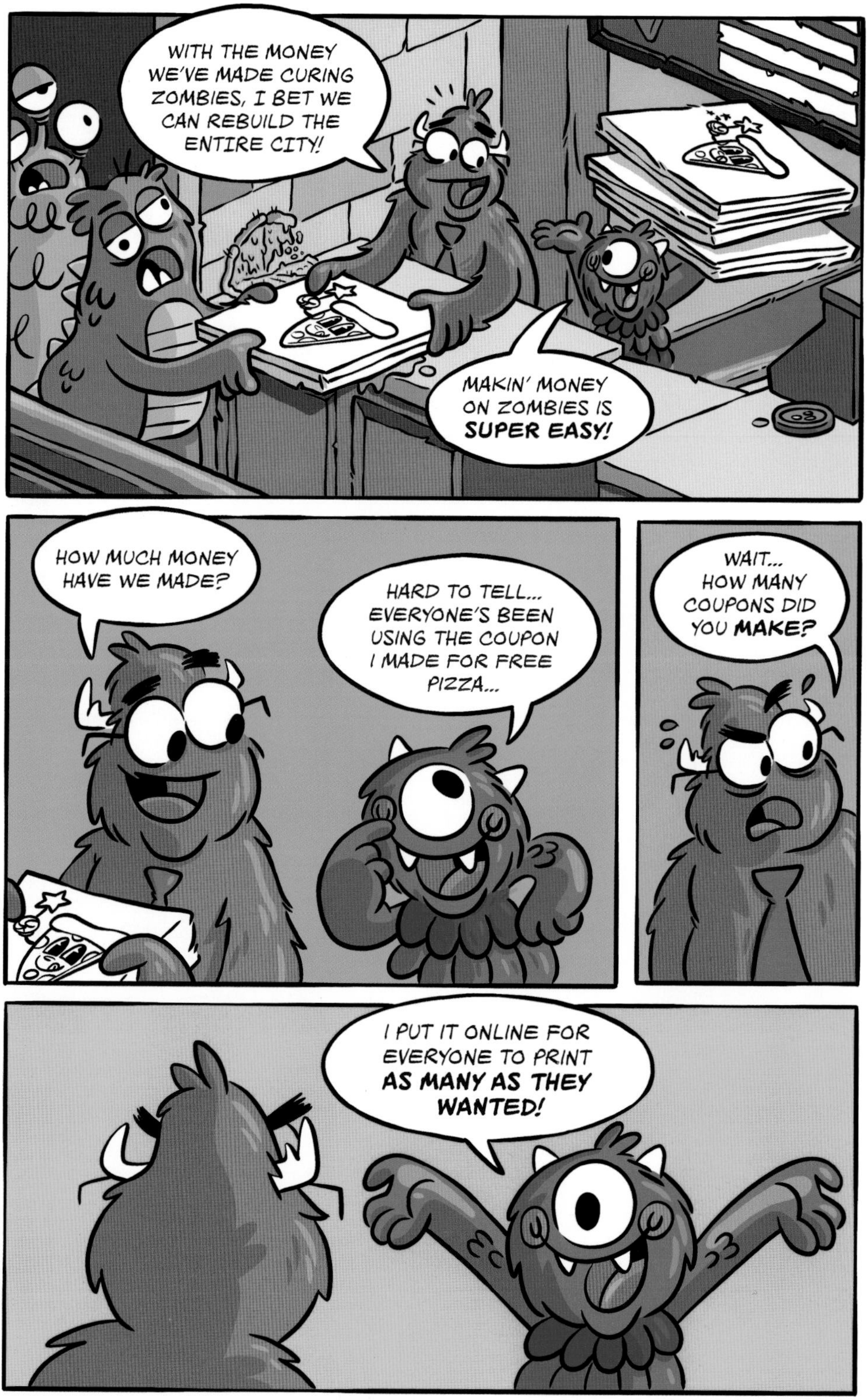
WITH THE MONEY WE'VE MADE CURING ZOMBIES, I BET WE CAN REBUILD THE ENTIRE CITY!
MAKIN' MONEY ON ZOMBIES IS **SUPER EASY!**
HOW MUCH MONEY HAVE WE MADE?
HARD TO TELL... EVERYONE'S BEEN USING THE COUPON I MADE FOR FREE PIZZA...
WAIT... HOW MANY COUPONS DID YOU **MAKE?**
I PUT IT ONLINE FOR EVERYONE TO PRINT **AS MANY AS THEY WANTED!**

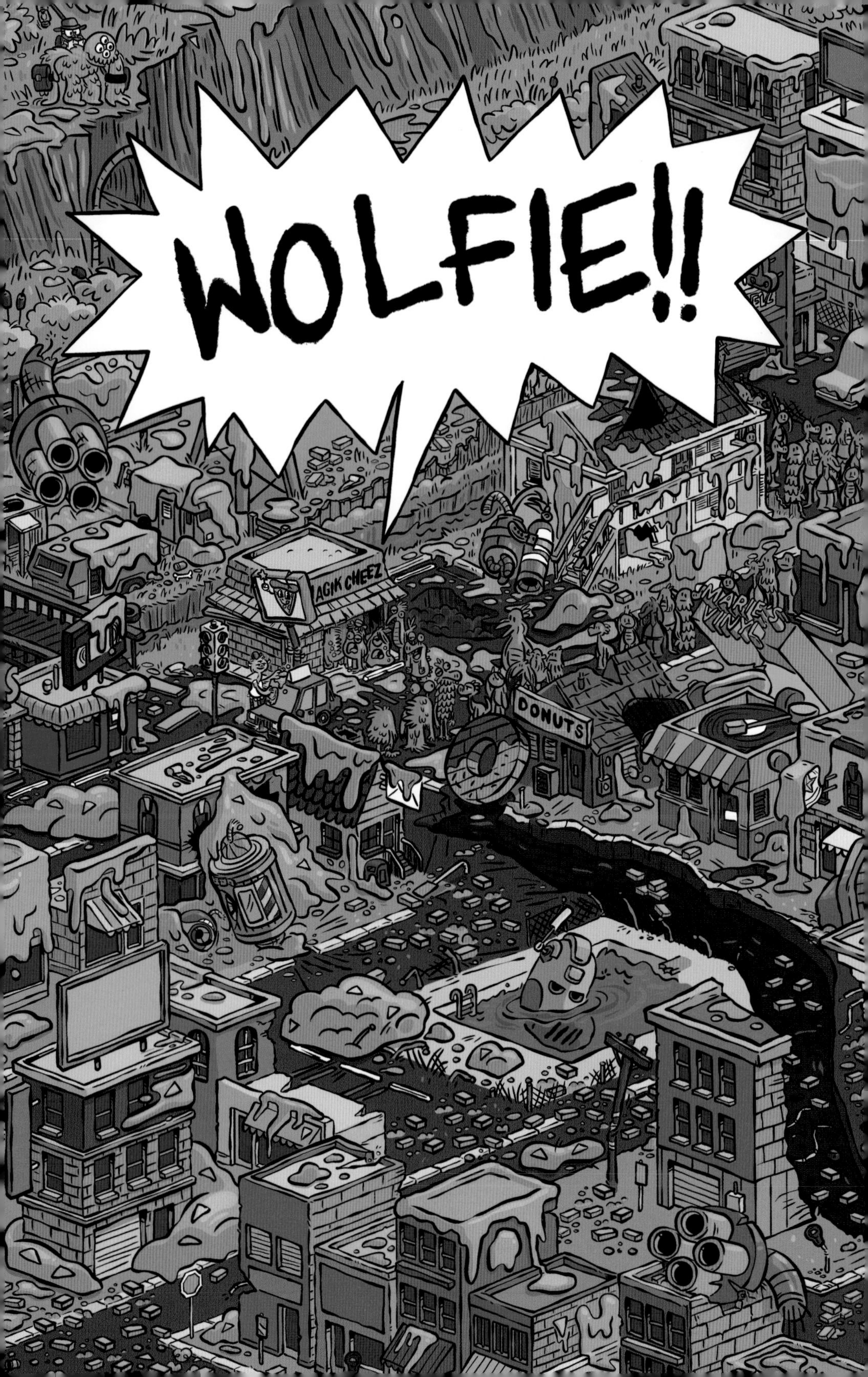
WOLFIE!!
AGIK CHEEZ
DONUTS

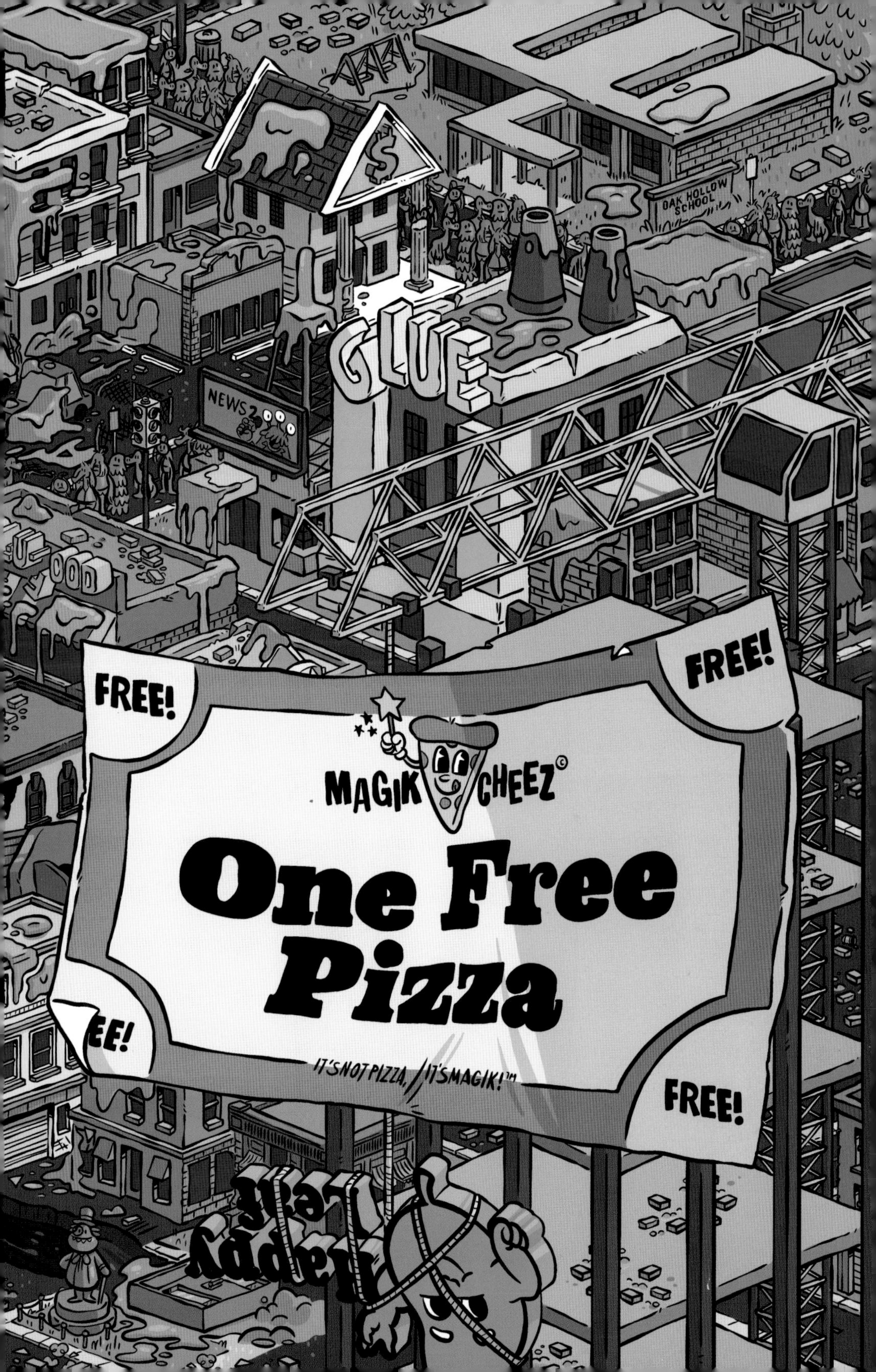
OAK HOLLOW SCHOOL
GLUE
FREE!
FREE!
MAGIK CHEEZ©
One Free Pizza
IT'S NOT PIZZA, IT'S MAGIK!™
FREE!

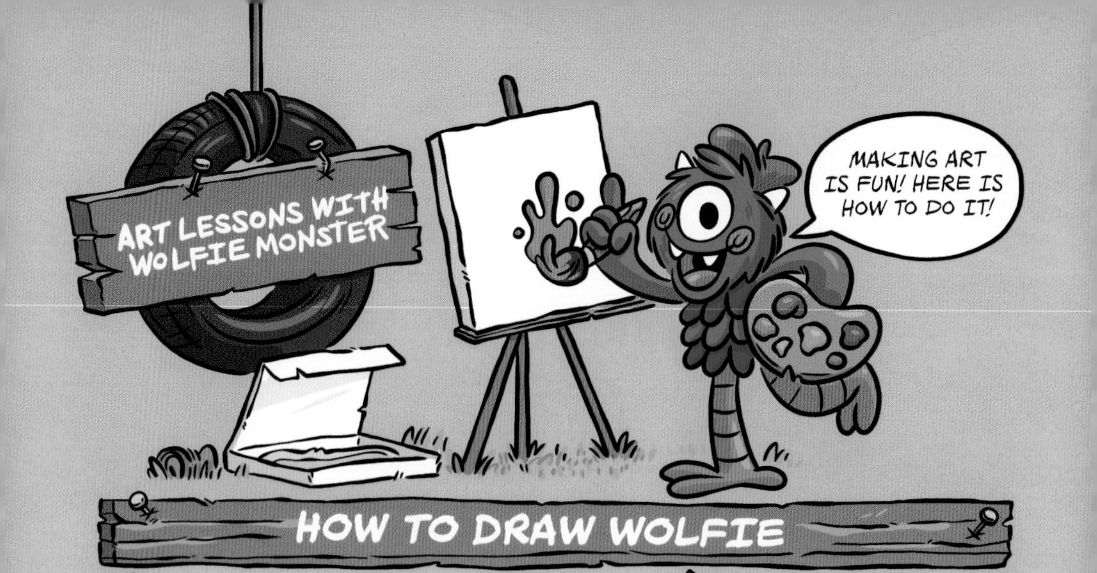
ART LESSONS WITH WOLFIE MONSTER
MAKING ART IS FUN! HERE IS HOW TO DO IT!

HOW TO DRAW WOLFIE

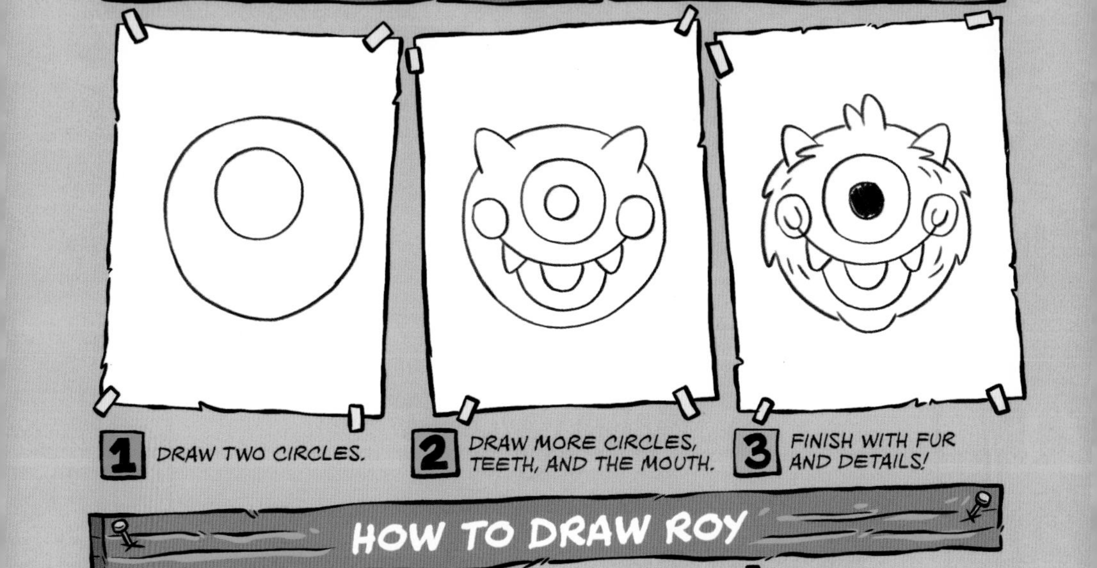

1 DRAW TWO CIRCLES.

2 DRAW MORE CIRCLES, TEETH, AND THE MOUTH.

3 FINISH WITH FUR AND DETAILS!

HOW TO DRAW ROY

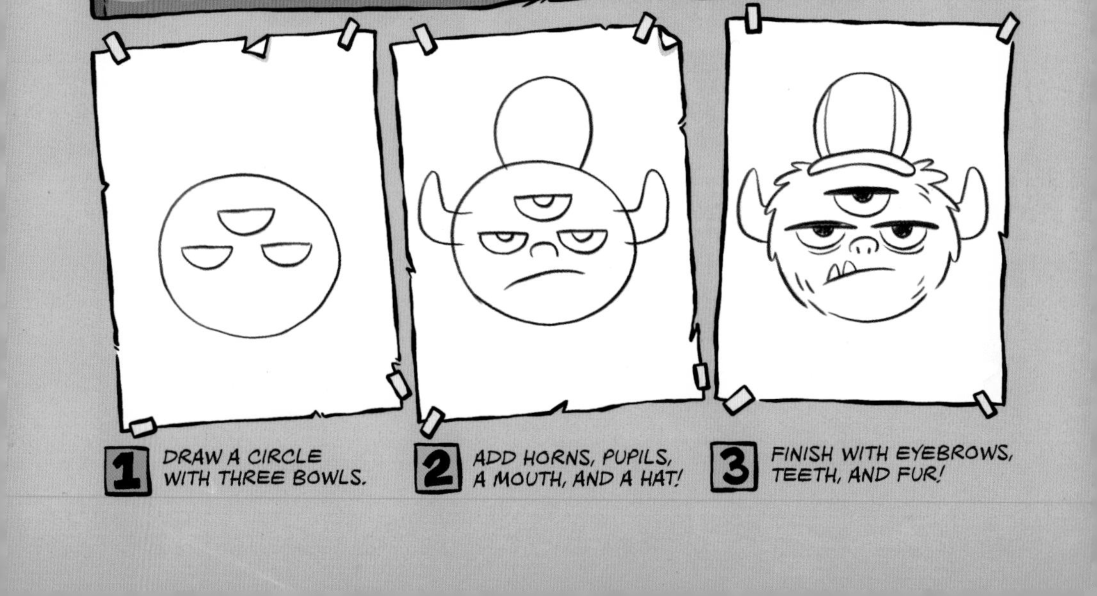

1 DRAW A CIRCLE WITH THREE BOWLS.

2 ADD HORNS, PUPILS, A MOUTH, AND A HAT!

3 FINISH WITH EYEBROWS, TEETH, AND FUR!

HOW TO DRAW JACKSON

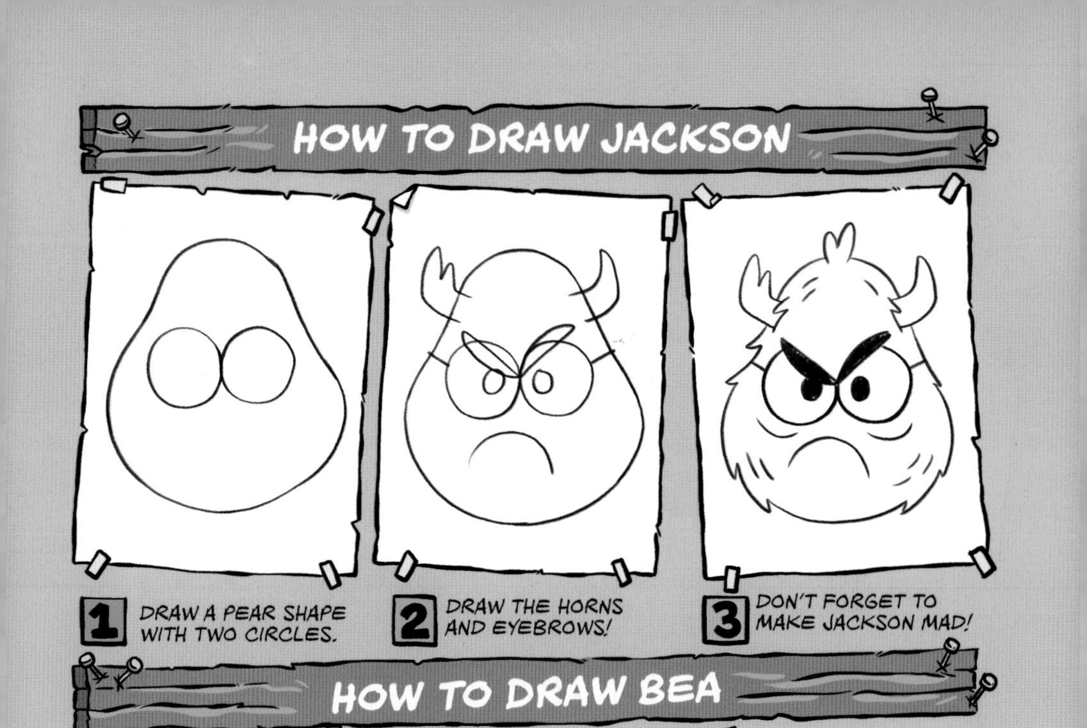

1 DRAW A PEAR SHAPE WITH TWO CIRCLES.

2 DRAW THE HORNS AND EYEBROWS!

3 DON'T FORGET TO MAKE JACKSON MAD!

HOW TO DRAW BEA

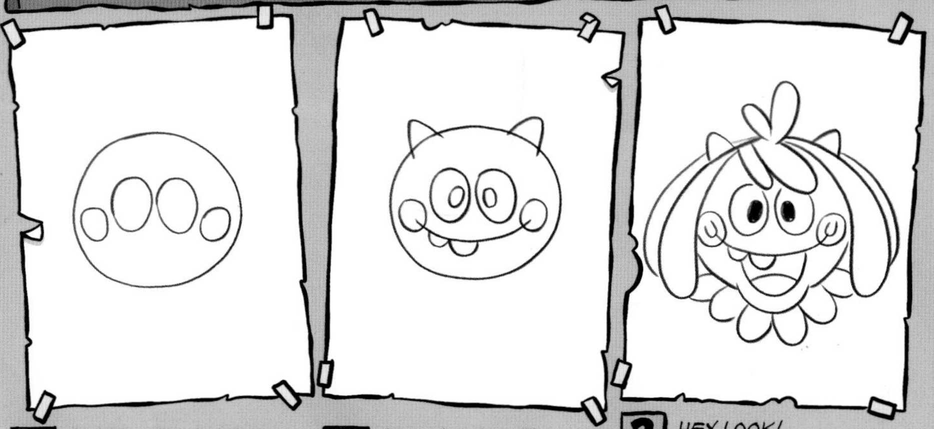

1 START WITH A CIRCLE AND SOME OVALS!

2 ADD THE MOUTH, EYES, AND HORNS.

3 HEY LOOK! IT'S BEA!

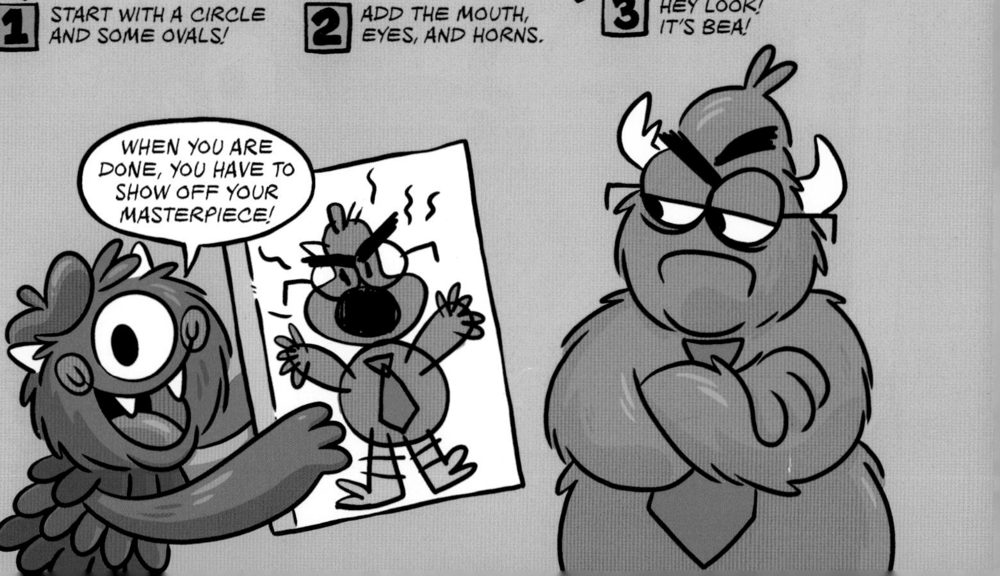
WHEN YOU ARE DONE, YOU HAVE TO SHOW OFF YOUR MASTERPIECE!

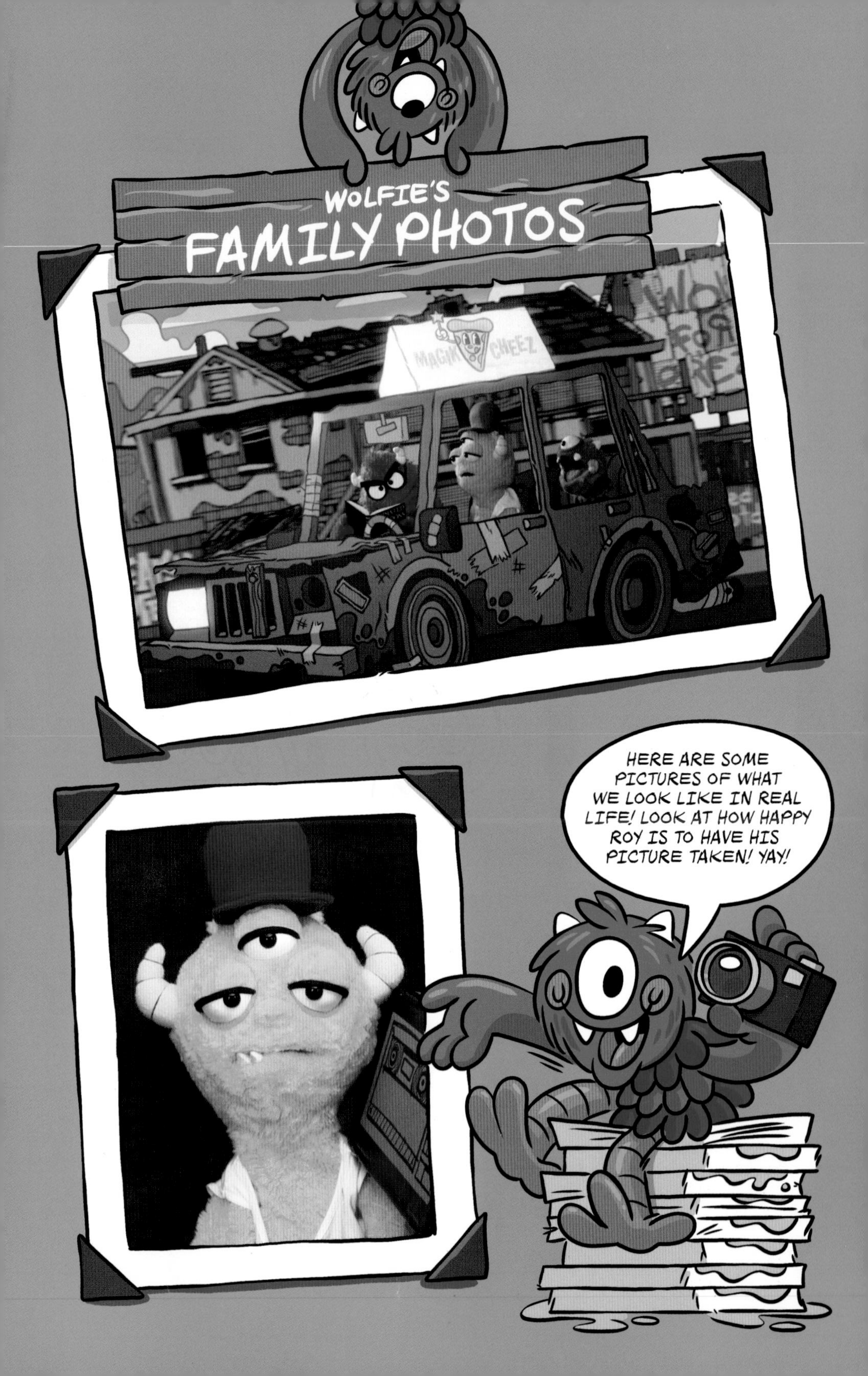
WOLFIE'S
FAMILY PHOTOS
MAGIK CHEEZ
HERE ARE SOME PICTURES OF WHAT WE LOOK LIKE IN REAL LIFE! LOOK AT HOW HAPPY ROY IS TO HAVE HIS PICTURE TAKEN! YAY!

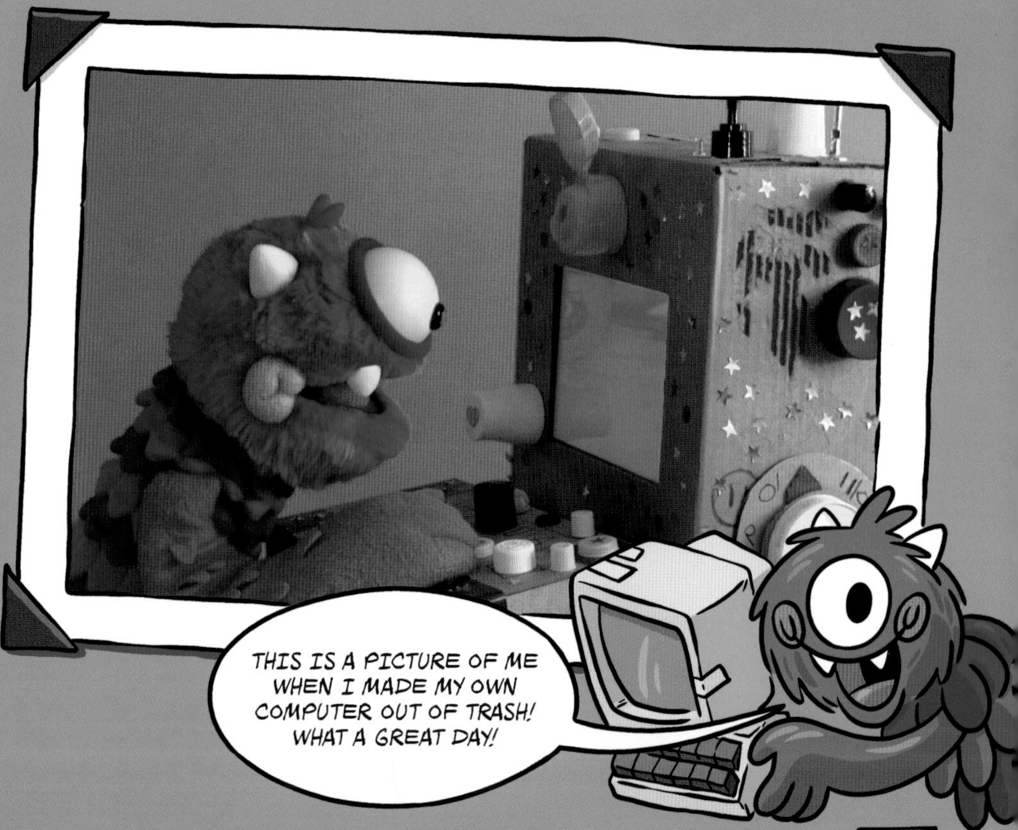
THIS IS A PICTURE OF ME WHEN I MADE MY OWN COMPUTER OUT OF TRASH! WHAT A GREAT DAY!

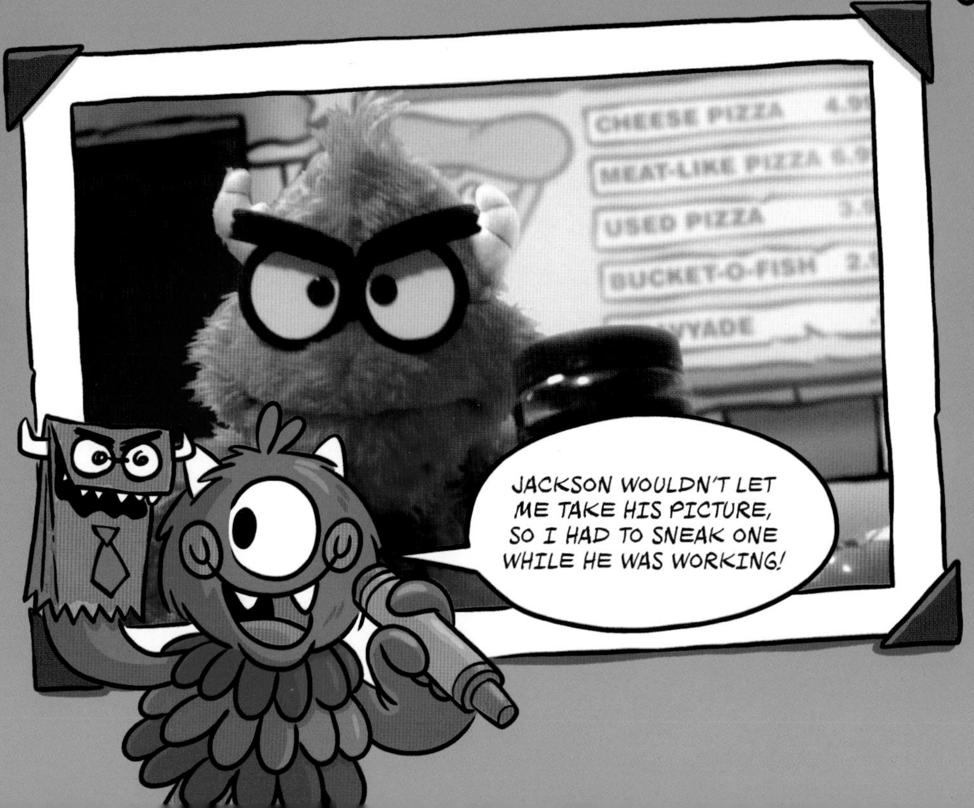
CHEESE PIZZA
MEAT-LIKE PIZZA
USED PIZZA
BUCKET-O-FISH
JACKSON WOULDN'T LET ME TAKE HIS PICTURE, SO I HAD TO SNEAK ONE WHILE HE WAS WORKING!

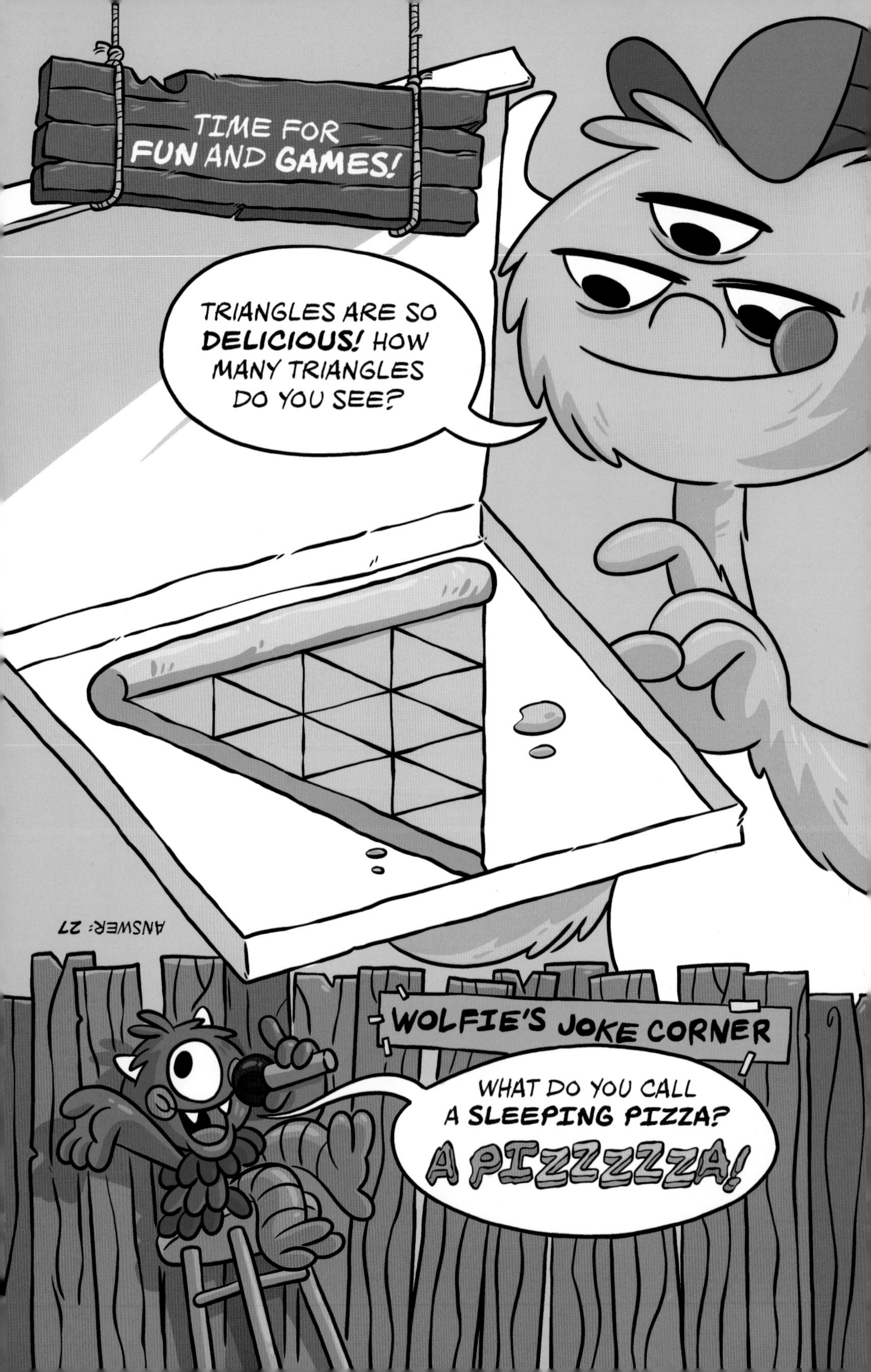
TIME FOR FUN AND GAMES!
TRIANGLES ARE SO DELICIOUS! HOW MANY TRIANGLES DO YOU SEE?
ANSWER: 27
WOLFIE'S JOKE CORNER
WHAT DO YOU CALL A SLEEPING PIZZA?
A PIZZZZZZA!

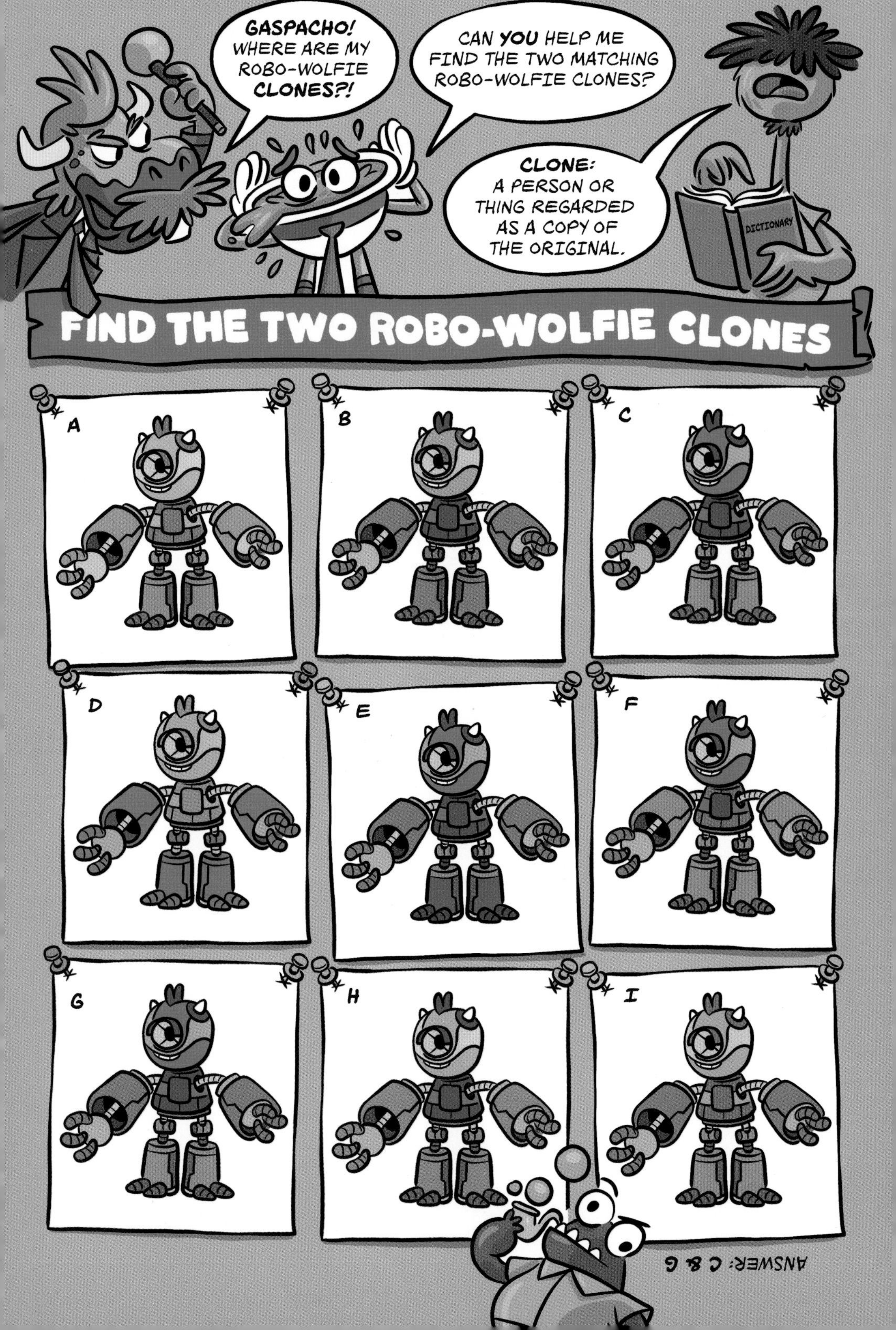
GASPACHO! WHERE ARE MY ROBO-WOLFIE CLONES?!
CAN YOU HELP ME FIND THE TWO MATCHING ROBO-WOLFIE CLONES?
CLONE: A PERSON OR THING REGARDED AS A COPY OF THE ORIGINAL.
DICTIONARY
FIND THE TWO ROBO-WOLFIE CLONES
A
B
C
D
E
F
G
H
I

ANSWER: C & G

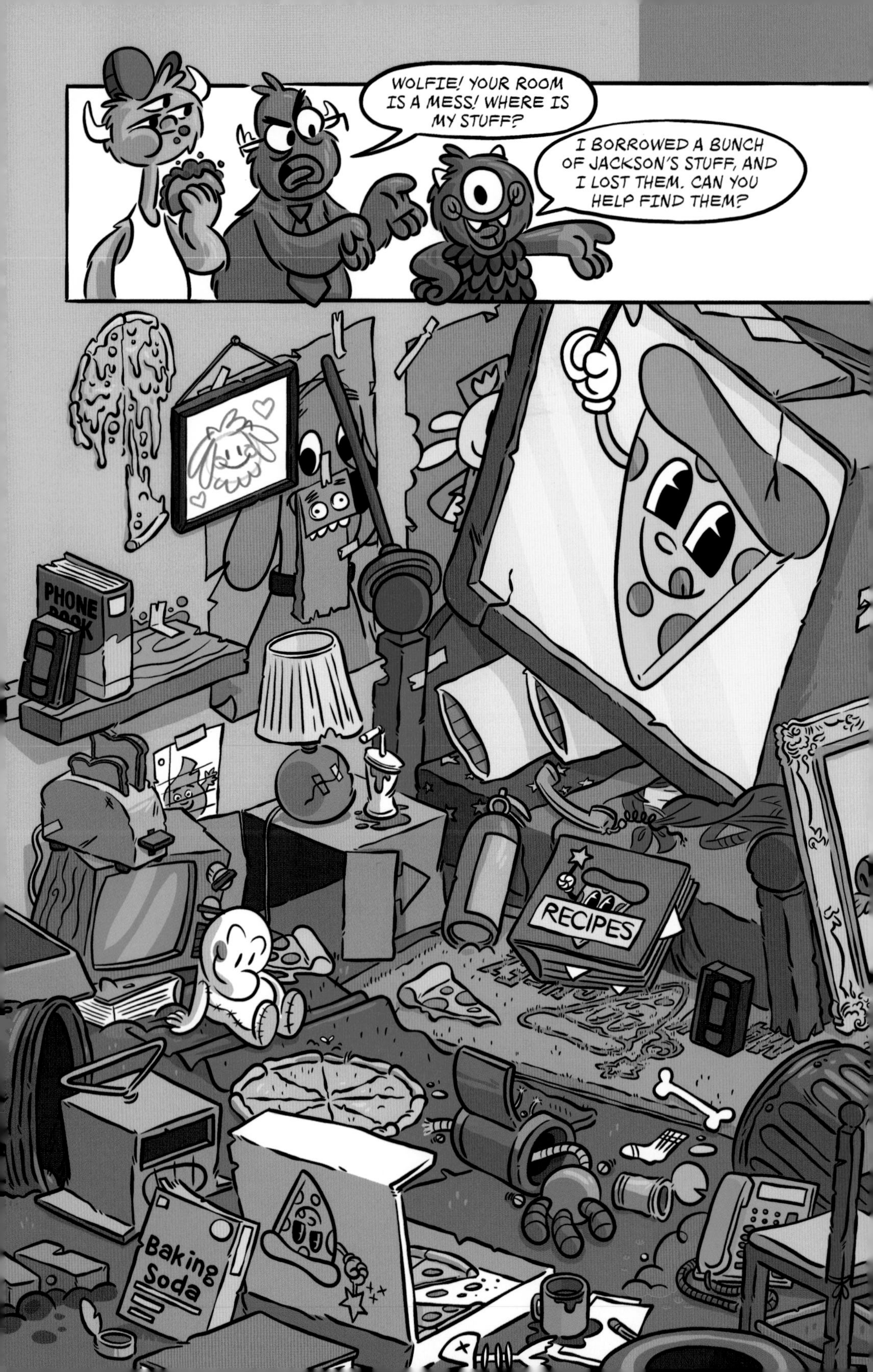
WOLFIE! YOUR ROOM IS A MESS! WHERE IS MY STUFF?
I BORROWED A BUNCH OF JACKSON'S STUFF, AND I LOST THEM. CAN YOU HELP FIND THEM?
PHONE BOOK
RECIPES
Baking Soda

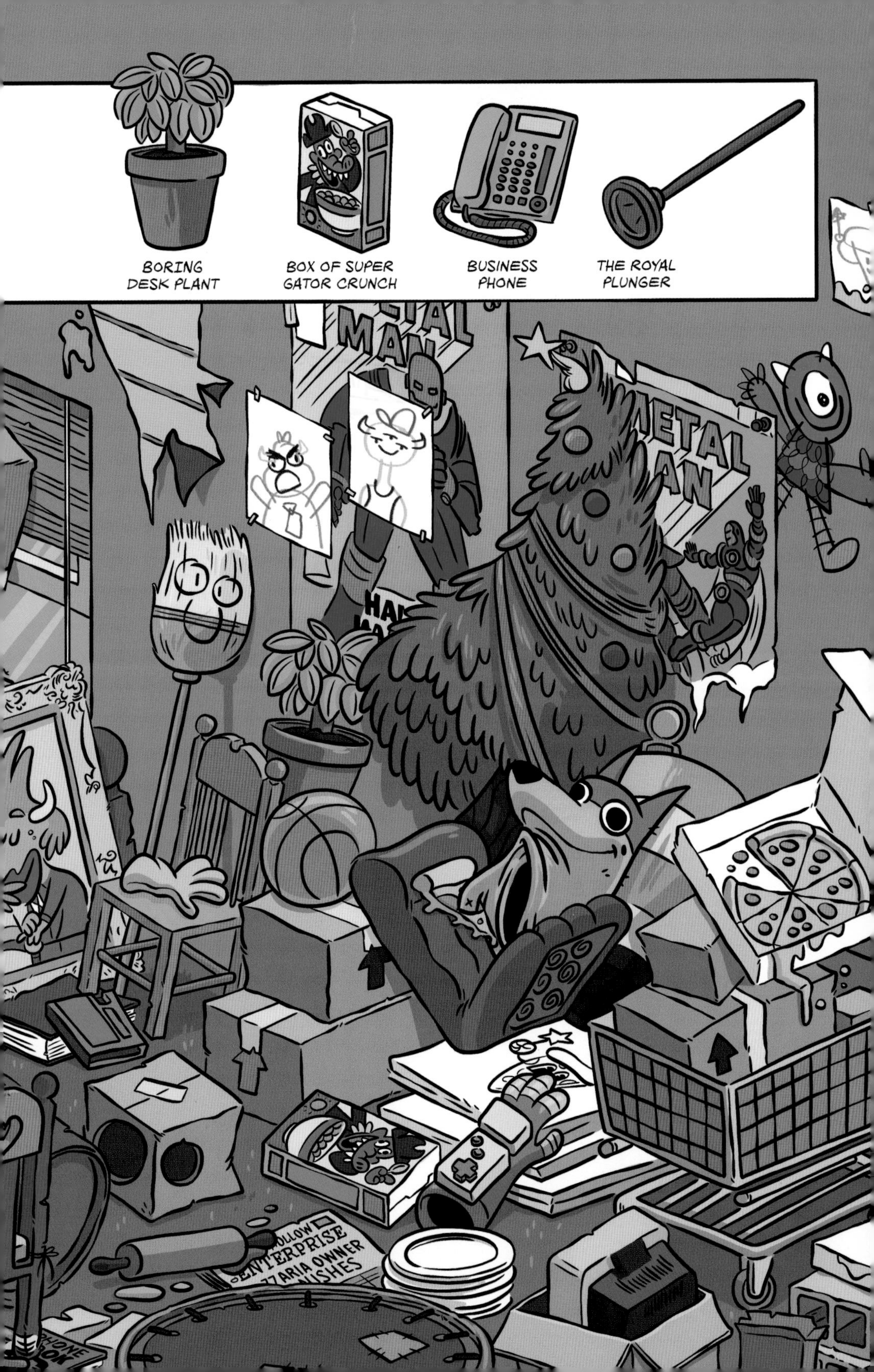

BORING DESK PLANT
BOX OF SUPER GATOR CRUNCH
BUSINESS PHONE
THE ROYAL PLUNGER
METAL
ENTERPRISE

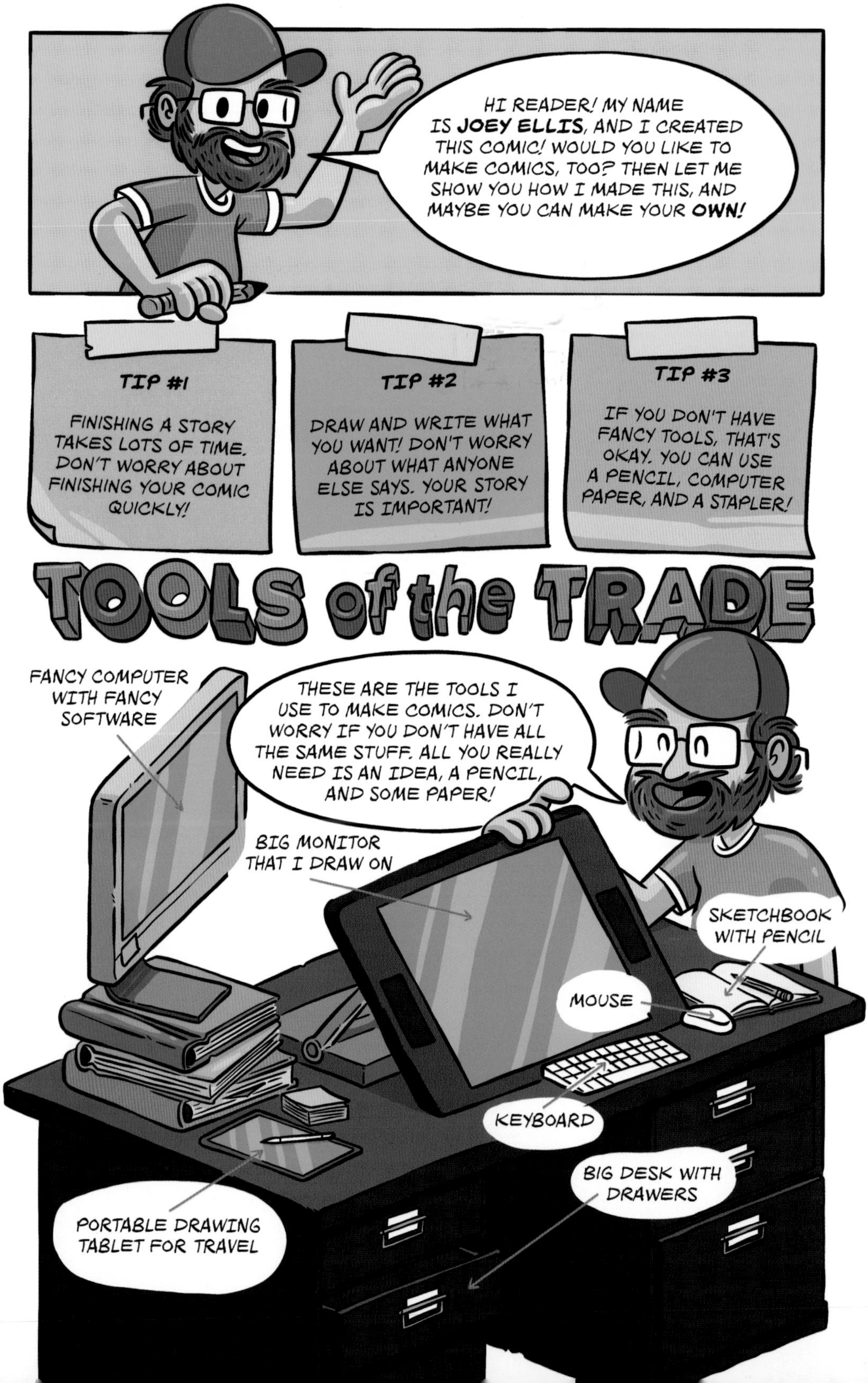

HI READER! MY NAME IS **JOEY ELLIS**, AND I CREATED THIS COMIC! WOULD YOU LIKE TO MAKE COMICS, TOO? THEN LET ME SHOW YOU HOW I MADE THIS, AND MAYBE YOU CAN MAKE YOUR **OWN!**
TIP #1
FINISHING A STORY TAKES LOTS OF TIME. DON'T WORRY ABOUT FINISHING YOUR COMIC QUICKLY!
TIP #2
DRAW AND WRITE WHAT YOU WANT! DON'T WORRY ABOUT WHAT ANYONE ELSE SAYS. YOUR STORY IS IMPORTANT!
TIP #3
IF YOU DON'T HAVE FANCY TOOLS, THAT'S OKAY. YOU CAN USE A PENCIL, COMPUTER PAPER, AND A STAPLER!
TOOLS of the TRADE
FANCY COMPUTER WITH FANCY SOFTWARE
THESE ARE THE TOOLS I USE TO MAKE COMICS. DON'T WORRY IF YOU DON'T HAVE ALL THE SAME STUFF. ALL YOU REALLY NEED IS AN IDEA, A PENCIL, AND SOME PAPER!
BIG MONITOR THAT I DRAW ON
SKETCHBOOK WITH PENCIL
MOUSE
KEYBOARD
BIG DESK WITH DRAWERS
PORTABLE DRAWING TABLET FOR TRAVEL

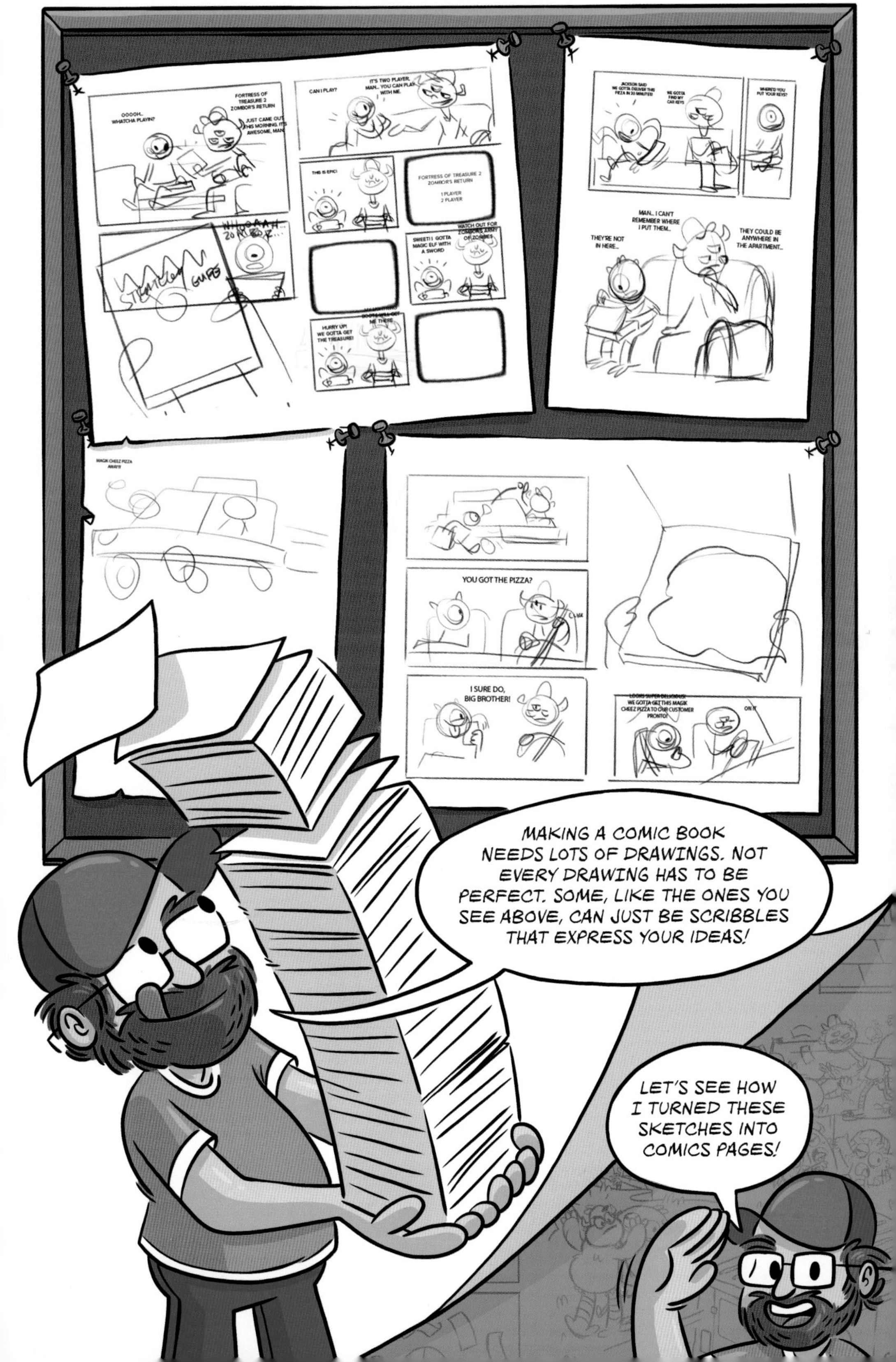
OOOOH... WHATCHA PLAYIN?
FORTRESS OF TREASURE 2 ZOMBOR'S RETURN
JUST CAME OUT THIS MORNING. IT'S AWESOME, MAN!
CAN I PLAY?
IT'S TWO PLAYER, MAN... YOU CAN PLAY WITH ME.
THIS IS EPIC!
FORTRESS OF TREASURE 2 ZOMBOR'S RETURN
1 PLAYER
2 PLAYER
SWEET! I GOTTA MAGIC ELF WITH A SWORD
WATCH OUT FOR ZOMBOR'S ARMY OF ZOMBIES
HURRY UP! WE GOTTA GET THE TREASURE!
JACKSON SAID WE GOTTA DELIVER THIS PIZZA IN 30 MINUTES!
WE GOTTA FIND MY CAR KEYS
WHERE'D YOU PUT YOUR KEYS?
MAN... I CAN'T REMEMBER WHERE I PUT THEM...
THEY'RE NOT IN HERE...
THEY COULD BE ANYWHERE IN THE APARTMENT...
YOU GOT THE PIZZA?
I SURE DO, BIG BROTHER!
WE GOTTA GET THIS MAGIK CHEEZ PIZZA TO OUR CUSTOMER PRONTO!
ON IT
MAKING A COMIC BOOK NEEDS LOTS OF DRAWINGS. NOT EVERY DRAWING HAS TO BE PERFECT. SOME, LIKE THE ONES YOU SEE ABOVE, CAN JUST BE SCRIBBLES THAT EXPRESS YOUR IDEAS!
LET'S SEE HOW I TURNED THESE SKETCHES INTO COMICS PAGES!

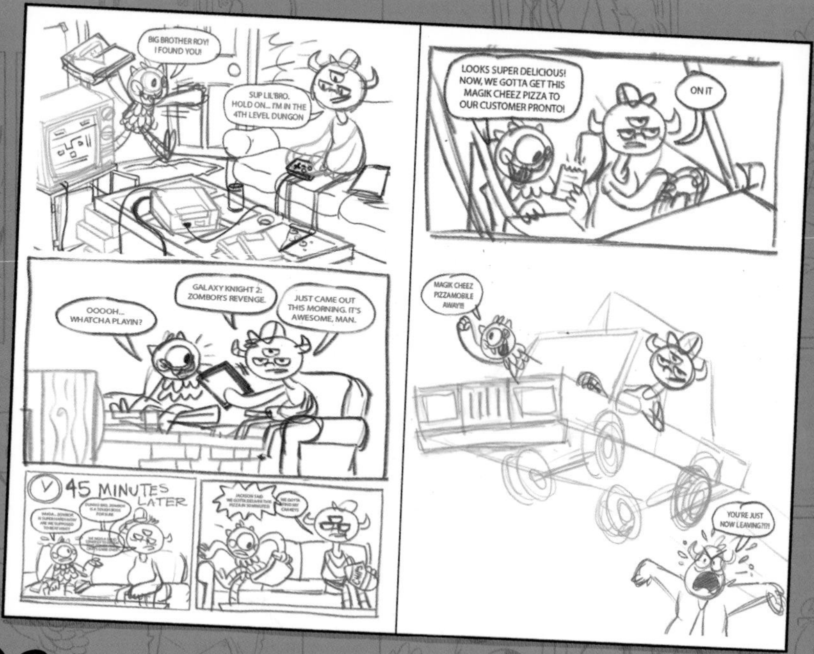
BIG BROTHER ROY! I FOUND YOU!
SUP LIL'BRO. HOLD ON... I'M IN THE 4TH LEVEL DUNGON
LOOKS SUPER DELICIOUS! NOW, WE GOTTA GET THIS MAGIK CHEEZ PIZZA TO OUR CUSTOMER PRONTO!
ON IT
OOOOH... WHATCHA PLAYIN?
GALAXY KNIGHT 2: ZOMBOR'S REVENGE.
JUST CAME OUT THIS MORNING. IT'S AWESOME, MAN.
MAGIK CHEEZ PIZZAMOBILE AWAY!!!
45 MINUTES LATER
YOU'RE JUST NOW LEAVING?!?!

AFTER I'VE WRITTEN OUT MY STORY AND FEEL GOOD ABOUT MY DRAWINGS, I WILL START TO ASSEMBLE THEM TOGETHER. THIS HELPS ME SEE WHAT THE PAGE MIGHT LOOK LIKE!

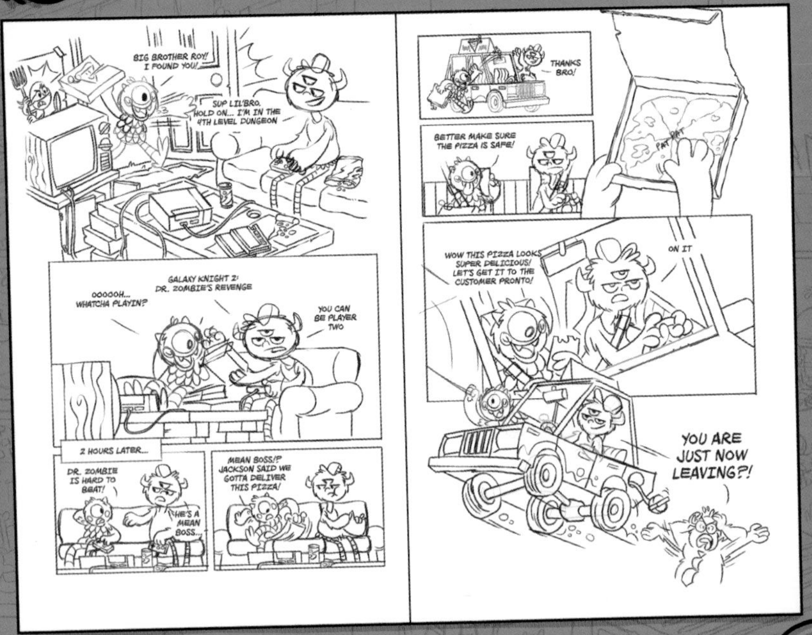
BIG BROTHER ROY! I FOUND YOU!
SUP LIL'BRO. HOLD ON... I'M IN THE 4TH LEVEL DUNGEON
THANKS BRO!
BETTER MAKE SURE THE PIZZA IS SAFE!
PAT PAT
OOOOOH... WHATCHA PLAYIN?
GALAXY KNIGHT 2: DR. ZOMBIE'S REVENGE
YOU CAN BE PLAYER TWO
WOW THIS PIZZA LOOKS SUPER DELICIOUS! LET'S GET IT TO THE CUSTOMER PRONTO!
ON IT
2 HOURS LATER...
DR. ZOMBIE IS HARD TO BEAT!
HE'S A MEAN BOSS...
MEAN BOSS!? JACKSON SAID WE GOTTA DELIVER THIS PIZZA!
YOU ARE JUST NOW LEAVING?!

I WORK WITH MY EDITOR TO "EDIT" OUT PARTS THAT SLOW THE STORY DOWN. THIS PAGE SHOWS MY "FINAL PENCILS." ONCE THIS PAGE IS APPROVED, I START INKING THE ART!

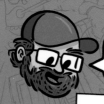

THIS IS WHAT THE PAGE LOOKS LIKE AFTER I'VE FINISHED INKING THE PENCIL LINES. REMEMBER TO MAKE ROOM FOR YOUR WORD BUBBLES! NOW, ON TO COLOR!

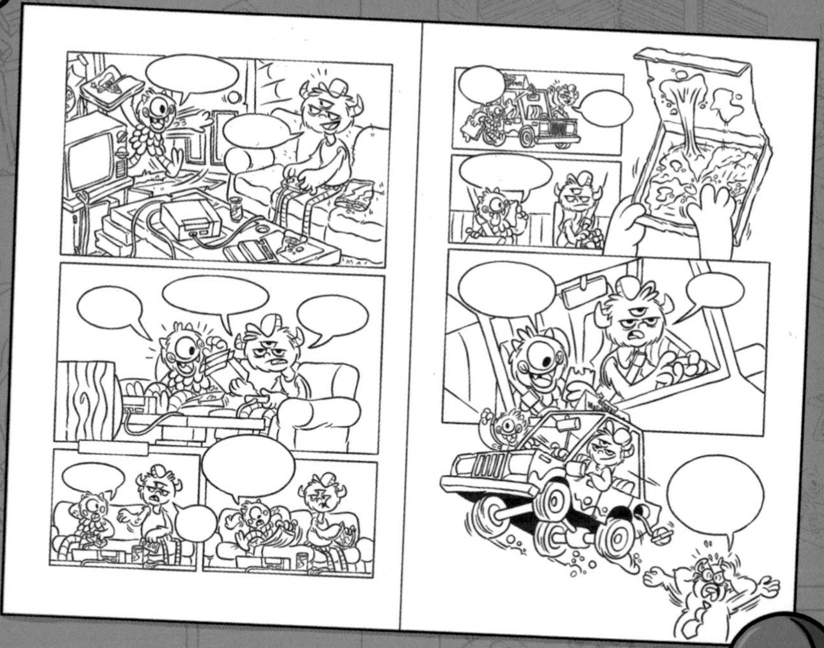

HERE IS THE FINAL PAGE WITH ALL OF THE INKS, COLORS, SHADOWS, AND HIGHLIGHTS! I BET YOUR BOOK WILL LOOK EVEN BETTER! I CAN'T WAIT TO SEE IT!

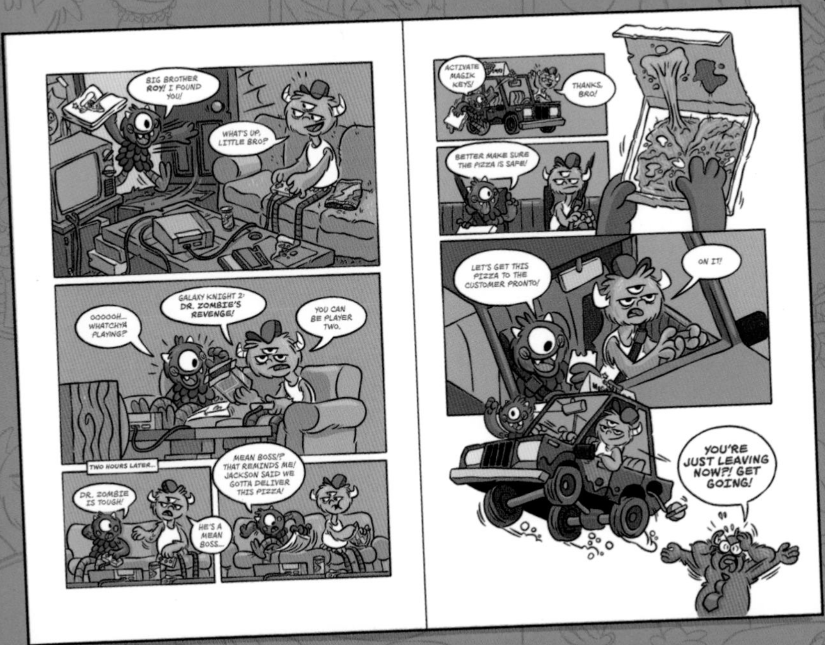
BIG BROTHER ROY! I FOUND YOU!
WHAT'S UP, LITTLE BRO?
OOOOOH... WHATCHYA PLAYING?
GALAXY KNIGHT 2: DR. ZOMBIE'S REVENGE!
YOU CAN BE PLAYER TWO.
TWO HOURS LATER...
DR. ZOMBIE IS TOUGH!
HE'S A MEAN BOSS...
MEAN BOSS!? THAT REMINDS ME! JACKSON SAID WE GOTTA DELIVER THIS PIZZA!
ACTIVATE MAGIK KEYS!
THANKS, BRO!
BETTER MAKE SURE THE PIZZA IS SAFE!
LET'S GET THIS PIZZA TO THE CUSTOMER PRONTO!
ON IT!
YOU'RE JUST LEAVING NOW?! GET GOING!

JOEY ELLIS has had his illustrations and character designs featured in *Highlights* magazine, *Boys' Life*, *Sports Illustrated*, ESPN.com, *Ranger Rick* magazine, The Walt Disney Company, and many others. Joey also performs puppetry and creates funny videos featuring his wacky characters. In his spare time, he collects toys and retro video games, and has fun with his family. Joey lives in Charlotte, North Carolina, with his wife, Erin, their two sons, James and Michael, and the family's sock-eating dog, Toby.

ACKNOWLEDGMENTS

Many thanks to Erin Ellis and Joey Weiser for their help with color flatting. Thank you also to Kyle Webster: This book wouldn't have happened without you. And Adam Rau, thank you for being my editor, you sweet and patient man.

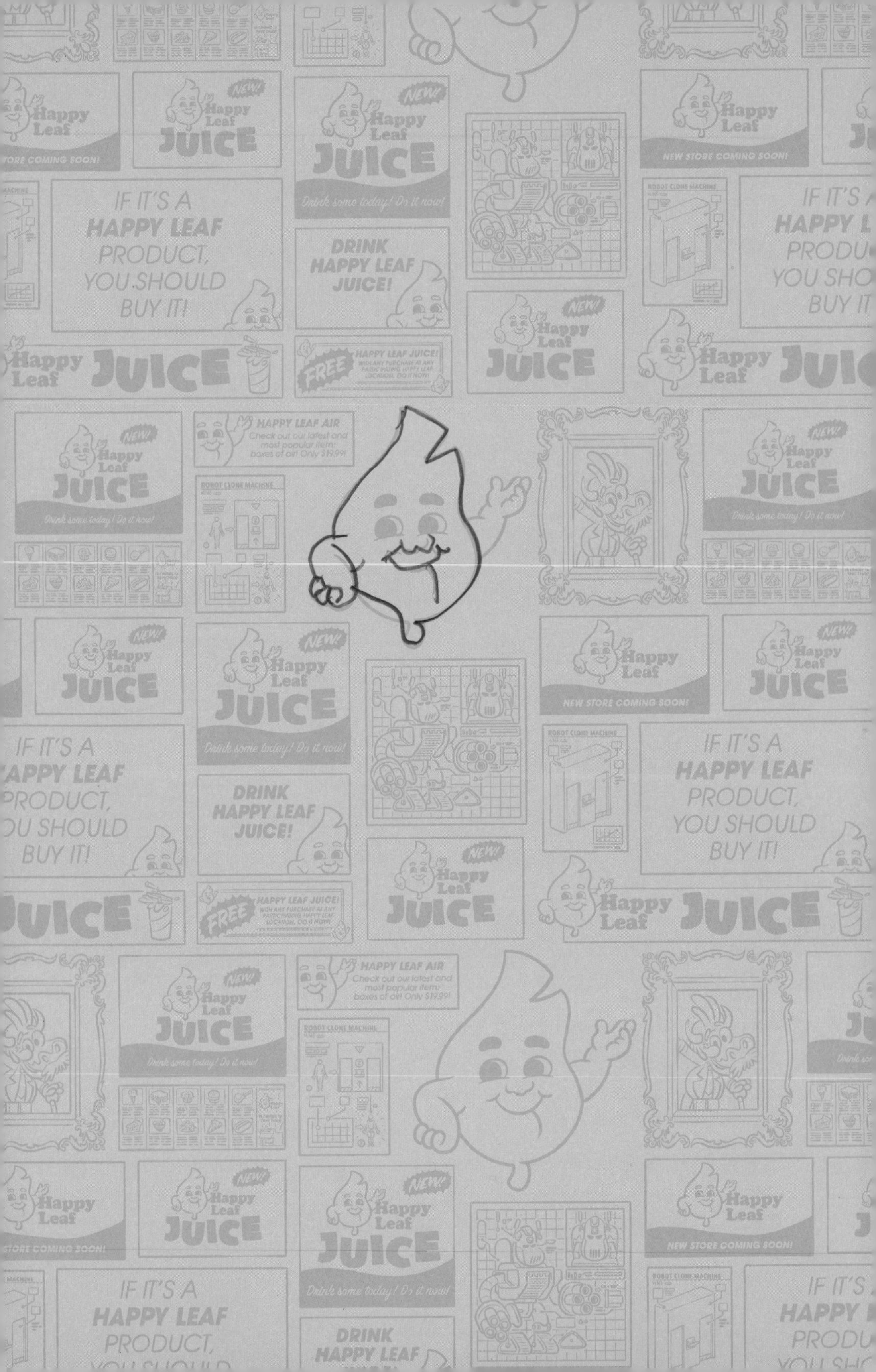

NEW!
Happy Leaf
JUICE
Drink some today! Do it now!
IF IT'S A HAPPY LEAF PRODUCT, YOU SHOULD BUY IT!
DRINK HAPPY LEAF JUICE!
FREE
HAPPY LEAF JUICE! WITH ANY PURCHASE AT ANY PASTIC PAVING HAPPY LEAF LOCATION. DO IT NOW!
HAPPY LEAF AIR
Check out our latest and most popular item: boxes of air! Only $19.99!
ROBOT CLONE MACHINE
NEW STORE COMING SOON!